GAY LYNCH

UNSETTLED

*To my children—Tiffany, Gemma and Cameron—
and their children—Hugo, Zoe, Oscar and Raphael; Hudson and Willow;
Isabella and Will and any others that might come along—
that they might imagine their Lynch ancestors.*

*To my Lynch husband Brian
who cried at the end of his reading.*

PREFACE

PORTLAND, VICTORIA (1870)

If Rosanna has a winter cough, Moorecke's must be worse and dangerous for a *Booandik*.

Holding herself upright, she feels as murderous as a snake. For
weeks before setting out she has hardened herself, preparing to gallop two hundred miles through swamps and low-lying coastal scrub,
along shores and riverbanks, and past townships; to press Lucifer
more than she should, to jump chaotically eroded creeks and fallen
red gums from Gambierton to Portland. Soon she will relinquish the
stallion and his colts to that tetchy lawyer employed by the actor's
Melbourne family. In their ignorance and pride, they have refused all
correspondence with her—have inflicted on her their grief and loss.

Unbeknownst to them she holds one more card. She knows how
to hide her feelings and will meet them on her own terms. Like any
brother, Edwin would not have wanted her company on this expedition had he known her plan.

The bullet-pocked signpost to the priest's hole barely registers
in her mind as she wheels Lucifer up the steep gradient to the head
of the valley. At the summit, he shuffles his unshod feet, setting off
a cascade of stones, and she drops back into her creaking saddle, an
un-gloved hand pressing against his broad black back, her thin wrists
gathered and laid one atop the other over the reins and pommel. She
holds herself stiff enough to be *feiseanna* dancing but her tanned, callused fingers belie such soft diversions.

Rosanna shakes the black boy's hand and rides the horse away from
the monastery, at least a mile, to squat beneath a peppermint gum and
relieve herself of all the irritation in her kidneys. No longer frightened,
she will wait with Lucifer, one hand cupping his nose, head resting
against his sweet side. For vespers. These men do not keep dogs and

leave their doors unlatched, but they have sharp ears. From beneath the tree she hears choral waves of thanksgiving rise in the air, and she reconstructs from memory the placement of items of interest in the fossil room. Then with this map laid out in her head, she sets off under cover of shadowy twilight. In full confidence, she locates the claw hammer, still faintly visible through the glass of the grimy hut window.

On seizing it, she begins to smash to smithereens his precious collection. Dust chokes her throat. Debris clings to her hair, spider webs and plaster. And what if he reports her to the Portland police? He will not have the hide, she decides, the yellow-bellied coward, saving her strongest emotion to slam an axe through drawer after drawer of the rosewood specimen cupboard: shattering bird bone, marsupial teeth, lungfish, vertebra, mollusc burrows.

PART 1

FRONTIER OF SOUTH AUSTRALIA
(1859)

I

DEATH OF A BULLOCK

It is a day for dying. Just this morning Rosanna has found a wombat that collapsed during its trundle to the water—now a cushion of bloated pink flesh, paws outstretched, eyes black and slitted. Too putrid to contemplate roasting a haunch.

The heat weighs on her skin. If she spat on her hand it would sizzle. Edwin says that the beds of swamps are crazed like china and birds drop dead from the sky. The silence swelling around her is broken by a new sound, like the sonorous boom of a steam ship's foghorn. It is the bellow of an angry bullock.

She waits. Listens. Lugging her water bucket, she lifts her skirts and moves forward to locate the bellow, following the trail of broken saplings and churned earth that mark the progress of a heavy beast. She approaches the bullock quietly. Something or someone has felled it between two trees; she watches its attempts to rise from its knees. White spittle froths at its mouth. Rosanna creeps closer fixing her eyes on the source of its pain. It scrabbles again in the dirt, fails to gain its feet, and falls to one side. Surely the front leg has broken under its great weight. On its side the Ashby brand, sunk in its neck is a spear. Rosanna stays clear of the thrashing limbs, gouging the earth. 'Poor *fullah ballum*,' she murmurs. Coat matted with filth and blood and eyes resigned, it has begun to dig its own grave. But whose spear? She turns her head away, bile filling her mouth. Softly, she calls for Moorecke. Would that lovely girl and her old man take an Ashby steer? For sure they would not abandon a week's feed? Rosanna scans the tree line. She has not seen either of them for months.

Left alone the bullock will die in its own time. But that is an end too slow and cruel to contemplate. She casts her eyes about for a waddy amongst the scatter of twigs and leaf litter covered in the white and desiccated trails of ants. Even if she finds one solid enough to strike the bullock's head, it would be a dangerous thing to do alone in the bush. Even in its death throes, it could knock her off her feet, trapping her beneath its mammoth body.

She imagines dogs tearing flesh from the live creature. And Mr William Ashby convulsed with rage at the loss of valuable stock setting off to punish Moorecke and Jack. If she shoots the bullock, quickly, kindly, and covers him with branches, who will know? Why waste fresh meat? She imagines her mother throwing her deft hands from the damper bowl to exclaim, '*Arrah*, what is it now?'

Father works for William Ashby but is opinionated about straying stock, and justice, being nothing if not practical because his first duty lies in feeding his family. What will the big man say about this spear? Mr Ashby nettles Father about justice being done; for justice *can* be found in the colony of South Australia. An Irishman has been hung for killing a black. Father told his boss that the Irishman was maddened by the English convict system. While he has never forbidden Rosanna spending time with Moorecke when the *Booandik* return to camp, nor does he approve. He is watchful—in some instances, grim.

She turns to the trees. Nothing stirs. The bullock heaves its head and rolls its yellow eyes. Fluid froths from its filthy mouth. She will stop up his bellow. Such dreadful suffering is wrong.

At the crack of a stock whip Rosanna stops in her tracks. A man's voice rises over the sound of cattle breaking from the scrub. She runs as far away as she can. By some miracle, the noise of the stricken bullock is subsumed by the bellowing of the main mob, stampeding towards the water. She hauls herself behind a stringybark, bruising her calf with her bucket, as the cattle followed by a fine white horse burst into view. Birds cry out in a mournful way. She hears rustlings and whirrings that she recognises as human tongues vibrating deep at the backs of throats, for so unnaturally long that she rams her knuckle against her heart.

Perspiration streams down the rider's unhappy face and darkens the waist of his moleskin breeches. It surely must be William Ashby. His hat jounces at his neck as he turns a large mob past the water and through the trees. Dust rises in filthy clouds around them and the squawking rattle of a wattle bird starts up. The tall man jerks around in the saddle to look behind him—not at her, she feels certain sure—gives the whip one more crack, then drags on his horse's mouth.

Rosanna turns her head to catch no more than a glimpse of ragged fabric, of net bags swinging over slim shoulders, of weapons angled over broader backs, of the air emptying behind them. She trembles. Prays. That he will not observe her or catch them, or ride on to see the bullock, for she cannot explain the spear piercing its hide and flesh.

She pitches stones in the opposite direction and, when they sing against the silky bark of a large tree trunk, the man turns his head once more. The moment in which they are both ensnared stretches until she fears she will faint with terror.

His eyes sweep the bush. The white horse shudders and bows its head. Moisture runs in streams below Rosanna's clothing. Parrots soar, marking human progress in the direction of the bay. The man will be angry if he sees the spear. She thinks the circus of sounds overwhelms his concentration. He will search for Moorecke and Jack, knock them down by chance or calculation. He will begin an investigation, which can never end well. A year or so after the Lynches' arrival, Moorecke, Jack and all their people drifted to Carratum Station, coming back only over summer to camp at the old places because Mr Ashby doesn't like black workers.

She wets her lips with her tongue. Slides the bucket more completely out of view. All the while crouching behind the tree her hands gripping the trunk. Around her, the bush stills and then hums again.

The man tugs again on the reins, his eyes scanning the horizon and then the breadth of the clearing, his legs locked around the grey's withers. It backs up, wheels, bringing its forelegs down in a show of strength, rearing up to jump the fallen branch of a shea oak. Man and horse plunge back into the scrub. Ashby will bank on scaring the pair, at least, before turning the cattle back towards the station. Rosanna's eyes track across the sky until the sound of their collective crashing fades away in waves. Then she runs.

2

DOING THE DEED

'You have the water?' Mother barks at Rosanna. She bends wearily to pluck a crying child from a box on the dirt floor; and looks too small to lift him. The child sags in her arms, his limbs limp, his chest concave through the thin muslin gown, his eyes dull. Eilish moves to a stool in the skillion kitchen behind the house, and balances him longways on her lap like a little boat, floating across her gathered skirt, enabling her to splay her hands in the small of her back. Leaning up against the smoke-stained wall, she rocks the child as best she can with her knees. How does she bear it, Rosanna thinks? It is not much to be the mistress of such a dwelling—two wattled and daubed rooms lined and pegged with bullock hides, a thatched roof and a stone chimney, box furniture wobbling on an earthen floor—when measured against the three story granite Irish public house they had left behind.

Rosanna hesitates.

'For God's sake, the children are thirsty. Can you not do anything right?' Eilish presses the flat of her arm against her temple, covering a streak of grey that runs like smoke to the coil of hair on her crown. Moisture pearls her upper lip. 'Today of all days, you soft *girseach*. You're old enough to help.' A feeble child's cry lifts, vibrates in the air and then falls. Eilish reaches out as if to strike her daughter, who jerks her hand to fend off an unlikely blow, dropping the bucket completely.

'I can, of course.' Rosanna's voice is hoarse from the dust and she wishes that the blue unrelenting sky would open up and swallow her. 'Mother, I need the gun before I fill the bucket.'

'Why do you need a gun to fetch water?' A wave of comprehension passes over Eilish's face. 'Is it a big one? Leave it.'

Rosanna leaps at this suggestion with relief. 'It is my own fault. I was dreaming in the reeds of Aoife and Cuchulain, right by a nest of little ones. By the time I saw the hatchlings their mother rushed out, reared up on her tail, and flicked her tongue at me like a serpent from hell. I threw the pail at her head.' Rosanna looks into her mother's face for effect.

A stream of perspiration runs down Eilish's tanned and grimy face. She dabs at it with the corner of her apron, steadying the plump baby on her hip. 'I need that water. Hugh is dirtying and dirtying himself. He is burning up with a fever. I should come with you.'

'I'll be all right, Mother. It's not such a big one, just a red-belly,' Rosanna skites, feeling as treacherous as the viper she has conjured for her mother. Thank God that Skelly hasn't lifted his luminous, boobook eyes from his sketchbook, to stick his phiz into business that need not concern him. She pictures him, pen in hand, day dreaming somewhere cool and sheltered along the creek.

'Where is St Patrick when we need him? God be with us in all hours, and that reptile and its hellish family slide back into the reeds, before you get there. Take the gun then, but be careful. And bring home the bucket. Brimful, and steady.' Her fingers part the baby's lips, coaxing him to latch on to her breast.

Rosanna lifts the gun from pegs above the fireplace and hurries away. Wobbling along the rim of the pond she carries the weapon above her head and into the bush to the wounded bullock. She glances about. Nothing stirs. No mushroom of dust swells in the sky. No bird cries.

Not wishing to blow the creature's head to pieces she measures up the distance and steps back to pull the trigger. The charge slams into the bullock's head. Red tailed cockatoos screech into the sky, wheel once, and descend in a moon-shaped spiral to settle in the eucalypts. The recoil throws her backwards and she falls down hard. Face collapsed in upon itself the bullock shudders one last time before ceasing its laboured breathing.

Rosanna remains sprawled, rubbing at her hip, listening for the sound of lithe feet in the grass or bodies moving through the scrub. Nothing. She approaches the bloody mess and tugs at the spear. It vibrates in her shaking hand, twangs. Uneasily, she glances around.

She covers the carcass with stringybark boughs, the dolomite baked too hard for grave digging. She shakes a branch, rattling its leaves, dancing backwards like Moorecke, to sweep the ground and cover her tracks; it is fear she feels. For she remembers the man turning the white horse, charging after Moorecke and Jack. Mr William Ashby must never see the steer. Not until she finds a way to remove the spear.

She carries the pail to the house, trips and slops the water levering it onto the wooden verandah. Her mother appears again in the doorway.

Rosanna stares miserably at the damp verandah planks lightening and drying, at the muddy puddle at her feet, sucked up by the fierce heat of the sun.

When she humps the brimming pail through the door her mother tugs at her arm with some relief. 'You took so long. So. But I'm glad to see you.'

'You act so brave with snakes. I am not fond of them, at all.' Rosanna shudders for effect. This was no lie.

Eilish stares into her daughter's eyes. 'I heard you. It was easy? Just one shot?'

Rosanna nods.

Satisfied, her mother turns away.

3

GUILTY PARTIES

Rosanna trudges back to the pond to fill a second bucket, scanning the bush for Moorecke. Now full grown, they need to look out for each other. But on her knees beside the water, her reflection confirms that everything is wrong: the high arch of her eyebrows, her strong nose, the slant of her cheekbones, the springing dark hair fizzing with perspiration at her brow. '*Thah*,' she murmurs to herself.

So much has changed since the Lynches came from Ireland. Too many people have walked away. Can land miss its people? Years ago when she rode with Edwin across the ridge on winter nights, campfires burned on the sides of the hills and beyond the swamp as well, blazed like beacons on the summit of the volcano, several hours' walk apart, more than the distance between smoke-stained Irish villages in which her own people gathered to tell stories about their old people. For a while the south-east Blacks have come in to the stations, agreeing to be paid in sugar, tobacco and grog instead of bullets, setting up new camps in old places near the Big Houses.

How long has it been since Rosanna woke in full moonlight to the whump of possum-skin drums, the tapping of sticks, the rise and fall of singing? Once, smelling roasting bustard, she had crept between the trees and hunkered down at a distance to watch Moorecke seated with the young women at the *murpenas*. Why had she not been paired with one of the *moorongal-ngara* who stamped a half-second behind the beat through the camp dust round the fire, spears quivering at their young shoulders, goanna fat and ochre glistening on their skin? Instead she had married that old man, Jack, who danced the kangaroo. Rosanna remembers his hair, grey-grizzled even then, and ochre-crenellated, his pock-marked face angled to catch the breeze, his broad nostrils twitching—sniffing *her* perhaps, from a great distance—one hand cupping his waggling ear, the other scratching his hard flat belly. The night sky had soaked up her rustling along with their ancestor voices. Father Tenison Woods says that in music, drums are the heartbeats, melodies the legs and feet. Rosanna thinks Irish music comes from the heart and *Booandik* music from the belly. It is the belly Moorecke clutches, when she is sad or frightened or angry.

She leaves the bucket on the step for her mother and stamps through the scrub on her way to warn Moorecke. In so many ways their lives are equally dutiful and dull. She arrives at the camp hot and bothered. A hot north wind puffs ash from the fireplace. Rosanna ignores the creaking lament of crows and parts the chewed-string curtain in the doorway of Moorecke's beehive-shaped wooden hut. Skins hang on the wall—a reed mat and some tools. They have come back for the summer and, no doubt, now, will stay awhile at MacDonnell Bay, to scruff crayfish from rocky ledges or to smoke sea eels with heads as big as dogs' and hang them in the trees. Rosanna will speak to Edwin about the bullock. If she can, she will concoct another great lie, for the occasion, and they will enjoy the meat. By dusk she will be capable of it.

4

BROTHER AND SISTER

Edwin and Father ride in, their horses so foamy and rank with sweat it is a wonder the saddles don't slide from their backs. Rosanna follows them to the rough yard behind the house, where they brush their horses down and hobble them. Rivulets of sweat run like storm-light through Lucifer's dark coat when Edwin applies the currycomb with long slick sweeps. Lucifer and Bran shoulder the men aside in the entitled way of stallions, to shake and rub themselves against the trunks of trees. They snort the warm eucalyptus air and whinny as they edge into the shade. Lucifer rolls exposing a cut on his cannon bone.

Father's face hardens when he sees Eilish's tears and he makes his way to the baby as if at gunpoint, parting its light wrappings with his fingers to examine its complexion, to rest his dark head against its frail chest. He curves his arm around Mother's shoulders, his deep voice cracking as he croons, mainly to comfort himself.

As soon as Father turns his back, Rosanna beckons her brother, leading him along a trail of flattened and bleached native grass past the pond. She carries his flensing knife in a fold of cloth and he tromps reluctantly along, toes turned out, legs slightly bowed as if his thighs are chafing after his day's ride. When they pass the water and turn into the scrub where the carcass lies, he tugs impatiently at her grubby apron string.

'How much further?'

She steps into the clearing. 'We're here then. Shut it.'

He flicks a chewed strip of leather against her cheek and delights at her recoil before he strides forward. A pigeon cavorts on the bullock's rump, then rattles away. Edwin kicks at the cloud of flies feeding on the dark contusion of blood. 'It is no prettier than houghing, and just as pointed.'

'What do you mean—houghing?'

'Back home, families were turned off their allotments because they couldn't pay the Burkes. So they slashed the hocks of his cattle.'

'I've never heard that word. But this is an accident, Edwin, or they would have kept it for a feed. You know that.'

'You'll have a problem persuading the Ashbys of that, with a weapon stuck in its throat.'

His sister shrugs. She sniffs the air. 'I'm not thinking this is a spear from around here, Edwin.'

He rolls his eyes at her and snaps it off, carves out the head and wipes it on his pants, then places it on the flat of her hand. 'Are *they* back then? Ask *her*.'

She turns her face away. Edwin rarely looks her straight in the eye. It will not be difficult to lie. 'They're not at the huts.' She lifts a lank plait heavy against her skin, and ducks her head to coil and fasten it at the back of her head. 'Likely camped in the cool at the port. Can we not take the meat home?'

'So we tell Father that the Blacks have driven this bullock from the other direction. That the beast was dying and that we put it out of its misery.'

'He doesn't have to know about every stray. In any event, he is pre-occupied with our baby.'

'I'll say I fought off a fierce man, bigger than Cuchulain, and blacker than a cockatoo. He had blood red feathers at his brow, and screamed worse than an Irish banshee. I'll tell him the man was blacker than an American negro come off a whaling boat at Portland. He was chasing the bullock when you distracted him, and mad with drink and loneliness, he turned on you.'

'Oh Edwin, you're such a fool to dream up black demons to cover our own thievery.'

'All right then, I can sell the meat and skin to that Kerryman O'Leary that I know at the bay, who doesn't ask questions about brands.'

'And why should you have the money when I did the killin'?'

'I am a man planning a business with a cart and a team of bullocks. Now that the spear is taken, and the carcass cut, the police troopers will be looking for a gun. I think you should lay low yourself.'

Edwin will make his way in the colony, Rosanna knows. 'I don't see why they would come out here. Swear to God, you won't say a word to

Mother and Father.'

'Why would I be blathering to them about their feckless daughter?' He grins.

Nothing dampens his spirit. 'Edwin, stop your teasing.' She picks up his hand and recoils from the smell on his fingers. 'God, you're such a reeky thing. The flies are loving you, now.'

Edwin snatches back his hand and returns to his task cutting through the flies and fat to the clean red meat beneath. It takes a long time—perhaps two hours—to butcher the beast. Mother will be chafing at the bit for them to return to help her with Baby. Rosanna impatiently watches her brother squatting in the dirt, his dark curly hair flopping into his eyes as he hacks and saws with concentration. Twenty year of age come Whitsunday, he is strong enough to do anything he wishes. She crests his shoulder but has not grown an inch since the year she first bled.

Edwin cuts slabs of meat from the bone and wraps them in Rosanna's cloth. He sighs, half rising to stretch his cramped body, wiping his hands from waist to thigh. 'I'll take some more of the hip. It's too fresh to waste.' He bends once more, sinking his blade deeper until she hears the crunch of bone.

EDWIN'S PLANS

Rosanna paces the perimeter of the clearing, anxiously listening for Ashby horses, and then returns.

'In God's truth Edwin, back in Ireland, why did they bring the cattle to their knees? It must be the cruellest thing.'

'Cruel that some have much and others little. Life is not like they say in your books.'

Rosanna nods and turns her face away.

'I saw worse when I went to the Portumna Poorhouse with Father to look for his brother,' he says.

'Edwin, I wasn't a baby then.' Rosanna thinks about Alice Spain and her mother, humping their belongings along the High Street, like broken-down mares in harness.

'The bliddy Burkes aimed to clear *Graíg na Muílte* by death or emigration.'

She prods his side with her finger. 'Burke's agent battered in Spain's roof. Did you know that then? They had to bury their baby in the ditch outside the Poor House.'

'We're better off here. When I have my own herd no one'll lay a finger on *them*.'

'I hate the Burkes.'

He tugs at her hand and peers up at the sky. 'Come on. We'd best not burn a carcass today. It's too warm.'

Four years ago fireballs fuelled by savage winds had hurtled past their house to the sea. For weeks they had kept vigil over smouldering stumps and prayed for summer rain. It is a beautiful thing to be so lucky when *Mar* is on a rampage. 'Why buy bullocks at all, Edwin? I thought you were going to the gold. I thought you might take me.'

He wipes his mouth with the back of his hand. 'When I was younger, sure, but I've seen them coming back, the seekers, and the brown and yellow creepers, from all the corners of the Empire. It is land they want, not gold. Even the Chinamen are returning.'

'How will you pay for land?'

'When I get my cart, chaps like Ashby'll ask me to carry their goods to the new port and back.' He curves his knife along the inside leg bone and cuts through sinew with a flourish.

'What else will you do?' she asks, arms folded, only half attending. He's pleased with himself, without a doubt. A puff of air ripples the corners of the meat cloth.

'Supplement my wages racing. Breed horses.'

She pushes irritating tendrils of hair from her face.

'Like Mr Gordon and Mr Livingstone on Carratum Station. Breed for the British Army in India. Then I'll buy land.'

'Land is what Father wants, more than anything.'

'Sometimes sons become more powerful than their fathers. God grant me good luck, I'll do well.'

'Well, you have plans, Edwin, and more chance than Skelly and I of them ripening. What of your sister, then, who loves you to death?'

'She should be grateful that her brother cleaned up a bullock and left her with a spear.'

'You'll be marrying soon, I suppose.'

'Good luck and prosperity never put off a wedding.'

'You're bummin' again, you great *shoneen*.'

'I heard about a meeting between small land buyers and the government. There's talk of dummying.'

'You'd never go to a meeting, Edwin. A dark lad like you. Always galloping to Miss Lallah's *síbín*, in the middle of the night your pocket weighed down with money, but coming home with none. You think I don't know, but I watch you in the moonlight. And so does Father.'

'It is a weight on a man with all this watching, watching.' Edwin kicks up sand at her, his face a study of resentment. 'The devil take the lot of you.'

She shields her face with her hand and raises her voice. 'A terrible life you lead, winning money for your secret business plans. I feel for you. I do. What about Skelly and me, stuck at home with Mother?' She steps back to slap her hand against the trunk of a gum. The sharp tang of eucalyptus and something else rises in her throat. She draws them deep. Then covers the remains of the bullock with branches and begins to sweep around it.

Edwin ties the cloth and hauls it with difficulty over his shoulder, glaring at her. 'You'll not marry a man or win your freedom if you are always spitting and grousing. For that matter, why should a man as sweet tempered as me be burdened with a sister so unlike him?' He marches away.

Pink moisture has seeped into his shirt and she stumbles after him to lift the heavy bundle away from his body, giving him at the same time a little bump with her hips. She will be the one to loosen the stain with dolly blue, for nothing draws attention to crime like the stench of drying blood.

'Shut your craw now. Come with me to the bay. We'll quickly tell Mother, while Father is busy at the still.'

She presses her hand into his shoulder blade and follows in his footsteps through the scrub and past the pond, where they wash their hands, before proceeding to temporarily wedge their heavy contraband in the fork of a large tree near the house.

REMINISCING PROVES A GREAT DISTRACTION

Mother waits, one hand raised to her forehead as she scans the scrub-line, the other lifting her skirt and letting it fall in a dance of grubby petticoats that cools her legs.

'Where have you been? You took your time,' she berates, relief pinking her face. 'Baby is sick, dangerously ill.' The line of her lower jaw hardens.

All skite and charm, Edwin presses his lips to his mother's cheeks, sliding an arm around her waist. He is taller now than Father, who is over six feet in his socks. He leans over the baby and feels its temperature with the palm of his hand. The baby writhes and screams. 'He's not too bad, just hot and bothered. Let Ro come with me to the port and bring back medicine for him. It is cooler by the water and it will do her good. Perhaps we could bring home a little crayfish for your supper.' Edwin raises his left eyebrow; it is a quirky thing he does to melt his mother's heart.

Emotions tangle up in Mother's face. Her mouth droops. Rosanna knows that more than anything she wants love between her children; and she has always talked of living in a more civilised place where her babies are safe and where her daughter will not be required to kill anything more dangerous than a quail or spatchcock. Rosanna knows these things, as surely as her mother pretends to be oblivious to the dark tides of discontent sweeping through her daughter's blood.

Eilish touches her hand to her face, where Edwin has softened her resistance. 'Apart from the worry of the child, Edwin, I need Rosanna to cook. I am faint with the heat. My head pounds like tunder in the hills. Where is your father *now*?'

Rosanna trickles water onto the baby's head, resists the urge to swing her head towards the creek. Edwin also operates under this restraint, for he throws his head in that direction but pulls it back to stare at her. 'Don't go worrying yourself about me, Edwin. I'll stay and take care of Mother and the baby,' she says prising the red-faced bundle out of their mother's arms.

'Well then, no snivelling,' he flings over his shoulder as he dances away, surprising Lucifer by vaulting onto his back. The horse leaps forward, black ripple-coated, pawing the air in indignation. He is ginger in the rear section. Oblivious, Edwin swings around in the saddle and dispatches a brilliant smile, for which he must surely have the patent.

Ceasing her fingering of the spear head in her pocket, Rosanna folds her arms against her own bad luck, and watches *him*, lanky as a stick insect, silhouetted against the rays of the grevillea sun sinking over the port, descending the hill on his horse.

When he pauses to gather the warm and laden cloth where they have placed it in the tea-tree, he lifts his hand in a laconic wave.

Rosanna calls pointlessly after him. 'If you see Moorecke, do not speak … about anything.' She follows her mother inside the hut.

FLOATING OFF ON THE TIDE

'Mother—tell me again why you brought us here to this drib-drab place?' She follows her mother inside the hut.

'At least help me while we blather.'

Rosanna croons. '*Tha*. Sit here and I'll finish off the dinner.' She moves a stool into the doorway and passes back the baby. 'I hope a little breeze will kiss you.' She damps a cloth and dabs at her mother's face, wipes down her neck and arms; then leans to kiss the baby's head.

Eilish holds him against her forehead and sighs. 'Some days I wonder if it was the best thing—to travel so far.'

'Oh you.' Rosanna kisses her cheek. 'I'm sure you wish you'd told us why. Even with Father stomping and banging, and the church bells ringing as we boarded the coach for Portumna.' She feels good at this—this reminiscing. It proves a great distraction.

'One day, darling. I won't forget, standing with our trunks on the step, the street a quagmire. Father Egan waving from the bridge. I wonder if he knew what your father had done—oh the shame.'

Rosanna shrugs at the idea of her father ever being called to account for anything. 'Skelly trailed behind you like a calf at foot. Lowing.'

'That he did.' Eilish reaches out to touch her daughter's hair. 'Oh I miss these people. Do you remember *alannahh* that Granny Walsh died seven years to this day? I had almost forgotten.'

'Didn't I nurse her each time you dropped like a stone in a bog into your rocking chair?'

Eilish angles her face away. 'Her chest was as hard as a rock, the pain as fierce as if someone was breaking into her with a spade ...'

Rosanna croons. 'And so we rocked along the canals through Meelick, Banagher, Balinnasloe and Shannon Harbour to the Dublin wharfs. Do the words sound like a poem?'

'More like a prayer. Or a song.' Her mother sways on the stool. 'The deck of that packet was as crowded as could be and I threw the contents of my stomach into the Irish Sea.'

'The old country melted away in the fog. Then England. Do you remember floating off on the Plymouth tide, aboard the *Emma Eugenia*?'

'I felt such a pang. Worse than childbirth. In either case, there was no turning back.' Eilish stills herself. 'Keep on with the dinner, Rosanna. Turn the meat and mix the boxty.'

Rosanna lifts the cloth from her mother's shoulder and folds it around her hand to protect it from the heat of the oven as she drives a long fork into the joint. 'I doubted we would ever find our way home again, Mother.'

'Your father's fingers dug so hard into my arm that I thought I would faint. Sorrow coursed through him. I knew he would blame me to hell and back for leaving Woodford.'

'It was terrible loud, with the roaring wind and the sound of the screw ...'

'The howls and cries from the deck.'

'And the whistling and banging on the rails. Even the petrels left us,' sing-songs Rosanna, beating plover eggs and salt into black potatoes soft and warm as gruel.

Her mother lifts the baby, limp as a rag, and begins to cry. 'I was praying everything was just a dream. That we were just in a curricle bobbing on Lough Derg—going on a pilgrimage to the Holy Island—instead of travelling to the other side of the world.'

Some days, Rosanna thinks, Mother enjoys her misery. Some days, homesickness and worry is all they have between them. She shapes the boxty in the wet palms of her hands and slaps them onto the griddle. The fat spits worse than black caterpillars and her hand rushes to her cheeks to take the sting.

As Eilish rises on her toes to gather bowls from the makeshift box shelf, she leans into her daughter's soft side, rubs her perspiring neck with the nub of her hand. 'It seems but a blink since we arrived here on this step. You and Skelly—my curly-haired boy, how blessed we are to keep *him*—your father and Edwin, riding away each day. Now, I am desperate worried about this one.' Eilish moves with the baby in her arms to sway before the window like a woman bewitched. 'And the first day across the *turlogh* we saw that other little family standing by the tillage for my new potatoes.'

'Moorecke,' whispers Rosanna, stopping her slapping and turning of boxty cakes to stare into her mother's face.

'Like they rose on a platform from the swamp. Not a bit like *sidhe* slipping out between the trees back home, dissolving in the air when I snap my fingers.'

'I thought I saw them today.' Rosanna bites her tongue, fearing for their safety. Her eyes fill with tears.

But her mother has already forgotten her and Moorecke, as the baby barks its croupy cough. As if it will never draw breath again.

8

SHENANIGANS BESIDE THE SINKHOLE

Skelly wears the feather of a firetail in his hat. Perched high in the foliage of a buloke tree, he spies on his sister chiacking with her heathen friend Moorecke at the edge of the pond. You would never know that a baby had died. Their washing basket lies upturned, rudely abandoned in the reeds. The sky is a clean strong blue and full of heat, broken only by the inelegant belching lines of ducks flying between the sinkholes and ponds. Skelly hopes that the eerie whine of the wind combing the buloke needles will cover the sound his pencil makes as it moves across the page. Mostly, everyone watches *him*. And he is sick to death of it. But where are they now, when he is way above the ground and could fall and hurt himself?

For three days he has watched his mother totally absorbed in the little blue figure laid out on the slab of stone beside the family altar. After fighting for its life, Baby had stopped breathing in sheer exhaustion. Each day, Mother lifts the delicate weight of her little son into her cupped hands and strokes the filegreed skin of his forehead, where the sun will never kiss or burn, and where fever will never rage again. Father had rinsed the limp body in his tears, turned it, as he might a fish caught in a net before throwing it back and stomping away to the stables.

Skelly has drawn the corpse of his little brother so many times that he has no tears left and the pages in his sketch book are smudged and soft. He feels empty and ready to die himself. At the sound of his sister's laughter, he angles his head to peer between the branches. Better for her here beside the pond with Moorecke than sliding off to the scrub to mope, as she has been lately. Stupid girl. Crying hysterically over the baby. He holds up a sun-warmed pink and downy peach from the tree behind the pit, fingering the luscious curves, before he eats it. He needs no reminding that he is almost twelve and his sketchbook contains the secret shapes of girls' *thóins.*

A pair of azure kingfishers bob and nod to each other in front of their excavated mud nest—like the little silk-clad Indian nabobs Mother once showed him in a book—and they interrupt his drawing. He takes up his pencil again and begins to outline their violet blue wing feathers, but suddenly they leap into the air—peee, peee—and, wings whirring, zigzag across the surface of the water. The spangle of birds and water is a gorgeous thing. If only he could paint in vivid colours, like a real artist. Father bought Skelly the precious sketching book. No one else received a gift—not Blinnie, nor Hugh; not Rosanna; nor Edwin—paper being scarce and expensive.

He peers over the branch at Rosanna and Moorecke lying full length on the stones ringing the pond, to skim water with the flats of their hands and behave like ninnies. Skelly likes their long bare legs— one pair shapely, more deeply golden than his morning *fúal*, the other spindle-shanked in all the shades of mushrooms. They have draped their skirts across the currant bushes and wear only their grubby chemises tucked in long pantaloons.

He stares at Moorecke for a long time. Some of the clothing she wears belongs to her husband, making her seem more beautiful than an ordinary girl. An urgent fluttering feeling begins in his pants, like a bird trapped beneath his hand. Half irritation, half longing, and the feeling confuses him. He rubs at the flannel of his pants, at the same time shifting his position on the branch to see more clearly. Sunlit leaves shimmer in sympathy. He stops and starts, tries to still himself but cannot. He pants softly, holding the branch with his left hand to keep balance until he feels spurts of joy. Do girls feel this too?

Sometimes he dreams of being suspended in the coolness of the pond– nightmares about being cut by the rocks beneath the surface, pink clouds of his useless blood suffusing the clear water until he is completely drained and fainting. *Musha*, with his luck, Mother would arrive too late to save him and he will be glad. By then he would be sucked through a crevice to the rock cathedral below the main pool and her constant fear would come to pass. It will be her punishment for birthing such a lag. The water in the pond is more than an Irish roadside flush, but calmer than a river. It is dark and deep. Full of ominous shadows. As chilly as a tomb. Skelly listens, intermittently sketching and thinking about joy and death. There is little else to divert him.

The girls' voices bounce up from the pool. He sees Moorecke sling an arm around his sister's shoulders as if to comfort her and then whisper in her ear. They duck their heads together.

'Why did Jack duff that *ballum*?' Rosanna raises her arm indicating the scrub behind the pond.

'Little Jesus sent the bullock right alongside our sit down place,' Moorecke shouts. 'He ran away from his mob.'

Rosanna smirks; then whistles through her teeth. 'And William Ashby very nearly caught you?'

'Cranky as *koo-no-wor*, came back to get the little fullah.'

'You were not frightened?' Rosanna looks suddenly worried and Skelly leans closer to catch their words.

'*Yooch-ba*. Off we ran to *Ngaranga*.'

'He chased you to MacDonnell Bay?'

Moorecke shakes her head. 'No. He turn around. With all those cattle.'

'Perhaps he only thought he saw you?'

'Later, Jack and me followed the tracks—*ngorn-da*—and we can see that bullock broke his leg. But no meat left. William Ashby got it first.'

Rosanna flips her body as she might a griddlecake on the slab of rock beneath her body and swings her head sideways to face Moorecke.

Why does she look so secretive? Skelly leans forward.

'Perhaps someone else, riding by. You were bold to touch Ashby cattle,' he hears. He always knows when Rosanna is lying.

9

SINK HOLES AND SKETCHES

Moorecke stands and dives in one long fluid movement; then makes languid sweeps with her arms, insinuating her body like an eel through the chasm between the rocks, holding her breath for a long time, until Skelly's teeth ache with clenching. He waits for her darting shadow until finally he sees her again, face swelling, big eyes opening like lilies, breaking through the skin of the water. He wobbles on the branch above her. His sketchbook slips in his sticky lap and he lurches forward to prevent it falling.

Moorecke flops as slick and dark as a seal onto the rock platform beside the reeds and Rosanna leaps up to run along the edge of the pond, kicking up water with her great long legs. They are equally brazen and Mother would despair. It is only because Father and Edwin have ridden away, swags strapped across their horses' broad backs, to help Mr Ashby muster more scrub cattle that there can be such shenanigans.

Once more, Skelly's pencil scirrs across the page, shading the curves of their bodies. Rosanna lies down again. Moorecke squats beside the water peering into the deep below, her body strong. The sunlight is much too bright for eels. But he has seen her trap them in woven baskets shaped like trumpets, and bait them too, with bone hooks—sanding her hands to kill them with a sharpened rock. The same rock with which she cut herself and, once, cut Rosanna too. Even after she twists their neck and decapitates them, running the point of her tool along the length of them, until their whiplashing frenzy slows, and she hangs them gently twitching around her neck. Appalling. What can be wrong with him that even girls are better at killing than he?

Rosanna squats too, her fingers tracing the corrugated burns on Moorecke's hips, caused by rolling into her campfire. Skelly holds his breath and stops sketching, his pencil just short of her belly on the page. He grips the branch. Almost yelps. He must not fall. But he has bitten his tongue and he is not supposed to be climbing trees. Ever. He does not bleed this time but, all the same, pain sings through his mouth.

Rosanna tosses water into the air. It is fey girls are, lucky, and he can never draw them well enough. They bend to the water, then shrieking like banshees throw back their heads to shake drops of water from their hair. Rosanna's hair is almost as blue-black and wild as Moorecke's. Eilish would reach for her wooden hairbrush and smack it smartly down on her daughter's head.

The sun beats down and the girls lie quiet as crocodiles on the edge of the hole, eyes flicking, tongues blatherin', all the while drying off Rosanna's washing on low dead boughs of the tea-tree. He cannot hear their secrets now but he sees two snakes intertwined in the highest branches. Shall he call? Or simply watch the snakes. Oblivious, Rosanna traces the pink soles of Moorecke's feet with a twig, then, swinging around, the tiny water drops on the crest of the girl's lips, and Skelly is sick with excitement, as if a thousand little people are running around in his belly. He wishes he could come down from the tree, and be with them.

Any minute now, Eilish will call. She can only sit so long in grief, with Hugh and Blinnie plucking fearfully at her dress. If she calls, or Jack comes for her, the black girl will skedaddle through the scrub. She drinks from the pond, through a reed. Skelly remembers her drinking vessel, years before—Jesus, Mary and Joseph; it was a skull, he knows that now—and it still shocks him. But it wasn't long before Father accused her of stealing their best bucket to carry water. The drinking vessel, the skull, whoever it was—perhaps her mother—has long since been abandoned. A more sinister idea enters his imagination, something he is forbidden to speak of—murder, Rosanna says.

When a bronze-winged pigeon rattles from the straggly trees by the water, he starts, twisting his head in fright. The sun disappears behind a cloud and Skelly senses change. Something has alarmed the pigeon and set the pelicans clattering from the lagoon behind him. Along the distant shore spumes of water rise and fall and, from a distance, Skelly begins to make out shapes.

It is the priest, black cloak flying out behind him, cantering towards them on his great horse, leading another weighed down with supplies and books and notes. As sure as Father Woods will need a Christian hearth for the night, Rosanna will be saying Hail Marys for the rest of her life. But, of course, he will be more interested in poor Baby.

Skelly hurls cones from the buloke tree until they splash beside his sister. Moorecke whips around like a startled adder and calls up to him. 'Might be William Ashby comes. Go home, Skelly boy, little booger.' How long had she known? He clutches his damp trousers.

Rosanna hauls her printed calico shift over her head and looks up at him with annoyance. '*Alilu*,' she shouts. Then leaps to her feet and scoops up washing.

Skelly grins to see the pair of them scurrying away like mad wombats in moonlight. What will he say to the priest when he offers confession? 'Father I have sinned, for I have drawn girls' *thóin*?' Never. And he has worse stories to tell.

He pinches his eyes shut in dread thought and scribbles across the folded page. Should he tell about the bullock? Skelly comes from a family of sinners. The priest must know that they use the creek water for illicit distillation. But, in any case, it will be baptising the Lynch baby and comforting Mother that will preoccupy him for the first while.

FATHER JULIAN TENISON WOODS

If Father Woods sees metallic, green wings flashing through the spraying water, hears the gurgle of girls' voices in the nearby trees, or wonders why an angry swan skids to a halt in front of his horse, he says nothing.

'*Faille*, Father,' calls Skelly, backing down from the buloke tree to drop at the feet of God's servant, 'are the flies troublin' you?'

'Good afternoon Skelly. I suppose they are. Thank you for enquiring. How is your family?'

'We have bad news.'

'Oh, indeed. I was saddened to hear from a stockman that your little one succumbed to fever.' Father Woods leans forward and pats Skelly's arm.

Skelly pulls away and glances over his shoulder, casting about for a new topic of conversation. 'What do you think about cattle duffing?' Oh wipe the imbecilic smile off your phizog he thinks. With the girls talking about the very same thing so recently and his little brother just passed into the next world. He grins to himself.

'It is the chief business of courts in all the colonies.' Father surveys Skelly, his face arranged in a pleasant expression. Curls spring over his ears where he has pushed them back in the heat.

Skelly purses his lips and glances around at the trees. Perhaps he will not tell. 'Isn't it warm, Father?'

'Indeed it is, but uppermost in my mind has been the thought of a cool drink from the pond and breaking bread with your family.'

Skelly sighs with satisfaction. 'It will be grand to have you, Father. Will you stay the night?' Skelly loves Father Woods so much he thinks his heart will burst. Everyone does.

'If I may. In the morning I'll ride to Portland to make my confession.'

Skelly tightens his grip on his sketchbook, his skin mottling into all the colours of a parakeet at the thought of confession. He must shade over his drawings of girls' *thóins*. And his sketches of their dead baby.

Father Woods dismounts to walk beside him. Skelly leads the horses to the water trough behind the house. 'We'll have good *craic* after supper?'

The priest stares into his eyes. 'We'll play and cry. For once I have brought my cello.' He taps a large case with his whip. 'And I have a gift for you from the gum tree at the halfway place where I say Mass. This swamp harrier fell at my feet. I fear it has lost its verve but you may like to sketch it before maggots set up their colony.'

Skelly unwraps a parcel containing the bird and turns the body in careful hands. Looks into her gelatinous eyes. Upends her. 'I like her rufous pantaloons.'

The priest smiles in a kind way as if Skelly can never upset him. 'Her tail is a little tatty.'

At the house Eilish rushes forward to greet the priest. 'Leave the damper and come,' she calls to Rosanna behind her.

Her daughter arrives on the step, face flushed from the fire, stockings rolled down to her boots, exposing her golden legs. Her plait is fuzzy and matted with azolla and pond-water. When she throws her head in a defiant way Skelly is filled with love for her and wants to reassure her that he has not confessed anything to the priest about duffed bullocks or afternoon shenanigans. And that she has flour upon her nose and a lacy spray of it across her damp black skirt.

'Rosanna, I am glad to see you looking well.' Father Woods takes her hand and turns it palmside up. 'I can see from these good hands that you have been helping your mother at this difficult time.'

Rosanna smiles in a wary way.

The priest guides Mother with his arm to sit in the rocking chair near the little corpse swathed in linen. They talk quietly for a very long time.

Later when Father Woods finds Skelly and Rosanna waiting nervously on the verandah, his eyes are red. 'I have brought you a book of poems by Browning, recently returned to me by my friend, Mr Gordon, all the lines of which, I swear, he has committed to memory. Sit with me.'

Adam Lindsay Gordon sometimes races against their Father and Edwin. In a steeplechase he is really something, everybody says so: like a wild bird clinging to the back of his horse, flying over fences that would make anyone else sick to the stomach; he is a horse-breaker. On other occasions, Skelly has seen him bobbing across the flats between the swamps, clay pipe clamped between his teeth, sometimes holding a book up against his nose, other times mumbling to himself, or reining in his horse to scribble verse into his notebook. He would drive a woman mad, Mother says.

Father Woods draws a slim book from his leather satchel, and opens it to a page he has marked with a satin ribbon. Rosanna and Skelly seat themselves on the step beside him.

'How it Strikes a Contemporary,' he reads:

> I only knew one poet in my life:
> And this, or something like it, was his way.

'The poem is like a friend telling you a great confidence,' Father Woods says. 'Read on a little, Rosanna.'

She places her finger on the page and commences:

> He walked and tapped the pavement with his cane,
> Scented the world, looked it full in the face,
> An old dog, bald and blindish at his heels.

'I wish I could look the world *full in the face*,' she says, shooting words at the priest like arrows.

'You do it now, Rosanna. It is one of the things I like about you,' says Father Woods. 'And you read well. Skelly, take your turn.'

He knows, Skelly thinks, how to make her happy and is devilish good at it. They read turn-about until Skelly takes the last two lines:

> Well, I could never write a verse—could you?
> Let's to the Prado and make the most of time.

'Mr Browning speaks directly to me, Father. I could never write a poem.' Skelly shakes his head, despondent.

'Perhaps he could not draw as well as you.' Father Woods pats Skelly's arm.

IT IS THE SADDEST THING

As the sun sinks low in the sky, the priest cleans and polishes his chalice and spreads his altar cloth on a red gum stump overlooking the pond. He carries two box seats from the house for himself and Eilish. Blinnie lies across her mother's lap, sticky fingers inveigling beneath the neck of Eilish's gown. They drink 'mops and brooms' brought by Father Woods in a hessian bag. Skelly watches him spooning black sugar into the twiggy brew and thinks how lovely it is to see his mother peaceful. Rosanna cannons off the verandah—jealous, Skelly decides, that the priest pays attention to anyone but to her. Their mother reminds Father Woods that not only have they lost the baby but that Hugh has always been a sickly boy even in the summer months and that she fears *he* will not survive another winter. Skelly edges closer.

'When I lived in Ireland, Father,' Eilish goes on, 'the church was next to the public house run by my family and every day I would slip inside to pray for Edwin and Rosanna.'

'And Skelly?'

'And Skelly, of course.' Eilish sighs and Skelly feels the weight of it.

'You've lost one child here, and none in Ireland. You are more fortunate than some.'

She nods and straightens her body, as if to shake off misery to please him. Then dabs at tears with her apron. She casts her eyes towards the small dirt mound beneath the buloke tree; awaiting the priest's attention. 'You have the strangest parish, Father.'

He stays her with a smile. 'It is my mission to carry God's word, on horseback, to all of you in the New Country.'

She swings her head to face him again. 'The church must fear your ministry will fall into savagery.'

'There are always some who think the worst.' He touches her arm. 'I prefer this work. Even though I travel hundreds of miles through floods and drought and bushfire, losing my way in places unmarked by roads or inns, my health improves. Indeed, I rarely cough now.' He turns to Skelly who feels swept up in the warmth of his gaze. 'Let us speak of Skelly's confirmation, in the autumn. I will leave him a pamphlet to read.'

Skelly blushes. White cockatoos rise on the wing, wheeling across a setting sun as plump and lustrous as an egg yolk. The rich fat smell of roasting mutton fills the air, and their Father and Edwin canter in, ducks slung across their saddle cloths.

It is always a grand night when the priest comes. The men sluice off their dirt in a barrel behind the house, before they come to Mass. If Skelly was a proper artist he would paint them all, weary and grimed by toil, their faces lifting in hopeful supplication, standing before their cottage with the lagoon spread out before them like a prayer cloth, a pallid cuckoo beginning the night's sonata.

Skelly lifts his head, takes the host in under the roof of his mouth where it sticks until he works at it with his tongue and swallows. Then crosses himself. Mother rocks her body, one foot before the other, stroking Blinnie in her arms, and clutching Hugh's small hand. Edwin pays scant attention, turning his hat in his hands, watching a blue crane take one elegant step and then another, before dipping its head to feed in the pond. Is he dreaming of girls? Skelly feels the weight of his sinful thoughts, and shifts his gaze to Rosanna.

Father Woods gifts them with his language until the loss of the baby burns like physical pain in them all. And then he releases them. There is something about hearing men cry; even Edwin bawls, shoulders heaving as he leans into his mother's side. The priest cries. Father too. After all the wailing, the clutching and hugging, he stands between his family and the bush, a giant black-bearded man slouching in the gathering dusk, coat riding up, hair sprouting from his ears and nostrils. He acts fiercest with Rosanna. This night, Skelly hopes for harmony.

I 2

AN EVENING'S ENTERTAINMENT ENDS BADLY

Clouds of mosquitoes hover round the lamps and supper is taken in slapping humour. Edwin and Rosanna skylark about, vying for the priest's attention, and Skelly wishes they would include him. Somehow the priest has settled their grief for the baby, now blessed, its small body resting beneath the mimosa trees.

The family press close together in one small room with smoke-grimed walls and a low ceiling. Rosanna has squeezed four wooden chairs around the table; she and Skelly share a box, Hugh sits on his father's knee. Blinnie snuffles at the bodice of her mother's dress, peeps out to grin at the priest, and then covers her face with her fingers.

'Edwin tells me that the little Irish girl, the overseer's wife who helps Mrs Ashby at the station, is awful melancholy,' says Eilish, her face filled with sympathy.

Father holds her eyes, lines softening around his mouth.

'One of the orphans that landed at Guichen Bay?' the priest asks.

'Not an orphan, Father, just a girl with enterprise. You being a wee bit Irish yourself, you would know that. Plenty of families got broken up by the Famine,' Mother says.

'Yes, I take your point.'

'She won't go to her work in the morning. Can't get out of bed,' Edwin contributes.

'Most of those girls begin in service and before you can blink, marry men in the district. Irish girls are plucky.'

'They say that she is useless, Mother.' Edwin sits up, his face creased and earnest. 'She won't lift a finger for anyone. Keening half the day and night, or silent as the dead. Her husband is losing patience.'

'Edwin, hush now. Have some compassion.'

'I will call on her in the morning,' offers Father Woods.

'Thank God for that. I would go myself but for Blinnie and Hugh.

And I would send Rosanna, but they might be too much for each other.' She throws a sidelong glance at her daughter, who glares, and looks away.

Father drinks steadily through the meal, his mouth loosening to accommodate his breathing, his great dark head thrown back, one hand dropping to lever his belly over his belt, two fingers resting against his *bod*. Each time the priest mentions temperance he takes another draught from his tin cup and wipes the thicket of his beard with the back of his hand. Skelly knows that his father stands on his dig about teetotalling but finds it hard, nevertheless, to resist the priest's remarkable charm.

The priest leans across the table to gain his attention. 'Garrick, abstinence is the only way.'

Father nods and takes another sip. 'You could be right.'

They lock eyes. The priest changes the subject. 'There is much talk of settlers taking up land in the new Hundreds.'

Now they will have a peaceful evening.

The meal cleared away the priest offers a blessing and takes up his instrument to play and sing. Since his last visit Skelly's body has changed. Now that his voice hurtles up and down a startling oral staircase, he no longer wishes to sing. Father Woods sits like a black grasshopper, tall and straight on the edge of his chair, legs straddling the cello, tapping out the music with his long fingers, his expressive voice filling the room. He is young and handsome, not much older than Edwin. By the time the little ones collapse in their beds, their heads full of laughter and music and talk, he and the Lynch men will be poking the coals, ready to talk deep into the night. And before he unrolls his bedroll on the verandah, they will play chess like the great Irish champion Cuchulain and his enemies.

Mother wipes away tears loosed by the music, pushes aside the table to clear a small space and hitches up her skirts. 'We must go on.' Seemingly eager to join her mother in a jig Rosanna leaps to her feet, her skirt spread around her *thóin* like petals around a pestle: flying up when she leaps and fluttering down when she lands. Toes pointed, her feet flip and bounce and kick as she attacks the beat. Her oval face looks like Father's, only much more beautiful. She holds out her hand to Skelly to jig along beside her—taking care not to bump him.

Skelly is not so young that he cannot remember summer nights outside Walsh's pub when Father leaned up against the wall with townsmen and travellers, his eyes on Eilish slapping tankards on the bar. He reaches out to catch his mother's hand. She misses a step to drop a kiss on his head; and scoops Blinnie from his arms. If only it were like this every night and Edwin and Father were not *lomicking* through the door in the wee hours, waking the babies when they knock cups and plates from the old box dresser, stumbling against the walls and urinating like horses until Eilish comes hissing to steer them to their beds, singing as they go:

> *Gra ma chrce ma chriskeen*
> *Sláinte gal mavoureen*
> *Ge ma chree.*

Abruptly, the music stops. Is the priest tired? Startled out of his reverie Skelly sees that Rosanna has knocked the mug of whiskey from her father's hand. She scowls up at him and then looks away. Unceremoniously dumping Blinnie in Skelly's lap, Eilish moves to her daughter's side.

'Git,' says Father in a voice as small and hard as the kernel of stone fruit. He raises his hand and slaps Rosanna's face.

Skelly's heart thumps against his rib cage.

'Garrick, no.'

Rosanna's body slumps and she transforms from a beautiful laughing girl into someone knotted up inside who cannot fly away.

Father Woods tries to draw her back. 'Be of good heart,' he says, picking up the first few bars of a new song. He nods to Rosanna.

'I hate you. All of you.' She murders them with a look.

Mother presses down her daughter's skirt, smooths out her clenched hand.

'Don't touch me,' Rosanna cries, throwing up her hands as if preventing a further attack, and leaves the room.

Mother ducks her head in mortal shame and presses tea on the priest.

It is a very long time before all the confessions are heard and Rosanna crawls mawking into Skelly's bed to recite poems about dying, wishing the priest were her real father, so that she could ride away with him. Father Woods has told her that in adversity she must be as brave and as good as little Dorrit, a girl in a book that he will borrow for her from the Adelaide Lending Library. That she is beautiful, and a woman, and that she must love God. With Father Woods's encouragement she could go into service or teach school. *This* is how Rosanna is to be rewarded for her carelessness.

'It will never happen,' Rosanna spits at Skelly. She will run away.

1 3

ROSANNA ABSCONDS

The next day is a Monday. Where is Rosanna? Skelly's heart bounces at the sight of her empty bed and her new green dress lying in a miserable puddle on the floor. He remembers the events of the previous night and his sister acting wild, throwing back her hair to laugh into the priest's face, prating about freedom. Has *he* noticed that Rosanna thinks herself a woman now, in her tightly laced dresses, and her skin turning golden like apricots in the hot Australian sun?

Apart from the soft *thwack* of Mother splitting wood, the house is quiet. Skelly should carry and stack the freshly cut shea oak logs from the back door but is never to use the axe himself; nor stand close, in case of flying chips. He has a vague remembrance of waking earlier to the laughter of kookaburras and the sounds of Father and Edwin's imminent departure: clanking billy cans, thudding swags, and horses snorting and neighing, backing irritably into each other in the morning chill.

Over the edge of his blanket he had seen Father kissing Mother, hard and angry on the mouth—how long has he noticed such things?—grazing his thumb against her breast as he pulls her up against him. Skelly imagines Father instead woad-painted: spear in hand, dark hair streaming out behind him, hunting deer, not chasing cattle. Last night Father had been a wild man. This morning, Mother had passed hats and food parcels warm from the stove, and warned Edwin to take care. Skelly thinks she had little to say to her husband but shook hands with the priest who would ride with the men as far as the station. Left behind, Skelly felt himself a gangly, soft, pink-faced boy. They will surely let him ride this year. He is sick to death of being mollycoddled.

Hugh curls like a limpet, his weight squelchy-damp across Skelly's middle, sucking at his fat fist. Mucous catches and turns at the back of his throat. Blinnie has crawled in beside him, and lies on her back, belching the air. Skelly prods at Hugh's soggy bottom and eases him off his pillow.

'Where is your sister?' Mother's eyes look black and darty; her face whiter than a corella's. 'I need her help.'

She is not worried about chores—only about her daughter. Rosanna is a runner.

'I will find her.' He kisses Hugh and clambers to his feet. This will not be the last time. Mother complicates her love by putting one child at risk to save another.

'Don't go past the pond.'

Even when the weather is hot, he wears long pants and a jacket to protect his skin. First, he checks on Edwin's horse, lame and hobbled by the still. He doubts that Rosanna would take off on him, for she loves horses more, he is sure, than people. The sun beats down on his head. Dripping spread hastily on a wedge of stale damper greases his hand as he climbs slowly towards the limestone ridge behind their house. He hasn't told Mother that his sock, stiff with washing, abrades his sore heel. He is sick to death of being precious.

The morning passes slow and steady like treacle poured from a spoon even though he hurries between Rosanna's favourite places: beneath the trees where she reads the priest's books; the small sinkhole; the top of the ridge where she shouts at swallows, making their way in clean swoops across the lagoons and swamps, to take her back to Ireland. At the mere thought of her leaving, he feels ill.

He turns his head and casts his eyes behind him. The sea is a thin ribbon of colour on the near horizon. It looks cool and inviting. Deflated by hot sun, he thinks of the times Edwin brings home bags of periwinkles, reef mussels, green whelks, cockles and limpets from rock pools. He loves the way the glistening flesh springs open in his mouth, releasing salt pleasure so intense that he rolls back his eyes until he feels the slide of skin on the back of his throat. Skelly licks his dry lips.

Then on he labours. What if Rosanna has been carried away by a hawker and set to scrubbing pots and pans, or kidnapped by a Chinaman to light his joss sticks? She would go anywhere with anyone and, he suspects, it is the heathens that she loves most.

Finally, he arrives at the last likely place, hot and tired and sore. Honeyeaters, attracted by the smell of water, dart at the lip of the cave. He rests his hand on the cool stone at the entrance before he picks his way inside through loose limestone rubble. The air smells damp and fetid. Dark walls close around him and he is overpowered by the peculiar smell of bent-wing bats as he steps into the main chamber, its great walls stretching thirty feet above his head. Motes surf the sunlight thrown from a small hole in the ceiling where reassuringly he sees grass and sky. A crow alights in the space. It cocks its head, making its mournful cry, as it peers in. It is looking for a snake, tumbled to the bottom of the cave, trapped. Skelly shifts his feet, uneasy. She isn't here.

I4

GOING FOR GOLD AND TINY BONES

Skelly settles on a large boulder, the small abrasion on his heel aches and he eases off his leaky *bróg*. Relief from the throbbing pain floods his white and wrinkled swollen foot, but if he can't put his boot back on, how will he get home?

The bats start up. Has *he* disturbed them? Dusk is the time to watch out for snakes waiting at the entrance of the cave for a low-flying bat. Bold bats roil about his head, flapping stale air across his face on their way back to their hanging place. Small dead bats lie scattered on the guano like leather gloves. Reflected in the dark sheen of sluggish water trickling past his feet he sees a yellow light.

It moves slowly along the shelf that links three tunnels to the main auditorium. His heart thunders in his ears until he sees, to his great relief, his sister looking annoyingly pleased with herself.

'Skelly, darling.'

'Mother is fretting.'

'Pft. Father won't be back for days. I'll make up for it by then.'

'Are you fine, Rosanna?' She couldn't care less he thinks, wincing as he lifts his foot.

'Even if I am, I'm not staying here much longer. It's all very well for Father and Edwin riding away like heroes every day. I am going to the goldfields. We only need one decent nugget to take us back to Ireland and live rich, just the two of us in a castle. Why should we be stuck out here in the middle of nowhere?'

'But we're here together. We're not hungry. You know what Father says about Ireland. We *had* to leave. Even Edwin remembers.'

'Do you believe them? We could have stayed in Woodford. Mother tells a different story in which she made Father leave because a soldier threw down a shilling. You are too young and you don't have the longing.'

'I aim to go back there with you.' How she infuriates him. He leans in. 'Rosanna, you smell like apricots.'

'I brought two in my hat. Have one. Skelly *alannahh*, I want to show you something grand.'

'I can't walk.' He eases his left foot onto the rock in front of him.

'Let me see.' Rosanna peels back his sock and peers at his heel, as her mother does. 'It's red for sure, but it hasn't broke the surface.' She moves her candle closer, dripping wax on the wound.

'That's hot,' he squeaks.

'Of course it's hot, you ninny. Come on now.' She leads him across the floor of the cave, up onto the smooth, cool surface of the shelf. Shoes in hand, hobbledehoy, he follows her into a tunnel.

'This tunnel links up,' she calls back to him, tucking her plait inside the bodice of her dress, 'with another.' Nosing around a tight bend, her skirt drags along the floor of the passageway and she gathers it up in a bunch at her hip. Eilish would be furious. He skims his fingers along the slimy walls, and shudders. In winter, they could both be washed away. The ceiling rises and the tunnel opens into a large antechamber where, backs slightly bent, they can stand together.

As if she is praying to Our Lady, Rosanna kneels below a shelf in the wall. 'Will you look at this,' she whispers.

Skelly leans forward to touch bones gracefully splayed on the stone in front of him. 'Is it a shrine?'

'It is, I suppose.'

'Is it a little wallaby?'

'No tail.'

'What then? A baby wombat fell down here?' Fresh grief determines that some part of him knows.

'Look at the skull.'

'Oh, it is not a sheep, nor a calf.' He bites his lip.

'It is a little human being, Skelly.'

'I am sick of sadness.' He drops his head. 'Do you think it was here picnicking in the caves with the station people and it crawled into the tunnels? That is why we are not to come here,' he reminds her.

'It has no clothes. I think its mother laid it here,' she says.

'Or its father?'

'I suppose, Skelly. More likely, its mother.'

Skelly stares at the bones a long time, imprinting the shapes and patterns on his memory, the ivory lattice of the ribs, the tiny skull small enough to cradle in his hands, the shapes and patterns. He wants very much to draw them. He imagines the little thing mewling in the chill darkness and wipes his eyes on the back of his hand.

'Oh, but you're a wet thing, Skelly. I think you're gorgeous.' Rosanna hugs him hard until he drops one of his boots, and slips sideways, knocking several of the bones.

'It makes me think of our baby ...' he says and his voice crackles. His face must look woeful.

'This one was very young. It hardly knew it was alive.'

'Did it breathe first do you suppose?'

Rosanna shrugs. 'No way of knowing, silly—but Moorecke cries *koongine* when she brings me here.'

'*Koongine* means son.'

His sister lowers her head. 'I don't know.'

'I want to go home, Rosanna.'

'We will. Poor Mother. It must be the worst pain to lose a child.' She raises her hands above her head, stretches, and flexes them against the curvature of the limestone, as if resisting being confined. 'On the way home I will tell you my plans.'

Skelly stands gingerly on one leg, stooping to gather up his boots. 'Plans?'

'To run away, to go to the gold.'

'No.' He limps miserably after her. A useless tearful *boccah*. Near the entrance Rosanna takes several bounding long-legged strides up the rubbly slope and into the sunshine. She walks strong like the Royal Emer, as if she owns the possum-poo–spattered path on which she walks.

When she turns back, her warm brown eyes are alive with sympathy. 'I'll piggyback you a wee bit.'

He shakes his head. Useless, and grown too big to piggyback.

The walk takes a very long time. Pain courses through the soles of his feet, even as he tries to touch the earth lightly, tries to prevent the blister breaking open, spilling his blood onto the path. Mother should not have to lose another son; even a useless one.

15

ENNUI

'*Ach*, may God help us,' Eilish shouts, crossing herself when Skelly limps in with Rosanna supporting his upper arm. A sour white mist rises from the marshy ground behind the house. 'Where have you been?'

'I'm fine if you are at all interested, but Skelly has a red foot.'

'Well, I can see that,' her mother snaps.

'He could not bear to put on his shoes. I helped him home along the creek.' This is wormwood to her mother. Rosanna arches her back, with virtuous weariness, and runs her hands down her spine.

'You'll rot in hell, Rosanna, if anything happens to this boy.'

Rosanna is not so much afraid of eternal damnation as she is of Skelly falling sick and leaving them before she fully furnishes her plans; for then his reproachful ghost will burden her journey. Let God come after her then. He'd be faster than the priest who visits them but every three months.

When they first arrived in the colony their mother had whispered that for all her sins, *she* had gone to hell in a bucket: tipped out in an upside-down place where the people were black and the swans too; and with all of them clinging on, at the bottom of the world, it sure was as hot as hell. How could it be worse? Soon enough, it was. So cold that grass couldn't grow and the flats flooded between the ridges.

Eilish pushes hair off her face. Swooping on Skelly, she presses him down onto a deal box at the back door and eases off his boots.

'I am fine, Mother—only tired,' he says.

'Tired ... of course you're tired, you daft *cratthur*, and flushed. Running all over the countryside after your sister, who is turning into a little savage. In the name of God what am I to do with her?' She dabs his foot with antimony. 'Say your prayers.'

Rosanna hovers, making rueful faces. What a fuss Eilish makes. Doesn't he look just fine? Blinnie appears, pantaloons atop her head, waggling her little *thóin* over her potty belly, like a duckling, tugging at her sister's skirt until she's scooped into her arms.

'Don't kiss her mouth, Rosanna,' Mother cries. 'Hugh has croup again and she is awful *bronickle*. Where *have* you been, girl? I needed your help.' Eilish places a poultice on Skelly's foot, ties strips of cloth around it, and shoos him hopping to his bed.

Rosanna tries to understand her fierceness. 'All right then, Mother. You rely on God's grace, but it didn't save Baby.'

'Oh no it did not. Dear Baby.' Eilish leans her belly against the chair and her fingers tear through her hair. She stops, sways then as if defeated.

Rosanna waits through the long silence. Tries not to think of Baby.

'Do you recall when that drunken linen-maker, O'Flaherty, shattered his glass all over Skelly?' Her mother speaks as if partially entranced. 'You were just a little girl.'

Rosanna winces, dancing her fingers across the top of the hot stove, blinking hard. 'I do, and I'll never forget the blood running down his cheeks and stopping up his mouth and ear-holes. It was a wonder he could breathe at all before I came to find you.'

Eilish draws Rosanna into her arms. 'He had bare enough strength to sip water from a spoon.'

'And you pressed cobwebs into his wound until the bleeding stopped,' her daughter murmurs against her chest.

'I did so. And I stitched tea and dog root into muslin bags to hold against his dilly downy head. I carried water from the Holy Well to sprinkle on his forehead. He was cold as a corpse. I thought he were extinct.'

For two days Skelly lies in bed, waking only to seize his sketchbook, work feverishly and then subside again. Adults in the family tiptoe around him, grief over the baby still whipping at their hearts. Mother knows the priest will once again advise them to take Skelly to a place in a town, to apprentice him to a soft trade or to allow him to serve the church in some small way. An adolescent appetite weighs on a frontier family. And Skelly brings little return. Father talks morbidly of funerals. Shamed, Rosanna stays close to home scouring pots and pans with sand brought by Edwin from the shore where he does his business. Skelly seems hardly to stir himself, while she runs ragged feeding babies and making soda bread.

'Don't you leave *that* sketch around,' she spits at him. So he *is* troubled by the scattering of tiny bones in the cave. It will not help Moorecke. Rosanna places a bat, fallen from the rafters, beside him on the bed wrappers, and watches him turn the creature reverently between his fingers. He must recover soon.

During the long afternoon next day, she hears the flap of a fan as her mother cools Skelly and the little ones. The persistent buzz of bush flies and the coughing of Blinnie and Hugh suck Rosanna into a pit of torpor. Everything is loathsome. How she had looked forward to wearing the green dress, but it has been as unsatisfactory as everything else. All she wants is to die. Father Woods says that dying is beautiful and he longs, when he has outlived his usefulness, to be with God. Nothing moves.

Why *should* she stay? Flayed by guilt and discontent. Skelly's sketch of the tiny bones brings on a yearning that comes only at certain times: when reading books or stroking herself in a gentling private way. Music brings it on. She leans into the feeling, and takes it up knowingly. Edwin feels it, she is sure. Father, also. It is as if they have been born with a piece missing.

The priest understands them. All of them. 'Settle yourself, Rosanna,' he says. 'Trust in God.' Perhaps he suffers himself.

Rosanna wonders if such restlessness is ever in her mother. When Eilish isn't watching Skelly and the little ones, her eye is on her daughter, earnest as a wedge-tailed eagle circling smoke. Her fierce love brooks no resistance. When they first arrived, she made all of them copy from old books brought from the Woodford National School. By then Edwin had taken up boundary riding with their father and begun the religious working of the ledger in his head. He had only ever cared for sums. And money.

'What else can I do,' she often said, 'in such an empty place? Not even a hedge school.'

Over and over, Rosanna read her only books, three volumes of *The Macdermots of Ballycloran*, until the pages wore thin and the ink came off on her fingers. Mother had come by the dog-eared volumes back in Ireland, by default, when an English lady with a belly as round and hard as a barrel of lard, but with such nice manners and a fancy wrap, was spied leaving Walsh's Inn without paying her chit. Running away, more than likely, Mother said; she had wanted her gone before a bloody wailing scrap turned up in one of the upstairs chamber pots. At first she refused the books as payment, then, when she saw the fierce look of pride in the woman's green eyes, took them with bad grace. 'Written by a postmaster in Drumsa, County Leitrim,' Mother said when she pushed them towards her daughter. 'What would a postmaster know about writing a novel'—she had been wrong about that, for now Mr Trollope was popular and famous—'and surely it will be dull.'

Every time the priest dropped into Walsh's premises for a drop of *usquebaugh*, Rosanna's luck would have him catch her before the fire with the kitchen hangers-on, head stuck in the book. Even the cheese-woman slummocking in the chimney corner had an opinion about the ill effects of a novel on a girl. Rosanna read and reread about the troubles of Feemy Macdermot, a girl without education, whose abilities were exercised in entirely the wrong direction—reading novels and taking up with a young lover. For years she felt uncertain about whether her mother knew their entire contents, feared she might remove them from her daughter's custody. Until lately, books brought by Father Woods quelled her need to run. But something has built up in her now.

Late in the night, rain stampedes across the roof as if their lives depend upon its rapid transit. Mother passes Rosanna reading and commandeers her candle on the way to tend her son. Rosanna sinks on her knees at the window and, clutching her book, stares into the murky darkness. It seems a very long time before Eilish returns the candle, taking care not to splash her cold hand with wax. 'The fever has broken. I have bathed him and his skin feels cooler. Go to sleep.' Her mother kisses her brow and creeps away. All is forgiven when danger passes.

Rosanna springs up and seizes the kitchen knife to slash at the sleeves of the green dress, opening up the long darts from breast to waist. Then, shamed, she stamps it into the earth by her bed—stamps out the smallest hope that the dress might bring redemption. Feemy Macdermot's life is far more interesting than hers. She will tear the pages, one by one, from *The Macdermots of Ballycloran* and stomp on them as well. Tomorrow she will leave for the goldfields.

16

A PALTRY THEFT

Today will be the day. Lucky Edwin, oh so lucky, Edwin, she thinks as he prepares to ride away. How she hates his good fortune. Raising her face to kiss his cheek, she passes him a parcel of meat and bread.

'Feed Lucifer extra oats and take him out for *light* exercise,' Edwin says. 'I want him fit for Saturday's race.'

When she turns away smiling, he seizes her arm and swings her back to face him. 'Grand to see Skelly recovering.'

Light exercise will not hold her or Lucifer. God love him, Edwin is a devil, too, so they are suited. She kisses her brother again before he swings his leg over his stock horse, and she runs to find Lucifer. She slides her hands down his muscular flanks—there is no heat in them now—and soft over the hocks, where only a faint scabby line remains. She flicks at the dry crust with her fingernail. The swelling has gone. She lifts the back hooves and examines his feet, like a blacksmith, like Father would.

'You're a begger, just like me. You want to go,' she whispers, lifting tack from a tree branch. If *only* she hadn't cut her dress. Her second-best will have to do. She pulls the bridle over his head, easing her fingers into the sides of his lips to open his teeth for the bit. The big horse sidesteps, ears twitching, swinging his backside about, snorting and breaking wind as he swishes flies with his tail.

'Oh, you.' She buries her face in his neck and breathes in his lovely smell. He blows out to prevent her tightening the girth strap. She balls her fist and punches him hard in the side until he lets go; then she tightens the strap.

Eilish and the babies will sleep for hours. She will only be an aggravation. And when Skelly hears Lucifer's heels drumming past the stands of wattle by the track and the indignation of the black cockatoos shattering the air around them as they pass, he will put down his sketchbook; he will know she is gone and wish that he was with her flying up the hill behind the house. But he will tend to the little ones if they wake: play games on their toes, tweak at their noses, and hold beakers of warm water to their fat lips. He will buy her time, while Mother lies abed clutching the baby's lace christening gown.

Rosanna stares up at the unforgiving blue sky before tying her reticule to the pommel. In it she has placed a handful of shillings earned from washing Father Woods's surplice and polishing his chalice and candlesticks. The heat is as strong and rich-smelling as leather. She uses a stump of wood to mount, shifting her weight in the saddle to encourage Lucifer to fancy-step up into the bit. He drops his head suddenly, legs splayed, all tug and temper.

'Oh, you'd like to throw me, you skittish thing. Get me into trouble with Edwin.' Not that she cares a *thrawneen* about that. Clear of the house she nudges the horse, giving him his head. He takes off in a startled canter, moving swiftly into a gallop on the bridle path leading to the ridge and the caves. Light on the reins, she gives herself up to the rhythm of his neck and the cooling rush of air in her hair. A mob of kangaroos surprises him and she drops deeper into her seat. Corellas split open the hum of the bush, flying up like a tossed hand of cards. He shies again. Each time he goes to market she moves her head to one side away from his neck and digs in her heels. Once he had broken her nose. It is best to push him forward when he rears; even Edwin says so. The sun beats down on her back.

Father and Edwin are miles away, mayhaps resting in the shade of a swamp gum, sucking on their pipes and pannikins of green tea, keeping an eye on a herd of yearlings they have driven from the scrub. Father will be reading dark, grave poetry. Edwin, all impatience, plinking limestone pebbles against a tree, or sleeping like a baby with his hat over his face.

Cresting the ridge she pulls the horse up hard, taking everything in: the track winding through the marshy flats, the smoking chimneys of the station house, the looming volcano behind it. It is like a park, she thinks, the muted greens of the stringybark forests to the east, the remnant pools of water.

She intends to gallop past the Big House where Father and Edwin draw their wages and on to Gambierton, where wagons and coaches pull up, and travel beyond. She cannot be trapped forever, helping her mother in a workman's cottage.

She wipes her eyes and looks behind her. Over her shoulder dirty clouds drift to the coast. A mere wisp of sea collars the tea-tree scrub. She will leave the horse in Gambierton with a note, and offer her services to a family with children, on their way to the goldfields at Ballarat.

She leans back in the saddle, allowing the horse to pick his way, sliding and clattering through limestone rubble as he descends from the lip of the ridge. At the bottom he bounds and eagerly skids forward. Rosanna rides him into the landscape as if she is entering a painting, rushing along between wind-bent trees, praying Lucifer will avoid hidden branches and boggy holes, past a flock of chestnut teal that splash and leap into the sky with crabbity quacks. Perspiration runs down her arms and back. Black horsehairs and filth speckle her dress where she has gripped the galloping horse. Not far now.

17

THE BIG HOUSE

After the worst flood, the Big House had been rebuilt on higher ground. Rosanna cannot resist a peep. At the gateway, she hesitates. For a little while her boldness ebbs away. Lucifer, sensing her lapse in concentration, flattens his ears and bounds forward along the avenue of trees towards the house. She hauls and hauls at the reins but the whistling of a hot and sudden wind excites him further.

At the end of the track, he lurches forward and pitches her onto the ground; she lands heavily, bouncing on her *thóin*. Fierce pain shoots through her lower back. Sprawled across the track she examines her grazed elbows. Lucifer pulls up at the last tree and stretches his neck to snatch at leaves. Rosanna limps forward. Praise God, she is not fatally hurt. She edges towards Lucifer, managing to gather up his reins and tie them to a branch. A dung-coloured dog barks.

She has never seen a house so commodious and white. Cut in square blocks of limestone the walls somehow seem to curve around the windows. Behind it, a small village of outbuildings have sprung up, for cooking, stores, meat and stabling. Overblown roses splash like blood against the walls.

Shifting shadows between the trees catch her attention. Trying to focus in blinding sunlight she sees Moorecke running through the yard, carrying a squawking bird beneath each arm and followed by barking dogs.

A small blonde woman with pale eyelashes and pearl drop earrings the size of grapes appears, pitching stones. 'You brazen creature. I will have my husband after you. I will use his gun.'

Moorecke is gone, quite likely streaking home across the mud-crazed, dried out swamps. And by now Rosanna should be on the road to Gambierton. The woman lifts her apron to her white face— then strides to free the dog straining at its chain. It bounces through a phalanx of turkeys wheeling across the yard. Alarmed, they gobble and break formation springing into the air. The dog, fierce enough to chew the tail off a bullock, bounds across the grass towards Rosanna, who crouches behind a spindly cherry ballart. It barks and circles.

Stick in hand, the woman marches towards her. 'I fear you don't speak English, but show yourself, now.' Pale and perspiring, the woman holds a stick out in front of her as if to ward off evil. The dog slathers at Rosanna's neck and she shoves it hard away before moving into the harsh sunlight. The woman suppresses a gasp and calls it off.

'Oh … oh.' She looks done-in. Her small round face crumples as she whimpers. This must be young Mrs Ashby. One word to Father and Rosanna is done for. She lifts her face to meet the woman's eyes.

One hand on the dog's collar, the other pressed for balance against the sky, like a statue in a garden, Mrs Ashby smiles in an insipid sickly way, sways and drops like a felled roo.

The dog licks her face, smells freedom, and scarpers. Rosanna falls to her knees beside the woman, attempting to smooth out her untidy landing, to lift her head and tap her cheeks, to push hair from her face. She runs to fetch water from a jug in the kitchen outhouse, and a cloth. A baby bawls from the dim recesses of the house.

Rosanna presses a wet towel against the woman's neck and brow and waits kneeling at her side. Almost immediately, eyes roiling, Mrs Ashby revives. Her head flops to one side and with some difficulty she pulls herself upright and vomits into Rosanna's lap.

They both recoil. Rosanna takes the cloth and runs down the slope to the edge of the swamp, where she uses her hands to sluice water down her front. Holy Mother of God, she is reeky. The woman struggles to her feet and Rosanna rushes back to assist her to the house, where Mrs Ashby collapses onto a chaise in the front room.

'I am most unwell. I fear it is the influenza.'

Rosanna brings a mug of water. Then she finds the baby, pink with exertion after its sudden squall. It whimpers, head down, bottom up, in its fancy cradle. Rosanna lumps it, sodden backside and all, to its mother, and prepares to withdraw.

'Can you not speak, girl?' says Mrs Ashby, over the baby's head. 'Make yourself known. Why are you so dirty?'

Rosanna struggles. She is in a binding chair. Damn the bossy

English woman, for it is she who threw her breakfast all over Rosanna's dress, which, but for a few horsehairs, was clean enough.

The woman drools and faints again. Rosanna plucks the baby to safety from the white frilled shoulder shuddering against the couch and takes more pity as Mrs Ashby rouses.

'I'll help you for now until you recover. Unless the boundary riders come ... until your husband ...' She cannot leave a sickly woman and a helpless baby. One more *day* will make no difference.

Mrs Ashby shows immediate relief. 'The Blacks have gone?' She looks around in trepidation, holding her forearm to her face. 'You're Irish. Tell me your name.'

'Rosanna.' It is only a whisper. Something inside her feels obliged, then, to speak about Moorecke, but she must not say her name. 'She is not fearsome, the black girl.' So much fuss about two fowls when the woman has flocks of geese and turkeys. 'She names this place her *m'rado*, where you have settled down. And she can get feed from anywhere.'

'I have no doubt of that, Rosanna, but this is my husband's land. He has leased it from the Crown.'

'*Booandik* people lived here—before your family came.'

'You are gabbling, Rosanna. You know this girl?'

'That I cannot say.' Rosanna turns her face towards the ridge, pressing her toe into the rag mat.

'Your mother should not allow you to roam about the countryside. There are rustlers killing our cattle, and Blacks. Why do you not stay at home and help her? Has she other children?'

Rosanna blanches, remembers the sweet smell of the baby. And the way he reaches out his little hands to be picked up. She thinks of *their* baby.

'Are you a wilful girl?'

Rosanna swings away, deciding, after all, that her shame knows no bounds. She will set off for Gambierton after all and then for the gold.

The woman relents and calls her back. 'Wait, I will pay you a penny if you can comfort the baby while I bathe.'

Rosanna is not mollified and stares her down. A penny will not take her far.

Mrs Ashby implores her, half expectant of mysterious dues. 'My husband is an affectionate man but he does not understand that the dearth of labour takes its toll on me, as well as him. Promises of scenic walks and sketching parties have come to nothing. All I do is work. Please look after the baby, just this morning, until I recover.'

She does not know real loss, Rosanna thinks. And what if Moorecke returns and Mrs Ashby shoots her?

18

MOORECKE IN DANGER

By the time the sun is sinking into the western sky, Rosanna has worked harder than all the slaves of Egypt, harder than her mother would believe likely, or even possible. She has no strength left to make a journey further away than home.

'I am going, ma'am. My mother will be worried.'

'Let us hope so, for we are living in a dangerous and uncivilised place. I will speak to my husband about the girl. He will locate her and make her understand that she must not steal.'

Rosanna thinks back to the day she shot the bullock and feels anxious to be off. It is not the black girl—her mother shot and killed by settlers—who is dangerous. Her first encounter with Moorecke occurred within months of their arrival. She had found her cowering in the fork of a tree, terrified by distant gunfire. Rosanna had settled down to watch her. After the gunshots died away—perhaps someone hunting ducks or geese—Moorecke had climbed down, digging stick in hand, wattle blossom in her smoky hair, lumping her dreadful skull. Rosanna had reached out to touch her skin, in all its shades of charcoal, ochre, midnight-blue. Seemingly oblivious, Moorecke had rocked from side to side, moaning and slapping at her small dark breasts for some time before she calmed. Rosanna thought her wondrous good at acting: either that or she was mad. It had been the beginning of their talking. Rosanna tried to mimic her but rued the difficulty of taking her tongue to the back of her throat, to utter any of the harsh words with the girl's fluency.

'Roanna,' Moorecke copied *her* quite easily, arching her slender arm to indicate where the sun rose in the east, and a fire smoked to the north, south where Rosanna had seen two brolgas rise like kites over the stringybark forests, and west where later, the sun would drop into the sea. '*M'rado.*'

Rosanna lies to Mrs Ashby. 'I have never seen her. She will run a long way and never come back because you have frightened her with your shouting. They are fey people.'

In the early years Father had been sent out to work on other stations, sometimes for a week or more, and Moorecke's people had camped closer to the house. If the Blacks approached the house in daylight, Eilish gave them tea and flour, and they brought her wood, which they stacked against the walls. Rosanna knew her mother had feared they'd burn the house down and had patrolled outside after dark, in a heavy coat and carrying a loaded rifle. As a show of strength she had shot swamp wallabies in the moonlight and cut them up for stew. Eilish was as tough as a tanner when protecting kin.

Mrs Ashby thrusts out her hand to clutch at Rosanna. 'Will you return in the morning to help me? I am stranded here and unaccustomed to this work. The overseer's slatternly Irish wife rarely gets out of bed to help me.'

The woman must be daft, insensitive, to speak in such a way to a girl from Galway. 'I might be leaving for Victoria.'

Mrs Ashby ignores this and sidles towards the window. 'In any case, she is gone, taken away this morning by the police and Doctor Wehl.' She looks out.

'Oh the poor dear girl,' Rosanna laments.

'Nothing could be done. She was quite hysterical, filthy, and tearing at her hair. They have taken her to the asylum in Adelaide.'

'My mother needs me,' Rosanna says, filled with uncertainty as she moves towards the door. She will get into a muck of trouble now because Eilish will be unhappy about the orphan girl.

'I will ask my husband to speak with your father.' A look of distaste plays across Mrs Ashby's face as she lightly touches Rosanna's soiled sleeve.

Rosanna rides through the late afternoon heat, emotions in a tangle. Why should she consider helping a strange demanding woman with a baby? If Mr Ashby had glimpsed her through the trees before she shot the bullock, he will recognise her. Safer to take Skelly to the goldfields as she has promised. Wages might afford her a coach from Portland. But if she works for the English woman her parents will have to know or they will forbid it. Father will be furious that she rode so far on Lucifer in the first place.

Her head muddles with conflicting thoughts. 'Mother Mary make me a better girl,' she moans to herself. Every so often, she thinks of the Irish girl shackled in a wagon, travelling across the mallee desert to the city; and of the Lynch baby's waxen face, as sheeny as orange blossom after it stopped breathing.

On the far side of the swamp she slides off Lucifer and leads him to slurp water at the reeds while she gathers swan eggs to appease her mother. It is a simple matter to chase the pen off the nest. Leaving several eggs behind, just as Moorecke has taught her, Rosanna backs away. The cob flies across the water, hissing fiercely at her, wings outstretched, feet ready to clutch her back if she turns. Lucifer throws back his head and whinnies, then drops his head to paw the water. The swan skids to a stop, bugling like an infantryman. Rosanna quickly mounts and hauls his head around.

On the spine of the ridge and near the caves the horse bucks. Two of the swan eggs catapult from her bonnet and crack open at his feet. His front hoof pulverises the shells. 'Such waste, now.' Swinging his great *thóin* against a tree, he kicks out again. Rosanna sits down hard in the saddle. When she leans back to run her hands over his rump, he dances, jumps. Blood drips from her fingers, wet first and then sticky as jam. Will Lucifer be killin' her next? The devil incarnate is in him this day. How will she explain his injuries to Edwin? She wipes her hand on the saddle cloth. Soon it will stink, for sure. Oh to think she had expected to be rattling along in a Cobb and Co coach by now, on her way to the goldfields, to Ballarat or Bendigo. It has not been a day for dancing.

19

HOMECOMING

At dusk, Rosanna rides into the yard, her hair mussed, filth on her shift and swinging a bonnet full of swan's eggs, looking no more mutinous than if she has been to the pond to catch little crayfish for their dinner. She shimmies off the horse, one hand looping his reins around the hitching post, juggling eggs with the other. Skelly stares at her face and the way she covers the horse's back with her cloak. He knows. Mother plies her rosary until his sister takes notice. It is not for lack of seeing that Rosanna is in trouble.

Mother spits words at Rosanna, 'I have been worried sick about you. How could you disappear again like that?' They hear the clatter of horses telegraphing Edwin's and Father's return. She turns. 'Hush up now.'

'I'm truly sorry.' Rosanna trails her mother, picking up Hugh and Blinnie who push at her like puppies. 'Sometimes I think I am dying. My head is full of bad things.'

'Hold your tongue, you foolish girl. It is a mortal sin you'll be committing.' She squeezes her hand. 'You're not dying, you daft *cailín*. Your thoughts have dwelled too much on Baby.'

Rosanna bites her lip.

Edwin has brought home a leg of mutton tied to his saddle rolls. Mother breaks swan eggs over a feed of potatoes in the camp oven. Running out to meet the riders, the little ones act as lively as chickens, after their long afternoon sleep. Holding Hugh high in his arms, Father fills the doorway, bending to search out love in Eilish's face. He kisses her like a drowning man, and then turns to his oldest daughter, plucking her hand and holding it hard against his chest.

'Have you been helping your mother?' He pulls her closer. Like a collared dog, Rosanna ducks her head against his.

Eilish inserts herself between them, pushing her daughter aside.

'Garrick, go. Blather with the little ones. Rosanna and I have work to do.'

Skelly concludes the worst is over. Unless Father takes hard to the grog. Through the door, he can see the men belting fleas from their bedding spread across the hitching rail and Rosanna creeping away from the stables.

On her return to the house, he surreptitiously watches her pour water from the jug into the bowl on the box between their beds, and turning her back to wash and change her shift. How thin she looks. He has not seen her rags for months. She must be ill or strange. Last night, he found the green dress that Mother made for her birthday, torn to pieces and stuffed behind the piss pot under their beds. First he arranged it on his pillow and made a sketch of Rosanna wearing it, before she became so sad. Then he returned it to its place.

At table, Rosanna is quiet, jumpy, watching everyone. Skelly turns the back of his spoon over the sweet curve of precious preserved apricots. One day he will leave home and become a famous artist. And he will draw girls' *thóins*—whenever he pleases.

Edwin begins to tap his spoon on the tabletop, just like Father when he is simmering over something. 'Rosanna, how is my horse?' he asks.

'I worked him well today. The leg is not warm. The swelling is down. Not one girth gall.' Rosanna licks her lips, and stares at her full plate.

'I am set on him doing well in the steeplechase on Saturday.'

'And I know it.' She lifts her eyes reluctantly. 'He'll be fine, Edwin, I swear by my Granny, who is in her grave.'

'Well what would the sticky mess on his backside be then?'

Her eyes skim over her father's head. 'I gave him light work. But you won't believe it. I saw a creature near the trees and he took fright and shied away. Backed into a tree.'

'A creature?'

'A native dog, maybe ... like a yellow streak, at the sundown. Big.'

'For sure, it is a good story, Ro,' says Edwin. 'But you know most of the dogs are dying.'

Rosanna bites her lip.

Father's face becomes severe. 'By all that's holy, Edwin, I'm surprised to hear you gnashing into your sister, after today's events.'

They fall into an uncomfortable silence. What has Edwin done this time?

THE IRISH ORPHAN GIRL

After dinner the older ones sit at the small deal table—Edwin, Rosanna, Skelly, Mother and Father. Edwin and Skelly begin a discourse about a dead rat that Skelly has found on the step. He sees Rosanna shudder, pushing her stool in, as she begins to gather up the plates. Hair snarls at the nape of her neck, where she has hastily washed.

'Rosanna,' says her father. 'Don't be long fussing; I want to hear about your grand ride.'

Her eyes shimmer with nerves. Skelly plays a game of chess with his father at the table. All the while he places the worn wooden pieces on the board, he watches Rosanna crouched on the step, washing crockery. A dish breaks against the pan.

'Take care. We have no more plates.' Eilish looks uneasy, stealing glances at her husband as she shifts Blinnie onto her shoulder and kisses her small cheek. Rosanna bends over the steaming tub, nose tilted, nostrils flaring like an animal in gun sight. When Father calls her she ducks her head as if she's a horse and he pulls too hard on her mouth. She skitters by his chair to wipe down the table.

'Sit,' he bellows. 'Tell us where you've been on the horse today.'

'Leave it. She's been helping me since then.' Mother knows about drink talking, after living in a public house.

'Why do you defend her when she's in the wrong?'

'I don't want a scrimmage in my kitchen, with Baby gone to God, Skelly recovering from illness and your daughter exhausted.'

Edwin fiddles with papers and tobacco. He has been waiting for such a scene, Skelly knows: Rosanna, too. Father holds her gaze, hauls on the bit some more, digs his heels in hard. Skelly makes a foolish move and loses his queen. Father sweeps up the pieces with his calloused hand. Rosanna is taking it hard.

Mother wants it over. 'Garrick, leave her. She'll not ride out again, unless she asks. Will you now?' she demands, turning to her daughter.

Father rolls his shoulders back, raises his glass to examine his drink against the guttering lantern-light, and places it down again. Leisurely, he fixes his pipe. 'Have you not heard, Eilish? Besides working the horse, Rosanna hasn't enough to do at home. She's working for Jane Ashby. Tell your mother the truth now and none of your lies.'

'It isn't exactly true. When she fell down in the yard I couldn't leave her. She was sick.'

It is like watching clouds pass over Eilish's face, Skelly thinks: heavy ones, lighter ones, then glimmering sunlit ones.

'What were you doing at the Big House? Is Mrs Ashby all right? And *her* baby?' Eilish crosses herself.

'She's fine.' Rosanna throws back her head. 'And I do ... I do want to work for her. I could ride over in the mornings, with Father and Edwin. Come back when they finish. I am old enough. It will be hard for you without Baby but ... she is offering wages.'

'Now, Eilish, you see how it is.' Father stares hard at Rosanna. 'I am to send my own daughter to Uncle William's cabin—to slave for his wife.'

'I want to go. Skelly can help Mother here. He is mostly well enough and careful. If only you would let me.'

Skelly loses sympathy for Rosanna and glares. Chops his fist into his hand.

She shifts her gaze from face to face, storms to her feet, twisting the end of her plait with her fingers. 'I hate it here,' she says, all stinging vehemence.

Father takes it personally. 'Oh do you, indeed? Isn't it enough that Edwin and I toil to put food in your mouth, and to save for land of our own ... after all we've been through?'

'I'll run then, right away. I'll ask the priest to find a place for me in the city with all those orphans.'

Skelly sees that she has forgotten her promise to take him to the gold.

'It's not the city needing orphans,' says Eilish, 'unless you've taken a fancy to living in the Poor House or the asylum. They're all being sent to the country, into service.'

'Mrs Ashby has no help in the house.'

'What can have happened to the overseer's little wife?'

'The police took her away to the asylum in Adelaide. Mrs Ashby says they tied her to the cart.'

Eilish stays Rosanna with her hand. 'Oh Mary, Mother of God, the poor little girl.'

'Rosanna, help your mother, now. Forget about the Ashbys.' Father speaks quietly.

But Eilish grips Rosanna's hand tighter and turns to her husband. It is one of those occasions when Skelly notices something fragile flashing between Mother and Father. The way Father arranges words upsets her. 'Did I not help my mother working in the bar?' she cries. 'Did I not raise our passage by doing so? Rosanna can earn money to help us buy land.'

'And what would she know about the kind of service the Ashbys would expect. You'd be laying her open to criticism.'

'She's as good as anyone, and bright. Don't frighten her.'

Rosanna flounces from the table and uses a cloth to lift the heavy kettle of boiling water from the fire. Edwin lights his pipe, leans back against the wall and winks at his brother. Skelly knows that he is awful pleased by this turn of events. He is glad to see Rosanna drawing heat, instead of him, for once. She goes back to washing pots. Skelly notices she has brought the crucifix threaded on velvet ribbon around her neck to her mouth, and is biting down on it while she beats the water with the soap holder.

'Rosanna.' Mother raises her voice. Rosanna lifts her head, deliberately placing her hand against the hot water kettle. She holds Eilish's gaze. Tears spill down her mother's cheeks. His sister appears to wait with perverse satisfaction for fierce pain to fill her eyes. What can she be thinking of? She lifts her injured hand like an indictment on the whole family and continues washing.

21

LUCKY EDWIN

Skelly cannot bear to watch Rosanna a minute longer and skedaddles
after his brother into the yard where Edwin is rubbing foul smelling salve into Lucifer's back. They mask a show of conversation, ears
cocked to the house.

'Will you be racing him next Saturday, Edwin? If he is full recovered.'

'I shall do that, God willing.'

'Where is the race?' Skelly leans forward to pat Lucifer, who nuzzles in his pocket.

'At MacDonnell Bay.'

'I wish that I might ride behind you in the morning.'

'Mother will worry and I'll have a lot on my mind. The steeplechase
is my chance to win a few sovereigns.'

'What will you do with the money?'

'Invest it in my business.'

Skelly knows that Edwin's dream of carting goods to the bay and
back is considerably hampered by his lack of a cart. He decides to re-
vert to the original subject. 'Do you suppose Lucifer can win?'

Edwin looks disconsolate. 'I sure could use the money, if he did.'

Skelly starts and lifts his head to face him. 'Why is it so upsetting
then, today?' Was he also saving for a wedding?

Edwin resumes tenderly rubbing the horse's coat until it gleams.
'Did Father not say?'

'Nil. Not a word.'

'I had such bad luck. Just when I saved enough money for a cart
and near enough for a pair of bullocks. I was mustering a mob of cattle
along the ridgetop. All of a sudden they charged and broke the line.
Mr High-and-Mighty Ashby, more-n-likely, set them off himself. Two
dead. The penalty is to come from my wages.'

'By the crass, Edwin. That is hard on a man.'

'Then, when I had to butcher them up for the Big House kitchen, not a shin bone did he offer a poor lad trying to make his way in life.'

'You should not complain. Every day things happen to you that are better than my dreams.' If only Edwin would talk to Father about taking him boundary riding.

'Lucifer's the best horse in the district. Even the poet says so. I'm thinking I might sell him for a lot of money,' says Edwin.

'I wish I could help you in your business. You're so lucky, Edwin.'

'I am, and I'm Irish.' Edwin lifts his eyebrow in his deliberate way.

Skelly laughs. 'We're all Irish but we don't feel lucky like you. Rosanna tore up her best dress. Did you ever hear of such a thing?'

Edwin sweeps his hand down Lucifer's hocks and the horse side-steps. 'Get out of the way Skel, or he'll step on you.'

Skelly sighs. 'I wish I might come with you next Saturday?'

'I'll be seeing about that.'

22

MOONLIGHT SONATA

Later that night, Skelly is tired and bothered by mosquitoes. Troubled by a bruise swelling behind his knee. At least his feet have healed since his walk to the cave. Inside he finds Eilish holding Hugh over a bowl of steam. The boy barks and throws his head like a seal pup. Rosanna is nowhere to be seen.

He crawls into bed and pulls a blanket over his head, longing to scratch at his bites. When he was little, Eilish made mittens to prevent him drawing his own blood. He hears Father raising his voice in the next room, Mother arguing as much as she dares, and he strains to pick out words over Hugh's wails and noisy exhalations at the steam bowl.

'Garrick, I can't hold her, not lately. She's got wind in her brain. I fear for her.'

Father snorts. 'Back home, what would we do? We'd take her to the sisters in Loughrea. Let them thrash a bit of sense into her.'

Skelly is suddenly afraid for his sister. But there are no nuns here. Only Father Woods. It would not be deemed proper for him to take her, although Skelly thinks she'd like it; Rosanna says that the priest is gorgeous. So disrespectful. God is good and so is Father Woods.

Hugh worms under Skelly's blanket, murmuring and wheezing. The smell of camphor, garlic and eucalyptus rises from his chest.

'Tell about Cuchulain,' the little boy begs.

'What about Maeve? They are both Irish royalty.' Sometimes Cuchulain is too much for Skelly, so strong and brave, leaping like a salmon at the throat of his enemies. Rosanna has a better chance of being a hero than Skelly. 'Maeve was the best of the King of Ireland's six daughters. She could take any man she wanted to be her husband.'

'Like Rosanna?'

'Not quite. Rosanna lives in South Australia, where there is no one good enough for an Irish princess.'

Hugh giggles. 'I will marry Rosanna, when I am grown.'

Skelly kisses his forehead. Emotion catches at the back of his throat. At night, his spirits drop like kestrels upon some worrisome thought he has put aside in daylight hours. Now he has a new fear, fuelled by his father's strictness in not letting Rosanna work at the Big House. She will run away again. This isn't a good story but the worst of bad ones. Surely to God, Father Woods will not act as her liberator, for he is also a friend to their Father.

Skelly stills himself until he can hear his own breathing, which he fears will stop when he least expects it. Is life just a kind of dream? He touches the part of him which is most responsive. His eyes grow heavy with concentration, until he forgets his mortal dread.

How long is it before the owl wakes him with its soulful 'Boo-book, boo-book'? At about the same time he hears Edwin and Father going hard at each other in the yard, slamming trees with their fists and stomping around the fire. Just after this he hears the creaking of a cart, of a large horse whinnying in pain or indignation and crashing against tin. Dainty breezes push the calico at the window, lifting Blinnie's wispy hair. She murmurs in her sleep.

Mary, Mother of God Rosanna's bed space is empty again. Will he always be afraid for her? He calls on the man above. Then holds his breath, listening again to the owl and the snorting of the horses. To more shouting. Warm air presses down on him as he crawls towards the door, glancing back at his mother, who sleeps with her worn elbow crooked across her face, a coverlet twisted around her legs, as if she too would like to escape but someone has tripped and tied her. Could she be pregnant again with a babe just lost?

He rushes into the yard carrying his boots in one hand to see his older brother clambering into the seat of a rickety vehicle, flicking the horse's *thóin* with his crop, and holding the sides of the cart to regain his balance as it lurches forward.

'Edwin,' Skelly cries out. 'Where did you get this contraption?' He lopes along behind, trying to attract his brother's attention.

Edwin lifts his crop, oblivious to anything but the way forward. The horse props. His brother swears and cracks the whip. As the horse takes off again, he begins to whistle a bullocky song that he learned at Ashby's; one he frequently sings when bored with Skelly's conversation:

> *Oh my hearty, that was a party*
> *Lots of prog and buckets of grog*
> *to swig at the bullockies' ball ...*

Edwin is all for show, its effect more than likely wasted now that Father has disappeared and Rosanna is miles away, probably skylarking with Moorecke. Skelly weighs the risk and leaps, scrabbling onto the back of the cart and pulling a tarpaulin over his body and head. The floor feels rough and dirty. He finds a space between several flagons of whiskey, before the vehicle picks up pace.

Edwin never once turns. The truth is his brother is probably fluthered and best facing forwards or he'll fall on his silly head.

23

AWAY, WAR AND CONTRABAND

Skelly senses rather than sees that they are heading in the direction of Miss Lallah's. They veer north-east and lurch towards the shea oak forest. When he lifts his head he smells wood smoke and fresh loam churned by the horse and a trickle of whiskey leaking from a flagon, which he winds around his finger in a sticky stream and licks. Branches whip the side of the cart, flicking back on Skelly, who protects his face and hands with the canvas as best he can.

The *síbín* is set back from the track behind a stand of trees. Edwin ceases singing, hauls the reins into his lap, and pulls up 100 yards from the door.

Skelly sits up and wills him to turn and face him. Edwin jumps out and whips back the cover to check his load, blowing like Lucifer in a show of braggado. Oh and sure enough there's no delight. No *I love your beautiful* gnúis, *Skel.* No *raise your glass to the sky for my brother has graced us with his company.*

Skelly has shocked *himself* in stowing away. He passes over the flagons one by one. Counts five. 'Why would you bring *poteen* to Lallah's when she makes her own fine drop?' he asks with unnatural alacrity.

'Oh Skelly boy. Such grand timing.' Edwin forms a gentle fist and rests it on the end of his brother's nose. 'Lallah had an accident this afternoon and needs her store refilled. I saw fit to offer our brew for a very reasonable price. *She* saw fit to lend me this cart before my heart swung as low as a fellow's can go.'

Skelly touches his arm. 'Poor you.' He feels a kind of hypocrisy in his sympathy. What has Edwin to complain of?

'Well she titivated me. If I can make some dosh at her tables, she'll consider my offer on this old bone-rattler.'

'Well now and what about Father's cut?'

Edwin flexes his fist and then runs it down Skelly's cheek. 'Lucky you're my brother or I'd thrash you. Sooner I'm off his hands the better.'

Skelly feels suddenly weary. 'I'll lie down. I'll wait. I shan't make a sound until we leave for home.'

'Well I did not invite you, so expect nothing. I'll come when I'm ready and you know it.'

Edwin thinks he is entitled to the best life. Some people are born this way. It's how they get things done. Always putting themselves in front of other people.

Shadows of flames flicker along the front of the cottage. Would it be amusing to join the drinkers by the fire? Of course, and it would. How long will *he* have to wait before he can move about the district and drink at Lallah's? Mother would say never. He'll probably be dead before she gives permission. Everything is hopeless. At least Father cannot whack him tomorrow; only his brother.

Edwin strides away, carrying vessels of whiskey in his arms like babies. After the third trip he does not return.

Not long after this, Skelly needs to piss and slides from the cart into loose scree, finding his way up the slope and behind a drooping conifer with a skirt as big as a whale. He kicks aside dry needles to wet his centrepiece with concentration; then covers the work and leans back on his heels to fasten his trousers.

From his slightly elevated position and through the branches he can see Edwin and a girl wrestling behind the washhouse wall. They lean in and out of his view, assuming one shape and then another, arms smoothing and retracting, gripping and fastening onto each other like the gluey tentacles of squid.

Then Edwin scoops her up as he might a load of wood, arms extended and braced beneath her skirt, mouth locked against hers, and lies her down on bracky grass, where they roll from side to side. Suddenly Edwin's right hand walks up her leg, gathering the gauzy fabric of her skirt, ducking his head beneath it to take in the view. Her fingers cling to his curly head and she twists about as if she can't decide whether to push him out or trap him in there and cry for help. Her mouth opens and closes, forming rubbery shapes that Skelly cannot interpret for he is almost out of earshot and hears only groans, small cries and murmurings. Such utterances can be disorienting. They often wake him in the dark of night or first light of the morning and are followed by the harsh sounds of Mother and Father's muffled quarrelling; then Mother panting and sobbing. As acutely as he listens, the sounds confuse him.

Edwin withdraws his tousled noggin and pushes it up the girl's body, seeming to search again and again for her lips as if he's furrowing a field, then covering his work in an urgent rhythmic way. Two men come into the yard and smoke and laugh and shake hands. How close his brother must be to discovery. But Edwin is nothing if not efficient and it seems no time at all before the girl ceases fluttering her hands at his collar and lifts them up to him in entreaty, because he has abruptly broken the grip on their suckers and leapt to his feet—backed away towards the house, buttoning up his fly, doffing his hat to the men as he passes them around the corner of the washhouse.

When the girl rearranges her clothing and completes her ablutions—a lot of squatting, dabbing and rubbing—Skelly feels he should belatedly respect her privacy and retreat to the cart. His body feels overheated; his hand clammy; his pants tight. Sipping the leaking Lynch vittles has not improved his mood. Oh Edwin is lucky, all right.

2 4

BATTLE ROYALE

Eventually he creeps to the front window through which he can see his brother hunched over a card table, playing against Mr Gordon. Clay mugs squat by their right hands, cigarillos burn between their smallest fingers—such pretence—candles flicker in jam jars on the deal tables. Around them several men commune by sign over their cards.

Below the table Edwin pounds his right heel into the rough floor. Skelly sees this when he plays against him at home. Father does this too, keeping tension out of sight. In the same way, no doubt, Gordon and Edwin bluff from the waist up, conveying calm as smooth as the surface of the table but below their legs agitate as fast as ducks' in lagoon water. Each one clever enough to calculate the odds. Each one furious with the other. Each one not wanting to show emotion. Each one desperate to win.

Gordon has the larger pile of sovereigns stacked in front of him. Edwin fans his hand of cards close to his chin, covering it with his thumb, rocks back on his chair and throws more coins on the table until the piles look more equal. Edwin takes his fingers to his nose and delicately inhales their perfume. This seems to spur him on and he leans forward with a determined expression on his face. Gordon, pulling at his linen collar, tugging at his blue coat tails, appears to ignore the crowd.

Suddenly, without warning, Edwin in great exaltation sweeps the kitty towards him. Gordon peers shortsightedly at him for a half second and then he is on his feet, jack-knifing his body to fling out his arm and retrieve the coins, to ward off Edwin. 'Hasty victory. Show me the cards you Irish *tórai*.'

'And you, you *swicker*.'

A blonde young woman—it must be her—accosts Edwin's arms but he flings her off as if she is a bothersome bird pecking at his jacket.

Skelly bites his lip. Everything happens very fast: faster and more frightening than the way Edwin and Gordon jockey their horses, bumping them up against each other close to the finish line of steeplechases. Now he wishes he'd stayed at home with the babies. Edwin glares at Gordon, who is rocking his chair in an aggravating way until he knocks him off it and topples the card table. Gordon leaps up to defend it.

Could men be any sillier? Young women hovering around the card table, jars in hand, jump back against the wall. Card players leap up and drag the light furniture to the perimeter of the room. Gordon has his dukes up and begins to circle his opponent on the dirt floor. Edwin strikes out at him and receives a punch on the side of his head. Gordon bunts Edwin in the chest before he grasps him around the shoulders refusing to let go. Trapped in his arms, Edwin tries to unhand him, to sneak a quick punch to the belly while he's in the vicinity. They topple to the floor and roll towards the fire, where a little girl not much older than Skelly jumps to one side and delivers one of them a kick with her work boots.

'Settle your bill. Be a man,' Skelly hears Edwin shout as he rolls on top of Gordon and over the other side. They find their feet at the same time. Edwin has a bloody nose. Gordon is panting with some kind of wild euphoria and begins to circle again. Oh and doesn't he love the bare-knuckle boxing just for the hell of it. Skelly has seen this before and he longs to take up a stick and send them both packing. One of them grasps the other's hands and attempts to lift his knee beneath the circle of arms.

Horsemen are fearless. Neither of them feint or dance back; both drive their bodies forward like the mad eetjits they are. Both are tall and slim as kangaroo dogs, but agile. Gordon tapers more to the waist, his wrists corded with muscle from dragging on the heads of unruly and unbroken colts; Edwin, strong-muscled in the buttocks from days of chasing cattle on horseback, plants his large feet firmly and launches his punches from his hard centre. They begin to play to the crowd who shout encouragement and abuse. One raises the flat of his hand straight, like a clockwork soldier and the other smacks it down. Chants rise to the smoky ceiling. A piper could transform this into a battle between the Celts, Skelly thinks, holding his head in his hands at the window.

Lallah arrives in the boxing ring and brings down a plank of wood on their backs. She is only a little woman—unhappy about cuts to her profit, about patrons drifting away. 'A round of drinks on the house. Restore the furniture and drink up.' A roar of laughter explodes on her use of the word *furniture*, for the deal tables and box seats make a poor imitation.

Edwin and Gordon are well considered because they are kings on the track. Skelly knows this. And with Lallah's persuasion they remove themselves to the verandah where they grimace, shrug their untidy coats back onto their shoulders, and brush down their pants with filthy hands. She helps them divvy up the money with a little extra thrown in. Demands they shake hands.

Skelly attempts to slide away from the window. Pipe dangling from one small gnarly hand, Lallah stays him with the other. 'Take your brother home. He has a headache.'

Edwin counts his money, a sodden rag pressed against his face.

'Make sure the bleeding stops,' she adds, kissing Edwin on the forehead. 'Come back tomorrow, darling. We can talk about the cart.'

She captures Gordon's arm and shepherds him back inside. His head droops, and he falls into his usual morose repose. Through the window they see him step up to the next table. Who is the more desperate for money, Gordon or Edwin? Skelly cannot tell.

He tugs his brother up the slope towards the cart.

'Shut it, Skel.'

'I did not speak.'

Edwin tries to shove him out of the way and climb into the driver's seat.

'She said I'm to drive you home.'

'And what will I be doing myself then?'

'Shutting it yourself.'

Edwin groans and relinquishes his position at the step, allowing Skelly to climb into the seat. He rolls over the side rails into the tray and lies down holding his head. The moon lights their way along rough tracks where stock have flattened the yellow grass.

In the distance, as they descend the hill, Skelly sees beacons burning on the coast and the sweet grey sheen of the sea. Edwin would have driven like a banshee bit his tail, with the cart jolting and lurching, and throwing Skelly up against the wooden sides, but tonight the ride is serene. He would like to stay out, to drive on forever. Unfortunately, he hasn't formulated a decent plan.

25

ROSANNA CONCEIVES OF A PLAN

Skelly creeps to bed, feels his way into the space where Rosanna usually lies beside Blinnie, and finds it surprisingly empty. He tosses; dreams a little; starts awake again. Later, he stirs when he feels her pushing in beside him, smelling of the charcoal painted on her face to drive away mosquitoes. In the moonlight he can see that she has tried to rinse off the black marks but they have streaked.

'Skelly, *alannahh*, I love you so much,' she whispers in his ear. Carried away with drink; its sweet smell exudes from her pores. She has tied a rag around her left hand, and winces when he moves against her.

He lifts it gently, as he would a dog's paw. 'I remember how you hurt your hand,' he says reproachful.

'I burnt it.'

'But you promised ...'

'Shut it, you great ...'

'Did Mrs Ashby really ask you to work at the station house?'

'She did, Skelly.'

'What was it like there?'

'It's a fancy house. A lot of rooms for only two people and a baby.'

'Are you very sad that you can't go?'

'I'll go, whether *they* like it or not.'

'Where have you been just now?'

'I went to the pond to dabble my feet. Edwin left me a little drop of the doings. I think he felt sorry, my trouble being entirely his fault. Moorecke heard the herons and came to me. A great moon as pearly as the inside of an oyster shell lit everything up as bright as day. Do you think it is the same moon, Skelly, as the one in Woodford?'

'I'm thinking it is, but it seems unlikely.'

She laughs. 'Some days I think I'll turn into a lunatic, start eating dirt and run at the walls, take all my clothes off and fall down screaming.'

Skelly jabs her in the ribs. 'They'll be taking you to the Adelaide asylum, to be with all the other mad girls.'

'Oh you.' She ribs him back. They sway with laughter muffled by hands placed over their mouths. 'Moorecke lit a fire and we smacked down little pond crayfish on hot rocks. They were cooked in no time. I brought two home for Mother.'

'Why do you hate it here with us so much?' His feelings overwhelm him. Is sadness a kind of cleverness? He can read near as well as she can, but Rosanna always knows what to do: since they first came she has run barelegged in the bush, and brought home wonderful surprises. She knows about rock-salting eels and smoking them on leaf-strewn coals beneath the stringybarks, about turning them until the oil runs into holes in their heads—about smoking ducks too—and hunting lizards. She knows how to steam a long-necked tortoise and an echidna.

And she is beautiful. Is that why Father keeps her close at home? She smells like honey. Adult breaths are reeky with tobacco, bad teeth, and grog—not Rosanna's. Her breath is always sweet; her skin always warm and smooth. She is as brown as a mulatto.

'It is because I don't belong here.'

'Why not?'

'I was born in another country and I remember it in my dreams.'

'Not only you, Rosanna. Tell about Ireland again.'

'We came in a ship, Eilish and Father, and Edwin and me.'

'And me, Rosanna.'

'And you, of course. I was just making sure that you remembered. After we landed at Portland, in the colony of Victoria, Mr Ashby met us—he'd been buying cattle—and he took us on a ferry across the river. Then in a cart over the border.'

'Was it a big river?'

'I don't know if it were as big as the Shannon. It was wider than the River Rossmore. There were high cliffs beside it and sand bars at the mouth. Mr Ashby and Father swam new cattle across. They rode together and talked about the wages and the work.'

'Were you afraid you would sink?'

'I was. The water was dark and dirty, and it was a long way to the bottom. Even though it was a cloudy day I saw eels and water snakes.

After we were safely on the other side, Father heard a story from Mr Ashby that chilled me to the bone. Once, the ferry went down and all the people drowned.'

'Oh no! And tell me again, about the murder.'

'When Eilish heard that, I thought she would turn about. Head straight back to the port, and get on the next big ship for Ireland. She was that frightened.'

'Tell, tell.' Skelly hugs her close.

Rosanna drapes her arm around his shoulders and kisses his cheek. 'Firstly, there was a ship ran aground in the bay. It wedged fast on the reef. The captain stopped on the boat to guard the stores, whilst all the passengers were rescued in lifeboats. Some ruffians from the station came riding down on their horses. They rowed out in a little boat and slit the captain's throat with a razor. Like this.' Rosanna slides her fingernails, across Skelly's neck, ear to ear. 'They stole money and galloped away.'

'What happened next?'

'One of them went to jail. The other one took the policeman's gun, stole his horse, and rode off again.'

'Did Father know those men?'

'Of course he didn't. We had only just arrived in the colonies. Mother was shaking and crying, wishing she was home again in our village.'

'Tell me about Ireland again.'

'I'm damned tired, Skelly. I'm going to sleep.' She kisses his forehead and wriggles out of his arms. 'It is green.' She yawns.

'Are there volcanoes?'

'No.'

'Caves?'

'No.'

'Wild animals?'

'No.'

'It doesn't sound much good. What else did you do by the pond?'

'I listened to Edwin and Father, rowing.' She moves her head in the direction of the window. 'Father pushed Edwin in the chest, like this.' She drums her finger into Skelly's solar plexus. 'Lurking about in the moonlight, they were, like a pair of great buffoons, and I heard them say my name.'

'Tell me what they said.' She thinks she knows everything.

'Shush now. It all went quiet. For a long time. Now I want to sleep.'

'And if I stroke your head, what say you then?'

'Great fools they are,' she slurs.

Skelly reaches up to smooth her hair back from her forehead, it being her favourite way to fall asleep. It is inconceivable that she might ask him about *his* evening. She would never think to ask *him* what *he* knows about the trouble between Edwin and their father.

'I say, I have a plan,' she adds. 'I'm going to Portland, before I am trapped by the wet, when even Father Woods has trouble making his way through the swamps. Then I'll travel on to Little Belfast, to Geelong, and to Melbourne. I don't know why we bother with Adelaide at all; it is so far away from everything.'

Skelly extends the sweep of his fingers from her thick and tangled hair to the hollows in the side of her neck.

She flicks them off and rolls away. 'I'll take you with me, Skelly, maybe not straight away. Now shut it. Close your eyes.'

And that won't be happening, he thinks. In chasing after Edwin tonight he has made a move in the right direction and it is better not to tell her yet. He does not want Mother and Father to know that he too has plans. Why should he be stuck here forever? Edwin will likely keep the night's events to himself but will have to explain the cart. He and Father will mumble and huff for a day or so. Soon enough, Father will find out about the fight with Gordon but there is no reason for Edwin to mention Skelly. Driving him home. It would throw an Irish hero in poor light. Cuchulain shone with his own light.

PART 2

THE STATION

26

I ONLY KNEW ONE POET IN MY LIFE

Edwin wakes Rosanna rudely, hauling on her quilt. 'Father says get up and help before you go.'

'Before I go where?'

'To the Ashbys'. We need the money.'

Rosanna feels a stirring sense of injustice. Her head throbs. Is this what Father and Edwin had been fighting about the night before? Is she expected to slave for nothing and hand over her wages, just like that?

By the time the sun throws pink rays over the eastern hills, Rosanna rides behind Father, a skilly cake clutched in her hand and Eilish's plaid cloak tied around her shoulders. Edwin and Father do not speak as they canter up the slope behind the house. But there is nothing uncommon about that and it is a grand adventure to be riding out with men; perhaps she will die of happiness. On the way to the Big House she rejoices in every sound: the jingling of spur and the creak of leather; the clump of hooves over hollow earth; the slap of reins on the horses' necks; the piercing scream of a swamp harrier attacking prey. She imagines the hawk gliding through pale grey skeins of clouds in the carded sky and returning to drop a wriggling morsel into the beaks of its chicks waiting in their platform nest above the swamp.

At the station yards mucky with the prints of horses, her father, Garrick, upright in his saddle, is all pride and assertion waiting for William Ashby to come to him. Mr Ashby is hunkered down beside a stockman carping with a stick at a slow fire and frying duck eggs. Meanwhile, Rosanna slithers to the ground, clutching her cloth bag and cloak. When Mr Ashby stands up she recognises the giant of a man who rode past her on the white horse, before she shot his bullock. He is taller than Father, fair, like his wife, with a fine blond beard and anxious penetrating blue eyes that might turn on you in a fit. Hands in his pockets, he walks towards her, head tipped on one side as if to cajole her into something disagreeable. Clearly, he does not recognise her. She is almost sure of this and feels glad.

'Rosanna, you look a good strong girl and smart enough. My wife slept poorly and is indisposed.' He uses his whole arm to wipe grime from his forehead. 'Later in the week, we are expecting guests from Melbourne. One is a famous actor from the Melbourne Princess Theatre. They anticipate leaving Little Belfast in the next few days. Will you help my wife prepare any way that you can?'

She has never met an actor—only the storytellers and musicians who frequented Walsh's Inn in their village back home. Tears of joy swamp her eyes. Her life is opening out like pig-face flowering in full sun. She nods and ducks her head in gratitude: first that he has failed to accuse her of cattle duffing and secondly that he has broken the tedious rhythm of her life.

As she moves towards the house she hears her father grim-voiced, remonstrating, 'Just for the moment she can help. Rosanna will make right Edwin's loss of the cattle.' This injustice feels like grit in her liver and her swift glance withers Edwin from ten paces.

Entering the back door, Rosanna hears the baby wailing up a storm and once inside she scoops it up on her way to locate its mother. Mrs Ashby's face looks pale and piteous—peevish, Rosanna thinks, like a survivor of a shipwreck, bobbing on the surface of her high bed, in a froth of white quilts. A jam preserving pan lies beside the huon-pine chest. Jars of smelly creams and unguents, pot pourri and lavender water commingle their scents with the pervasive stench of vomit. The room smells like an old biddy's breast.

Mrs Ashby impresses on Rosanna the urgent need for the house to be set to rights by week's end when the house party may arrive from Melbourne. If Rosanna can clean the house, including the kitchen out-house, and bring the baby in for feeds, her mistress will rest a further day and then, recovered or not, she will resume her duties. While Rosanna jiggles the baby and swings her head about in curiosity, Mrs Ashby composes a great long list of chores and then, eyes beseeching, subsides upon the pillow.

'Don't break things, for it is hard to replace them in such a place as this.' She turns her face to the wall.

Rosanna imagines her composing a letter to her family:

> The Irish serving girl has cracked the vegetable tureen and is working her way through the entire dinner service. Scarcely worth keeping for wages. There is no hope for me in this God-forsaken place. I daresay you are heartily sick of hearing my grievances.

Nevertheless, Rosanna feels optimistic; she has ridden out to meet her fate; she has left the stultifying boredom of her own house and chores; the English baby is curled against her neck and gently snuffling. When she has earned sufficient money, and she has found a way to take what is rightfully hers, she will leave. She refuses to include Edwin's debt in her calculations.

Mrs Ashby remains in bed the entire morning. Once Rosanna has fed the baby and changed his linen, he falls asleep. She scrubs the kitchen table and stews green apples for his dinner. She stokes up the copper and boils the vomity sheets and towels that she finds lying putrid in a basket at the bedroom door. Even this can't dampen her mood.

It is a grand house and Rosanna tackles its surfaces with damp cloths and manic energy. Mr Ashby and the Lynch men have ridden out and won't be back 'til dusk. Holy Mother of God, perhaps Mr Ashby will soon forgive Edwin and she can pocket her own money, or at least a bit of it.

HOMESICKNESS

By mid-afternoon, the house is almost silent, apart from yellow-tailed black cockatoos gnawing and scraping their beaks on the wooden shutters. What a mess they make and she will have to clean it up. She beats her knuckle on the window, then she hears a faint sound. Is the baby wailing again? Why doesn't the woman feed it?

But is not the baby crying. It is Mrs Ashby, who has arisen to sob her heart out over a photograph resting in her hand. Her fingers smooth and smooth its creased sepia surface. Then she clutches it against her bosom and looks up at Rosanna who hovers in the doorway before moving with caution to her side. 'Ma'am?'

House silver is strewn across the dining table. Mrs Ashby rises to her feet in a rush and thrusts a cloth into Rosanna's hand before she runs from the room holding the photograph against her hip. What can be wrong now? Rosanna bends to the task, no doubt one abandoned by the orphan girl, and rubs the black stains from the fine cutlery until it gleams. She sees herself indistinct but eminently present in the bowls of the largest spoons. When she looks up she is also present in the mirrors of the rosewood sideboard and the marble-topped credenza by the bay window. If she lived in this house, she would check herself for happiness a hundred times a day.

It puzzles Rosanna that Mrs Ashby acts so unhappy. Through the window she can see the great red gums and the house cattle grazing beneath a mottled sky. She holds a spoon against her cheek and sighs, then spits on it and polishes some more. Does Mrs Ashby have the longing for another country? Is she not happy in her big station house with her husband, who is arrogant but, like as not, kind to someone of his own class. Everything in the house is elegant. It is a mansion stuffed with beautiful things: furniture, cloths, china, silver and pol-ished wood. There is meat aplenty. The cellar holds flagons of port wine, and boxes and tins of every kind of provision. Has Mrs Ashby's white skin soured like milk in the hot sun, her body shrunk from feeding her baby? Rosanna imagines life as a fine lady, a pastoralist's wife, riding out on her horse each day. Preparing for house parties is the only work she would do.

For the rest of the afternoon she labours over cruets and pickle jars, tureens and vegetable platters. She lays her head on the table and stares dreamily at her reflection in the polished surface of a silver teapot, noticing that she has touched her face and blackened it. 'Look at you,' she mouths, 'as dour and privileged as the little Queen of England, sitting on a balloon-backed chair, in such a grand palace.'

What would she be doing, back in Galway—helping in Walsh's bar, getting married? She is, after all, seventeen. Seven years she has been in exile. It is such a thrilling word: *exile*. It is not a word that Father likes.

'Exile! Don't be blathering, Rosanna. It is a new life we are making for ourselves,' Eilish had berated her once, 'and no more than a calculation. You make us sound like the Israelites rushing across the Red Sea. We more resemble geese, flying to all the corners of the Earth, with a kind of compass in our hearts. When the wind is right, and the seasons have turned, the fat and prosperous flocks will fly home. Irish people have been doing this for centuries. My own father went regular to England for work, cutting the harvest. And his ancestors came from Wales to mine the iron.'

'Why do you fill the child's head with such nonsense, Eilish?' Father had said.

'And what of your mother's name ... Spain? I'll wager her family did not come from Peking,' Eilish had retorted.

'I'll not be going back. We are family enough on our own.'

'Garrick, no.' Eilish had kissed her cup and offered drink to him. 'We left our dead behind. Pitched like sea biscuits in the Poor House ditches and under the yew tree in the church graveyard beside our inn. You know I miss them. I visited them every day.'

Kookaburras had started up as Father stormed away along the pathway to the creek.

'Shut up your gobs, you heathen jackasses,' Edwin had bellowed from the rough bush table where he worked plaiting leather. He grinned at his sister. 'Exile!' he ragged.

'I had to bring your father away. People were dying.' Eilish had said. 'Now he is hard on himself and on everyone around him.'

'He doesn't like to talk about death, Mother. It is morbid.'

'It *is* exile then, if we don't bring the memory of our dead. I *like* to think of them, especially Granny Walsh.'

'Rosanna,' Mrs Ashby admonishes her from the door. 'Stop your dreaming. I am feeling better now and there is so much work to be done, I dare not think on it.' Slight and bony as a bird cage, Mrs Ashby is swaying on her feet again.

'Are you wanting me to come?' Rosanna looks helplessly at the unfinished silver.

'No, I am recovered. Thank you. I will bake the cakes. Please clear away the silver before you go to the stables at five o'clock. But first, gather me some eggs. Hurry, I had quite forgotten about them, and they will be ruined by the crows, or lifted by black hands. I think you remember that girl absconding with my Sussex.'

Rosanna hurries to the nests beneath the trees. The sun dips in the west; the hens squabble as they roost. Every day will be a grand day now, she decides as she prances between fallen perches like a sword dancer. 'Think before you go flying off,' is what Eilish always says. Rosanna gathers twenty eggs in her hat and tries not to think at all. She sinks them in a pan to test their freshness. Only three float. Mrs Ashby is a small soft woman. Surely she could not harm Moorecke.

2 8

A HOUSE PARTY AND ALL MANNER OF DIVERSIONS

Each morning, without complaint, Rosanna lifts her weary body from her bed and swings up onto the horse behind Edwin or her father, for the ride to Ashby's Station.

'Perhaps it will be the making of her,' she overhears her mother telling Father. 'Work brings a kind of happiness.'

Although she feels too tired to plot right now, she has not given up on the idea of running away. And she will not wait much longer. The baby is needy. Mrs Ashby is polite enough as she continues her great preparations for another weekend of house guests. Rosanna runs ragged, fetching and carrying: linen from trunks to make up beds; bacon and cheese from the cellar to the pantry. She sweats over the blazing fire, turning sides of beef in roasting pans, cutting and mincing, kneading and rolling, working knobs of suet into weevilly pastry until her arms ache and her body slumps.

On Friday she waits as usual in the stable for her father. Next week he and Edwin will camp away for several days and nights and Rosanna must ride over alone and find her own way home. Taking up her mother's shawl she shapes it around her head and shoulders lying full length on the stable floor. She likes the smell of hay and liniment.

A small bat swings from the joists, its wings folded around its body. Rosanna feels like the bat, in her shawl, toes pointed, staring ahead to the inky sky: suspended in time. She does not want to fall asleep, but some part of her seems to know that Edwin and Father will not return for hours, and Mrs Ashby, pressed and stressed by the demands of hospitality, will not be Rosanna's responsibility. That is the beautiful thing about being Irish, she decides. Mrs Ashby cannot push her.

While the sky turns oyster dark she thinks of that hero Cuchulain slinging stones—killing Queen Maeve's pet bird and her marten nestling on her shoulder. Even then things were hopeless. And she remembers Eilish's stories about the warrior princess Aoife's gifts: embroidery, chastity and hunting through the night. What can Rosanna's gift be? She draws her arm across her eyes. Is it nodding off that sets her lips twitching, turn her limbs to liquid, cause her to hopelessly flip her hand like a hooked fish against her thigh and beneath her skirt? Do dreams keep her alive—being the only vivid parts of her life?

When she hears the clatter of hooves outside the stable she starts and clambers up the ladder into the hayloft, where she can safely observe the horses and their riders. Through a small wall aperture, big enough for a rifle barrel and designed to defend the house against Blacks, she sees that it is not Edwin and Father come to collect her but two strange men, one tall and thin, the other small and plump, and that they have come some distance. Foam sets like chantilly around their horses' mouths.

The men lead their mounts down to the swamp to drink, walking like pregnant women, lifting their heavy legs from the hips and clumping their feet down. Baby curled on her chest, Mrs Ashby appears at the gate. Will she send them on their way and return to sipping Madeira by the fire, loaded gun at her side? She has told Rosanna how she shudders over tales told by the Arthur brothers, and the Leakes, their homes attacked by marauding *Booandik*.

When the men return they spring forward and hold the gate for Mrs Ashby, remove their hats and point away down the track to Punt Road leading to Nelson. Hand outstretched, her mistress directs them to the stables, then takes her hand to her forehead. Is she perpetually giddy?

Rosanna crouches in the semi-darkness listening to snippets of conversation wafting up to her in the loft: a carriage and a broken axle, not far, south. One of the men will take fresh horses to Mr and Mrs Brigstock, who wait resting beneath a river gum. Men will ride out early in the morning and repair the wheel. The other man, eyebrows meeting like spitting caterpillars in the middle of his forehead, clutches his belly and shakes his head. He rushes towards the privy. Mrs Ashby disappears into the house.

The taller man leads the horses towards the stables. Rosanna darts away from the aperture and back against the wall; she slides to the floor, arms hugging her knees. As he pushes through the doorway leading the horse, his boots crunch on the compacted earth floor and leather creaks; the horses thud and snort, jostling against each other. He secures them with a rope and removes their saddles at the hitching rails.

'All right. Wait.' The horses thrust their heads towards the loft, excited by the smell of chaff, and he climbs the ladder. She shrinks into the shadows, closing her eyes while he sweeps hay into his arms. To her surprise, he suddenly strides across the floor to crouch on his knees beside her. Her eyes widen as he stares into her face. Even in poor light she notices his well-shaped head and delicate features. Damp wool, perspiration, and tobacco smells rise from his clothing.

He laughs. 'And who are you?' he asks, his face inches from her own. 'I spied you from below. Are you an Ashby daughter?'

'My name is Rosanna Lynch.'

He throws back his head in mock surprise. 'I am rehearsing a play about Lynches. A father and his son. I play the son.'

'And why would *you* be taking the part of a Lynch? I'm sure that you know nothing about them.' She brushes down her dress and struggles to her feet.

'The play was written by Mr Edward Geoghegan, an Irishman.'

'Anyhow, I don't believe you.'

He raises his eyebrows. As soon as she has let the words go, Rosanna wishes she hadn't. It is not her place to argue with Ashby guests.

'They are Irish Lynches—the father and his son, in the play,' the actor says.

'I am an Irish Lynch. From Galway.'

'Then it is fair that I show you the playscript. Mr Geoghegan tells me that it is based on a Galway story.'

'I would like to see it.'

He snatches her hand and holds it against his tweeds. A long moment stretches its muscles between them.

It brings raw feelings, she decides, to look up at a grown man and see moonlight dancing through the dormer window onto the tiny yellow hairs coiled against his collar, to see him looking back at her, his fingers all the while moving in delicious rhythmic motion on the inside of her wrist. Over her heartbeat she hears the plonking sounds of frogs. Oh it would not do, if Father came now. She pulls her hand away.

'Can you read, then?' he asks.

'I can, of course,' she throws back at him and pulls her hand away. 'I know about the abolition of slavery everywhere in the Empire excepting Ireland, about the Zulu War, and the Afghan War as well.' She sounds bad mannered, desperate, a boundary rider's silly girl.

'I will bring the play here tomorrow.' He backs down the ladder.

She peers over the rim of the loft after him. Is he a dream?

29

THROW DOWN YOUR COIN

No sooner does the guest disappear into the house than Mr Ashby and his men arrive home. Through the window of the loft she sees the men shake hands. Then Father calls out to Rosanna and she scurries from the aperture and down the ladder to the yard, where the men wait on horseback. She mounts behind Edwin, who is always in a desperate hurry to get away.

'Did you see a man, Edwin? Riding out when you rode in?' She stretches up to shout into his ear as they set off.

Edwin grunts.

'There were two men—the advance party of the Ashby's house guests.' She says *house guests* like an incantation. 'Their buggy broke down.' The sky is clear and cloudless; the Pleiades sparkle over the volcano. 'One of them was ill. The other must be the *actor*.'

Edwin snorts. 'An *actor*!'

'What do you suppose an actor looks like?' She touches her fingers to her lips.

'He'd be a great lunk of a man with a red cravat and a beauty spot.'

Rosanna laughs.

'And a massive chest like Lucifer's and mighty lungs. And he'd be full of horse droppings.' Edwin rises in his stirrups, and leans forward to pat his horse's neck as he urges him over the rise. 'All right darling, we're almost home.'

'Edwin, I don't mind going to the Big House after all.'

'Well stop blathering and tell me about Lucifer. Did you look to him before you left home this morning?'

'He's full recovered. It was nothing—just a wee graze on his rump. Felt like a mosquito bite to him.' Rosanna warms her hand inside Edwin's coat and croons, 'Edwin, *alannahh,* I could ride him tomorrow; there's a ladies race after luncheon. Remember you told me that I might, that day we played swordfight among the grasstrees.'

'My boots need cleaning. All day, I've been chasing Ashby cattle through the swamps.'

'I will do everything you say, if you let me race,' she says. Father draws close. As they turn the horses south to face the sea, salt wind stings their faces. 'And Lucifer is grand. Didn't the poet make you an offer for him after his last race?' Surely Edwin will let her race.

'You're not thinking to sell that horse, man?' Father asks.

'I might need money.'

Rosanna rests hard up against Edwin's shoulder as they lurch to a stop beneath the wattles. 'If only I could buy him with my wages.'

Her father turns. 'By the holy Virgin and Saint Patrick, what would *you* be doing with a stallion? Shut your flighty gob, and go inside to help your mother. Edwin and I will tend to the horses until you've learned some sense.'

Rosanna gathers her shawl around her shoulders as she slides off the horse, and savages her father with a look.

'Go inside. Edwin needs to stop lommicking about and making promises he can't afford to keep. If it weren't for your great *gramog* of a brother living so hard, bringing trouble on all of us, you wouldn't be slaving at Ashby's place; you'd be helping your mother at home until you married.' He reaches into his pocket and takes coins from a leather pouch. 'Take your earnings and give them to Edwin. Or else, the only racing he'll be doing tomorrow is past a debt collector.'

Rosanna knows so very little of Edwin's doings in the wider world. She fingers the shape of the coins before she flings them at him, and turns towards the house. She will go to the race or run in the opposite direction.

30

RACE DAY

On Saturday, the sky breaks open the colour of eggshells with dark clouds looming on the horizon. A sweep of chill wind shepherds his sister from the privy, along the walls of the house. Crested pigeons rattle beside the path, crouching like pomaded Chinese gentlemen in tangerine slippers. Even the birds, Skelly thinks, know that Rosanna is out of sorts: her mood as grey as the morning ash that she carries in a metal bucket to the toilet pit. She may go to the races to buy fresh produce for Eilish from the carts, but is forbidden to harangue Edwin about riding Lucifer. It is a victory of sorts for her.

Skelly watches her sullen efforts to make purchase on the day: pulling on her second-best gown, braiding her hair and fastening it with a bodkin at the nape of her golden neck, attaching Granny Spain's claddagh brooch between the wings of her starched linen collar. Blacking polish used on Edwin's boots rims her fingernails and stains the palms of her hands. Happily, Mother can spare Skelly too, for Hugh is well again and Blinnie has cut her final tooth. As he slides his sketchbook into his knapsack, he stares back at the house with all its certainties. Rosanna's intensity wounds him. In his mind's eye, he paints the blue and meat-fat yellows of bruises beneath his skin.

In single file they follow the boreen over dips and rises to the bay, the mood of the group subdued. Edwin makes no comment about Lucifer's tail, plaited and threaded with coastal daisies. Skelly carries a leather water bag, a pumpkin, and jute sacks for Eilish's produce, and he sticks like a burr to Rosanna's unresponsive back. His sister slouches on Glorvina, a mare of twenty, purchased because she was solid and reliable enough to be left at home for Eilish in the event of an emergency. In the early days they had lived in terror of emergencies.

Edwin whistles in his irritating way, in much the same way that he taps his foot beneath the card table; no doubt he is focused on his race-plan. Seven days ago he had ridden to the bay, ostensibly to sell his skins, but at the same time to help the other men who frequent Miss Lallah's to clear away the bush, using ropes to set up fallen logs as jumps, to build a dry-stone wall at the half-way point of the race circuit, and to mark a finishing-line. It is only a picnic race meeting, but Skelly has heard from his father that the stewards have raised eighty sovereigns for the steeplechase and that the poet will ride a young horse named Ivanhoe. This fact will not have escaped Edwin's attention. For forty crowns, he will have Lucifer in a complete lather.

Near the shore the horse spins about, nipping the mare on the shoulder. She squeals, splays her legs and drops her head to mouth the wound.

Rosanna raises her crop to him. 'What's got into you, you useless thing?' The sea breeze catches her scarlet petticoat, exposing her darned stockings.

They cut across the point and around the last curve on the track to the bay. Alongside them surf crashes against the rocks; wind sprays them with salt. Skelly ignores the pitying glances of the lady-folk as they ride in. Edwin stalks away to take a drink, perhaps to lay a wager with his friends near where Miss Lallah dispenses punch from her cart in front of a pair of spindly windblown trees.

Skelly finds a log on which to sit and watch the men sauntering past a thoroughbred marked for sale. At the same time he keeps an eye on Rosanna. Wind tosses her dark hair and she pushes it from her face to glare at Skelly, then at Edwin and his friends. Forbidden to race, she looks angry with them all. He sketches her woman's shape as she leans her hip up against Lucifer's side to plait his mane. He supposes that her eyes are casting around for the station party, hoping that they will offer her French wine and snipe pie. Skelly admires the fine hats and elegant habits of the ladies, the way they strike light whips on the ground. And he imagines their *thóins*, round as wombat's heads, beneath their habits.

Rosanna looks redder than her dress, he decides. Surely, her heart must be smarting at being denied a chance to vie for the saddle prize offered to the winner of the Ladies' Race. She feeds Lucifer a coddly apple and adjusts his halter. He refuses her, spraying skin and juice.

Her body is angled to survey *Booandik* people sitting cross-legged under a stand of trees, weaving rushes into baskets. Even with possum-skin tied around her body, her friend Moorecke looks thin. Two cousins, coats dragging in the mud, cabbage-tree hats askew, slide between the horses of their employers from Carratum Station. Old women, smouldering pipes resting in their straggly beards, sell boomerangs and woven mats and baskets to passersby.

Father can be seen with a pannikin in his hand, knocking back the raw liquid he purchased fair and square, above Lallah's makeshift counter, and the policeman from the Gambierton station stands nearby. When Father and Edwin return, Rosanna pounces. 'Well, look at you both thinking you're so grand. Leaving me here, like a damned stable boy.' Her eyes flash up at Edwin. 'You should have put me down for the ladies' race. I could win if I so wished.' She leans up against Lucifer's withers, obstructing Edwin's efforts to tighten the girth strap.

'Give over, Ro,' Edwin blusters, pushing her aside to spring up into the saddle.

'I hope you're enjoying yourself.' She folds her arms and digs her heels in.

'Hold your tongue. Do not shame us in front of the station people.'

'*Shame.* What about your promise? I cleaned your boots.'

'You won't get within a chaff bag of my horse the way you treated him, you *cailleach.* You might have ruined his chances galloping about on him before he's healed. Giving him a new injury to boot.'

'And bad luck on the day I got a brother like you.'

Skelly sees that Rosanna is spoiling for a fight: a fresh gum shoot strangled by her family.

31

THE TURF FLIES

Edwin rides away, shoulders hunched, cantering Lucifer to the starting line. Turning up his collar against the cold Skelly follows him on foot. The wind keens. Predacious clouds threaten the day.

The poet also rides away from the saddling place, waving a dismissive hand at bookmakers as he passes. Skelly garners barely a glance. He is too young, just a younger brother. Beneath his notice.

Ahead at the starting line, a handsome barrel-chested bay goes to market, kicking out at a chestnut stallion pulling into place behind him. They both jump sideways, crashing into the judge's dray, scattering boxes and papers and bumping an official as round as a scallion down on his back in the mud. Unnerved by the whinnying of the horses, the thump of their hooves on the turf, and the grim lines of the mouths of their riders, Skelly retreats to a safer observation place, where his father joins him.

The first jump is a fallen blue gum propped at one end. The second, twenty yards in front, a tea-tree brush fence bolstered by saplings, while the third is the stiffest jump of all: a dry stone wall, stacked with limestone to an alarming height. Jesus, Mary and Joseph, if one of the horses clips it, they'll all go to God in the falling stones. But Lucifer will sail over the remaining six.

On the starting line, Ivanhoe, the poet's horse, and Lucifer move together like two boats in choppy water at the dock.

'Mr Gordon likes stiff timber,' Skelly murmurs. 'He won on that horse at Guichen Bay, but I fancy Edwin's chances.'

'Gordon will win,' says Father. 'He is fearless.'

Edwin is just as reckless, Skelly thinks. Why doesn't Father believe in his son?

'I'll end up carrying the boy home.' Father spits, and makes to turn away. All show for the Ashbys.

The starter's flag cuts through the hazy afternoon, and they're off. Edwin takes the log easily, the horse stretched out beneath him like black silk as he pounds towards the tea-tree brush. The poet, close behind him, leans back in the saddle like a lunatic swept into Hades, head thrown back in his peculiar fashion, one hand outstretched as if to balance the horse's spirit against his own. They wheel around the trees, four horses bunched in the lead, the sound of the drumming hooves drowning the crash of the surf. They soar over four more jumps. The poet's horse moves out strongly, and then a length in front. Both horses slip once or twice on the wet turf but retain their balance.

On the second lap the small crowd chants: 'Gordon, Gordon. Bravo Gordon.' But Lucifer looks steady, striding out with complete ease; he has not put himself out yet, even for Edwin. Mr Gordon's horse approaches the stone wall, a beat out of rhythm. It hesitates, recovers, and throws itself into the ascent. The poet stands up in his stirrups as the horse leaps.

In mid-flight they clip the wall, setting off a cascade of stones. Skelly's fingers clasp his face. Lucifer comes down behind Ivanhoe like a dancer picking gaps between swords, leaps sideways, thrusts out his back legs like a spring, and takes off again. Behind them, a horse clips Lucifer's heels before hitting the wing of the jump. It crashes onto the stones and rears up on its massive *thóin*, throwing its rider. A squeal pierces the steady sounds of heavy thudding hooves. The rider rolls away, narrowly avoiding falling beneath the horse. Then he leaps to his feet, striking his whip in disappointment against his side, before rushing to tend to his mount, now thrashing in the mud.

Skelly drags his eyes back to the race, trying not to turn back to the jockey hauling on the reins of his horse in an effort to bring him upright. Lucifer and the poet's horse tear away and down the straight neck and neck, towards the finish line. Lucifer edges out in front and Father's eyes well with tears.

Lucifer wins by a nose. Grinning at Skelly, Father dances a proud jig on the spot. The horses pull up yards past the line and Mr Gordon reaches over to lay his hand upon Edwin's arm; then offers his hand to shake. Surely they have not forgotten their boxing match at Miss Lallah's? Gordon rubs the twitchy bits of Lucifer's ears—'Well done, old cock,' he says—and Skelly suppresses a smile. Ignoring Gordon's hand, Edwin bows and turns away grinning.

But they are all distracted when a shot rings out. Skelly hears a horse scream and a wheezing spasm emptying its bellow-like lungs before it stills. A ring of officials gathers around the jockey collapsed upon his horse's neck. The crowd's mood becomes subdued, eyes drawn to the abjection of the rider sprawled across a mound of inert horseflesh beside the track.

Father tells Skelly later that as just deserts, Mrs Ashby disdains to shake Edwin's hand, preferring a fainting fit. A Mrs Brigstock from Punt Road, Melbourne, who looks as solid as the Bank of England and robust enough to do the honours, takes her place. Gordon stands with his back to the proceedings, head low, cap clamped against his thigh. He stares out to sea as if it holds the answer.

32

ROSANNA FORCES HER WAY

Skelly runs to find Rosanna, cross-legged and absorbed in Moorecke's nimble fingers threading weaving reeds into the shape of a mat.

'Lucifer won!' he shouts.

She tilts her face to the leaden sky. Moorecke elbows her in the side and grins. Edwin leads Lucifer past a gaggle of servant women from Sutton Town in tow. Who is the freckled white-faced girl who steps out first to greet him and pat his horse? Is it the girl from Miss Lallah's? Edwin loops his hand through her arm and she laughs up at him. Oh there is no doubt about it: Edwin is lucky. Lucifer, all rippling muscle and shining coat, picks his way back along the hoof-carved track, shaking his head in a distracted way. The end of a race is nothing to a horse; all it wants is a feed or the beach, to lunge into the water, and swim powerfully past the breakers to the sand bar.

Father strides forward to reach for Lucifer's reins, his expression unreadable until he grasps Edwin by the shoulders and kisses him on the mouth. 'Good, Man. Begone now and deal with the money-lending leeches.'

Edwin's face works, and he wipes his eyes with the back of his sleeve. He steers his father away from the pale girl, who fiddles with the sash of her blue dress and prinks her hair with licked wet fingers. Father walks around the horse, and praises him as well. Edwin nods, pointing in a careful way to Rosanna, now bent over a game of cat's cradle with her friend under the shelter of the gums. Father and son confer. Skelly strains but is unable to hear their conversation over the wind. They straighten and nod. Father claps Edwin on the back. He will agree to anything now it seems, on this grand day for the Lynches.

He slaps the reins into Edwin's hands and retreats. Edwin leads Lucifer towards his sister. Stranded, the blonde girl twists her gimcrackery ornamented fingers and pivots her slippers in the mud. She turns on her heel, throwing a backward smile at Skelly. Her dainty skirt moves in two-part harmony over the gently undulating ground.

Skelly pulls his eyes away in time to witness Rosanna standing up to her oldest brother, like a small bearded dragon, her collar flipping in the wind, her body angled towards him. Edwin dangles Lucifer's reins behind him like a bribe, and the horse, head down, is pulling. Suddenly he thrusts the reins into Rosanna's hands.

'By all the swans on Lough Derg, Rosanna, pull yourself together—because I'll have more than you think riding on this race, before the starter drops his silk,' shouts Edwin.

Rosanna glances across the track at the fancy party that Skelly is sure must be the Ashbys', and steps into Edwin's hand to mount. She takes up the reins, and lifts her head as if smelling the sea will clear it. 'More fool you then, you dirty *spalpeen*. Show some decency and get out of my way.'

Members of the Ashby house party cast oblique glances in their direction—must be enjoying the Irish spectacle. When Edwin bends to shorten the stirrups, Rosanna snatches the crop from between his teeth and taps his ear with the tip. Skelly holds his breath. His brother rises up beside her. Subsides.

'Edwin,' one of the racing men calls, and laughs. 'I'll wager four sovereigns on the little hoyden in the red dress.'

'It is indelicate,' another calls. 'Feminine exhibition on the Turf.'

'But supported by her father and brothers.'

Father starts towards the pair of them.

But Rosanna is away and Edwin is not out of the Derrycrag Woods yet. All his life, Skelly has seen them going at each other: one minute spitting and screeching, the next larking and rolling in the long grass beside the pond. Intent on winning, Edwin's emotions rush through him like electric storms. And Rosanna is never happy; but if her life is dull, Skelly's is worse. She should spare a thought for him—always the watcher.

She canters Lucifer to the starting place. The ladies ride their health-giving flat race in a circuit set around the judge's cart, newly restored to its wheels. Head in the air, nose tilted towards the northern hills, Rosanna appears oblivious to bystanders casting glances in her direction. Will Father smack her down?

By turn Lucifer prances, then paws the mud; she walks him to the line, turning him in tighter and tighter circles. Skelly imagines her half-attending to instructions from the stewards about the course, too proud to wave to Edwin's friend, who sweetly tries to catch her eye and wish her luck. Lucifer throws a tantrum on the line, spins, lifts his front feet and considers rearing. The steward brings down the flag.

Rosanna eases up on the bit, using her legs to send him forward. Skelly sees the shapes of words on her lips. Away they go. Three take a wide arc around the swamp gums, bunched together, up to their knees in brackish water. Two fall to the back of the pack. Before Rosanna takes the first bend, she leans to one side, her hands following the rhythm of Lucifer's lunging neck. The horse slips in a slushy hole and stumbles forward but quickly rights himself. The rider in second position seizes her advantage and surges past. Rosanna crunches down, pushing Lucifer back up to the grey to snatch back the lead. It will be close.

As she takes the bend Skelly watches her face: the wide mouth, the quick eyes darting across the uneven ground, the jutting chin, the braid flopping on her shoulders. He knows that she is mad to win, and nothing else will do. The crowd roars, and black cloud rolls in from the sea. The red skirt flip-flaps in the breeze. Eerie light douses everything in silver; the air is expectant; lightning flashes across the water. Everything is caught up in the same electric moment. Lucifer's sides heave as Rosanna powers down the western side of the track, drops of rain glittering in her hair, delirious joy painted on her face, her dress swirling around her.

'Who is the girl in red riding that great horse. Is she bolting?'

'Nein, no, the Lynch girl it is. Ride she can.'

While Skelly knows that Lucifer isn't bolting, there is something not quite right about his sister, her lungs full of vindictive freedom, taking the lead by three lengths: is she riding for a fall? He sucks at his fist. Pounding down the track, Rosanna flings a fleeting uncertain glance at Edwin who, all cool appraisal, rests his arm lightly on the elbow of his girl. Not a doubt about it. He thinks the money as good as in his pocket.

But to Skelly's astonishment Rosanna refuses the finish line, savagely hauling Lucifer at an angle across the track, heading for the dry-stone wall. The crowd groans. The horse whinnies in surprise.

'Damn,' Skelly mouths, for it is a grim jump, and she approaches it too fast. But Lucifer takes it in his stride and soars, like a bat across the night sky. In agitation, Edwin brushes off his girl.

Rosanna lands, her body jolting like a bag of potatoes on a dray. She slips sideways, just managing to hold her seat, and Lucifer gallops on. Within seconds they are no more than small dark shapes moving across the parkland towards the trees; then they are gone.

33

FATHER AND SKELLY, BAFFLED

Three times Edwin pounds his fist into his hand. 'The curse of Cromwell on her. Why did she not cross the line? The vixen, the bitch, the damned tosser! The loyalty of a death adder she shows. She damned well won.' Edwin leaps onto Bran, his father's horse, and gallops after her.

Black cloud casts shadows over the course. Men from the Ashby party pack up their trestles and seats, and their picnic hampers. The presentation to the winner of the ladies' race proceeds through rain splashes. Gulls and cormorants fly inland, away from the rising sea and the weather. Malingering crested terns dive for fish. A grey shape rises and falls between the white-capped waves beyond the reef. During the ruckus, Moorecke and her people leave without notice. It is as if they had never been present, in the space between the trees.

Father shakes hands with station boundary riders; one of them has won well enough to make an offer for Lucifer. Kow-towing to others sticks in his craw like dry cheese. Abandoned, with only Glorvina to carry them home, Skelly hopes they will arrive by midnight.

The old mare plods along the coastal track. 'Edwin and Rosanna'll be scaring the birds out of the trees with their screeching and cursing,' his father grouses.

Skelly lifts his head from his father's back to shout into the breeze. 'No one will hear them.'

His father laughs. 'Only emus pounding in the opposite direction.'

'Edwin will thrash her.'

Father grunts.

'Are we shamed?'

'Shamed? Not by the likes of them, nor for a peck of high spirit. There's no rule says you have to finish the race, just because you happen to be a length in front on a magnificent animal and it could save your brother from the debtor's prison. That'd be far too grand a plan for Rosanna.'

Father's emotions shift like the vast plates below the Earth's surface, explained to Skelly by Father Woods.

'Might be the poet'll save Edwin's neck. He has a good eye and he likes the look of Lucifer.'

'Do you ever wish, Father, that I was more useful?'

'You silly *gossoon*. No one could be more useful than you. Now that Rosanna works up at the Big House, Mother needs a man at home.'

Skelly sighs. He is taller and stronger now at least. He looks down at his feet and feels himself flushing.

'And what about your drawing, man? When Gambierton is as big as Dublin, and twice as sophisticated, they'll hold exhibitions of Skelly Lynch's work in the main street.'

'My sketches are paltry—just birds and animals.'

'Well and won't that be something to make people sit up, one day, when all the birds and animals are gone to God because the damned Ashbys have shot them.'

Skelly laughs. 'That will never happen, so. Kangaroos are hardier than corncrakes. Moorecke's people have been killing them for years, Rosanna says. And you'd hardly know it, to see so many mobs.'

'Kangaroos, at least, have freedom. Hanging round the stations, slaving for Englishmen can wear you down, kill your spirit. It can bring fearful sickness. We need our own land.'

'Are you afraid we'll become ill, Father?'

'No, *alannahh*. People with a bit of get-up-and-go will do just that. See which way the wind is blowing and leave. Like we did.'

Skelly lays his head against his father's shoulders. 'And what if your blood is different?'

'You have to listen harder, to all the voices in your head. Blood runs in families. You have to be tough and brave like the people you came from. Take heart from being here at all.'

'I'm not like Rosanna, or Edwin. Mother says I was suckled behind the bar.'

'She's a wise woman. I don't know how I'd live without her.'

'And why would you want to?' Skelly presses his head against Father's back. 'If it weren't for my drawings, no one would know I'm here at all. I want to work and make my future, move around like Edwin, like Rosanna, like the bats.'

'Rosanna's impatience will be her undoing. I saw her with the Blacks today. Did she say anything about Moorecke's mob?'

'Rosanna thinks they won't stay long. Awful sick some of them've been. Did you see the scabs and scars on the old woman's face? Mr Ashby's onto them about killing a bullock.'

'A bullock?' Father's voice catches. 'She told you this?'

'I heard them speaking by the pond.'

'Is it to another station the blacks are headed?' He sucks deeply on his pipe and coughs.

'She doesn't know. They might go to the lakes.'

'Like us, Skelly. They'll leave when they have to.'

34

PLACATING THE PUNTERS

Dark descends quickly on a moonless night. Rosanna snatches her father's oldest oilskin jacket from a stable peg, and flees across the boggy yard, scrambling up into the branches of a blue gum, from where she has a perfect view of Edwin's arrival in the yard.

'I hate her. Why is she so wild?' he shouts at Mother, throwing down his crop. 'You'll regret it, Rosanna, I swear to God,' he yells into the bush, as he kicks the verandah posts.

It is all about her timing; she will not climb down until Edwin settles, his belly lined with food but not too much of the drink. She also waits until her father and his lantern bob past the tree and back again—long enough for Mother to have swept the hearth and arranged the chairs for the comfort of the dead before the fire.

When she creeps inside, Edwin is asleep with the others, an arm curved around his head, still wearing his dirty riding shirt and breathing through his mouth. Rosanna, as cold as a hag's *diddy*, places her hands on his warm chest, allowing them to rise and fall. It is no surprise to her that Kitty of Dismal Swamp fancies him, his hair coot-black and curly, his broad face open and friendly. Hauling on a horse's neck all day has made him as lean and muscled as a working dog. When he simmers down they will laugh together, perhaps tomorrow, and she will hand over her wages, for a sin nowhere near as bad as Feemy Macdermot's in her book brought from Ireland.

At breakfast Edwin averts his face from her. Mother whispers that creditors may come for his money and that, as usual, Rosanna has been a foolish girl making everything worse for herself and people who love her. She has only just managed to keep Garrick's hand from his stockwhip.

Rosanna has not slept enough to be cheerful but her face is pink from the splashing of icy water, and the steaming pannikin of tea set before her. Skelly goggles his eyes at her. Intent on her soda bread and boiled moor-hen's egg she will not say sorry, yet, and Edwin knows it. On the way to the station he rides close beside her, huffy, knocking his horse up against hers amongst the trees, trying to unseat her.

The day is long and slow. The baby has a loose tummy and cries half the morning, beating the air with his little fists, peddling his knees with gripe. The house party has abandoned coats and umbrellas and boots beside the fireplace in the dining room, and the ladies of the party remain abed until after noon, while Mrs Ashby struggles to prepare broth and meat for the men branding cattle.

Rosanna is surprised that her mistress, such a grand lady, has ridden home at dawn from the dancing and piping at the bay, but not at all that she is as tetchy as a goanna, especially with Rosanna. Mrs Ashby chips away at her about 'decorum' and 'dignity', about why a girl would bring disgrace to her employers and her family by throwing a race, like a tinker, and by cursing at her brother in a public place, for all of society to hear. Rosanna is on trial. It is a revelation. She works and works until she aches with tiredness.

In the middle of the afternoon, Mrs Ashby runs out of steam and subsides on the *chaise-longue* in the parlour. 'God's truth, Rosanna, I am at my wits' end, but I cannot do without you.'

Rosanna drops her head and bites her lip. She will not be rude to Mrs Ashby. Confined to the kitchen, she bakes lady-finger biscuits and fruit scones, which Mrs Ashby arranges on dishes painted with blue and white pictures of a willow tree and some orientals standing on a bridge.

'Take care carrying the Spode,' she snaps, pushing Rosanna towards the door. 'Before you serve the tea, check you have made the beds, and cleaned the floors,' she orders, 'but leave the front room with the bay window, where the child and his mother lie sleeping.' When Rosanna is done, Mrs Ashby wafts a handkerchief before her face and rolls her eyes. 'Rosanna, wash yourself in the copper with a rag—you smell.'

Clean and sullen, in a worn gown as pale yellow as early sunshine, lent by Mrs Ashby, Rosanna prepares to serve tea. When the door springs open, they both start. Three men from the house party enter Mrs Ashby's domain, in a lather of excitement about a kangaroo-hunt arranged by Mr Ashby for their amusement that very afternoon.

'Why, I do believe we have a champion jockey in our midst,' says the shortest gentleman, his fair but ruddy face alight with interest, as he turns to face his friends.

'Jove, it is. The Irish bolter,' says a taller one, fingering his drooping moustache in a contemplative way.

Rosanna blushes, conscious of the third man with swamp grey eyes and a delicate mouth that she feels sure must be the actor, now that she can clearly see his face.

Mrs Ashby instructs her to address them as Mr Melvin Brigstock, a grazier from Portland, who is the father of the small child; Mr Laurence Colyer, a lawyer from Melbourne who wishes to speak to Mr Ashby about buying land; and their friend Mr George Sutherland— an actor, lately on the Melbourne stage. She must remember exactly how they prefer their tea. Instead of bobbing, as Mrs Ashby would undoubtedly prefer, Rosanna straightens up and holds the actor's gaze before she turns away. It is a powerful thing to be stared at by a man.

She returns with heavily laden tea trays. As she passes milk and sugar she sees Edwin and her father through the window, erecting a stockade for the kangaroo hunt. By the time she clears the table they have begun digging pits.

The hunt will be held at dusk, when the kangaroos stir from their sets behind the stringybarks and move out to feed between the grass-trees. Edwin and Garrick Lynch, Mrs Ashby says, will be required to assist with the flensing of bodies and the disposal of carcasses. Does she suppose Rosanna is an orphan or simply invisible? Reversing through the doorway to the hall she half turns, and catches Mr George Sutherland's eyes whipping up and down her back.

3 5

THE KANGAROO HUNT

Rosanna retires to the stables to wait for the men, wondering if from there she can watch the hunt. The stable bat flitters past, its wings grazing her face. Light from a smoky crescent moon illuminates half a dozen horses stamping their feet before they take off into the belt of bush at the back of the house. Father says Mr Ashby never tires of hunting. And the mobs of kangaroos never diminish in their plenitude. Creatures of habit, they move through the corridors of trees, descending on the swamps and the station garden at night.

Rosanna watches the horses wheeling away behind the scrub and, although she can hear the bark of dogs, the crack of breaking branches, the excited whinnying of the horses, she sees nothing more for several minutes until hundreds of animals come leaping from the scrub, down the gradient towards the pits.

'Tally ho,' a fool cries. Shouts, rifle cracks and whistles pierce the night silence. Rosanna thinks she smells the kangaroos' panic as they smack up against the makeshift walls of the stockade. Most crash where they are shot and fall back into the mob, scrabbling for purchase amongst fallen bodies; some fly over the rails, veering suddenly across the path of galloping horses. Mr Gordon stands up in his stirrups, silhouetted against the remnants of a sunset as pink as a parrot.

A large buck swerves and is driven back by the lash of Father's stock whip, smashing to smithereens a section of the stockade. The roo sprawls amongst the broken timber, struggling to right itself. Rosanna sees it stand upright, claws lashing, blood rushing from his massive tail. Is it screaming she hears, high pitched whistling? Edwin will be grinning like a loon, bare headed, his *caubeen* lost in the scrum. Finally, she sees George Sutherland galloping towards the roo.

Mr Ashby shouts out to him and waves him round to cover a breach. But the main mobs have passed and are bounding away. She sees Edwin take off in pursuit but it is pointless. The roos will scatter in panic along the edge of the swamp. Some will leap into the water and, with powerful thrusts, swim out to wait, the swinging lanterns reflecting in their eyes, their ears twisting against the sounds of the killing. Others will leap left and right, deep into the scrub, following the remainder of their old man mob, away from the smell of blood, in a desperate race to meet the dawn. Rosanna likes eating meat but the twitching bodies are bad *cess*. She leans up against the rain-stippled wall, attempting to blot out the distressing sounds.

The men complete their work, roping and hauling corpses deeper into the pit, making their careful way around the thrashing limbs. The station dogs run back and forth, dropping their heads low to the ground to bark. A small roo jerks its head around and a porridge-coloured dog is on it, worrying at its throat, keeping clear of the powerful legs until it sustains a lashing wound across its belly. Mr Ashby puts a bullet in the dog's brain and drags it to one side. Rosanna gasps to see the flop and sprawl of the mutt in the dirt; wishes she might gather it up and give it a decent burial.

At the end of the killing the men gather like primitives in a circle. Rosanna creeps closer, sheltering behind a cart, to listen to the chorus of men. No doubt Skelly would like to sketch Mr Colyer, acting such a champion, one foot on the largest buck, rifle thrust to the sky. Mr Brigstock wipes his face with his handkerchief. Is he overwhelmed by country hospitality?

Edwin is sent to the cellar for the finest drop of porter and the men raise their glasses to Mr Ashby for the excellent sport he has offered for their enjoyment. What a fine upstanding occupier he is, with so many estimable qualities, bringing order to the land and its inhabitants. They toast God and the Queen. Rosanna senses Mr Ashby's excitement, his pleasure heightened by his responsive audience. But his face looks as soulful as a British bulldog's, as he stands on a rise by the pit. Removing his hat he sweeps it upward in an emphatic gesture towards the Southern Cross. A faint breeze dances along the branches. The leaves shiver and still.

'We will tame this place,' he says. 'Make it safe. It is unfortunate that these creatures, gentle enough, must feed our sport. They know no better than to tear the livelihood from our grasslands, cutting out the cattle for whom the feed is intended, to come bounding from the scrub we have allotted them, when we could hunt them on fair terms, on their own terrain, give them a fighting chance, as we would elk or deer or pig. They are opportunists, marauders. I toast Queen Victoria and her Empire, and you, my worthy hunters, for your energy and courage during this successful foray—at least one hundred pesky kangaroos felled, meat for the dogs and for us all.'

His voice carries clearly across the yard until cockatoos interrupt him. The men drink quickly; Edwin refills their glasses and, Rosanna sees, turns his body to swig sly and quick from the bottle. George Sutherland angles his face in the moonlight. Has he spied Rosanna retreating towards the stable doors? Even from this distance she feels she knows his deliberate gaze and is warmed by it.

36

THE ACTOR TEASES HER WITH A PLAY

Rosanna slips into the shadows of the stables and, from some distance, observes Mr Ashby drawing her father and her brother aside. Edwin ropes two dead roos to the rumps of their horses. Surely they will not be required to finish the work at the pit tonight, covering the sticky flesh before the native cats and dogs arrive. Rosanna hears one howling now.

Father squelches across the stable yard, carrying ropes. He brays, 'Rosanna, are you there, *alannahh*?'

'I am,' she calls back, as loud as she dares. He will be smarting over the English toasts.

A hand touches her skirt from behind. She leaps in fright. Then remembers to whom the hand must belong. The actor has entered the stables from the rear door. She steps forward, brushing his hand in a less than decisive way.

'Edwin is skinning the good carcasses to sell at the port,' her father adds.

'Fine then. I will be all right.' Mr Ashby will take half of the profits, she thinks, and burn the hides not worth huckstering.

'Stay where you are, until I come for you. Do not fall asleep.'

If she calls, 'Father, I will,' he will cock his head, uncertain, for Rosanna is rarely biddable. She waits, throwing uneasy glances into the darkness behind her.

Father forms a solid presence in the doorway, blocking out the moonlight. Can his eyes penetrate the darkness of the stables? 'What are you doing, girl? Show yourself.'

George Sutherland's fingers seize hers. Little goosey bumps trill along her spine. Such audacity! She throws his hand off and steps forward.

'Whose fault is it that I am waiting and waiting, while men make such a display of killing that it makes the bile rise in my throat?' She will act, and well enough. But her father is not amused. She remembers that it is another slight to have a daughter speak this way in the vicinity of William Ashby. 'It is only Edwin that you care about. But you have made him pay his own debts until now.'

Rosanna smarts over her own stupidity. Reckless, she has uttered a truth. She rushes forward. 'I am tired, Father. Finish your work so that we may go.' Even if the little queen herself begs her for the sake of the Empire, she will not say sorry.

Her father reaches out to strike her, hesitates. He wipes a weary arm across his brow and strides away.

'Why do you creep about like a bushranger?' she throws into the dark recesses of the stable.

'So Miss Rosanna Lynch, all the South-east of South Australia and half of Victoria knows your name, since your ride on Sunday.'

'Pft.' He is teasing her.

'What made you throw the race at MacDonnell Bay? It put your brother in a funk.'

'My brother cares only for the timing. It is none of your affair.'

The actor moves closer. She can smell perspiration and brandy. Glancing up at the ceiling she notices that the little bat has gone— flapped into the night to feed. Safe. At a distance she can see her father leaning up against a horse's side, lifting its front hoof to examine it for a stone. He picks with a sharp stick. As if sensing her surveillance, he turns his head, and Rosanna raises her hand to him before moving deeper into the darkened stable.

'You will show me the play tomorrow, while it is still light,' she whispers.

'If I promise, will you bring the stallion you rode on Saturday?'

She feels the actor's breath on her neck, his hand on her shoulder. 'Lucifer belongs to my brother.'

The actor moves to a saddle bag slung from a peg and reaches in to lift out a sheaf of papers, which he rattles in front of her face. 'I will tease you with an extract.' With great inflection, he rolls out a line he knows by heart and claps the pages against his chest.

She suppresses laughter. 'I don't know what you mean.' Are all actors like this, their voices dark and rich as molasses, their mannerisms so fey and affected?

He shrugs.

Rosanna feels self-conscious. 'Until now, I have never met an actor,' she says, by way of conversation.

He slaps the papers against his side in mock exasperation. 'You must have heard my name? I am well-known in Sydney and in Melbourne. I have worked most recently at the Albert Theatre in Geelong, with Mr Geoghegan, the playwright of this play.'

Rosanna is inexplicably filled with longing; for what, she can't ascertain.

He puffs his chest out like a pigeon. '*The Hibernian Father* will eventually have a Melbourne run at the Princess Theatre.'

She reaches out to snatch some pages and steps more into the moonlight spilling over the stable door. She checks on Father. The sheets are loose and covered in an elegant sloping script. Angling the title page she tries to decipher a few words. She feels his eyes on her face; his hands come creeping to her waist.

He fiddles with her yellow sash and continues speaking about the play as if hands and minds are not connected. She struggles to control the papers slipping through her fingers until he takes them from her. He leans so hard against her that she feels a kind of pain, and she turns ever so slightly towards danger. When his mouth opens over hers the feeling is more delicious than anything in a book. She pulls away. Mr Trollope had not included a great deal of detail about Feemy's first kiss.

'Has anyone told you that you are beautiful? They must have.'

'Everyone is beautiful, in their way. I don't like to be discoursing about it.'

'Last night I dreamt that you had the legs of an untried two year old at a St Patrick's Day race meeting,' he teases.

'I am not a horse.' She snorts.

The actor laughs.

'Rosanna.' Father's voice booms across the yard, like thunder cracking over the ridge behind the house.

She hurries forward, without a backward glance, repairing her hair and dress in the same movement.

'Bring your things, darlin',' he calls. 'We are done here.'

Her father waits for her on horseback in the yard, preoccupied with Mr Gordon, who is reading a poem aloud in a low, loud, monotonous voice. Rosanna takes his arm, and vaults up behind him. It is not the way she cares to ride, any more, like a trusting child behind her father. The wind catches her hair.

When the actor materialises from behind the stables, she presses her face against her father's shoulder blades. Alert in the moonlight, Edwin walks his horse between them and the man, and subdues her wind-ruffled petticoat with his crop. She looks up, mortified. The actor grins.

Mr Gordon lifts out a tatty piece of paper and recites on and on to her father, head high, hand on his pommel; he seems arrested by the beauty of the words released in the moonlight.

Impatient with poetry, Edwin walks his horse forward.

'Wait,' the actor calls. 'I want a word with you.' But Edwin ignores him and moves along the track. It will be about Lucifer, Rosanna reassures herself. Mother must never hear that men look at her daughter.

The poet tails off his recitation, closes the book, and nods to Father. Then he smiles at Rosanna; looks at her as he has never done before. It must be the race that has transformed her from Edwin's sister into someone else, she decides, one hand fluttering at her neck.

37

ROSANNA FORFEITS HER WAGE

They canter along the boggy path beside the water's edge, the moon bobbling on its surface like a Chinese lantern. Does God love her, after all? It is a new space Rosanna inhabits on a sunlit plateau, with a bigger sky opening out around her, the old dark chasms receding on either side.

She looks back at the station, outlined in the moonlight. A pair of brown kestrels hover over the kangaroo pits. When she turns again, a large doe materialises waist-deep in the water, beating at her shoulders with her claws; drawing blood. Has she lost her baby or her mob? Rosanna curls against her father's back until the image recedes.

'I hope that you'll learn more sense working like a gin for Mrs Ashby,' her father shouts. The horse slows as they bound through the shale at the crest of the ridge. Twenty yards in front of them, Edwin takes off on a mad gallop, roos' legs slapping against his saddle. Garrick calls after him. 'Watch out, or you'll be losing your stirrups, man.'

Edwin's careless laugh frightens a possum across the track, and Rosanna holds her breath as it skitters beneath the hoofs of Garrick's horse. She waits for the crunch of gristle and bones; but somehow it emerges squealing on the other side, looking back at them with its aggrieved saucer eyes before darting up a tree.

'I like working at the station. It is like another world. Could I keep a little money for myself?' Rosanna asks. She will need cloth for a new dress when Mrs Ashby takes back the lemon gown. She would never, not in a hundred years, have thought to meet an actor, and it has come about because she is employed at the Big House. Jaysus and the little virgin; or is it the grand wild women of Connaught, from Eilish's stories, coming into play? Up until this point, her life has been so dull.

'I'm not promising anything, when your own mother is making do every day. But you can stay on for now, until we've saved enough for land of our own and quit your brother's debts.'

Edwin slows and turns his head, throwing murderous glances at his father. Lucky Edwin, to call in favours, as sure as God forgets her. At least the dead bullock remains a secret. But now perhaps everything has changed.

She closes her eyes, reliving the moment of the actor's mouth nudging hers, his fingers at her wrist, his hand upon her waist; she shudders with pleasure. And she thinks of the poet holding her gaze. Has she committed mortal sins—worse than running away? She can hardly wait to return to the Big House, even if her money finds its way into Edwin's pockets. Now that she is no longer invisible it will be worth it.

3 8

WHILE THE MISTRESS IS AWAY

In the morning creeping fog blots out any memory of the heightened atmosphere of the night before, and Rosanna feels cheated as she carries the coal bucket to the yard where Edwin and Father have finished skinning roos, jerking meat, and burning the remains of bodies in the pit. Some of the carcasses have been dragged by dogs. It is not a pretty sight. She scrubs muddy and bloody boot treads from the verandah, face averted from the stink of bodies. It would not be good for the actor or the poet to see her now.

Skinned roos covered in flies, like clove-studded roasting meats, sway and creak from the verandah rafters of the outhouse. Each time Rosanna attends to chores outside, she feels her stomach churn, but she is buoyed by the memory of the actor's promise to read from the manuscript at dusk.

Edwin and Father wash their flensing knives in the creek and cover the kangaroo pelts with tea-tree branches, then ride away to check on a shepherd camped near the Ellis's station boundary. They will remain at his hut for the night to rake the coals of his fire for ewe bones. It is rumoured that he has taken to the drink and run off, leaving his sheep for dingoes. The following day they will count the remains of the flock and check them for coastal fever and ticks. Thus, today, Rosanna will ride home from the Big House alone.

Soon enough she hears the actor's mellifluous voice carrying from the breakfast room. She ducks away to wash her face and hands, but her ablutions come to nothing. George and the other houseguests set off for Gambierton on business and to partake of luncheon at the Farmer's Inn. Rosanna watches the horses gathered by the wagon at the lip of the ford. Overnight showers in the far hills have caused a meagre channel to rise.

Mr Ashby stomps about in the middle of the stream, water rushing past his thighs, as he determines its depth. He pronounces it safe by raising his hat and then strides out to lift his wife and baby into the cart. She looks fragile. Kept awake half the night, she said, by the interminable howling of dogs. Beside her Mrs Brigstock nurses her own small boy. On horseback and in single file, George Sutherland, Mr Colyer and Mr Brigstock follow the lurching cart through the water. Rosanna wonders if it may be presumptuous or familiar to wave them off. George looks neither left nor right.

Back at the house, she wipes the dust from polished wooden surfaces, scrubs meat-encrusted pans, and washes breakfast dishes before returning them to the dresser. She neatens the piles of books and papers on Mr Ashby's massive wooden desk, and crushes inch ants between her duster-clad fingers as they climb an invisible sticky ladder up the side of his whiskey glass. Water bubbles in the cauldron on the stove and Rosanna hums with fresh anticipation. She has half-filled the hip bath with cool water from the lagoon behind the house and a plan is crystallising in her mind.

Why should she wait for Mr George Sutherland to read the play? First, she will take a bath, and then ... she hardly dares to think upon it. She must be a fool to put everything at risk—for curiosity. God's truth, she can hardly imagine herself bold enough, to intrude on a gentleman's privacy—but now her work is done, she has half the afternoon to read at leisure. Why should she not search for something that rightly belongs to her family? She will find the Lynch manuscript and read it herself.

First she will enjoy the hipbath. Dare she touch the lily-of-the-valley perfumed soap on Mrs Ashby's washstand that she has lifted to her nose and swooned over? Better to use the old soap chips rattling in the metal holder to stir some suds into the tub. Everything unfolds in an instant; each new decadence more exciting than the next. Should she not wash her mother's blouse, at the same time? But merciful Mary, Mother of God, she couldn't be getting about the house without her clothes. How would she confess such a thing to Father Woods?

The next thought comes easily, rolls into her consciousness like a soft cloud on a summer's day. Of course, she hadn't planned to be rifling in Mrs Ashby's Saratoga trunk, nor her huon-pine robe, her red hands touching scarves and ribbons, and fancy garments—*flick,*

flick, flick—this way and that, drawing in the smells of French cologne, and dried lavender sewn into muslin bags hanging from brass hooks. Womanish she feels, and no harm in that, she thinks, the moment before she plucks out a robe the colour of moss, and slips it on over her clothes, before the dressing table mirror.

Gazing at her dishevelled face for a pleasing novel moment, she senses why she has drawn the eye of the actor: noting the dark wings of her hair scraped back from her high brow and braided and looped at the nape of her neck; her strong cheek bones; her flushed lips. She pinches her cheeks. At last, she really exists.

Now she vows to leap headfirst into adventures—not just mending and fetching and carrying like Little Dorrit in Mr Dickens's book, nor waiting, waiting like Mr Trollope's Feemy Macdermot. She dances along the passage, one hand unbuttoning her blouse, the other holding up Mrs Ashby's robe as she crosses the cobbled yard to the kitchen, where she has placed the hip bath beside the fire. After rinsing her mother's blouse, she hangs it over the rail of the cooker.

It is the grandest feeling, she decides, as she sinks deeper in the water, pulling up her knees to rock herself back and forth along the base of the tub, enjoying the warm trilling of the water around her legs and hips, the swirling around her shoulders. It feels so pleasant that she almost falls asleep, but then racketing yellow-tailed black cockatoos rising from the gums behind the stables spoil her reverie.

She rises abruptly to her feet, clutching the wash cloth, straddling the edge of the tub, snatching up the green robe from the chair. Condensation frosts one small window; the other is ajar.

Dear God, it is Gordon the poet passing the window, an open book in his hand. He walks with his head thrust forward like an emu. He is ever so quiet. And now he approaches the kitchen door, stumbling a little on the cobbles. Rosanna's heart hammers. Pulling the gown tight around her waist she calls out to him. 'Please. Wait outside. I have had an accident with hot stew and I was forced to bathe.'

39

THE PRICE OF A BATH

Indecisively, he steps inside. 'Did you burn yourself?'

'All is well. Please go away, Mr Gordon.'

'I would like some tea.' Light blue eyes fix on her; brown curls frame his face. Up close his face is gentle, lachrymose. He wears a blue shirt tucked into his corduroy breeches. Chafing his hands together, he stamps his knee-high Wellington boots on the hearth. 'I am a great admirer of your brother's horse.'

'Edwin won him at cards from a drunken shyster at Miss Lallah's.'

'I was present, and I think that an unfair construction of what really occurred.'

Rosanna draws in a sharp breath. Oh my goodness, had he lost to Edwin? She casts her mind back. Had there been a quarrel? She will ask Skelly.

'Larking about on your brother's horse must be more enjoyable than working at the house,' he continues, as if to smooth out the doubly awkward moment. He stares into her face. 'I had two sisters,' he says, and then recites with great intensity:

> For we have played in childhood there
> Beneath the hawthorn bough,
> And bent our knee in childish prayer
> I cannot utter now!

Rosanna feels heartsick. *Had two sisters*. Rumour has it that he disgraced his entire family. While they are speaking she manages to fasten the green gown tightly about her waist. 'I will make your tea.'

She brushes past him to the hob to shake tea into a pannikin and fill his flask with water from the faucet. If he betrays her to Mrs Ashby for taking a bath, they will surely not dismiss her while so desperate for help in the house?

But then she remembers that the poet is very sniffy about station people; thinks he is a cut above them. She thinks perhaps he would *not* tell. Once a pastoralist directed him to the workman's quarters and, for this slight, the poet rode away refusing to do business there again. This is one of the things Father likes about him, and the way he can hold his tongue for hours.

Leading him to the door she points to pelicans drifting as solid as barges across the low sky towards the sea.

He cocks his head, refusing all distraction. 'Did you get a ragging from your brother when you flogged his horse off the course on Saturday?' Again he peers into her face. Can he be that short-sighted? She feels his arm pressing against hers. 'You look a strong girl. Sensible.'

'I do my work. I must do it now.' After all, he must be a ladies' man? She blushes, attempting to manouevre him towards the door.

'I would like to do my work reclining in a tub,' he says.

Fear strikes her heart once more and when he pulls her hard against his chest she tries to rear away, laughing inappropriately. Oh what is to become of her? The actor will soon return from the town. If he sees the poet with her he will not like her for sure. If either of them tells Mrs Sutherland or her husband, Rosanna will lose her job and with no hope of finding another.

Thoughts and feelings slide so fast inside her, she feels as if she has lost her compass. Perspiration beads her forehead, runs down her cheeks and under her armpits from the heat of the bath; all this sensation—twice within the week—cannot be her fault, and she knows this before the poet places his mouth on the side of hers and turns her head towards him. Oh he is the best rider in the district and unwed, the cleverest and most well-read.

She feels little trills beneath her skin that will not quieten and lie down. Had the actor not told her about the Lynch play, she might have been completely swayed. She should be proud that Gordon has finally noticed that she is a girl, something separate from her brothers, away from the track. He is a fine-looking man. All along she had only wanted to converse with him about the poems he read and wrote and discussed with Father. She is sure of this. Absolutely sure of this. But he kisses her and kisses her until she can hardly draw breath. Until her belly and legs begin to dissolve in strange sensation. Until she feels so self-conscious she laughs. Why had she not stayed home with Mother and the children?

'Laugh again,' he says, as if she had deliberately enchanted him instead of simply falling into hysteria.

She tries. He slides his tongue into her mouth and cuts off her small utterance. Perhaps she will cry in all the confusion. Doubts rise up. Her heart attempts to harden. What if she'd been riding a donkey rather than winning a race on Lucifer? What if he had not encountered her alone with all the station people away? Perhaps he had been reading romance before he came for tea; instead of working? He is unusual—everyone says so. He must be overheated. What will people say if he tells? She steps back and untangles his arms from hers, urging him towards the door.

'Perhaps Edwin will sell the horse back to you. I will tell him you are keen.'

He relinquishes her fingers last, a look of dumb suffering travelling across his face. But that cannot be. Such a strange fellow. She will need to look out for him from now on; at least until she makes up her mind about him.

Eventually, he leaves. Later, she thinks, she will tell him that he must never speak of what has passed between them. She is not herself.

Jesus wept. Rosanna wipes out the tub and runs back to the house. When he turns the corner of the outbuildings and crosses the yard, her thoughts return to the second part of her plan. The actor has forgotten her while gadding about the town. He is late but she still has time. Why had she let Mr Gordon spoil everything?

She slips along the passageway between the buildings to the box-room, which has been set up with three makeshift bunk beds for the male guests. Only the Burkes of Portumna Castle have guest beds enough for large house parties. On the surface the room looks neat. She carries her duster to the window and swishes it around the architrave, glancing out; seated beneath a tree, the poet cradles his tea and stares off into the distance.

Gathering her robe tightly around her waist, she tidies and straightens items on the box shelves—a mustachioed cup, a shaving brush—then pokes like a possum into saddle bags and boxes, seeking to identify their owners. Is it Mr Colyer who smokes the briar pipe, and if so, why has he left it behind? If not, perhaps it belongs to Mr Brigstock, who smokes but rarely. She is almost certain the slightly dandified and foppish embroidered vest belongs to George.

Where can it be? The search takes longer than she expects and she casts frequent frantic glances through the window to see that the poet has returned to lunging the mare. While patting down a coverlet she stubs her toe on a metal box and lo, it contains the manuscript.

She snatches it eagerly and begins to flick the pages. Almost in the same moment, she hears a piercing shriek.

40

THEFT OF GOOSE AND MANUSCRIPT

'*Yaki yak!*' Moorecke's face appears at the open window.

Rosanna leaps to her feet. 'Holy Mother of God, you'd scare the skin off a lizard. What are you doing here? Will I never have peace?'

Moorecke lays a large bedraggled goose on the grass before springing through the window. Rosanna peers into the yard. The poet is using a long-handled whip to encourage the mare around the circle. Surely *Booandik* be wilder than Irish girls and twice as strong. 'Not a word have I heard from Ashbys about that bullock, but Moorecke, you should leave soon for Carratum. The cold is coming: *koo-na-maa*.'

'Pilfering from the bosses.' Moorecke touches the green gown with her fingers and laughs.

'What about the goose?'

Moorecke grins. 'We can cook goose together.'

'You must be more careful. Think now, what happened to your mother.' Rosanna's eyes fill with tears. 'Quickly, go home.' She snatches at Moorecke's hand and squeezes it. 'It is not safe here. You must not let the poet see you.'

'Why so cranky?' Moorecke's voice is soft. She pats Rosanna's arm before swinging her long thin legs across the sill. 'I go.'

Rosanna waves her off. Then makes a split-second decision to lift Act One, leaving behind the cast list and the bulk of the manuscript. George will never notice and, in the meantime, she and Skelly will copy the words by candlelight. Will he begrudge the last clean pages of his sketchbook? She must hurry. All stories make life endurable, exciting even, but this story belongs to Lynches.

Running along the passageway to Mrs Ashby's dressing room, she rebuttons her mother's damp blouse. When she returns the gown to its hanging place, she delicately sniffs the underside of the sleeves—sweet enough—and tucks the manuscript inside her blouse.

Moorecke stands outside the open bedroom window ignoring Rosanna's frantic waves. '*Winana yon.*' A smile haunts her broad face. Her luminous eyes stare back at Rosanna. She has tied the goose around her waist with dirty string.

'Go *now*,' Rosanna calls, leaning on the sill, then flies through the house checking every room on her way to the outbuildings. She places more logs in the kitchen stove and closes it up; carries the bathwater to the straggly rose garden beneath the bedroom window.

Little birds start up, as they do when telegraphing snakes; geese and turkeys join in the chorus—dear God, Moorecke, do not be excessive. It would not make sense, carrying two heavy birds across the ridge. Something else must have set them shrieking.

A shadow darkens the window as she slips into the study. Rosanna leans over the sill to scan the yard. A cloud has covered the sun perhaps. She flips through papers on Mr Ashby's desk, but they are covered in palimpsest, paper being so awfully expensive. On what can she copy the words that tell the Lynches' story? Almost certainly, Skelly will lend her *some* pages from his precious sketchbook; he loves her, does he not?

Rosanna runs to the stables. It will take longer to make her way home on Glorvina. Edwin is resting Lucifer again—no doubt just to spite her—dare she ride him tomorrow? Whatever would become of him if a creditor came? Edwin, with all his money problems, would have to let him go. Sell him to Mr Gordon.

FLIGHT FROM GUILTY SECRETS

Cantering along the edge of the swamp, Rosanna sees the poet riding slowly in the opposite direction along the track to Gambierton, body slumped over a book, and she sighs with gratitude.

Sour smoke from the Big House chimney hangs over the valley. Has she over-stacked the stove? She sniffs the air. The manuscript crackles against her skin as she moves. When she glances down she can see the edge of the pages frilling the neck of her blouse. Will the play be like books by Mr Dickens, in which the reader has to wade through words as dense and sweet as treacle, trying to make sense of them, all the while revelling in their richness?

Her mind leaps from one thought to another; images appear, unaccounted for; she sees things, but doesn't see things: an echidna hurrying beside the track, a man and his son playing chess in a glade of oaks, and a woman screaming. Moorecke believes that the dream of a woman can bring sickness in a man.

Pounding hooves penetrate her reverie. Someone has followed her. Who can it be? Not Mr Gordon. Miles away, Father and Edwin must be coming to the end of their day in the saddle; and the station party returns by the Gambierton road, from the other direction. But there is no one to be afraid of. South Australia is the safest and most enlightened of colonies—hardly a convict or a bushranger; well, some old lags, on the lam from the east. Most camp on the boundaries of the runs—shepherding sheep—or live in rough shacks at the bay.

She urges Glorvina on in the dusk light. Fierce wind scours the hilltop. Gulls flap inland, keeping ahead of black clouds building on the coast. Behind her, the hooves beat louder. A branch cracks as she passes. She startles and shivers. Her mother's blouse cools against her back.

On reaching the summit she can safely gallop for several hundred yards, leave the track and plunge into unmapped scrub. Then she remembers that the caves lie just ahead. She will hide there until the stranger passes. She swings into a clearing and dismounts to listen, tying the mare's reins to the low branch of a tree. Will the rider look for Glorvina's veering tracks? If he finds a riderless horse, he will know that someone hides close by.

Taking off her boots she scampers in her home-knitted socks, leaving tracks invisible to a white man across the clearing to the entrance to the caves. Down she climbs between rocks the colour of kangaroo pelts, stained and smoothed by underground water, her heartbeats matching the whumping sound of leather and the heaving of a horse's sides as it labours up the slope. Scrambling the last few yards, she flattens her back against the walls of the main chamber from where she can observe the entrance. She tilts her face like a goanna at the point of a stick: shoulders squared, head thrust forward, eyes shrewd but not accepting.

4 2

WHAT CAN AN ACTOR PROMISE?

A horse treads the hollow ground above her, dislodging clods of earth that shower through the entrance to the cave. Rosanna clutches her throat, swallowing dust at the lift and fall of fetlock, knee, hock, hoof. Horses and carts have disappeared through the collapsed ceilings of caves. Go, she prays, glaring out. Today she is facing a plague of men, she decides, and hugs the manuscript to her body. The chestnut, seventeen hands high perhaps, resents the evenhanded tug at the bit, the pebbles moving beneath its feet. It throws its head as it backs up.

The rider wears breeches and a black dress-coat, and when he turns the horse to face the sea she cannot see his head, but there is something familiar in the way he holds himself, the impatient way he taps his whip against his legs. While he faces the downward path winding through the hillocks to her home, Rosanna holds her breath and shrinks against the wall of the cave. Water drips onto her hair.

'Rosanna,' the man calls. After all, it is a god, not a stranger, for he knows her name. It does not sound like Gordon.

She concentrates on the voice: deep-timbred, penetrating, practised, with a small inflection. Her heart hiccups. George. What should she do? '*Che shin*? Who is speaking?' Her hands flutter and curl around the edge of the manuscript.

His horse dances sideways and throws its head in her direction. Rosanna pokes out her head as he dismounts.

The actor pleats his brow. 'Where is your horse? Do you live near by?'

He asks too many questions. 'No,' she lies.

Knotting his reins over a branch he bounds into the cave.

Anger surges through her. 'Why not call out earlier? I heard you flying up the hill behind me and thought you were the devil incarnate, come to punish me.'

He places his hand upon her head as if she were a child and he an angel of the Lord. 'I hear a guilty person speaking.' He sweeps hair from her face. 'Tell me how you discovered this cave.'

A shadow of regret crosses her eyes. Perhaps only the cave holds his interest? Will he tell the Brigstocks and Mr Colyer? The station people must know about it, for she and Skelly have seen the evidence: a broken chair, an English flint, a kerchief. George places himself beside her—everything he does seems deliberate, rehearsed—except his hands smoothing down his thighs, head swivelling in wonder at the stalactites and stalagmites, the cathedral ceiling, the gloomy offshoot passages, the glistening stream.

Rosanna remains standing, deciding whether she should run away. She focuses on the last column of sunlight, near the entrance, the shimmer of fast-moving wings above her head. 'I am very late.'

He tugs at her arm and points at the ceiling. 'What is all this scritching and flapping?' He drops his gaze.

'Bats,' she whispers, folding her arms across her chest. The manuscript rustles against her skin. The actor's arm encircles her waist; his fingers move swiftly to the edges of the stolen pages.

'Father Woods can tell you a great deal about the caves,' Rosanna waffles. 'He has published papers in Melbourne: "Observations on Metamorphic Rocks in South Australia".' She prates to cover the sound of the paper moving beneath the actor's fingertips. It is guilt she suffers—he is quite correct—and something else.

'Rosanna, there is no doubt you have starched your undergarments until they can stand without assistance in the corner of your sleeping quarters.' He walks his fingers to the height of the paper. The pages slide smoothly past her breasts, before he lifts them clear.

Her eyes fill with tears. 'It is a sinful thing I have done. Why did you not come at five o'clock, to the stables, to read the Lynch story with me?' Oh, she is disingenuous. She tries to forget about Gordon. The actor inspects the rims of his fingernails and she reminds herself that although pretty, he must be a pompous man.

George's expression turns down in seeming disapproval. He pinches his lips. 'Do you know that the author of this play made but one copy to submit to the colonial secretary, and then two others, for the actors. How would he view such a loss?'

Rosanna quivers, then fires up. Her mother would accuse her of being overtired. In fact, it is something much worse. She is overexcited. She quivers with emotion. 'I ask you again, sir, who is Mr Edward Geoghegan to be writing about Lynches? Who does the story belong to, if not to a Galway Lynch?' Now she will lose her job, for sure.

He pulls her down beside him. 'You are a little goose.'

Her heart palpitates again at the thought of the goose recently lifted by Moorecke. She struggles away from him, shaking with nerves. First Gordon and now the houseguest: every moment feels conflicted; she wants to go and she wants to stay. The actor reaches out to draw her back.

Rosanna resists. He holds the sheets of manuscript behind his back and leans towards her, until his mouth is poised but an inch from her own. She suspects he must have commanded girls like this before. She concentrates on breathing smoothly.

'You shall read the play, I give you my word,' he murmurs.

'I can take home Act One then?' She reaches behind him to gain purchase on the papers.

'I'm afraid not. The play is to be performed soon. How can I trust you now?' He draws away from her.

She bites her lip in aggravation. Over his shoulder she sees bats swarming through the entrance to the cave and leaping into the dusk. The air feels warm; bark blows across the pathway. They will fly out for hours, perhaps until the early hours of the morning, feeding on the wing and returning to their young ones.

She remembers the tiny bones in the alcove. Caves hold secrets, but please God the actor will not tell hers to Mrs Ashby, for Rosanna has never thieved before.

43

THE WAY OF MEN

'What are you doing?' she jerks her head, as he levers her back on the smooth rock, one hand securing the small of her back, his fingers working at the buttons on her mother's blouse. He seems no longer angry about the manuscript. She is accustomed to the sharp smell of guano, but not to the full weight of a man's body. She feels a frisson of fear. Her mother has told her about drunk and violent men. She is never to walk on the streets of Gambierton after dark; she is always to be careful at the bay; and when riding out she must never lose sight of Edwin. But Eilish can't mean to save her from a man like George. Or even Mr Gordon.

'Mr Sutherland, you would not hurt me?' Rosanna is reassured by the clever sweetness of his face, his pale skin beneath the clipped beard, which tickles her throat. Had she ever been so clean that a man would want to run his tongue inside her waistband? He murmurs reassurances, steadying her body with one hand and pushing hair from her face with the other, as he hovers over her. When his mouth covers hers, sounds overwhelm her: water gurgling over the stones on the cave floor, his horse snuffling in the twilight, the *tenap, tenap* of a cuckle of frogs deep in the chambers, the scuttling of native rats, the electricity of the bats.

'George. No. Do not be rough.' She struggles against him. He presses her down, hands and mouth placating her. A feeling resembling the yearning she has at first light—half irritation and dissatisfaction— tugs at her will. He feathers his fingers where she touches herself, finds his way inside. At the same time he clamps his mouth over hers as if he is sucking her between his teeth. She is dragged by the tide, like a starfish from a rock pool.

He holds the back of her neck until her head tilts forward and she bucks against his *boddagh,* soft at first and then rigid. Then he seems to forget about her feelings, bunting and tearing the last shred of her resistance. When she gasps he takes her top lip between his teeth as if to transfer her pain. She strikes at his face with her elbow. He cannot know how he hurts her and continues to do so until she relents, loosening her legs, opening them wider to ease the pressure. His *thóin* moves as emphatically as Lucifer's straddling Glorvina on a sand hill. But he has not pushed his face into the stream of Rosanna's *fáel*, nor screamed with excitement like a horse.

Finally, he sighs and moans, rolling aside to cup her knee and lift it to his lips. His face is mournful, comic, as pink and beautiful as a girl's pinched for effect. He tugs a linen handkerchief from his pocket to wipe blood from his fingers and dew from his *bod*. Rosanna feels shamed by this fastidiousness. A gust of wind swirls through the cave attacking moist trails cooling on her legs. Why had Eilish not told her about this? It is better than the thought of dying. The actor must love her and she is only a girl. But tomorrow she will stay home and never leave again. Ever. She floats out of her depth.

'I will assist you to find your horse,' he says, as she leaps in a panic towards the entrance, one hand on her skirt, the other in her hair. Bats swirl around them, faster than the eye can see, zig-zagging past their heads, swooping over the trees, their movement not the least like birds. She hears the flap and creak of their wings as she gingerly steps along the path. A soft body dashes against her face, drops and rights itself. Even after the wicked thing she has done at the Big House, she is not in trouble. One event has collapsed into the next. Rosanna touches her fingers to her face and croons. Father and Edwin will have swagged down at the shepherd's hut. Only Eilish and the children wait for her at home.

The moon is rising in the sky when Rosanna descends too quickly on Glorvina, down the steep track to the house. She has not once turned her head to observe George cantering back along the ridge and over the other side. She feels damp and loose-limbed. Without trying she has had her way. Tomorrow, George has whispered into her ear, they will read the play together. She rides with her face thrust up against the sky, using the back of her hand to wipe away tears brought about by bitter wind. She smells the sea. It must be a mortal sin she has committed but it doesn't feel important.

44

DUPLICITY DOES NOT BECOME HER

Brandishing a stick, Skelly takes her by surprise at the last bend in the track. Glorvina cat-jumps and spins around in fright.

Rosanna struggles to keep her seat. 'Skelly, what are you doing out here in the dark?'

'Mother is asking the same question of you.'

Rosanna drops her head. 'Why are you limping then?'

'I ran out to wait for you and I fell.'

'Why do you crash about like a stupid emu? The Ashbys went to Gambierton. I awaited their return and I'm not so *very* late.'

'Let me on the horse. I have a terrible bruise on my knee.'

Rosanna flings out an arm and braces herself to help him climb up. 'Skelly, I missed you, *amadan*.' She closes her arms around him.

'That is so far from God's truth, Rosanna, you should be struck down. It is lucky Father Woods comes to administer the sacrament again this Friday.'

Something heavy settles in the pit of her belly. Father Woods *cannot* know what she has done. She kisses the top of Skelly's head. 'What would I do without you?'

'Shut it, Rosanna. I'm sick to death of you caterwauling over me.'

'Well, that's grand, and what if it were me that was doing the leaving—not you always threatening.' She will beg the actor to take her away with him. He loves her half to death, already. Mr Gordon would never be so serious. Mother finds him queer.

'What about your job at the Big House, then?'

'I can get another. I have experience now.' She drops her lip and looks away.

'Moorecke has been looking for you. "Long time," she said. I thought you must have fallen off Glorvina.'

'God save Ireland. Hold your tongue.'

'She has brought something to the house for you. Green stuff. Mother says it is silk.'

'Did she leave it?'

'The answer to that question would be no. She's camped near the still, with Jack, and I smelled a good smell, like roasting bustard. It *is* the best place to camp, like Father says.'

'Black or white or yellow ... everyone wants to camp in the best place, you daft thing. I'll go to her. Tell Mother I am tending the horse, and sorry to have troubled her.'

She hobbles and waters Glorvina, stopping only briefly to kiss Lucifer's nose and offer him a handful of chaff before rushing through the scrub, following drifting smoke. Moorecke beckons Rosanna from behind a fallen tree where she sits, patting a blackened hole in the underside.

'Green bees?' Rosanna squats beside her.

Moorecke laughs. 'Pretty, like green bees.' She curls her hand into the hole, easing out a bolt of filthy cloth.

'May the holy virgin save me, for all my sins, is it Mrs Ashby's robe covered in goose fat and feathers? Did you drag it along the ground behind you? Oh my *Croí.*' Pray her mistress thinks that the robe has gone to God? Now she will surely lose her position. Her head swarms with terrible lies. Moorecke pirouettes, throwing the robe out from her shoulders like a brolga displaying its wings, and mimicking Rosanna's pose in front of the dressing table mirror. She holds Rosanna's gaze. 'That Missa Ashby has plenty of clothes,' she sing-songs.

'Don't speak like that. You sound like a minstrel.' She supposes Moorecke has stolen the gown to please her. Edwin will not be the only one to fear the policeman from Gambierton and his bung bung. 'You watched me at the mirror?' Rosanna sighs. 'Where is Jack?'

'Bringing *kang ngaro* for his *mala.*'

'You have a feast already.'

'Take some for Skelly boy, the little booger.'

Rosanna hurries home clutching the grey and oily breast of the goose in a curl of bark.

Mother waits in the doorway, arms folded, a small pannikin of tea in her hand. She wipes her apron over her face in pretence of great relief.

Surely Skelly passed on her message.

'What have you got there? You smell like a chimney-girl.'
'Bustard.'
Rosanna attempts to pass between her mother and the door, but is caught by the waist. Eilish splays her fingers across her daughter's bodice, brushes them through her hair, and arches her eyebrows. 'My blouse is damp and the bustard has a curious smell.'

Rosanna paves the way for the play. In any case Mother would never tell. 'Did I mention yesterday that Mrs Ashby is awfully pleased that I can read and write? She may lend me some important documents to improve my mind.'

'She is a lonely woman. Like me. With only her baby for company.' Mother kisses Rosanna's cheek. 'Bring the documents home, and read them to us while we're raking a pot of tea. It will be a treat for Skelly and me. But now, I need your help. Make a steam bath for Hugh and rub some Holloway's ointment on his chest.'

'I'll help you too, I swear. And I'll always love you.' The mention of love sends raw feelings surging through her. Does the actor love her? She feels sweet and ginger, bleak and tender, all at once; her father must never know. She turns away and sniffs her fingers, wets her mouth with spittle, tastes her breath, and it is changed.

Mother tugs her back and scans her face but only for deceit, Rosanna feels sure.

PART 3

THE PLAY

45

ROSANNA PLAYS HER PART

'You will do as I say,' her father shouts the next morning when she feigns illness.

She had not expected him home in the early hours of the morning. Had rain washed them out? Back to work she will go. But what if she encounters Gordon and George at the same time?

She puts her panic aside and gathers her cloak, crossing her fingers as she rides. Surely, she will get to read the play and, God be with us in all hours, George will not tell the Ashbys that she stole it.

'If we are late tonight,' her father says, 'ride home before us.'

At the station she finds the household quiet. The guests must have returned in great frivolity from their long luncheon in the town the previous day, because she finds the evidence: empty bottles of porter, sticky glasses, dirty plates and musical sheets spread across the top of the piano. The Brigstocks and Mrs Ashby spend the day in their rooms.

A note on the kitchen table instructs Rosanna to bring sandwiches and coffee at five o'clock. At three she sees the Brigstock child and his father walking along the edge of the swamp. Soon after that Mr Brigstock and Mr Colyer play backgammon at a round card table they have carried beneath trees in the garden. The small boy falls asleep on his father's coat. If only propriety would allow her to ask one of them, 'And where might Mr Sutherland be, sir?' She thinks she may have glimpsed him smoking with Mr Ashby in the gunroom, but the door stays ominously closed. Surely he will come before she bites off all her fingernails.

Apart from the occasional cry of the Ashby baby, not a sound emanates from the north wing of the house while Rosanna makes pastry, washes dishes and folds linen on the scrubbed pine table, all the while keeping an eye on the kitchen clock. No riders approach the house or outbuildings. Perhaps Mr Gordon is breaking horses miles away. Had she not seen him ride north the night before?

All day she longs to meet the actor and read the play. Other thoughts pull at her mind but she brushes them away. At five minutes before the hour of five she taps on the bedroom door with a tray. 'I am going to the stables, Mrs Ashby, to wait for my Father.' But she is not.

'Is everything all right? There is no disturbance?'

'No, ma'am.' Rosanna has seen her mother sit bolt upright in the dead quiet of the afternoon, prepared to defend her babies against God knows what. Living on the edge of civilisation unsettles everyone. Mrs Ashby seems half-glad to see her and she struggles from the bed, fastening her bed jacket around her body as she crosses the room.

'You may enter. I have something. A little paste-and-glass brooch for the neck of your blouse.' She upends a silk drawstring bag on the dressing table, pursing her lips and cocking her head like a curious parrot. Mrs Ashby is indecisive in all her dealings with Rosanna. On the one hand, she is only a young woman with a baby and in need of her maid's assistance. On the other, she looks half afraid as she shakes out precious jewellery, perhaps remembering that she employs an Irish girl not to be trusted with anything.

'Turn your back.' Mrs Ashby's lips flex and purse. 'You are lucky, Rosanna, to remain in the care of your family.'

'I am, ma'am.'

'My father is unwell. I was loath to leave him when I married Mr Ashby.'

'You must write and tell him to pay you a visit.'

'I fear not, ever. He is too frail to leave Hobart Town. Turn again. Hold out your hand.'

Rosanna swings around to face her. 'I am sorry about your father. Thank you for the brooch.' The gift confuses her further. What will accepting it cost her?

On the way to the stables, she fears that George will not come, is convinced he will not and that Gordon will appear instead; but finds him already ensconced, leaning up against the door of the tack room, a cheroot dangling from his fingers. Full throated, unselfconscious, he throws lines of verse into the musty room, pausing only to draw in fragrant smoke. She has not seen him the entire day.

He feigns surprise at her arrival and his tone mocks her. Filled with delicious dread, she fingers the new brooch in her fingers. Will he speak of what happened in the cave?

'Such a face, Miss Rosanna.'

She keeps her distance. Seating herself on a barrel she opens *Little Dorrit*, lent to her by Father Woods. She is suspicious that he has borrowed the book from the Adelaide Lending Library for the purpose of her instruction. Little Dorrit is very humble, a much better girl than Rosanna, and takes great care of her father in the debtor's prison. For the life of her Rosanna cannot understand why the girl doesn't run away. It makes no sense in a book, when Mr Dickens could allow her to do anything he wished.

'I am not crabbity at all. You rehearse the play?'

'Indeed, those harsh and dutiful words with which I greeted you belong to the Lynch father.' He lifts his boot, twists it at an angle like an Irish dancer, and extinguishes his cheroot.

'The Lynch father sounds so pompous? Is he a weak thing, then?'

'Pray no.' George angles his head to make a more expansive 'o' of his mouth. 'Some Galway people consider him a hero. A paragon of moral conviction.'

The actor strides towards her as if she has displeased him. Disconcerted, she returns the book to her cloth bag. He drops the manuscript onto her lap.

'I dislike moral conviction,' she flusters, 'and I can't read this. Not while you stand so close.'

'Why not, when you went to all the trouble of bringing Mr Dickens's book. It is no great shame, not to read, when living on the edge of civilisation.'

'I can read, you ignoramus.' How bold she feels lifting the manuscript from his fingers and marching to the tack room, where she spreads the pages over the wooden bench on which her father sometimes works repairing leather or greasing saddles. The actor follows her like a dairy cat.

Rosanna lifts a slush lamp from the shelf behind the door. He takes a flint box from his pocket, fusses with the lint and cotton, teasing it up with his fingers. She hears the sharp nick-nick-sound of his flintlock. The flame flutters into life, emitting a fatty smell.

She leans over the bench. '*The Hibernian Father*, in five acts.' Her finger travels across the page and stabs down a cast of characters:

Walter Lynch	A wealthy merchant & Warden of Galway
Oscar Lynch	His son
Alonzo de Velasquez	A young Spaniard
Rupert d'Arcy	A pirate disguised as Father Oswald
Martin Blake	A principal Burgess of Galway
Anastasia	Ward of Walter Lynch betrothed to Oscar
Morna	Wife of Gerald

The actor observes, seemingly amused as she devours the words.
'Oscar Lynch. You take his part?' She snaps the question.
'Certainly.'
'And the magistrate—the father?'
'Mr Geoghegan pines to hire his dear friend, Mr Nesbitt, who was famous for the role in Sydney. Like me, Nesbitt was an extraordinary judge of horseflesh, with a preference for Irish fillies.'
Rosanna blushes. 'So he will play the Lynch father?'
'Sadly no—he died in Geelong before the Melbourne production could be brokered. Mr Geoghegan says that Nesbitt made his reputation dying on the stage, and at the racetrack. He was a great tragedian and made the Magistrate famous.'
'Tragedy, please not that for Galway Lynches.' It is unsettling, him always speaking in riddles. 'I shall read on; I must.'
'Read from the beginning, for you cannot understand the full tragedy unless you know the historical background. Read, while you can,' the actor says, leaning up against the door.
'Oh.' Rosanna sucks in her breath. He would not take it from her now. She places the first page behind the others and reads aloud.

> *Scene I. Mountainous pass. With view of sea—Cave Right.*
> *Rupert D'Arcy and Bernard Enter from cave.*

'Well, it is not Lough Derg, nor our village. A sea cave, how wonderful.' She returns to the cast list. 'Rupert is a pirate—disguised as Father Oswald? You know this already, for you have been practising your part. But it is confusing.'

The actor grins, places his hand on a feed bin and hoists himself upon it, brandishing his crop snatched hastily from a peg. He menaces her with his prop, taking on the visage of a grimacing pirate. 'On a mountain pass overlooking the sea cave, I plot revenge on Walter Lynch.' He laughs at her.

It is infectious. She laughs back. How handsome he looks. How sure of himself. Not a bit like Mr Gordon. She tidies Mrs Ashby's yellow dress with her fingers. Does he love her enough that she can read the play whenever she wishes? She reads on:

> *Rupert*   I am resolved—and not e'en Hell itself
> Did Its black yawning gulph before me gape
> And from its depths the Demon thunder 'Hold!'
> Should shake the stedfast purpose of my soul.

'Oh he is fearsome. And what reason can there be for all his misery? Can it be famine times?' Rosanna picks up a stick and points at George, as if to place *him* in the dock.

'Were you to ask him, Irish maid, he would say—'

> *Rupert*   My Father whose proud barque so long had swept
> Triumphant oer the vassal seas and borne
> The Rover's gallant and unconquer'd flag,
> Was prisoner taken, by this Walter Lynch
> And, through his means, received a pirate's doom.

'Oh I doubt that.' Rosanna turns back to the actor, her eyes dark with terror. 'Will he kill the Lynch father?'

George leaps from the feed bin brandishing his crop, whipping the air in front of him, until he brings the tip to rest below her chin:

> *Rupert*   I would not take his life—but I would fain
> Rob him of station and of fair repute,
> Poison the source of honour, yield him up
> A prey to all the bitter anguished pangs
> Of blasted happiness and hope o'erthrown!

'He will then, I know it.' She pushes at the crop.

Rosanna tastes the actor's breath; he smells of apples and tobacco. Time slows. Nothing is real: not Lynches in a story; not an actor from Melbourne fingering the folds of a borrowed dress, lifting the hem to stroke her legs, long and strong from years of running in the bush with Moorecke; not the wicked things he whispers. He eases off her shoe and kneads the arch of her foot as Mother might a ball of dough when she is pensive. Rosanna curls her foot around his thumb and bucks against the wall, where he has pressed her, raising her right knee. She knocks her head. Wiping her tears away, he increases the pressure on her foot; next kissing her with great deliberation, taking up her lips as if lifting whelks from a shell. She does not like to look at him.

Does she look like the idiots of Woodford: liquid streaming from their mouths, eyes rolling one without the other? She nuzzles delicate ecru hairs lacing the inside of his wrist. He has not pinioned her below the tack hook. Her legs clutch his waist as Hugh might or Blinnie desperate to be carried close. When he snatches her fingers and places them inside his breeches she feels alarm but his skin is soft—softer than the skin of her *cíochanna*—and warm. She touches the tip of his *boddagh* with trepidation, as she might approach a small sea creature that twitches and trembles beneath her fingers, oozing silky liquid. He sighs and shivers. She hunkers down over a familiar ache in her lower back that she remembers from the aggravating few days before she bleeds, when she can't keep her fingers from her *fáel*-flaps. The iron and grit smell passing from his fingers over her cheekbones and into her hair belongs to her. She savours it, crooning, pushing her chin into his shoulder. Then he lifts his *bod* inside her—pressing, pressing—into the beautiful aching part of herself. It appears her feelings are to be left behind; he jolts inside her and then subsides. Jesus, Mary and Joseph; she begins again to cry. He stares, unblinking, into her eyes, as guileless as a goanna disturbed while feeding but then relents, kissing her breasts back into her bodice, easing her off the wall onto her unsteady feet.

'I cannot get enough of you,' he says.

She wipes her eyes and slaps him.

46

STRICT IMPARTIALITY REIGNS

'I longed to read the play and now you have hurt me again. I want to go home.'

'Why not finish our reading first? This is a grand story. Important to the Lynches. And bound to cheer you up.'

Rosanna seizes the manuscript and holds it over her face.

'You must be dying to know what happens,' he says. 'Let me soothe you.' He dabs at her eyes with his handkerchief.

'Nothing soothes injustice.'

'You're no pirate's doxy, Rosanna.'

She hides her face as she straightens her gown. 'The play is very complicated with all these pirates, fathers and sons.'

The actor reads at a pace through the next scene in which the people of Galway celebrate the Lynch father's election as warden with a banquet in the Town Hall. Rosanna feels transported.

> Blake   (to W. Lynch) We hail you then, Sir
> The representative of our liege lord
> And Warden of this ancient loyal city.
> And now by right prescriptive do invest
> You with all full authority and power
> To wield the sword of justice, and maintain
> Inviolate the sanctity of Law
> Within your jurisdiction.

'It is wonderful eloquent you are with your actor's voice—quite changed. I doubt that I should trust you.'

'It is your decision. You are the mistress of your destiny.'

Rosanna hesitates.

'Let us read on,' he says, 'and I will decide if I can trust *you*.'

'If you only knew me better.'

'It is my ambition to do so.' The actor throws back his head and takes up the gruff voice of the Lynch statesman:

> *Warden*   With gratitude elate I do accept.
> And, as the guardian of my country's laws
> I will as zealously discharge the trust.
> As their unspotted purity demands
> Within our courts, corruption ne'er shall stalk,
> But strict impartiality shall reign.

'What is his meaning?'

'He will favour none—not even his son.' The actor puffs out his chest and resumes the magistrate's voice:

> *Warden*   Nay, here I swear that though the guilty one,
> Were to myself in tend'rest ties allied
> And to my bosom dear as son to sire,
> If to conviction were a crime brought home
> Repugnant to the laws I've vowed to guard,
> I have enough the Roman Father in me,
> Though, in the effort did my heart strings crack,
> To seal his doom and lead him to the Scaffold!

'Why does he call on Romans? Do they not protect their sons?'

'He alludes to Brutus, a Roman consul who, in antiquity, slew his son.'

'In Shakespeare's play?'

'Shakespeare's Brutus was also interested in murder and justice but no, it was the elder Brutus. You know Shakespeare?'

'Is it as Mr Shakespeare's fool you are casting me, in your superior melodrama?'

He strokes her face, his brow knitted in mock contrition. 'Believe you a father should place his principles before his child's survival?'

Rosanna shakes her head.

'There are plays within plays, as you may well know.'

After all, he is wonderful, astounding and magnificent: brighter than a cockatiel. If only he will stay long enough for her to know the whole play.

'George, could I be following the words, while you recite them into the air?'

'You may be my prompt, and more beautiful than any other from whom I have accepted correction.'

He is funning her. Grinning like a loon he swoops up the pages and proffers them to her. 'Better still. Let us take the parts together. You must be the voice of Anastasia, affianced to Oscar Lynch.'

Rosanna is not sure that she wishes to play Anastasia. George's fingers trail down her nape. She shivers. It is a prideful thing she has done, agreeing to read. Lynches are proud people, Mother says. They bow their heads to no one, not even God, to their shame. Her eyes dart towards the door. Dusk gathers. Her father's horse cannot be far away and they have read little enough of the play.

'In this scene Oscar Lynch returns from business in Spain. His father awaits him on the shore. I will play the magistrate.' The actor stands tall, using his thumbs to outline an imaginary regal garment, swirling it out behind him before placing one hand upon her shoulders. 'He is *miadh*. What is that, Rosanna?'

'*Miadh*,' she corrects his pronunciation, 'means most awful sad. Is he sore with longing for his son?'

'Indeed, he must be, waiting on shore for him. Beside the magistrate stands his ward, Anastasia. Do you suppose that on disembarking, Oscar will pluck a kiss from Anastasia?'

'Has he done such a thing before?'

George leans over Rosanna and takes her bottom lip between his teeth. She leans away to take a ragged breath. 'If it is in the play, I may play it.'

The actor laughs and plumps himself up, fingers at his fob, face set in an arrogant expression. Rosanna thinks him beautiful, terrifying. She imagines him on stage.

'Anastasia is Oscar's childhood playmate.' George lifts Rosanna's chin, in a paternal way. 'The magistrate finds their new love *exceeding* convenient.'

'How does Anastasia respond, then? It is my turn to speak back, to take her part.'

'Speak then, lo.' He points to her place on the page.

   Anastasia   To Oscar, playmate of my infant years
                    I deemed I'd yielded but a sister's love
                    'Till separation wrung my soul with grief
                    And self-examination brought to view
                    The true state of my thoughts. Since then how oft
                    I've trembled with emotion when his name
                    Was uttered in my presence, and his praise
                    (Sweet music to mine ear) became the theme
                    Of conversation. Then I've felt the glow
                    Of pleasure kindle in tumultuous rush
                    Upon my brow, but dared not yet to join
                    My voice to that of general commendation
                    Yet when alone, my heart devoted still
                    To one loved object.

Rosanna likes the sound of her voice, quavering in the musty stable air. It reminds her of the times she reads aloud for Father Woods, but more exhilarating.

'You must come with me to Melbourne. What a fine actress you will be.' George touches the tip of his tongue on the salt skin below her lashes.

Melbourne—her heart skips. Perhaps he makes fun of a frontier girl. Everything he says is sugarcoated.

When she hears the sudden thump and jingle of horses and men in the yard, she pushes him away. 'George,' she whispers, 'will you not, after all, allow me to take these pages home and read them with my brother?'

'After yesterday, I am a fool to consider such a thing. I should have you dismissed … If I allow you one scene to share with your brother, you must promise never to trespass on my privacy again.'

There is something clever about the actor's words. Fear trickles through her veins, and cautious optimism. She blushes. Why had she thought him a fool? 'I promise.'

He passes her several pages. 'Place them beneath the stable lantern, the moment you arrive tomorrow.'

She rushes from the tack room, feigning a yawn when she catches her father's eye, and bends to pluck straw from the hem of her skirt.

'Rosanna.'

'Here, Father. I am waiting, waiting.'

47

SONS AND THEIR DUTIES

Rosanna has secrets now, perhaps as many as Edwin. For two weeks, she has ridden away in milky morning light and returned at dusk, looking tired but excitable. Good luck stalks the pair of them, ignoring Skelly. In the twilight he can just make out the silhouettes of his older brother and sister racketing into the yard. Edwin runs with Rosanna's bridle towards the pond and she follows, snatching it back and holding the reins over her head.

Father yells, 'Stop your fooling, the pair of you, now. I'll not have decent leather spoiled.'

Edwin swoops to pull her down by her skirt, tugs at her hair. He gives up the bridle and flings it onto the grass, then lifts her around the waist to dangle her legs over the water. Rosanna shrieks. Eventually, they arrive laughing and gabbing at the door.

'Skelly darlin', I missed you.' His sister tries to catch his eye. He turns his face away. Life is all about luck.

After supper Edwin and Father take the newspaper and their pipes to the verandah and Skelly follows. Father reads about the war in Europe. As soon as he can, Skelly decides, he will enlist. The army will not treat him like a cripple because they will never know. He will lie about his age and his frailty and run away. He will die bravely at the front.

Edwin acts so confident. 'If my business doesn't profit I'll take myself off to war.' He looks raffish, his long legs resting on the water barrel, dark hair curled over his collar.

'I will come with you,' Skelly interjects, and Edwin cuffs him.

Aggravated sucking on his pipe makes Father's speech sound sloppy and careless. His nose is red with drink. 'Irish boys have always run off to fight other people's wars. It is a mark of their desperation.'

'The Irish have a reputation for soldiery. I could be a hero. Bring home medals,' says Edwin.

'Who would you save?'

'Go away with you, Father, there's action everywhere in Europe. And talk of a volunteer fighting force from South Australia.'

'I was once offered a commission with the Army.'

'And what happened?'

'Instead, I took a chance on forty-five pounds a year and rations here. Honest labour. You earn good money. If you weren't so careless losing it at Lallah's you'd have your bullocks by now.'

'You only know about slog. I'm planning a different life.'

'Gambling eats profits. Don't come to me for loans. Your mother and I have saved seven years for land.'

'If the bullocks don't give me a start, I might import cases of Kinahan's Dublin whiskey. Or port, champagne, claret, colonial wine, brandy, rum, gin and gineva.'

Father holds out his newspaper. 'Land is the only way to get ahead. Listen—the following leases of Waste Lands of the Crown are being offered for sale in lots of twenty-two square miles, in the Hundred of MacDonnell—Surveyor General's Office.'

Edwin takes it from him. 'Skelly darling, look at this. Moffat's Vegetable Life Medicines: for flatulence and foulness of the complexion ... Shall I order some for you?'

'*Pog mo tóin.*' Skelly carries his sketchbook inside in a huff. Seated at the table, he takes a cloth parcel from his pocket, from which he unwraps the desiccated body of a bat. He manipulates the limbs, tests joints where the wing bends like a hinge. He strokes its tiny head and the seamed underside of the wing and begins to sketch the bat in sections. So many bats have died in the drought.

Rosanna slides in beside him. 'You've been to the cave,' she whispers. 'Mother won't be happy.'

He looks up from his sketch of the bat, turns the shrivelled body in his hand, and stares into its eyes. 'If I had not come back, she wouldn't know now,' he snaps at his sister.

'Darling, can you help me? I brought home a wonderful surprise.'

He wants to resist her wheedling voice. 'Is it a secret, then?'

'Well it might be. I was hoping, Skelly, that you would allow me a page or two of your sketching book.'

He curves his arm around it.

'Don't be sour. Where did you find the bat?' She strokes it lovingly. 'They're quiet now, preparing for the winter. Only a few come and go for food.'

'A hole opened up behind the cave. I almost fell in. The little bat flew into my hand and died.'

Rosanna turns the bat over. 'Sad. Skelly, the actor, George Sutherland, has allowed me the privilege of reading a play. You'd never guess what it is about: Lynches from Galway! George plays the part of the Lynch son.'

'Are you sure he isn't skiting so you'll kiss him?'

'Please don't say that in front of Eilish. Look. I have two pages of the playscript, to share with you.'

How pretentious, calling Mother by her name. Skelly scuffs the floor with his foot.

'Spare me a page or two of your precious book. I'm sure Father Woods would not want you to act so mean.' She pinches him, sly. Reaching across his body she flicks the pages in an idle way until she lights upon the picture in which the trunk and branches of the buloke tree frame the page on which she bathes with Moorecke in the pond. 'I knew you were there that day, amongst the leaves—hiding, watching—quieter than the Blacks.' She moves her fingers across the shaded pond swarming now with creatures. She lingers.

Does she see?

She flicks over the next page, clicking her tongue. 'What does Father Woods say about your perspective—the little animals and giant birds?' She takes the pencil from him. 'How can you draw with that? It's stubbier than a koala's nose. You'll smudge your work.'

He snatches it back. 'I'll scrape the point with Edwin's knife.'

'Oh no, you're not to. Why risk cutting your finger when your sister, who loves you, wants to do it for you?'

'Give it back; I'll do it myself.' The first mistake he made was to trust his sister. Always treating him like a cripple or a baby. Nothing has been the same since she began riding to the Big House. He feels caught: one hand clutching the bat, the other hopelessly lunging for his book and pencil.

Something snaps inside him and he reaches further across the table, and strikes her face hard with the flat of his hand. Rosanna's head snaps back against the dresser. Her mouth falls open. Her hand cradles her cheek. To his horror the sound has resounded through the house. He drops the bat, picks up his book and pencil and dashes outside. Darkness swallows him. Shame.

Father bellows from the verandah, 'Eilish. Is this progress in the evening—fighting and screeching? The boy should go to bed.'

And Mother retorts from the babies' beds, 'We're not so poor that we cannot afford a candle or two or some sperm oil to light a lamp. Skelly needs society in the evenings, just like you and Edwin.' Within minutes she flows across the back step and tracks him to where he now sits shoulders hunched, head in his hands, beside the pit. 'You must apologise, of course.'

Through his fingers he sees that she looks severe, her arms folded, her face creased with tiredness and worry.

'Rosanna, bring a quart pot of tea for your brother and me,' he hears Father call from the verandah.

4 8

SKELLY LONGS FOR LOVE

Skelly creeps in the rear door and slides back onto his seat next to Rosanna. In the lantern light he can see the red mark on her face, moist now from carrying tea to their father and brother on the verandah. Straightening a page of the manuscript he begins in tiny script to transfer the words from the play to the last half a dozen blank pages of his sketchbook. He will not apologise. She should show him more respect.

Rosanna allows armed truce, seeming desperate to copy the manuscript. 'Fancy, a Lynch story, a Galway one at that, and we were never told.'

'Difficult it is to read, in parts, with the ink fading.' Skelly's voice breaks.

'Better if you know it well, like George. His eyes are not troubled by it.'

'*George*?' He fixes with a rude stare the bruises on her neck. Then drags his gaze back to the page. 'I never heard of a warden.'

'Nor I, apart from the warden in Trollope, a fusty old church man— not at all gorgeous like Father Woods.'

'*George*,' he mimics her voice again. He will see what Father Woods thinks about *George*. 'The Lynch warden will be quite important to the story.'

'Heavens, he must be. The play is named for him. *The Hibernian Father*.'

Skelly's head hangs over the page. 'They are in a splendid garden, decorated for a festival. The Lynch warden waits for his son Oscar to return from the Citron groves of Spain and marry his ward Anastasia. He speaks to his friend Blake.'

'What is the Lynch father saying?'

'Bragging. About his son.' Skelly raises one eyebrow thinking this ridiculous. '*Seastachta*.'

Rosanna reads aloud with him:

> *Warden*   Were he but here how he would shine tonight,
>   Pre-eminent above his youthfull peers
>   The bravest gallant in the courtly throng!

'Can you imagine our father blustering prideful about us like so?' she says.

Skelly laughs. He knows Father would never speak up for him this way, but especially tonight. 'And what else do they say?'

'That they are too old to care about women.'

> *Blake*   Ah, my good friend, the time
>   Indeed has been when woman's witching smile
>   Fired our young blood ... but that time's past with us.
>
> *Warden*   Aye, so it is.

'Have they wives?'

'I haven't read that far yet. There is only Anastasia, who is to marry Oscar Lynch, the warden's son. Perhaps she will refuse him.'

'Oh, for sure she will.' Skelly looks at her and crosses his eyes. 'Do *you* not crave a wedding?'

'I never think about it,' she replies; her face looks shifty. 'I'll speak to Father about organising a few head of cattle, a hundred guineas, and two feather beds.'

Skelly bunts his head against hers. 'I was wrong to slap you.'

She jerks away. 'Perhaps I forgive you. Now read and copy. Soon after, the boat anchors in port.'

Writing out the play, Skelly forgets his misery, stopping only to pass his blunted pencil across the table to his sister. Anastasia, who the warden compares to a rose, admits to her lady in waiting that she loves Oscar. Skelly sighs with satisfaction. Of course, she will say yes to a wedding. He likes the setup. His eyes track back to the word breast and he rocks a little in his chair.

The clock on the mantel whirs and stops. Rosanna leaps up to find the key and wind it. 'How far have you read? A terrible tragedy happens at sea.'

'I know,' he shouts. 'And Oscar's friend has drowned. He can hardly bear to tell it.'

> *Oscar*   That night, that dreadful night, Alonzo was
>   By the impetuous fury of the waves
>   Washed from the forecastle into the deep,
>   Which, quick as thought, engulphed his struggling form—

Skelly coughs to cover his emotion. 'Alonzo's father had entrusted him to the Lynches' care. To lose a son must be unbearable.'

'And a daughter also.' Rosanna shrugs as she eases herself back behind the table, appearing to calculate his mood. 'I'm tired. Will you copy the rest for me?'

'All right.' Skelly bends to his task.

She kisses the top of his head and he shrugs her off.

Panicky thoughts break his concentration. The play is the most exciting thing that has happened to him this year—and the beginnings of a beard. Hair grows in other places too—bound to be the wrong places, for doesn't he fail at everything. Edwin will soon leave to become a soldier and Rosanna will go to the gold or marry the actor.

Skelly hopes that one day, Father Woods will take him on as a geological assistant—perhaps if he peaches on his sister. For now, he has the manuscript.

49

A MELBOURNE INVITATION

Bertram, the Brigstock child, has translucent skin like that of an albino and he appears to have no sense. Rosanna has watched him standing stock-still in the yard, at a distance from his mother, completely covered in ants. Once she saw him running into the swamp as if he expected it to lift him up. He will follow a dog outdoors and up the hill without a backward glance and yet is afraid to come to the table for his porridge.

It is burden enough to work in the kitchen without a child underfoot. She is surprised that Mrs Ashby will allow it but the truth is that she is desperate. Poorly or not, Mrs Melvin Brigstock—Rosanna has heard Mrs Ashby call her Olivia—has set off riding with her husband and George Sutherland, along the river, leaving behind her child. Today Rosanna feels sorry for her employer. Her face looks peaky, her eyes tired. They are standing in her dressing room—it reeks of mouse droppings and camphor balls—and she has placed her white hand with great delicacy upon Rosanna's forearm.

'Have you seen my green silk peignoir? I was sure I hung it in the huon-pine robe.'

Rosanna lowers her eyes, and flushes. Can she mean the robe taken by Moorecke? So soon.

'You must help me find it.' Mrs Ashby places her hand at her throat, retracts it, and moves towards the door.

Rosanna stares at whirls of dust on the floor.

'By the way, the day after tomorrow my husband and I have planned an excursion to Mount Schanck, a picnic,' Mrs Ashby says, 'and I will need your help. Wear the yellow dress and braid your hair tightly away from your face. Nothing looks worse than hair dangling in food. Eating outside will be tedious enough. Let us hope the weather holds.'

'Yes, Mrs Ashby. Will a picnic be amusing?' She is disinclined to be more gracious.

'I dare say it will to our guests.'

Rosanna's heart rises and falls. Then she thinks about Friday's out-ing. She has never been on a picnic. But she will be at the beck and call of all the houseguests, including George Sutherland. All day she feels on edge, deciding that she must speak to Moorecke and that perhaps the actor does not care for her at all. Well then, if he does not come to the stables at five o'clock, she will keep the scenes from Act I and go and look for the girl. What a fool he was to trust her. And Mr Edward Geoghegan will have an actor who knows but half the play.

For at least a quarter of an hour she waits, conflicted over whether to stay, or go and speak to Moorecke about the robe: 'Oh Villain, Villain. Deceitful Smooth-tongued Villain,' she casts at him, on his dishev-elled and late arrival through the stable door.

He grins, as unrepentant as any boy. 'You have uncovered Lynch treachery?'

'I know Alonzo drowned. A tragic accident. All will be revealed at the climax of the play. Of that you can be sure.' She lifts her carriage to express her confidence.

'What if the ship's crew and Gerald his faithful servant are in agree-ance that Oscar betrayed his friend?'

'A Lynch would never do such a thing. Anastasia loves Oscar and his father is rich and stiff with virtue. It is not such a blighted life that a boy should commit a crime.'

She knows George pretends to show forbearing.

'Ah, but he is yet to be acquainted with her changed love, which has ripened into something more seductive than sisterly affection. Show me do, how she shall act to signify it.' He roughly pushes up against her, crushing the pages of the manuscript. 'Kiss me that I might forget my saddle weariness and the prattle of Olivia Brigstock. Then we can rehearse until your father and amusing brother come.'

She sees that George is not all sweetness. 'It is boisterous you sound and not sincere at all.'

'It may be foolish to sacrifice my sensitivities for the manuscript, Rosanna. Are they not inextricably intertwined?'

She concedes this, one hand cupping the nape of his neck. He smells of horses and perspiration. Unperturbed he smooths the flesh beneath her pantaloons. So urgent his will, ear pressed against her own, head ducked over her shoulder. No one will come.

Her hand moves beneath his shirt, stroking his chest in agitated rhythm as if his nipples are her own, and he begins to rub against her like a horse against a tree, only half-attending to her and his surrounds. He curves his hands around her *thóin* and she rocks her hips against him. If a coach comes by, she decides, she will still go to the gold. With or without him. But he makes room inside her with his fingers for the rest of him and plunges in. Her hands curl like a suckling babe's, her mouth loosens and falls open and she makes sounds similar to those Baby made mouthing Mother's breast—until she feels she has expelled her insides. Even love is ridden at a gallop now. They straighten up and disentangle limbs and clothing.

George buttons his breeches and worries his fingers through his hair. 'Such tedious telegrams I receive from the playwright Edward Geoghegan. Now he is in lather about backers. He asks too much. I cannot rush back to Melbourne before I have concluded my business here.' He kisses the top of her head. 'And he is always unwell.'

'When I am an actress, I will meet the famous man.'

'Oh, he is not so famous. With his disreputable background, I am sure that he would like an Irish girl like you.'

Such diminution jolts Rosanna. Love-making does not always bring out the best in George. 'Let us act then.'

'I doubt that you are acting, but have your way. We may as well rehearse.'

She settles huffily on a box beside the chaff barrel, one eye on the door.

5 0

A MURDEROUS LYNCH SON

Back turned, George smokes a cigarillo in the doorway and Rosanna reads avidly on. He returns jingling coins, an impatient look on his face.

'The pirate is disguised as a priest. Imagine that,' Rosanna call out to him from her box seat. 'He has heard a terrible secret under the false seal of confession. Now he announces to the Lynches and all assembled that Oscar cannot marry Anastasia.'

Rupert My sacred duty calls me to denounce
     The guilty spoiler of another's life
     And to avert from your confiding maid
     The dread calamity that must accrue
     From mating with a Murderer!

            (Fixes his eyes instantly on Oscar)

Omnes A Murderer!

Rupert The word once spoken cannot be recalled
     And here before the burgesses assembled
     In presence of thy father and thy bride
     I do attaint thee Oscar of that crime
     The murder of Alonzo de Velasquez!

'Murder ... a Lynch.' Subdued, Rosanna reads on. 'Anastasia begs him to defend himself. The poor Lynch boy. Mother would be aghast.'

Oscar My father. My Anastasia! I cannot—
     The scorpions of remorse invade my breast
     And conscience, the unfailing scourge of crime,
     Forbids denial. In mercy take me hence!
     My life is hateful now, bereft of honour;
     Bear me then to the dungeon or the rack.
     For indeed I am—

Rupert *(triumphantly)* Guilty!

Oscar 'Tis too true.

'Oh,' Rosanna's eyes fill with tears. '*The scorpions of remorse*—is that not beautiful? Imagine them scorpions stinging his heart.' She leans back in her chair.

The actor sits beside her. 'The warden is a man of honour and justice is his first love. If his son broke the law, he will swing. You can rely on it.'

'There is nothing just in that. This is all the pirate's doing, somehow. And dressed like a priest, the black devil?'

'He is well pleased with events.' The actor straightens his jacket and settles his collar.

'Like you.'

'It is love, Rosanna, I feel for you.'

'Oh, you sound perfunctory.' She looks sideways at him. Does he mean it? Can it be true, after all his rudeness? If only she had not read *The Macdermots of Ballycloran* in which a girl's trust is betrayed. All the same, she kisses him. 'Read on, George.'

He stops to lick his fingers and thumb back pages. 'Anastasia is much cast down.'

Rosanna takes up the page. '*All is melancholy, dark and drear.* She worries on Oscar's behalf, but she has felt this way before, I swear.'

'Like Mr Geoghegan, you sometimes share her feelings?' Pensively, he rests his hand upon her arm.

Rosanna lifts her face to his. 'Oscar's predicament has infected her. It is natural to feel a loved one's pain.'

'But she is serious in wishing she were dead.'

'Why do you say so?'

'Mouth the words, Rosanna. Mouth them sweet.'

Rosanna trembles as she reads. The words cut deep inside her. She has felt like this—not for love, but for lack of it:

> *Anastasia*   Oh Heaven in Mercy snatch me from a life
> Where nought for me exists but misery
> Despairing wretched days and hopeless nights

'Oh, dear girl. Sweet, *Mavourneen.*' Rosanna flattens her hand against her skirt. 'The Lynch boy has caused this storm in her but he will be suffering more.' Being with George makes her belly churn so.

George takes back the pages and rifles through for earlier evidence of Oscar's mercurial shifts of temper on the voyage home to Galway. 'No doubt, his beloved friend Alonzo bears the brunt of them. Hear witness from Oscar's attendant, Gerald, on the voyage with him from Spain.'

> *Gerald*   But ere five days had lapsed, the former grew
> Reserved and sullen, and his spirits lost
> Their wanted buoyancy. Absorbed in thought,
> He frequently would pace the vessel's deck,
> With moody sadness traced upon his brow.

'It is a terrible feeling, when it strikes. Moorecke and I agree.' This irony puzzles her for *Booandik* lives seem harder compared to Lynches' in Galway or the colonies. Restless, Rosanna stands suddenly, her face pleated with sympathy. 'Why do you suppose he feels so sad?' she ponders.

'Read for yourself.'

> *Gerald*   And when at times, his eye would rest upon
> Th' unconscious object of his vengeful thoughts
> His angry glance would kindle to a glare
> Of settled hatred and a withering scowl
> Proclaim the conflict raging in his breast
> Alonzo, unsuspicious of the cause
> Of grief which seemed to prey on Oscar's mind.

Rosanna stumbles over the words. 'Oh, George, he is jealous of his friend but ... he cannot be faulted for thoughts springing from within.'

'They come from somewhere.'

'Dreams perhaps.'

'Mr Coleridge believes so. Oft loosed by the poppy. Unreliable. Read on. What think you now?'

'During a storm, a quarrel arose. Oh no!' Rosanna brings the page close to her lips in agitation:

<blockquote>
Gerald   'Twas on that night of horror, whilst around
Raged the fierce war of elemental strife,
That, unawares, Oscar Alonzo seized
And hurled him headlong in the wild abyss
Of foaming ocean!
</blockquote>

'*Unawares* note. He is in a dreamlike state, George.'

'Haughty spirits, I say.'

'Father is haughty but only on his family's behalf.'

'We shall see what haughty fathers do to their sons. Are you, Rosanna, haughty?' He reaches over to touch her face, creased with irritation.

'I am not,' she cries, pulling away from him, moving again towards the door.

He grins and follows her, holding out his hand to take back the pages.

'It is not such a Lynch trait,' she says, 'but I have seen it here in Ashbys.' She turns and skims the words. 'His father will free him. Apply clemency. The Spaniard's death a tragic accident. A young man's temper.'

The sound of hooves startles her. Is Mr Colyer riding out again?

'Rosanna,' her father's voice booms from the yard.

Heart jumping, she hesitates. 'Let me take more pages.' She leafs back through the pieces of paper in his hands.

'You must tell no one about reading the play with me,' George hisses in her ear, bending over her. 'It can be our secret,' he whispers stroking the underside of her arm. 'If any awkwardness should arise I shall say that I bring letters for you to deliver to your brother, whom I have met on business at Miss Lallah's.'

'But you have not. Have you?'

'You don't know that.'

She unfastens the stable door. 'Father, you bark louder than an owl. How you startled me.' She secretes several scenes under her plaid wrap.

George melts into the shadows.

'What are you reading?' her father asks.

'Something the poet gave me.' Oh fool, she thinks. But God smiles on her because Father is in too much haste to question her further. She steps away. He loops the reins over his arm and leans against his horse's flanks to lift her into the saddle.

'Am I haughty, Father?'

'Haughty. What kind of language are you speaking now—English language?'

'Skelly taunts me so,' Rosanna cries. '"Hoity-toity," he says. Where is Edwin?'

'Edwin has business at MacDonnell Bay. He cut away through Benara and south. Take that look off your face, girly, or you'll have people believing this haughty toity.'

Rosanna is satisfied that Edwin is once again at the centre of Father's thoughts, God bless him, and that she is safe from interrogation. She leans her cheek against her father's back and fingers her mouth. Her chin feels rough, abraded. Mother must not see where the actor has rubbed his beard against her tender skin. Rosanna feels an urgent love for him despite his roughness. Not that he has offered to take her with him, yet, but has he not said that he loves her? What a fool she was to tell Skelly anything about him.

51

WHO WILL STAND BY A LYNCH BOY?

Skelly waits while his sister makes a show of scraping turnips and taties from the pan. She clanks and grouses as she rinses the supper bowls. Then comes to sit some distance from him at the table, her hands fiddling with papers in her lap.

'Rosanna, and so?'

She smiles a queer smile. There is no doubt that it pleases her to gripe him. She could not be more smug if she'd laid an egg.

'Have you brought more pages from that place?'

'Perhaps the play will upset you, darlin'.'

Skelly rises up, fists clenched, and kicks over his stool. Rosanna glances over her shoulder to locate their parents. Will she peach?

After the meal, Mother and Father had disappeared, whispering and crooning, to share a cup at the edge of the pond. He does not wish to rouse them.

'All right then. May the blessings of light fall upon you, if you promise to keep your temper.' She pushes the lantern towards his place at the table. 'Pick up your seat.'

Rosanna's company has become scarcer than butter. Skelly calculates the cost, hooks the stool with his fingers, and straddles it.

'You will soon see why I was loath to show you.' She pushes a page in front of him. 'But I'm desperate to read on myself.'

He snatches up his pencil and sketching pad and flips the manuscript page. 'I am not a baby.'

Rosanna acquiesces. It is what she wants, after all. 'In this scene, Mr Geoghegan reveals something terrible. We must determine the likelihood of such behaviour in a Lynch.'

'Don't be so tragic.' Skelly copies while Rosanna reads and reads deeper into the manuscript. He watches her out of the corner of his eye, turning pages, racing ahead of him.

'Recto, verso,' she mumbles as if demented. Had Father Woods taught her this?

'Please, Rosanna. How can I keep my hand neat? Stop biting the inside of your mouth or I'll call Mother.'

Rosanna's mouth sets in a grim line.

'It is clear that Oscar and Alonzo are at odds,' he says eventually.

'What do you suppose to be the substance of their quarrel?'

'It must be the girl, Anastasia.'

She looks smug. 'Only a brother would blame a girl.'

'I would not *blame* a girl.'

'I love this playing, but I am sick with fear,' Rosanna whispers.

Skelly shrugs. All very well, for a girl who works away from home and enjoys the best life. What does she leave out when she talks of the play—apart from the bruises on her shoulders.

'Read Anastasia's lines and all will be revealed.'

With more suspicion than a black boy offered food, he approaches the lines:

> *Anastasia*   My brain is seared the thunderbolt of fate
> Hath rived my heart and every sense is locked
> With the iron rasp of dark despair
> Withhold me not—for I myself will forth
> E'en to the Council—in their sight I'll kneel
> Myself will be my Oscar's advocate
> Will plead for him with love's persuasive tongue.

'*My Oscar*. Mother would say as much.' Rosanna sniffs.

'That is very true. Mother would run to the public house and raise a crowd.'

'Or hire a sharp-tongued Galway lawyer to get him off.'

Rosanna eases her stool along to sit beside him at the table, appearing to calculate his mood. 'Will you finish copying these pages now?'

'I'll be doing that.' Skelly bends to his task. For a long time, panicky thoughts break his concentration. His hand rushes over the pages in an attempt to catch up with his sister. When he reaches the revelation about the priest, he averts his head. It is just a story but he dreads so to know how it ends.

> *Oscar*   Almighty powers! Hast thou no ready store
>   Of sudden death and quick annihilation
>   To rid one of this hated load of life?

As the import of the Lynch boy's confession compresses his heart, Skelly's eyes fill with sadness. Oscar too longs for death. Oh *fein*. Skelly hadn't lived long on that wet island. He has not done anything half as terrible—but he understands self hatred. It must be a terrible mistake. 'A Lynch boy would never kill.' When Mother returns from the pond, she will be aghast. Of course, Rosanna could not tell him. He had to find out for himself.

He rushes outside to evacuate turnip weighing down his gizzards. Then returns to the table more slowly. Filled with melancholy, he reads on and on, copying by candlelight until all that remains is a sputtering stub of wax.

His sister has lain her head on the table and closed her eyes. He prods her arm. 'It is a foolish play, Rosanna. He wouldn't have done the crime in the first place, but if he did, the family would ride to the Loughrea assizes and defend him in their own tongue.' Does she feign sleep?

Skelly closes his sketchbook and wraps it in kangaroo hide. He pats at his sister's shoulder. 'I do not believe the whole story.' She does not stir. In the morning he will ask her the next bad thing. Perhaps she will tell him. He places the paper in her lap and rests his cheek against hers before he moves towards his bed roll. Her sweaty smell is womanish.

Tomorrow or the next day, Father Wood is expected at the little house, and he and Mother will speak about Skelly's future. If he has one at all. Rosanna's secrets gyre in his mind. It will be hard not to speak of them.

5 2

A SCIENTIFIC EXPEDITION

Skelly bides his time. Father Woods is as curious as a newborn about the world. Together they gather rock and fossil samples along the karst until a heavy sky rolls overhead. Perhaps the storm will travel through quickly, not linger until the next day to spoil the picnic that Rosanna is in such a lather about. She has ridden away to the Big House early to prepare more cakes and jellies but also, Skelly suspects, to avoid Father Woods.

'Describe these tiny invertebrates for me, Skelly, and note their resting place.' Father secures a page of his morocco notebook and scribbles furiously. Black coat flapping around his legs, silver hammer in hand, he examines shards of volcanic rock with his thumb and forefinger in great concentration. His leather sample bag lies at his feet. Scattered silver and indigo lights spill through the clouds; lightning forks in the fringe of trees behind them.

'We must hurry or we may be caught up in the storm.'

Seconds later thunder and lightning split the sky.

'I can take you to the bat cave. It is only a short walk.' He will show Father the little human bones and then speak to him about Rosanna.

The priest's face lights up. 'What a pleasure that will be and the storm is only a passing one. See the sky rinsed clean beyond it.'

To Skelly's satisfaction Father Woods caresses the cold smoothness of the stalactites, cups the dripping water and tastes it on his fingertips. From the moment he strikes the sulphur match and lights a candle his countenance is filled with wonder. Thunder rips the sky again. Skelly feels the violence of it beneath his skin. Pounding rain sends rivulets of water rushing over the lip of the entrance, cascading over the roots of the trees buttressing the cave walls. He and the priest stand side by side breathing in the clean wet smell invading the cave.

'The last time I came here I was sick for days afterwards. I dreamed terrible hot dreams, that I was covered in blood and my clothes were saturated with it,' Skelly says.

The priest squeezes his shoulder and moves away to stare up at the ceiling. He seems troubled. 'I also dream about blood but Our Blessed Mother comforts me.'

'The blood in *my* nightmares is true. It began when I was a baby, mother says. A linen-maker threw his drinking glass into my cradle and it shattered on my crown and coverlet. She says that when I am sick, blood floods my mind.'

Father Woods places his arm around Skelly's shoulders. 'Drink can be an evil thing.' He shivers. 'How cold it is below the Earth's surface, Skelly.'

'Come and see the bats. Last time I came here, it was hotter than the furnaces of hell.' He crosses the main auditorium, ducking through an archway into the second largest chamber. Bent almost double, Father follows him, holding a handkerchief to his nose at the smell of guano. 'Is it warm enough now for you, Father?'

'It is very ripe.'

Skelly stoops to pick up a tiny body splayed across a rock. 'This one has crashed. They do not like to fly low.' Tenderly, he cradles it, fingering its woeful snouty mouth and pointy ears, its fine leather skin, outlining fine blood vessels from membranous wing to ankle. Their candlelight illuminates the bat's changing colouration: golden lights on the fur of its back; pink limbs and ear holes.

'Look at the little ones, Skelly.' The pups pulsate, their thin feet clinging to the limestone dome of the ceiling. A small white bat stands out like a cabbage moth against the dark fur of the bumping humming throng. 'See how they pet the albino. He seems curiously well accepted.'

Skelly continues to stroke his specimen. 'I don't suppose babies know about colour. Father, it is fearful hot in here. I am sweating like a horse.' He wipes his face with the back of his sleeve. 'Rosanna loves this cave.' He raises his voice over the din.

'She should not come alone.'

'Once she brought a houseguest here.' He claps his hand across his mouth and looks away. Rosanna is not the only actor. A pang of guilt shoots through him and he refuses to meet the priest's eye.

'Do not further breach your sister's confidence. I will speak to her. Perhaps I should write her a letter about teaching little ones at my school,' says Father sharply.

'She cares for the actor at the Ashbys more than me. Will you ask her to confess?'

'All in God's time.'

Skelly feels diminished.

'Other people's lives are never as simple as we believe. How few people know you as a fine zoologist. You know the creatures of the caves, the ponds, the sky, and the bush around you. I could not wish a better assistant.'

In God's time again. Skelly sighs.

Father Woods fingers his beard. 'How long will it be before these babies streak across the night sky, feeding on the wing?'

'Perhaps they go now, riding on their mothers' backs.' Skelly laughs, dissolving the tension between them. 'They grow quickly in a month or two.' He resumes stroking his specimen. He will sketch the parts and label them—phalanx, forearm, tibia, metacarpals and *penis* in English, as Father prefers. More than likely the priest will confront his sister. She will be sorry.

53

MRS ASHBY CONFIDES IN ROSANNA

All morning Rosanna has sole responsibility for the Brigstock child. It is the last day before the picnic. At ten o'clock she takes him by the hand to the stable yard to pet and feed coddly apples to the horses. Mrs Ashby weighs each request: afraid perhaps that a silly Irish girl will run off in the middle of a chore, never to return. True enough, but at the moment it does not suit her to run away to the gold. At dusk she hopes to read the play with the actor although she has not set eyes on him the entire morning.

The boy lags and with scraps of pastry she coaxes him further away from the verandah, eager to feel sun on her face. He drags on her fingers, head down, picking his way behind her. As they cross the yard to the horses, he wipes his fingers, distractedly, on his silly frilly shirt. He fusses and grizzles, pulling at the breaking yard rails. She will not lift him for he is a solid child. Perhaps a new tooth troubles him. Revealing himself too timid to feed horses, he screams like a barn owl in their proximity and, cursing, she carries him on her hip to the back door.

By eleven o'clock he has fallen asleep in a dappled pool of sunshine on the chaise and Rosanna is once more unencumbered. On and on she works. After the dining room clock chimes twelve she hears voices in the yard and she makes her way to the window to see the actor returning from a ride with Mr and Mrs Brigstock.

Mrs Ashby has cheered a little and relates to Rosanna the many entertainments available in Hobart Town, and the perils of her journey to South Australia. She tells Rosanna about her plans for the picnic at the volcano. It is always diverting to have society, particularly in a place of scientific significance. Why, it is from the vantage of Mt Schanck that Mr Ashby and his father, awed by park-like heaths and lush stringybark forests rolling to the sea, made the decision to purchase the lease for the station. The party will travel by spring cart and on horseback to the small crater at the base. Only the men will proceed on foot to the top of the volcano.

'You will take care of my little man, Rosanna, and serve refreshments. If Mrs Brigstock is well enough to accompany us'—Mrs Ashby raises her eyebrows and then retracts them—'and indeed, I hope she will be, for it is for her benefit and entertainment that the excursion is planned, you will have the care of Bertie, as well. Since her illness he has been difficult to quieten.' Bertram sleeps on, serenely, fist in his mouth. Rosanna enjoys this irony and smiles, as she considers the plan. Mrs Ashby stretches, fans her fingers over the sash at her waist and tentatively smiles back.

All this Rosanna hears, and more; Mrs Ashby's tongue runs on at astonishing speed, while they roast mutton, beefsteak and shanks of kangaroo, assemble Scotch eggs and short crust pies, bake cakes and custards. Sent to the cellar with steaming victuals for their jaunt, covered with floury cloths, she is disconcerted to find it occupied.

'It is not safe, Mr Sutherland.'

Rosanna sounds terse even to herself. Her voice reverberates around the room. Her face works in strange ways as if sinful thoughts have broken through her skin. Has he lain in wait for her? It seems she cannot help but agree to almost anything he suggests. Now Mrs Ashby calls a list of items over the balustrade above them. Rosanna's shaking hands shift earthenware bowls in pretence of searching for preserves. Fingers wet with spittle, he seeks her breasts inside her bodice, ducking his head over her shoulder to bite and fondle her neck, moving at the same time against her *thóin* until the shelves rattle and she turns her head towards the staircase thinking that she might faint. He laughs as he swings her around, sweeps up her skirts and manoeuvres her in clumsy fashion to the flagstone floor; she thrusts her tongue into his mouth to silence him. Life is no more than a game to him. Edwin acts the same with his lovely girl from Dismal Swamp. Rosanna had once observed them partly screened by trees behind the store at the bay, wind covering the girl's soft moans. But surely, George's feelings are too frequent; excessive. Rosanna feels hot. Is her face red?

'What can be taking you so long, girl?' Mrs Ashby scrapes the rickety cellar gate across the stone steps.

Rosanna raises her head in fright. If only the baby will bawl. 'I'll not be long,' she cries out. 'I cannot locate the mustard.'

'Bring a jar of pickles and some cheddar,' Mrs Ashby calls.

Will she descend? 'Oh, I have it now.' Rosanna twists away from George, and rises on her knees, brushing cobwebs and filth from her gown. She straightens her apron and rushes across the room to the wooden shelving to gather food and hurry, arms laden, up the stone staircase. When she glances back, she sees George's face, floating gloomy as a ghoul in the cellar darkness.

Mrs Ashby sets her to work squeezing the juice of lemons into jugs of boiled water. Soon after, she hears the scrape of the cellar gate and George's footsteps in the hallway.

54

SECRET LETTERS AND LOVE

Next afternoon, Rosanna waits and waits in the stables—prays to the man up there—fearing that George will not come to read the play after all, having already flustered her below the stairs.

'Miss Lynch, I have a letter for your brother,' he calls, unnaturally loud when he finally ducks beneath the lintels.

She hesitates, looks up; how strange that he has brought Mr Brigstock with him. She gathers her shawl closer around her shoulders. 'A letter?' she hisses. 'He is working at another station.'

George passes her the note sealed with ruby wax. 'Remember our previous discussion about delivering this to your brother.' He repeats himself as if he considers her a half-wit or wishes to convey this idea to Mr Brigstock. She holds out her hand to take the note. She had thought talk about the letter no more than a ruse for their playing in the stables, but it is, after all, written and sealed.

'Come, George, we can bag a duck or two before dark,' begs Bertie's father, moving towards the doorway.

'I shall be with you shortly, Melvin. You might fetch some bread and wine to carry with us. The air is cooling rapidly.'

'Melvin ...' a voice calls.

'Go to your wife; I wish only to speak with Miss Lynch about the importance of speedily delivering this letter to her brother.'

The man looks torn between duty and pleasure. He hesitates and then hurries off.

'How many acts and scenes are in your play?' Rosanna snaps at George. Saddled and tied to the hitching rail by the stable door, Glorvina lifts her feet against gusts of cold wind. Rosanna shivers.

George opens his mouth over hers, and holds her hard against the wall. The stone abrades her skin through her thin dress. She flattens out her back, then softens, and like a water snake moves her body in sections, to accommodate his fingers. He lifts her higher. He cannot get enough of her; it must be love he feels.

'Sir, Mr Brigstock may return,' she whispers as she twists his hair around her fingers.

'Do not fear, Rosanna. You may take more pages with you, when you go.'

His chin rests on her head. She slides her hands inside the neck of his shirt. The feeling with George is not unlike drinking Father's *potoín*. She wants to resist, most times, but once she feels it under her tongue, the smoky taste of it moves swiftly into her veins, and she is helpless, languid, laughing, not herself at all.

It is as if she floats disconnected from her troubles but never for long enough, before guilt comes seeping in. She is a bad girl, that is certain, but will not end up like Feemy Macdermot in Mr Trollope's book—dead.

George disentangles himself. 'I will check on Brigstock.'

He hurries away. Rosanna slides down the wall. Straightens out her petticoat. Pretends to look away.

Within seconds, he returns from the tack room, bouncing his crop against his hip and holding a sheaf of papers. 'Through the window, I saw Mr Brigstock held captive at the gate. William regales him with frontier tales, no doubt, while Jane packs victuals and fetches a lantern for his hunting expedition. I swear he will be too terrified of Blacks and bunyips to depart.'

Rosanna rifles through the pages of the manuscript; her expression imploring but all pretext: 'Let us read Act 3, Scene 4.'

'Ah, set in the Galway Council Chambers, where events of consequence transpire.'

'George, do not forget your promise. That you will take me with you, when you leave here.'

'It would be most unseemly.'

She raises her eyebrows. 'Pish. I will ride out with you at break of dawn or fall of dusk.'

'On Lucifer?'

'It might be so.' Everything is bluff. After all her criticism of Edwin, now *she* gambles with his horse.

'You *have* finished with the Lynch family dramas?'

Rosanna eyes him, speculatively. 'We shall bring the play with us.' She holds his gaze. 'You are just like my brother—vainglorious. I will not allow you to rile me.'

'How ungrateful you sound, saying such outrageous things.'

Rosanna blushes. George only half attends her, his interest being in his own performance.

She holds the page up to the lighted doorway and skims the text. 'It is all repentance, guilt, and *no* mercy. His son has one week to prepare for death. What you have told me is true.' She gathers her breath in a little choking sound. 'The Lynch father is torn between his love of justice and his son.' But he cannot believe Oscar a murderer.

'*The father in the judge is wholly merged,*' George recites.

'No.' Rosanna sucks in her breath. 'Sure he might relinquish his son to the courts, but he is Irish. There is more to it, rest assured.'

The actor staggers across the stable floor, pressing his hand to his heart.

> *Warden*   This woe fraught task. But no, it cannot be.
> I cannot, will not falter with my trust!
> Nor e'er shall it be said that Walter Lynch
> Permitted aught to interfere between
> His duty to his Country and his God!
> Enough, proceed we with the case, and now
> The father in the judge is wholly merged.
> Bring forth the prisoner! Now support me Heaven
> In this sad agony!

'George, this does not bode well. Tell me if the Lynch boy can be saved. You have read the whole; you have seen it played.'

'Throw yourself at my feet and beg for mercy,' he mocks. 'This is what the play asks of Lynch's fiancée Anastasia.'

Rosanna looks askance, calculating how many minutes of light remain before she must go. 'Oscar is as good as dead but I'll not beg, George.'

'Ahah! Then you have not loved.' He ducks behind her, brandishing the page. 'Read on, then. Take Anastasia's part.'

She snatches at the page, and lifts her head assuming the wracked attitude of an imaginary actress:

'*And spare his life or kill me by refusal.*' How bravely the girl acts, standing up to the Lynch father. She goads him:

> *Anastasia*   It is not Justice rules thy stubborn heart
> But reckless Stoicism and haughty pride
> Within thy ruthless breast triumphant sway
> And freeze sweet nature's genial current there.

'Oh, but she is dangerously wise,' Rosanna cries. 'I can hardly bear to read on.'

George's lips tease along the yoke of Rosanna's blouse.

'How can you be so distracted, when it is a young man's life at stake?' Rosanna stamps her feet and moves away.

Mr Brigstock calls from the yard and then bounds rapidly into the stables.

Flourishing his pen and an envelope extracted from his pocket, George smiles benignly at Rosanna and lifts his hand to speak in a loud voice: 'I will await your brother's reply to my letter tomorrow.' As if he is no more than one of Edwin's horse cronies. George acts continually. She doubts the letter is of much import. But how infuriating if he and her brother have spoken about Lucifer.

55

PICNIC AT MT SCHANCK

Rosanna is not afraid to make her way to the Big House alone. She has been sleepless with anticipation about the picnic. The volcano looms in the distance, the sun's arresting pink rays scattering the plain before it. Swamp gums poke their twiggy fingers into the sky: gnarly-skinned hags up to their knees in water, peering through their dripping hair. Rosanna ducks cankerous boughs. Wind blows drifts of cobalt, splotches of grey, and banks of dirty wool-coloured clouds over her head to the sea.

It takes a full three hours before the gay station party sets out: women and babies on the cart, men on horseback. Mrs Ashby smiles at her husband as he converses with the men. Mrs Brigstock's pale face peeps from her voluminous coat and hood. Rosanna balls her feet to grip the boards of the cart, one hand steadying the food hamper, the other on the Brigstock heir. Baby Ashby sleeps in a Moses basket at his mother's feet.

Happy in their separateness, the men throw courtesies at the cart, swinging their faces, back and forth, between the mountain and their companions. George makes reconnaissance forays, cantering ahead and back, eager and impatient. If only Rosanna were free to gallop across the plains with him. If only he would look at her as if she were a plate of cream again instead of paying compliments to the ladies. She feels the grit of his affection. He will not acknowledge her in station-company.

They follow cattle-crushed rutted trails to the mountain. The men shoot an emu running beside the cart. Unsuitably dressed in velvet and soft-shoes, the Brigstock heir laughs with delight at the bedraggled body pulsing by the track.

At the lower crater the men unpack hampers and boxes beneath the shea oaks. Mrs Ashby passes a canvas water bag amongst them.

Rosanna uses a small branch to sweep clean a picnic place and they spread rugs and cushions, onto which Mrs Brigstock subsides like a collapsing parasol. A fire is built for the blackened kettle. The men shade their eyes, preparing to climb the steep path to the summit, which is partly obscured by spindly wind-bent shea oaks clinging to the crater sides.

Bertram whines softly, tugging at his papa's breeches. 'Bertie go?'

His father brushes him off. 'Olivia, he must stay with you. Keep him, do. He'll not manage, and will be such a pest.'

'The maid, surely, may take him part the way.' Mrs Brigstock turns to Mrs Ashby. 'Do say she may, Jane.'

Rosanna turns her inscrutable face to her employer, who bows her head. 'I will serve tea to the ladies until you return with Bertie.' His confidence has much improved, Rosanna thinks as she plucks the child's hand away from his mother's. He pulls away from her as soon as he takes to the path in his ungainly way. George and the men are already striding away and soon it is only she and the child, following in their wake, their echoing voices winding up the steep incline until they become quite faint like the gurgle of a distant spring.

Within a hundred yards, the boy breaks completely away from her, running up the grassy track pressed down by the men. Rosanna tails him, intermittently calling his name. But soon he is well ahead of her and apparently deaf to her calls. The path steepens and she lifts her skirt to hurry forward. Subsumed by guilt she glances frequently behind her. The dark eastern walls of the lower crater resemble the walls of a house, its roof long blown away into the big sky. The women have settled like cabbage moths beside the shining lake.

'Wait, Bertie!' she calls, startled by a fall of stones above her. 'Stop at once or I'll take you back.' Her threats waft away on breezes sculpting the shea oaks. She wipes her brow. The little beast is as slippery as a water rat. How much trouble will afflict her if he slips and falls? She labours then, for several minutes, halting only to listen over the drone of insects, for Bertie's childish panting.

'Bertram!' she cries again. With some of Edwin's luck, just a wee drop, she will overtake her renegade without alerting the men. He will tire: such a weakly boy, to be cantering up a mountain, like a goat or a pony.

Rosanna's yellow gown is drenched with perspiration; her heart beats like a bodhran at a wake. A formidable rock-face lies before her, pigface flowers rioting across its surface. At first she focuses on the solid and immediate: silver grass, igneous bubbles in the rock face—the traces left by volcanic gas.

On the last part of her ascent, she traces a whorl in a rock with her fingers, a pine-shaped hole; then she lifts herself forward over the dolomite rim of the crater. On the far side she can see the men marching around the rim like eager Lilliputians. Their voices have ebbed away. Singing and carrying flags, they should be. What if Bertie's little body lays splattered on the base? She holds her breath in terror. Holy Mother of God let him be safely perched on a ledge.

Her head spins when she finally looks down, searching the red rings like the contours of cut gum that encircle the unbroken walls of the crater. A wagtail aggravates a flock of swallows, resting on their tails and diving off, riding invisible currents over the startling void. Not a flutter of childish frilly clothing. Father Woods and Skelly have long conversations about the Pleistocene period, when molten lava cooled forming the solid parts of the south-east landscape and great seas retreated, leaving behind corals and small crustaceans. Moorecke has told Rosanna *Booandik* stories about giant *Craitbul*'s cooking mound, for that is what *she* calls it. Now the volcano has taken a small boy. Rosanna begins to sob. May all the saints protect him. And her.

What will Mrs Ashby say, about her deplorable state, her windblown hair, her dirty fingernails—and Bertram missing? A skink runs out of a rock crevice. It blinks and stares, slides away like mercury. Anchored by a hardy bush, she casts her eyes every which way, then past the north rim of the volcano. She shakes convulsively. If only, after all, she were in Gambierton boarding a coach for the goldfields. She thinks of people climbing in and out of the spring-fed cave by the policeman's hut, walking past Mr Crouch's store and the telegraph station—not one of them concerned about Bertie. What a fool she feels.

The shadows of two kites suspended in the shimmering air darken the rockface; will Bertram Brigstock be their prey? Their black shoulders tilt as they glide in a wide arc away from the crater and towards the sea. The men look up. Rosanna removes her hat and waves it in the air. The men keep up their progress around the rocky rim—oblivious—how absurd they look, like gambolling boys. Her knees quiver. Light-headed she turns away. What a daft *gommach* she was to let Bertie get away.

In her imagination, molten mud has risen up and snatched him. Perhaps he failed to reach the summit and, first playing along the western scarp, then hurtled like a cannonball to the base. She shifts her gaze over chains of swamps and forests to the east, follows the fuzzy blue line of the ocean to the port. It is only that he is such a tedious child that she steals a moment of peace. He cannot be far away but all the same, she must own up to his mother; perhaps by some fluke he has descended and reached her already.

Rushing down the mountain path, eyes darting left and right, she prays to the Blessed Virgin for the little *maneen*. Surely, she will find him on the way and haul him back by his pudgy arm. 'Cooee!' she cries at intervals, tearing aside tangled brushwood to clamber onto large rocks overlooking the lower crater—in vain. She imagines George selecting meat for her plate, whispering in her ear, 'I saw a yellow bird upon the summit—too small to be a honeyeater—perhaps a wren or a European thrush.' She imagines a happy picnic reunion between mother and son. Breaking from the last stand of shea oaks, she pants towards Mrs Brigstock, who reclines against a mimosa.

'Where is Bertram?' Mrs Brigstock jerks upright. Then scrambles to her feet to tap her finger against Rosanna's shoulder like a mother bird pecking an enemy. Within minutes of her scream the men come running down the path. 'Melvin, Bertie has disappeared.'

'We must all search. The boy cannot have wandered far,' his father says.

'He ran ahead. I could not catch him,' Rosanna cries.

George asks of the women, 'You have been here, beside the water? He has not returned?'

At this new terrifying thought Mrs Brigstock swings her head towards the lower crater.

'We'll work our way up the path, fanning out at the sides,' Mr Colyer instructs the men. 'The Irish girl must retrace her footsteps.'

Mrs Ashby holds her friend upright. 'Oh poor, dear Olivia, do not grieve. He will be found, your lovely boy.'

56

THE LOST CHILD

At dusk they return to the house. Something terrible has befallen Bertie and Rosanna must take the blame. As stiff and proper as a coachman, George helps Mrs Ashby from the cart in the station yard. Mr Brigstock half carries his wife in his arms. Mr Colyer sets off on horseback for Gambierton to raise a search party.

'Go home, girl. There is nothing more you can do.' Shamed, she jumps down. Mr Ashby has lost his hat. His face is sunburnt and distressed.

Rosanna will not give up and she canters back and forth in the scrub on the way to the volcano. She dare not follow Mr Brigstock and Mr Ashby, who have returned to the lower crater, where they will work their way to the summit one more time. Resigned to changing feet, Glorvina trots left and then right. Bertie could never walk so far. He must have fallen. The gloomy braying of the bittern will surely frighten him. The light is fading.

A mile from Mount Schanck Glorvina stops dead and Rosanna is hurled onto her neck. Hand to her forehead to block the last dazzling rays of the setting sun bouncing off the lagoons she sees two figures walking along the shore: one tall, one small; one light, one dark. She gallops towards them. Moorecke has knotted a blanket around Bertram's shoulders.

'God, Mary and Patrick to you, and what are you doing with that child? His parents are distraught,' Rosanna barks at her.

Anger flashes like summer lightning across Moorecke's eyes, and she drops the child's hand. Bertie continues sucking at a piece of tuberous grass-tree root. She pushes against the small of his back, and begins to march away. Rosanna seizes her hand.

'Moorecke, I'm sorry. I was wrong. You took me by surprise. Where did you find him?'

'He walked a long way, poor *wunine-wunine.*'

'No, that's not correct. He has a mother.'

'He fell down tired in the swamp. I shook him and shook him. Make him cranky enough to cough up all the water.' Moorecke's shoulders slump.

Bertie begins a soft, slow whine, holding his arms up to Rosanna. Moorecke lifts the child into the saddle.

'It is a miracle you saw him. And he is alive. We must take him to his parents. He is not hurt,' she adds, more to calm herself.

The boy places his thumb in his mouth and curls into her body. Moorecke scans the horizon, her face hostile.

'Get up, behind me, please. You're wetter than an eel. We must take him back to the Big House and then go home.' Moorecke hesitates and then assents.

'Bertram, you frightened us. How did you walk so far from our picnic? That was very naughty. Now, Glorvina will be dancing a polka around the wombat holes, in the dark. All because of you. You don't care about *my* mother waiting at home, nor about Moorecke's killed by squatters.' She knows she is being absurd. The boy droops against her chest. A chill settles on their shoulders.

When Rosanna sees the Big House chimney smoke she is filled with apprehension. Lantern lights bob along the path and she can faintly make out the shapes of horses and their riders. The boy whimpers as they canter down the slope to the house. 'Shush now, Glorvina is like a rocking chair.'

Mrs Ashby stands at the stable doors, a shotgun breeched against her shoulder. What is she waiting for—Red Indians with a ransom note? Rosanna arranges her hands over the reins in a show of composure. It is difficult to ascertain who is frightened *most.* Moorecke grips her waist tighter, quivers. Rosanna imagines her friend's eyes widening with terror, her fingers twirling in her springy hair. Does the gun trigger terrible memories of running for her life through the bush—of her mother struck down from behind? It really is too much. These people.

'Olivia, Bertie is back,' cries Mrs Ashby over her shoulder, holding the barrel steady. 'He is alive.'

Mrs Brigstock runs from the orchard. Stands stock still at the sight of Moorecke.

Rosanna affects a confidence she does not feel.

'Let him down. Let him approach his mother so she can be sure that he is unharmed,' orders Mrs Ashby. Rosanna turns Bertie's shoulders and lifts him free of the pommel. The boy bounces as his toes hit the ground, rights himself and runs to his mother. Safe in her arms he begins a terrible wailing. Mrs Ashby throws venomous looks at Rosanna and Moorecke. She lifts the gun. 'You, girl. I remember you,' she flings.

Rosanna feels as if something delicate has ruptured. If only *she* had found the boy. 'No, ma'am. Stop. Bertram walked into the swamp near the volcano. It is lucky that Moorecke saved him when his lungs were full of water.' She backs Glorvina into the bit and swings her around.

'You know this black girl, then.'

Nails dig into Rosanna's hips. When she turns in reassurance, Moorecke's eyes remain fixed on white-faced herons wading serenely through pools of water in the yard. She will not speak to Mrs Ashby. Rosanna knows this.

'We must go,' Rosanna says. 'My mother is home alone with little ones.'

Mrs Ashby gestures with the gun. 'First ride out to tell the men. Mr Ashby will want to speak with you, and with this girl, tomorrow, after the child has been examined by Doctor Wehl in Gambierton.'

'Light a fire behind the house and they will come,' Rosanna suggests. Surely soon her mistress will rush inside, take her own child into her arms and almost squeeze the life from him. She digs her heels hard into Glorvina, and they take off at a jolting trot.

It seems an interminably long time before they see a rider cantering towards them. The rising moon lights the shape of the dark monolith behind him. When Rosanna turns her head she sees that Jane Ashby has done as she has suggested. Flames dance behind the house. Smoke surges on the breeze. Mr Ashby has seen the fire and turned for home. She calls out to him over the wind riffling the surface of the swamp, 'The child is home, safe with his mother.'

'Thank God,' he answers in a rasping voice and uses the back of his hand to wipe away tears of relief. When he notices Moorecke, he stiffens.

Rosanna squeezes Glorvina's belly.

He fires his gun in the air, three times, and two more riders arrive. 'The fire?'

'To get your attention,' Rosanna says, turning Glorvina in a small tight circle around him. 'I cannot stay, sir.' At that moment he looks uncertain and then, buoyed by relief, he hauls at his horse's mouth and gallops towards the station. The men ride after him. The actor stares back at her as if she is no more than an animal emerging from the landscape.

There is no knowing what the station people will make of Bertie's rescue. Jane Ashby will think it one more trial to endure. At the very least, she will admonish Rosanna for losing a child and then for consorting with Blacks.

On the ride home, Moorecke is silent and unresponsive. Before they reach her camp she suddenly slides from the back of the horse and, without saying goodbye, walks away in the opposite direction.

'Wait. Where are you going?' Rosanna calls.

'To catch wombat.'

'For your dinner?'

Moorecke halts, turns, nods, face impassive.

'What were you doing by the mountain in the dark? Where is that old man, Jack?'

She hangs her head. 'We started a growling and then fighting. Jack hit me. I wanted to kill him and have his fat. The policeman in Gambierton gave me blankets and food. I stayed with our *druals* until late. But I came back.'

Rosanna extends her hand to touch her shoulders. 'It was grand that you saved the boy. Tell Jack you are a hero, when you take him his tucker.'

Moorecke shrugs. 'My *koonge* also lost. No more *moorongal.*'

Rosanna stares at her, swept by a sudden wave of comprehension. 'You lost your child in the cave?'

'*Yanang-a.* I am going now.'

'You did not pinch his nostrils?'

'*Yaki yak.*' Moorecke begins to slap in a fury at her thin dress. She shoves the horse's neck away and turns on her heel. Screeching over her shoulder at Rosanna she turns back to thrash at the horse's rump. Glorvina startles into an untidy trot. Moorecke pitches stones.

Rosanna's heart immediately swells with self-loathing. She is worse than the Ashbys. Twice she has betrayed her friend. 'I am sorry,' she calls after her. 'Please do not walk near the station tomorrow. You may not be safe.'

57

SNAKES AND NARRATIVE SURPRISES

The light at the skillion is a welcome sight. Mother waits tight-lipped on the verandah near where she has hung a storm lantern from the rafters. Creases in her face have deepened in the hot Australian sun. And from worry.

'You took your time,' she says, before retreating behind the hessian curtain to put her little ones to bed.

Skelly looks pale, weighed down. Rosanna gulps mutton stew straight from the camp oven.

'Why do you eat like that ...?' he says.

She swings her head towards him in surprise. 'Shut it. You don't know what I have endured today.'

He flushes miserably.

'If you ever betray my confidences I will beat you with a poker, until you wish I had left you back in Woodford to drown in your own blood.'

'Worse than *an cailleach*, you are,' he counters. 'Father Woods wants you to make confession.'

'I have been to the volcano. I have worked all day. The Brigstock child almost drowned. Moorecke is now in danger for saving his life. Why?' Lately she feels older than Methuselah. Like Mr Trollope's Feemy she will ignore her priest's advice. What would he know about love? Or hate?

Skelly bites his lip, glancing uneasily in the direction of the bedroom where Mother can be heard singing an Irish song. 'I sketched a beautiful snake.'

Rosanna calms herself. 'Well now, that is good, if you were careful.' She wipes her hands on her dress and ladles water from the barrel. 'Show me then.'

He opens his sketchbook to the page.

'Holy Mary, Mother of God. Why did you place the snake beside the babies' bed?'

'*They* were not in the bed but down at the pond with Mother. I drew the reptile as it passed me here at the table. I heard a little sound, like a shiver.'

'It might have bitten you.'

'I did not shout out in case Blinnie or Hugh ran inside or it turned on me. I watched for an eternity until it passed.'

'You drew it while you observed it?' Rosanna slaps her forehead, her eyes wide with admonishment.

'Only a few strokes of the pencil. Just for a short while. Eventually Mother came and took the pitchfork to it between the beds.' Skelly's face is damp and pink with shame. 'How could I kill the thing—with my pencil?' Now he looks close to tears.

'You did right. Father said *you* should never kill a snake.' Rosanna hugs him and strokes the hair at the back of his head.

He ducks away. 'It is late for a brown snake.'

'They move about more than people think. You know that.' Rosanna decides not tell her mother about Bertie. Perhaps she may try to keep her daughter home.

After the children fall asleep, the three of them sit close by the fire. Of late there has been sewing from the station and Mother bends over her needle by lamplight. More and more, she appears fascinated with Skelly's talk of the play, and her face lights up as his sister relates to them the developments in recent scenes. If Rosanna is careful in the way she talks about the actor, she decides, the play may prove a bargaining chip to win other privileges from her mother.

'The Lynch father has cast his son into the dungeon,' says Rosanna.

'No!' Mother ceases sewing.

'Skelly, let us take turnabout. I will first read and you write. The first scene of Act 4 is set in a rocky place beside the river, in a cottage.'

'Much like this one.' He laughs with deep pleasure. Skelly is growing tall and thin. His bony face more like a man's every day. He must be relieved to be alive after his ordeal with the snake. Rosanna knows he looks forward so much to her homecomings that she wants to cut herself with guilt. Soon she will ride away with George and then where will Skelly be? Even the little ones will leave him behind.

'We need to purchase paper. I have few pages left.'

'Write tiny, like the water snail.'
She begins to read aloud:

Scene 1   *Enter Alonzo de Velasquez from cottage.*

'Alonzo!' squeals Skelly. 'But he is the murdered Spanish boy, on whose death the whole play hinges!'

Rosanna checks the line. 'By all the goats in Galway, it is so. Fancy Mr Geoghegan misleading us. There we were, worrying about a murder that has never happened.'

'None but an Irishman could do it!' says Mother. 'Explain.'

Rosanna scans the page ahead. 'When Oscar pitches him overboard, Alonzo keeps his head above the water, struggles ashore and is rescued by a fisherman.'

'He is alive,' says Skelly with satisfaction. 'The play can end well, after all.'

'Perhaps he is not himself, and he will die, all the same,' says Mother. 'Read the verse, Rosanna. We do not know for how long Alonzo has been waterlogged and sorrowful.'

'Poor Alonzo has visions,' says Rosanna. 'Hear this.'

Alonzo   A dread presentiment of evil weighs
                Heavy upon my heart—last night in sleep
                Anastasia stood beside my couch
                Her beauty blighted by affliction's hand
                With hair dishevelled eyes bedewed with tears
                As in the piteous accents of despair
                She called on me besought me to arise
                And save the life of Oscar.

'He is raving mad,' Mother concludes. 'I fear for him.'

'Fear for the Lynch boy, if Alonzo does not live to tell his tale.'

'I could not blame him if he does not wish to save Oscar, and I am the mother of Lynches. After all, Oscar hurled him overboard. Read on, Rosanna.'

'The fisherman reveals to Alonzo that Oscar has confessed to murdering him,' cries Skelly. 'How strange.' And then, much cheered,

'Huzzah, Alonzo wishes to go to Galway, straightways, and save his friend from the gallows.'

'He is a good man, this Spaniard.' Mother rolls up the sleeve of Mrs Ashby's gown and snaps off her Loughrea thread. 'Your father's mother was a Spain. A common enough name in Galway.'

'The journey is a perilous one,' cries Skelly, 'descending along a craggy path to Galway town.'

They read and exclaim late into the night until Mother tires of reminding them of their beds and goes to lie with the little ones.

'We must finish the last scene, Skelly.' Rosanna turns the page and crosses herself, in her worry for the Lynch son. 'You read and I shall write more swiftly. The gloating and vengeful pirates plot to capture and kill Anastasia, who tramps the mountain paths, on her way to petition the Viceroy for a pardon for her lover. The pirate boasts that the beautiful Anastasia of *peerless charms* and *witching loveliness is in his power.*'

'He will attack her, of course,' calls Mother from her sleeping place. 'Mr Geoghegan has written a most exciting melodrama. Murderous pirates, fathers as hard as granite, mountain passes and evil priests—what would Father Woods think of it? We must use my sewing money to purchase more writing paper, Rosanna. When is the actor expected to leave the station? Do we have time?'

Can Mother see her daughter's face bloom in the lamplight? What might she think of her acting the part of Anastasia on a Melbourne stage? Rosanna turns her face from the lamp. Her voice catches and slows in the reading—refines itself. Tomorrow, she must find out from the actor how many scenes remain. But she must first find a way to explain to him about Bertie running away.

58

MOORECKE AND ANASTASIA IN DANGER

Edwin arrives home next morning, as grumpy as a bear. Anyone would think he owns all the problems in the world. Rosanna watches him snatch up food and the actor's letter before he rushes away to the Suttons' station from where he will carry goods to the port. Perhaps he has been forbidden to see the girl Kitty, or he hasn't the time. Father arrives minutes later, cursing his son; for had not Edwin lit out for Miss Lallah's the night before and not returned, leaving him to ride home alone? He and Rosanna leave for the Big House.

Rosanna works unsupervised until midday, when Mrs Ashby runs from the bedroom to the yard to greet Mr Brigstock and his wife, returned from Gambierton. Rosanna follows her, holding out her arms to lift Bertram down from the cart and kiss his downy head. Mr Brigstock passes two brown paper packages and a wad of letters to his wife. The women duck their heads together, periodically glaring out at Rosanna, like native bees from a honey nest.

'What is Doctor Wehl's opinion?' she hears Mrs Ashby ask. Mrs Brigstock withholds her reply until Rosanna carries her child away. Is the wee boy sick, after all? Has he taken swamp-water into his lungs, sucked in dreaded hydatid? She settles him in his bed. The party retires to the sitting room to read their mail. After several minutes Rosanna opens the door to offer tea and finds Mrs Ashby walking back and forth before the fireplace, her nose red and her eyes streaming. The Brigstocks look up from their conversation by the window.

'Please knock before entering a room,' Mrs Ashby scolds, and stops her pacing, inelegantly sniffing as she dabs at her forehead with *Eau de Cologne*. A curtsy seems politic and Rosanna executes one hovering in the doorway. What can be wrong? Is Bertie dying? Her employer follows her to the scullery to instruct her about cakes to serve with tea.

'Imagine if my child had been taken yesterday,' she says, tugging uncertainly at Rosanna's arm. 'It was only a matter of chance that he wasn't. Oh, I cannot rest easy after what has happened.'

Is Jane Ashby mad? 'Can Bertie be having a relapse? He looks so well.'

'The boy is fine. The doctor has given him a clean bill of health.' She hesitates. 'But you must care for my husband if I leave.'

Rosanna purses her lips over the chaotic conversation while arranging cups and plates on a tea tray. Has the woman been drinking?

Mrs Ashby leans into Rosanna's face. 'My nerves are shattered. News has come by telegram that my father is gravely ill in Tasmania. In truth I cannot bear much longer to be alone in this dangerous place. I must go to him.' First, she must put on a mask of gaiety for at least ten more days, until she farewells her houseguests. Then she must make preparations to leave as well, perhaps for several months; perhaps forever. From the outset she feared for the baby's safety.

Oh, my, Rosanna thinks—such hysteria. Had Jane Ashby not shown powerful industry when preparing for the picnic? And, after they returned the boy, a frightening steadiness, looking down the sightline of her rifle at Moorecke? Rosanna lays down the tea tray and takes a step back. She turns the pot with one hand and pours a good strong cup. Then wonders how she might feel should Father take ill. She places the cup in Mrs Ashby's hand, who nurses it like something newly hatched, first warming her hands and then lifting it to cradle it against her cheek.

'Rest here for a moment,' Rosanna urges, guiding her mistress through the door and towards a chair by the stove. 'I will take the tea and Madeira cake to the guests.' Mr Ashby will not allow his wife to leave the house in such a state and while caring for his son.

Of course, when George Sutherland leaves, and that thought is contingent on the surety of ongoing drama, he will make arrangements for Rosanna to follow him to Melbourne. Events unfold so quickly at the Big House. And yet, George rarely hurries. All his previous urgency for the play production seems lately forgotten, engrossed as he has become with bloodstock. She hasn't read the last pages of the manuscript. Skelly must finish his transcription for Mother to read, and for the little ones, when they grow older.

Mrs Ashby ceases her swaying and subsides into the chair. 'I hope my leaving does not bring William low, for he takes things very keenly. The money he owes his father for the land. The unreliability of labour. The scab and the sheep ticks. The Blacks—although now, there are fewer of them.' Her eyes bore into Rosanna's face. 'Oh.' Mrs Ashby dabs her handkerchief over her mouth, as if she has been indiscreet.

Rosanna digests this.

'You must make this house a haven for my husband. But you will not go to the cellar alone, for I know how you Irish like to drink.'

'Then I'll take your husband with me to the cellar, ma'am,' Rosanna feels rage boiling up inside her, 'if that would suit you better.' She thinks of George accosting her in the cellar and flushes.

Incensed, Mrs Ashby carries a linen napkin from the table to her brow. 'Never speak like that.' She stands abruptly and tweaks Rosanna's blouse with distaste. 'I will return with at least two gowns, suitable clothes for you to wear in service.'

Rosanna half turns her back and steadies her hands on the dresser.

'In the meantime, you will do your best for Mr Ashby during the day. But each evening, you will return home.'

The woman's mood flows as chaotically as quicksilver, in one direction and then another.

'Mrs Brigstock tells me that she has seen the black girl in the town making a spectacle of herself in a green robe with gold embroidery.'

Rosanna senses menace or at least confusion and tries to move away.

Mrs Ashby tugs at her skirt. 'Would you not say, Rosanna, this description matches that of my missing gown?' She turns her head to one side in distress. 'The very thought of that girl touching my clothes ...'

'I doubt it could be yours, ma'am. In the town.' Her skin feels clammy and despite the heat, she shivers. She must warn Moorecke. She will ride to the camp as soon as she is dismissed.

59

MRS ASHBY THREATENS MOORECKE

The morning seems interminably long; the station folk act tired and snappy. Light rain falls. The Brigstocks confine Bertie to the house but no one speaks of Doctor Wehl's assessment. Rosanna finds herself caught up in the bustle and preparation for impending journeys that have no departure date; washing and drying; listening to instructions about the household and advice about consorting with Blacks. After she serves late luncheon and clears away, she is permitted to take her pick from the table-scraps, before feeding the rest to the poultry. Mrs Ashby dabs her nose with her scented handkerchief as she conveys this information to Rosanna, as if she is afraid of contamination. When the ladies retire to the morning room, Rosanna takes her bowl of food to the stable.

The actor has lately taken to leaving his manuscript in the iron box in the tack room and, huzzah, this day is no exception. She has taken one last sheet of paper from Mr Ashby's desk, it being an emergency. Between bites of mutton and dripping, she begins to copy Act 4, passing the time while she waits for George and Moorecke.

Rosanna writes as quickly as she can. Scene 2 opens with Oscar's three young Galway friends plotting to storm the castle and rescue their friend—*Huzzah.* How frustrating to see their plans stymied by arguments about guilt and the law. She feels the magistrate father's pain, but how can he be so cruelly intransigent, when the life of his son is at risk? How can a parent's instincts be so confused?

Rosanna fears equally for herself. She will trust in God, as Father Woods has taught her. The play will work out well, of course. Even in the books she reads, the authors try their best to terrify the readers. Plays are written to torment the emotions of the audience, following an unlikely sequence of events decided by a playwright. Mr Geoghegan would be a bleak Irishman to dash an audience's need for resolution.

As well as that, Lynches and their families are lucky, and all the people they hold dear. Despite floods and fires and epidemics, vicious snakes and felonious lags, nothing terrible has happened to their family. Edwin owns his carting business, and Father will soon own land; Skelly will sell his pictures and Rosanna will become an actress. If not, or if she does not fancy acting, she will take care of George, who worships her skin, her teeth, her hair, her smile—other unmentionable things as well—and is forever kissing her to death. He has never lied to her like Feemy's Captain Ussher in Trollope's novel.

She writes in tiny hand-cramping script, on and on, until her arm aches and the last two pages are covered. Palimpsest is something she will not contemplate. Skelly will never follow it. Rosanna reads as she writes.

On her quest to save her fiancé's life, Anastasia tramps through the mountains, to seek for him a Vice-regal pardon. Unbeknownst to her, Rupert D'Arcy and his henchman stalk her. Oh, it is too much to bear. And Oscar Lynch's life is more than ever in peril.

'Rosanna.'

She starts. Guilt swamps her and she lifts her pen to peer out into the rain. Why, when she has never been a good girl—nor a bad girl, neither?

The voice belongs to Mr Ashby, booming from the doorway, droplets of water cascading from his hat. He is a big man, not unkind, but often reserved. His eyes whip over her in a precise way, as if checking an inventory.

Rosanna is startled to her feet, most particularly by her apparent sudden materialisation in his eyes, as if she now exists in some more substantial way than she did before.

'What distracts you from your duties in the house?'

He has been sent to look for her. This thought relieves her anxiety about the play but he cannot know that a houseguest loves her. 'I was writing a letter to America,' she lies, with equal equanimity, bending over to gather up her paper sheets and moving towards the door. 'To my mother's family. I have finished now.'

'Sit down upon the blacksmith's stool. I wish to speak with you on matters of importance.'

Rosanna finds that she cannot do this thing: make herself low, allowing him to tower over her. In this she is her father's daughter. Some things stick in her craw. 'Thank you, I'm fine, Sir.'

'Stand, as you wish,' he replies. 'You know that Mrs Ashby plans soon to return to Tasmania. Her father has been ill for some time and has taken a turn for the worst, but I must surmise the speed of her plans connected also to Bertram's mishap. Doctor Wehl pronounces the boy completely well, and we must thank God for that. My wife, however, has lost confidence in station life. We are waiting on the blacksmith to complete repairs on the Brigstocks' conveyance that they may depart.' He steps towards her and she is glad to be on her feet. 'Deuce, we may have a little time but I blame you for not keeping a closer watch on the boy,' he says.

Sympathy momentarily lightening Rosanna's heart is swiftly extinguished.

'I hear from the policeman in Gambierton—and it seems he is acquainted with your brother—that choice cuts of my beef find their way to MacDonnell Bay.' He stands hand bracing his back and rocks back on his heels, like a bullying schoolmaster.

Rosanna bristles. Father would forget about saving for land and knock him flat. 'I doubt it would be your beef, sir. Edwin tells me that you keep excellent stock records.' Compulsively she seizes her own wrist and feels her pulse betray her.

Undeterred, Mr Ashby glares into her face. 'Many of our misfortunes are a consequence of that black gin and her man camping on my land.'

Rosanna's fear takes a new turn. It is not Edwin but Moorecke who is at risk. 'Sir?'

'My wife has seen the black girl on two or three occasions. There has been a matter of filching—poultry, several bullocks, and items of clothing. The girl has been seen in Gambierton wearing, in ridiculous fashion, a silk robe of my wife's. I cannot rule out that girl enticing Bertram from Mount Schanck.'

'But she saved Bertie from drowning, after he wandered off alone.'

'Well, we shall never know. Nevertheless, I find her involvement unsettling. The girl belongs to an old man who has made himself a nuisance at several stations.'

'They are married, Mr Ashby.'

He dismisses this with an imperious wave. 'As a pair, they seem curiously healthy. It is only a question of time before something worse occurs. Tell me where they camp. Mr Colyer has agreed to ride out with me in search of them.'

Rosanna is stricken by this detour in the conversation. 'Moorecke belongs on this land. It is her *m'rado*, Mr Ashby, but they are rarely camped here. Her husband works at Carratum. Perhaps they have gone there.'

'Is their camp near your hut?' He says 'hut' as if it could be expected that Irish and *Booandik* people could be relegated to the thin edge of civilization.

Rosanna grimaces; then tries to transform her physiognomy into an arrangement more benign. 'They visit several camps, depending on the weather and the game. I am sorry but I cannot help you.' She curtsies. It is a great actress she has become, for she has one more line left in her, to throw him off the scent. 'It is rare that I see Blacks, now that the country is settled. You know how they walk about. I would be thinking of asking the poet, Mr Gordon.' Obsequious tones have infiltrated her speech.

'Perhaps I shall. My wife will leave soon; nothing is more certain. And the *Booandik* gin will be the cause.'

'I am sorry, sir, that you think so.'

'It is disappointing that you see fit to withhold information which could render our home safer. It brings to mind my initial doubts concerning your employment. During my wife's likely absence there will be little work to do about the house.'

Rosanna looks at her feet. He threatens her, but Moorecke is more at risk. Men are dangerous creatures if thwarted. When she looks up, he has gone. Rain drums on the roof of the stables. There will be no rehearsal this afternoon and she must speak to George but she dares not leave a note. She wraps a page or two of the play in her mother's shawl. First she must warn Moorecke. She hurries inside.

'Rosanna, you look discomposed.'

'I'm sorry, ma'am, but I cannot stay. My mind flies constantly to my mother sick at home. I did not like to mention it this morning. And as well, my brother has taken a turn for the worse; he suffers from a terrible illness. If I could go now, it would set my mind at rest to see them both alive.'

Mrs Ashby continues feeding her baby. The little thing looks up at the spoon arrested in its flight to his mouth and smiles at his mother. Immediately smitten, her face softens. Rosanna sees weary lines around her eyes, and she reaches out to stroke the baby's pudgy hand.

'Is he not delicious, Rosanna?'

She nods. 'All babies are delicious, ma'am, but if I could take some buttons to sew on at home, I could also tend my mother.' Through the morning-room drapes, she sees Mr Ashby, Mr Brigstock and Mr Colyer riding towards the ridge, rifles scabbarded to their saddles. She waits. Waits. Until the atmosphere thickens and her throat constricts with terror.

Mrs Ashby waves her hand in a desultory way. 'Go to your mother. Although, God knows, she is not my responsibility.'

Rosanna stoops to kiss the baby's fingers and pulls away. 'I beg your pardon, Mrs Ashby, and God bless you.'

60

VIOLENCE IN THE *BOOANDIK* CAMP

What a fool she is to believe that she can warn Moorecke in time, when the men have already ridden over the range, although their relative unfamiliarity with the location of *Booandik* camps reassures her. The rain eases as she reaches the last hillock before her ascent. Rain does not bother Glorvina as much as wind and she manages something close to a gallop across the ridge. Mist drifts through the low hills, settling in the trees like a snood. A slippery track means Rosanna must be satisfied with a long loping canter through the back hills. If only she were riding Lucifer. At the last fork before their home she urges Glorvina east through the scrub. There is not a puff of smoke.

She will watch from some distance. She pulls Glorvina into slightly elevated light scrub and reins in behind a large gum. How long should she wait? Gunshots explode nearby and Glorvina leaps sideways. Rosanna slides about clutching for the pommel.

'Moorecke,' Rosanna's voice catches in her throat. No one shoots *Booandik* now. Silent rain drips from leaves, heightening the scent of eucalyptus and mimosa.

As she urges Glorvina towards the camping place, three riders on horseback emerge from the trees. Mr Brigstock bounces untidily at a trot, plump belly overflowing his shirt, jowls wobbling above his cravat, unused perhaps to dealing with refractory servants and Blacks. Has exertion made him ruddier? Mr Colyer mops his face with a yellow kerchief and reloads his double-barrelled shotgun. Rosanna glares at them as she crashes into the camp.

The *ngoorla* has been ripped asunder, its tea-tree logs piled onto the fireplace; its cutting grass thatch pitched around the camp. All that remains is an untidy pile of bark and branches, little-used bowls and crushing stones. In the old days, Jack would have stood up to these men, shaken his spear and threatened their horses. Now he is old and fat from white man's tucker. His creased old face hides behind a wild black beard and he can't make Moorecke's babies stick.

'Return to the station, girl.' Mr Ashby gestures, one hand steadying his gun across his horse's neck. His expression is severe.

He cannot make her. She has rights. She is sure of that. And even if she hasn't … Her mind churns with fear until she alights on an idea.

'Sir, you must go quickly. Bertie's signal fire has reignited. Mrs Ashby, fearing it burns towards the house, sent me after you.'

The men shift in their saddles and nose the damp air. She has created a poor diversion. She should have burned down the storeroom before she left. Rosanna pulls her head in like a tortoise, manoeuvring Glorvina out of their way, as they canter off.

A wattle bird rattles in the near distance. She eyes the scrub. Run. Run. No. Inspecting hoof prints carving up the desecrated campsite, she finds a bullock skull. Moorecke always carries flint and digging sticks, baskets and her water vessel. Jack would take his tools and traps and *catum catum*. She finds no evidence of these. She waits. Calls. Nothing stirs. Her heart lightens.

THE IMPORT OF A SECOND LETTER

At home, Rosanna finds her mother attempting to dry linen squares over a smoking stove.

Eilish lifts the kettle from the fire and pours tea. 'Why are you home so early?'

Rosanna seats herself. Her head flops into her arms on the table. 'Moorecke has gone.'

'To the harbour?' asks Mother. 'It is bitter cold. The season is turning.'

'Mr Ashby and some men on horseback came after her with guns.'

Her mother rounds the table, touching a cloth to her mouth in dismay. She grips Rosanna's arm. 'Go to the camp and suggest that she and Jack return to Carratum.'

'I have been there. The men wrecked the camp but it is deserted. It is as quiet as the bottom of a sink hole.' Rosanna sobs.

'More than likely you'll find her along the creek, driving a feed of mallards into a net strung between the trees, and Jack waiting in the water to grab their feet and twist their necks,' her mother soothes.

'I wish that it were true.' She imagines Moorecke halfway up a large gum, smoking out a possum, her slim back leaning way out from the footholds scored with a small axe, thrusting a smoking branch into the hole at the first fork. Possum screams rupture the air; blood spraying like red-gum blossom from its ruff. Moorecke springing from the tree to neatly skin and peg the pelt. Jack is a law-man; his young wife fitter, with powerful arms and legs. Rosanna knows—they will get away. But then why does she feel so wretched?

'Look again for her. You must warn her of the danger.' Eilish untangles Rosanna's hair with her fingers; then reaches for her brush. 'I am more concerned about Edwin than Moorecke.'

Rosanna lifts her head, mouthing mock surprise. 'He is so lucky, all his life. Why would you gnash your teeth over him?'

'While he lines O'Leary's purse for his connections at the bay, his nerves jangle in his head. Night after night, he goes to Lallah's, making good his debts and losing more. I would not like to get in his way if this carting business fails. He has set his heart on it but your father cannot lend him another penny. We are struggling ourselves to feed you all.'

Rosanna sighs. 'Edwin is like winds along the coast. He will change his tack. He will becalm the gobbity Mr O'Leary, and then he will blow him off his feet.' Moorecke has more to fear.

'Your brother would not see you shamed, *alannahh*.'

Rosanna feels colour suffusing her neck. 'He has forgiven me throwing the race on Lucifer. He is no saint himself.'

Mother exchanges the hairbrush for her rosary beads and begins to finger them. 'I pray for you all, especially your stubborn father.'

'Do not waste your prayers on me. I'll be fine. Lucky like Edwin. Pray for Moorecke.'

'I love to watch you riding off to the Big House with the men. I am envious. I am. Until now, work has lifted your spirits. We can do little for Moorecke when so many wish them ill.'

'Will Father ride home tonight?'

'Tomorrow. Edwin too. He has business in Gambierton.' Eilish moves swiftly to the dresser and passes a note to Rosanna, who blushes. 'It is from your brother, *mavoureen*.' She eyes her speculatively.

Rosanna reads quickly, her eyes filling with tears. 'Oh, the fool, he is—the daft *oinseach*.' She beats her hand against her head and stands to face the back door, through which she can see the horses feeding.

'What is it? What has he done?'

'He has been dilly-dallying at Miss Lallah's with the actor who is houseguest at the Ashbys.'

'No harm in that. Why should you mind? You read the play with Mr Sutherland, and Skelly enjoys the drama of it all. Do you want to have him all to yourself?'

Rosanna runs crying into the yard and lays her face against Lucifer's.

Mother pants behind her. 'What is it then?'

If only Rosanna could gallop away. 'Mother, why did you not tell me that the actor had made Edwin an offer for Lucifer?'

'And how would I know that? It is men's business the buying and selling of thoroughbreds.'

'Mr Sutherland has bought our horse to resolve Edwin's debts with O'Leary.'

'Oh, *alannahh*, no.'

Such fuss brings the children running from the bush, Hugh coughing with exertion, Skelly clumping along beside them carrying a bucket of mushrooms. Blinnie, winsome child, tugs at Rosanna's skirt and throws back her head, to read her sister's expression.

'And what shall I do about Moorecke?' Rosanna hugs the babies and then cries afresh. Lucifer backs up, bunting his head against her waist, kicking out his back legs to catch the tree to which he is tethered. She pulls down his head and cries into his face, traces the soft vein on his nose, and his whiskery lips, and rubs his twitching ears.

'Rosanna, do not upset Lucifer; he's mighty flighty already without you keening in his ears. Come now, and tell us what is wrong. What else has Edwin written?'

Blinnie wraps her arms around her sister's neck and cries along with her. Skelly's face strains with anxiety as he digs the toe of his boot into the mud.

Rosanna takes the letter from her pocket, unfolds it and reads it again. Fresh tears spill. 'I am to take Lucifer to the bay, where the actor will inspect him, before giving me the money. I am to count it. Then I am to hand it over to that reeky turnip, that *gombeen*, O'Leary, at his shanty.'

Mother kisses her mouth. 'Go then. It is better not to build up a head of steam. You are upsetting the children.' She wipes Hugh's face on her apron and lifts Blinnie onto her hip.

Rosanna's last thoughts drown each other out. If Edwin's debt is paid, perhaps she can claim her wages. But, no doubt, there will be another. If George sponsors her as an actress, she will ride Lucifer to Melbourne. But nothing is guaranteed. Old plans to ride to the goldfields run through her head.

62

LOVE, PRIDE AND LUCIFER

It is a great pity that her last ride on Lucifer will be at a paltry canter. How her gradgrind brother can bear to part with him she will never understand. Setting out from the house she sees two trading vessels anchored a mile out to sea. On her way criss-crossing swamps and water-courses she thinks about his business; he hopes to cart wood, tallow and home supplies from the lighters. If it is successful, that is if he can keep his axles out of the bog to the north of the bay settlement, he will not be so dependent on his boundary riding or the sale of skins. The building of a lighthouse, and a causeway over the low-lying ground near the new port, will help everyone. Now Edwin takes casual work as well as his wage from Mr Ashby, taking goods to the boats. Already she misses him.

His letter relates how Mr O'Leary takes forty per cent for all the goods he carries from the bay to Gambierton and the stations. It is a deuced large cut, and one that Edwin can ill afford, until the year is out and the bullocks paid for. He should not go to Lallah's. She sniffs the salt air. Soon, his letter reminds her, he will have regular customers, more than he can shake a stick at, and perhaps a business partner, perhaps a wife.

On the way to the meeting, she rides south towards the *Booandik* summer camps in the sand hills beside the sea to look for Moorecke. Why should she not keep O'Leary waiting? All the clouds are moving in the same direction as if God hurled them in a hissy-fit or blew them out to sea. Lucifer likes the warm sun on his face; he steps out nicely. Leaping across bogs and pools he tugs at the reins. If it weren't for poor old Glorvina hog-trotting behind he would kick up his heels and gallop to the shore. Instead he wends his way around sandy pathways between the tea-trees and over the smooth tracks of copperhead snakes until she reins him in hard. The mowed down *Booandik* coastal windbreak pains her. The station men have been here too. Rosanna shivers. The sun disappears behind dirty streaks of yellow striating sky like potato skins or one of Skelly's bruises.

George waits for her on horseback at the back of the shipping office. Were it not for the circumstances she would be glad to see him alone. She straightens her carriage, sitting up tall. She and George stand up to each other like a pair of dogs. Their horses dance beneath them. He need not think that she and Lucifer do not belong together. She turns the stallion sideways to show off his beautiful flanks, his coat as glossy as a seal's, and the great black orbs hanging between his back legs.

George tips his hat. 'Fine horse, Miss Lynch.'

They conclude their business on the ground, George counting the money into her hand, she concentrating, not wishing to contradict him in a public place. He takes Lucifer's reins and attaches a lead rope to his borrowed horse. Rosanna thinks the contrast between the two horses heartbreaking, his being little more than a station hack.

George touches his fingers to her puffy eyes. 'This is a good solution for your brother, Rosanna. And perhaps you will see Lucifer again, before too long.'

Her mood lifts as he leans in to kiss her. His intentions are surely clear.

Outside his small establishment Mr O'Leary slowly turns his head towards her, like a bloated toad on a mud heap.

George moves away from her.

'I have to take the money to Mr O'Leary, for my brother,' she enunciates in a clear loud voice, trying to stop her lip from trembling. She will put on a good show.

'I will wait for you at the point.' He waves his crop.

Her heart leaps. 'French's Point?' She jerks her head towards it in anticipation.

63

O'LEARY PRESIDES OVER BUSINESS AT THE BAY

Mr O'Leary has risen from his seat beneath the sagging verandah to bark orders at a young man rowing a skiff thirty yards out in the water. By the time she arrives at his door he is seated at his desk and she can smell his fishy unwashed skin. If she were a fly she would alight on his bulbous head and enjoy good pickings.

'Where is your horse?' He looks down on her standing uncertain on his step. She lifts her head and points to Glorvina, tethered near the pathway. Does he know about Lucifer? He has struck the first blow.

'My brother is in Gambierton and would have me make good his debt.' There is no doubt that if an Irishman is on a spit over a fire, another can be found to turn it.

'Place it on the table then, and we will see.'

She leans forward to count the money out in front of him. His chair creaks and she can smell his crapulous breath. Her stomach turns.

'Where is the rest, girl? Have you been buying prinky-trinky things from a hawker?'

Rosanna stiffens. 'This is the figure agreed upon. Edwin wrote it down. I counted it. I am following his instructions.'

'You Lynches are all the same. Don't think I don't know about you. I had money on your horse at Racecourse Bay.'

'I am sorry about the race.' She lifts her head to meet his eyes and thinks that she may asphyxiate with loathing.

'Your brother also owes me for goods I disposed of some months back—a little matter of some meat.'

'I will speak to him. It is nothing to do with me, Mr O'Leary.' God forbid, but it was. 'I would be obliged if you would make my brother a receipt for the money I have brought you in his stead.'

The toad shifts his weight. Has she gone too far? His eyes linger on her neckline; his hand hovers over his ink pot. Outside, the lad calls out his name.

It is a thick and dirty sheet of paper he pushes at her across the desk, on which he has scrawled the amount paid and the amount still owing. When she notices a corner lifting on the paper, she carries it carefully, using both hands, to her face to read. A page is stuck, one beneath the other. Rosanna is exultant.

O'Leary noddles his bulbous head over the desk drawer in which he places Edwin's money. He licks his fingers, lifting a piece of fishing line from the drawer, before ushering her out and locking the door behind them both.

'Tell your brother he has two days. After that I will take evidence of our previous transactions to the police at Gambierton. If I am not mistaken the brands were sliced.'

Pride is a sin. She folds Edwin's receipt and the additional sheet of paper into her reticule and sweeps forward. Gaining an extra page on which to copy another act of the play is a small victory, compared to the aching loss of Lucifer and the terror of O'Leary's threats. No brain at all has Edwin, dealing with a crook, who is never satisfied. What will her brother do about the remaining guineas? How will he get about the district without a decent horse? And now it seems that he has become the victim of blackmail.

64

ANASTASIA AND ROSANNA IN DANGER
AT THE BAY

Making her way along the boggy track to the sea, she ties Glorvina to a
stunted blackwood tree beside Lucifer and George's splay-toed station
horse. From here she observes the antics of O'Leary on his way to the
boats, shouting across the water at his boy. Bent over his oars the lad
lowers his head, cowed by the man and the choppy swell. Rosanna
feels equally subdued by the time George and Lucifer come galloping
along the beach and stop before her in a flurry of sand.

She brushes down her skirts. They make a pretty pair, she thinks—
the blonde actor and the black horse—until Lucifer, in a fit of exuber-
ance, ducks his head and snorts into her lap. Tears come to her eyes
and she dabs at them with the sleeve of her jacket.

'Rosanna.'

'That loathsome man filling his jowls with clean sea air and turning it sour.'

'He was disrespectful?'

Rosanna shakes her head. 'No.' George would never understand.

'Shall I speak with the cur?'

'I'm all right,' she says. 'I can look after myself.'

George dismounts falling to his knees in the sand. Hair flops in his
face.

'How comic you look.'

He bounces up playing for a laugh, settles for a watery smile.

'You are a handsome fool.'

'Act Four: Scene Three. Let us begin.'

'You have the play? Here?'

'It is a great scene—full of drama. Alas, I do not carry it with me,
but I know it well. I will guide you through it.'

'Indeed? You know it by heart?'

'I will feed you lines. The scene opens on a moonlit night, with Lynch's betrothed Anastasia unconscious, insensible on a mountain path, awaiting rescue. Lie down, like her, dear girl.'

Rescue, indeed. Rosanna flicks him a look usually reserved for Edwin and settles her frock back against the slope of the sand hill. It is secluded enough. The bruised sky rolls over her head, so swiftly she fears that she is moving also, in the opposite direction, and that she must close her eyes to retain her balance.

George crouches over her. 'How beautiful Anastasia looks, says Rupert D'Arcy.'

'The diabolical pirate speaks?'

'Indeed.'

Rupert	With all the fury of despairing men
	The victory is ours and the rich purse
	I scarcely hoped to win is now mine own!
	How beautiful she looks e'en thus bereft
	Of sense. How lovely! Tis indeed a prize
	A prize Good Bernard must not slip my grasp.

Lulled by George's worshipful face, his hands unravelling her hair, Rosanna dares not tell him that she has read thus far and imagined Anastasia's terror. 'How can she save her beloved Oscar?'

'Can you believe that the pirate attacks her?' George slaps Rosanna's face, as if to bring her around: 'Stir, Anastasia, wake.'

Rosanna gasps. It is just play. She flutters her eyelashes and struggles up against him. Presses her hands against her cheeks just as she imagines an actress might do. 'She will defend herself, of course?'

'Recite Anastasia's words, Rosanna. Say them after me. Lunging behind her, George mouths her ear. A sea breeze plucks at his shirttails, and swishes around his breeches. She repeats the lines into the wind:

Anastasia   Methought my path by ruffians was beset
                 And the rude clash of weapons, dying shrieks
                 And groans of anguish smote my frightened ear—
                 Ah, how is this? Where am I? Speak. Oh heaven
                 Twas not a vision. Say, if ye be men
                 In aught but outward bearing, say what means
                 This dreadful violence? If your purpose be
                 Pillage, you your object have achieved.
                 Oh then in mercy let me speed from hence
                 For life and death hang on our promptitude
                 And urge me to exertion—

George grips her hard as he apes the pirate:

Rupert   Let then the puny minion, Oscar meet
                 The sentence for his crime has been adjudged
                 While thou shalt revel in far brighter joys,
                 Shalt hence with me the Pirate's chosen queen
                 Pride of the Rover's barque—the Darcy's bride!

'How can you bear to play such wickedness? Is Anastasia not to your liking, George?'

'She is only as good and virtuous as Mr Geoghegan's lines will allow.'

'That is not an answer. What happens next?'

'She begs the pirate for mercy: *Release me and permit me to depart.* If ransom be his object, she will support a generous payment. Saving Oscar is uppermost. She must free herself. *Stay me not for on my haste a life most dear depends.*'

'Rupert D'Arcy the pirate has no heart.'

'There is more craft than heart in melodrama, whereby he will have murderous revenge and the girl as well.' George lifts Rosanna's hand and kisses it. 'He professes long love for Anastasia and invites her to embrace her destiny as a Pirate's dame.'

> *Rupert*   No, Anastasia, thou art now mine own,
> Safe in my power the Rover's destined bride
> And all the force of Heaven or Hell alike
> Were vain to tear thee from my grip unscathed—
> And hark! The promised signal doth announce
> The boat approaches which shall bear thee hence
> This night shall view my bridal. Come, my fair,
> Thy bridegroom pants to take thee to his arms.
> Nay seek not thus to coy it—

Rage and anxiety rise in Rosanna's heart. 'How can Anastasia break free? In melodrama, do girls die?'

George leaps to his feet and plucks a piece of driftwood to make a show of swordsmanship. He looks young and happy, not especially fiendish. How can Rosanna resist him when he plays like one of her brothers? When George scoops her into his arms, she winds her arms around his neck and kisses his eyelashes, thumbs the delicate tracery of veins at his temples, mouths the lemon hairs below his ears.

On and on, he prates. 'The pirate curses her and mocks her then. He will have her anyway.'

> *Rupert*   Th' enraptured blessings of a grateful heart
> Poured forth on her who yields him life and love!
> Than meet your destiny—the Pirate's dame,
> The fair companion of his hours of love
> When he unbeds himself to dalliance—
> His slave—His captive—Lady, such thy doom!

George is as rough with Rosanna as any pirate, surely, as he forces his knee between her legs, bunches up the fabric of her dress and flattens his hand around her hips. His touching brings on a raw, sad feeling. A rush of blood low in her body. 'I don't know what Father will say about my acting, Mr Sutherland.'

'Tell him that I love your acting.'

'To what effect? Can Anastasia escape that devil's clutches any more than I can yours?'

'She has offended him.'

'Offended him. That's rich. Have I offended you, George?'

'*Oh villain, villain* ... The play, it is Gothic, Rosanna. Whisper lines back to me.'

'Oh villain, villain,' she whispers against his lips. They taste of salt and sweet wine from his silver flask.

As he shifts his weight his arm frames her face and he stares into her eyes, then moves back and forth inside her. 'When the play opens, its Melbourne audience will turn wild with confused desire,' he says. 'They will boo and hiss and stamp their feet. They will throw their black silk hats into the air. Gaslights will flicker. When Rupert D'Arcy seizes Anastasia and drags her to a little boat set upon the stage, they will erupt in joyous anticipation that he will ravish her.'

Rosanna is felled by such an image; she cannot think past 'joyous anticipation' as her body twists beneath his and then stills. Cool air roils over; sand swirls through her hair; Lucifer snorts and she sits up.

'Is Anastasia doomed?' Rosanna feels suddenly subdued.

'Aha—the audience will swoon when in one swift movement she exposes a dagger in the bodice of her gown.'

Rosanna mimes this action, raises an imaginary knife above his head. 'Thank God.'

He stays her hand.

'She will defend her honour against this swill—D'Arcy and his men?'

'Sadly, no. You are mistaken. Say these lines, Rosanna, with desperation in your heart:

> Anastasia   Life hath no charms for me at honour's cost.
>   Thy fate is sealed, or I depart from hence.
>   Free, unimpeded to pursue my way
>   Or rather than be yielded to your power
>   This dagger in my heart should find a sheathe.

Rosanna leaps to her feet. 'Mr Edward Geoghegan plays her for a fool. What point in disposing of a girl like that? Why would she kill herself when she has done no harm to anyone? And then who will save Oscar Lynch?'

Something impels her to cast her eyes along the beach to the store where O'Leary and a police trooper stand on the verandah, pointing to a lugger at anchor. Now wouldn't that be right, the little wart consorting with police, and Anastasia dead. Injustice masses like magma inside her chest. She raises her voice.

'When I meet Mr Geoghegan, I shall ask him why he dealt so harshly with Anastasia.'

'Perhaps you will. He was once an Irish doctor who had bad luck in business—criminally bad luck. Not unlike your brother.'

Her mouth falls open in dismay. 'I cannot bear to know what happens. I must go.' She tidies herself and darts to kiss Lucifer's nose, scattering mountain ducks—*chank chank*—camouflaged against the rocks. 'George, next I see you at the station you will tell me how it will be with you and me, in Melbourne.' She feels as desperate as Feemy Macdermot in Trollope's novel. She has a yearning in her belly, for what she does not know. Poor Anastasia.

Unravelling Glorvina's reins from the blackwood tree she hauls the horse up the sandhill in search of a convenient place to mount. To her dismay she finds Gordon, sitting unaccustomedly straight in the saddle, beribboned pocket book propped against its pommel. A severe expression plaints his mouth as he surveys the sea, ostensibly paying no attention to Rosanna or his open book until Glorvina flounders in the sand before him.

Rosanna feels mucky: a fright, with hair awry and sandy petticoats. Throwing a furious glance behind her, she hopes that George has galloped away but Lucifer whinnies and rears, draws attention to his new owner.

It has been a long time since Gordon kissed her but it is not difficult now to discern that looking down on her he views her with disdain. Head bowed, Rosanna mounts Glorvina. The horse sinks in the plurried sand. Gordon offers no assistance, merely doffing his wide-awake hat before cantering away, his face a picture of doleful tragedy. His horse picks up speed as it streaks past the township; his figure diminishes in size as he rises up the bridle path to the cliff and veers east.

65

ARRESTS AND A PITCHFORK

A few days after Rosanna delivers Lucifer to the actor for Edwin, Skelly hears his brother and sister going at each other on the front step.

'Rosanna, did you not pay that corpulent bag of pus, O'Leary?'

'I did, of course,' his sister shouts, stepping down from the vegetable patch, 'but he wanted more. How could you sell Lucifer? Even in debt up to your lumpy neck. You still are!' She pulls the receipt from her pocket and throws it towards him.

He lunges forward as it flutters to the bottom of the steps.

'Why did you let him blackmail you?' she says.

'For the privilege of using his contacts on the boats.'

'He knows about the dead steer. You did not mention the spear?'

'I may yet.' He smooths out the paper and turns his body on an angle to decipher the sum. It enrages him further and he turns back to Rosanna.

Skelly pulls his hat down and peers up at them from his seat on the verandah. He takes perverse pleasure in their cussing and slapping the posts, their marching towards each other and backing off.

'It's just a small thing I overlooked. You're only a girl. What would you know about getting ahead in the colony? All men carry debt. Only women save pin-money. I have to take risks, forge ahead.'

'No doubt you will and leave the rest of us behind, but don't forget my wages saved you from the debt collector. And you left me to deal with that Barbary ape, O'Leary.'

'I will buy another horse—better than Lucifer.'

'Lucifer wins races now. He'll sire champions.' His sister sobs. 'He is worth more than gold. He would have brought you luck. What will people say about Edwin Lynch, so successful he cannot afford a decent horse?'

'I'll buy him back before too long.'

Mother drops a basket of dirty linen at Rosanna's feet, and points to the pond. Skelly sees that she is sorely tried by their ruckus.

'You'll never be rich enough, ever, to be happy,' Rosanna shouts.

'Shut it. You're got so sour you could pickle cucumbers!' Edwin kicks a clump of mud whistling past her head.

'Edwin.' Mother's voice is cool and tough, as she steers him into the house.

Skelly helps his sister carry the basket of washing to the pond, where they kneel beside the water. Rosanna's reflection is dark with misery and worry: lips down-turned, hair dishevelled, skin sallow in the pale sunlight, eyes large and swollen. Why does she bother to quarrel with Edwin? Even when he is losing an argument, he is ferocious. Skelly peers at his own reflection in dismay. Just when he had thought to make some progress with his skin, his face erupts like a lava field. He breaks up the painful image with his fingers.

'*Thar ...*' Rosanna croons, stroking his arm. 'You'll grow out of your bad skin—unlike Edwin, who will always be selfish.' She drags wet linen up against her washboard and thumps it down, glancing up at her mother, now digging in the potato and carrot patch. The last thing he needs is Rosanna's pity. Edwin will become successful. Just last night he had confided in his brother that the bank has promised him a loan.

Not long after this Skelly hears the beat of approaching hooves, and finally, the jingle of spurs. Even from the pond, Skelly recognises his mother's look of consternation as she rises above the lacy carrot tops to wipe her face on her apron, and walk slowly towards the front of the house, where a black-suited man reins in a splendid barrel-chested grey. Rosanna drapes a chemise and nightgown across a slab of rock and backs up on her hands and knees.

'Is Mr Edwin Lynch at home?' the man calls out. His voice breaks the silence.

66

THE LYNCH MEN STAND UP AGAINST LAW

Screened by the black-wood trees Skelly creeps behind his sister towards the house. Edwin and Father appear in the doorway.

The dark suited man, gun at his side, is as fat as a turkey cock and pompous looking, his jowls wobbling over his collar, his purple hands bunched on the pommel. He looks like a renegade from a boxing tent. 'I am assistant bailiff to the local court.' The man throws out his authority, by way of introduction.

Father stands rigid on the step, food in his beard, eyes glittering like snakes'.

'You are the defendant, Edwin Lynch?'

Skelly sees that his brother has clenched his fists and he feels a rush of love for him. Alarmed he must be—much more than his face shows.

He creaks forward in the saddle. 'Edwin Lynch, I have a warrant against you for debt and the theft of bullocks.'

Skelly thinks Edwin jinxed by bullocks. With so few Blacks remaining, surely his brother should change to breeding sheep like the Arthurs.

Edwin finally steps forward, fist raised, tongue belligerently thrusting against his left cheek. 'It would take a better man than you to arrest me.'

Skelly gasps.

Rosanna pushes her fist against her mouth. Something impels her forward. Father scans natural detail in his vicinity: the muddy track, the corridors of trees, and perhaps the pathway to the privy. Edwin bounces on the balls of his feet, looks poised to run, if necessary up the walls of the house and onto the roof. What is to become of him? Skelly's heart begins to thunder.

After the expeditious issuing of his warrant, the man seems surprised by this resistance. He shifts in his saddle, lifting his right hand to flick an imaginary insect from his fleshy cheek. 'You will accompany me to Gambierton.'

Father takes three strides, seizing up a pitchfork angled against the side of the house. 'Leave now—before I pitchfork you off the place.'

The bailiff loosens his left rein and circles his horse in the mud before putting him up to Father. 'You Irish are nothing but trouble.'

'Get off your horse and say that,' says Father, brandishing his fork.

When Rosanna comes walking from the trees, dragging a broken branch along the ground in a loud disruptive way, the bailiff swings his head, uncertain. He glances back at Edwin. Skelly grins, watching his brother, cocky now, hands in his braces like a Whiteboy, back swayed, belly and bottom sticking out. Father lunges forward to restrain the bailiff's horse.

The horse jerks its head; a bewildered boyish expression darts across the law-keeper's face. He reasserts his authority, swinging his legs to the ground, and leading the horse away from Father to lay a hand upon Edwin's shoulder. Edwin throws it off. Father slashes the air with his pitchfork. It is like a call to battle. Skelly feels inexplicably excited. Will his father claw the seat of the policeman's pants and catapult him to Mount Schanck?

But Mother rushes between her husband and the bailliff, placing the flat of her hand on her husband's chest. 'Garrick, leave it.'

He stabs the air once more with his pitchfork, offering Mother a look that would throw a man on his *thóin*.

The bailiff backs up, one arm slung across the horse's neck, and feels with his other hand for his stirrup.

Skelly and Rosanna step out from behind a blackwood tree.

'Look at yourselves,' the man adds, 'coming out of the woods—like Fenians.'

Rosanna appears to take offence at this and pitches up a piece of limestone, then another, aiming for his head. Skelly joins in, half proud, half apprehensive. Edwin punches his fist into a post. Father sweeps Mother's hand aside and then, when she totters, lifts it again to steady her. Hugh coughs until he cries.

The bailiff ducks the hail of stones as he throws his leg over the horse and retreats. Rosanna throws unlettered Irish after him and his horse: '... Nothing wrong with Fenians or Finn Macumhail! Don't come back or we'll cut off your leg!'

Skelly feels faint with terror.

'Rosanna,' Mother admonishes, 'we're in trouble enough, girl,' and turns to her husband, who is steering Edwin towards the still.

'The darling boy,' Rosanna sobs, staring after Edwin, hat pulled down, shirt riding up, an arm around his father's waist. 'It is my fault for upsetting O'Leary.'

This will not be the end of it and Skelly knows it. Rosanna takes her melancholy face back to her drubbing at the pond. Throughout the afternoon Skelly hears his father's low serious voice and occasional outbursts of vehemence from Edwin. Mother cries in the potato patch. He watches her move up and down the furrows between the beds, pulling weeds, straightening to peer at Rosanna hunched over the washing and, every now and then, to wipe her face with the back of her hand.

67

LYNCH ARRESTS

It is not until the pale sun drops half way to the sea that Edwin and Father return to the house, just in time to greet the bailiff cantering in with two policemen. Seated on the verandah, Mother throws back her head and shakes her fist at the suety sky. Then, her eyes fixed on the intruders, she continues to lightly beat her fists on Hugh's back, using her knees to steer his head over the steam bowl. Rosanna has disappeared, perhaps to the cave to search again for Moorecke.

This time the lawmen stay seated on their horses to deliver their decree; in the manner of the magistrate in Mr Geoghegan's play. 'Garrick Lynch and his son Edwin Lynch are called, upon information, to answer a charge of assault preferred against them by John Duncan, assistant bailiff of the Local Court, in revisiting the execution of a warrant for debt issued by the said Court against Edwin Lynch, whereby the said Edwin was rescued from lawful custody.'

Edwin and Father hear them out, fists in their pockets, legs crossed, deceptively laconic, leaning against the verandah posts.

Skelly holds his breath, his eyes almost crossing with the effort of staying calm, as father and son raise their fists at the lawmen. In the end they go in a volley of cusses but with no further physical resistance.

When the shouting is over and the Lynch men ridden out in handcuffs, Skelly retreats to the step, and sketches the incident from memory, while Blinnie and Hugh play conkers at his feet. He tries to ignore a kernel of fear hardening in his belly. Without Father and Edwin's wages, the family will surely starve. He pushes the children away and goes inside to warm himself.

When Rosanna returns from the pond she sits by the fire with Skelly and Mother. Scratching at the coals, they kiss the cup they pass between them.

'Search no further than that filthy O'Leary,' she says. 'I blame him. He sent the law to persecute our family.'

'You paid him, surely?' Skelly asks.

'You saw the receipt did you not?'

'Edwin would not lay a hand on anyone's stock,' Skelly says, his face intent on gaining Mother's attention. He is hardly ever included. Why should he not play the devil's advocate? 'But he would be a fool not to.'

Rosanna flushes and prods Skelly with her foot. 'He is no less than any opportunist.'

Mother stares at her, her knuckles white against the drinking cup. 'You know something about this?'

'Edwin is unlucky this time. Sometimes it is an accident that bullocks go missing.'

Skelly lifts his pencil and places it in his mouth—satisfied. He casts his mind back to the day he listened from the buloke tree, while his sister swam in the pond with Moorecke. Avoiding Mother's eyes, he snots on his sleeve. Truthfully, even he does not know the entire story.

Mother stands up and reaches for her husband's coat. 'I cannot stand the lot of you. I'm going into town to see for myself.'

'Wait until tomorrow.'

'I cannot bear not knowing.'

'Mother, I will go,' Rosanna says. 'You must stay here with the little ones.'

'I will go too.'

'I need you here, Skelly. I have no men in the house.' He is not fooled by this but concurs. Rosanna is already up and running through the doorway.

6 8

PRISON VISIT

Late that night, his sister relates the story of how she urged Glorvina through wind and rising water, at times up to the pommel. She had never ridden alone up the mountain between the blue crater lakes and down the steep track to Gambierton. She found Father and Edwin chained to a cart near a young policeman shaving, who waved his blade above his cup: 'Move along.'

'I have food for these men.'

He fluttered his hand at her and returned to his ablutions.

'You must tell him that we found that bullock,' she had hissed at Edwin. Skelly thinks that she has forgotten he is not supposed to know this and it feels like a victory.

'How should I do that without the detail of the spear?'

'Explain how the bullock broke its leg stumbling into a wombat hole.'

Father took the parcel of food and pushed her away. 'Go home. Your brother is accused of hocking more than one bullock.' Dark circles swelled beneath his eyes.

It is Father Woods who eventually brings home the news that a Mr Corcoran has appeared at the policeman's hut for Edwin and Father. The magistrate reprimanded both parties. Had it not been for the presence of Mrs Lynch, he said, Mr Lynch might have gone wild with the pitchfork.

Eilish blows out her cheeks with indignation. It is the same hot breath Father will feel when he returns. All charges against him have been dropped but Edwin has been sentenced to four months' hard labour for debt and, as the Gambierton gaol is full and Guichen Bay gaol as well, he is to be transferred to Adelaide. The charge of theft has been put aside due to lack of evidence.

'Why not release him then, if all the jails are full?' asks Skelly.

'It is not for us to say, but only to pray,' replies Father Woods, holding out his hand for Skelly's sketchbook.

Skelly prevaricates.

'My son would never steal a bullock,' Mother snaps, scrubbing at the table with soapsuds and a bristle brush. In her distress, she turns her face away from the priest.

'O'Leary lied about the money. I took it to him and I counted it,' Rosanna says, blushing.

'Such a story, Rosanna. I wish I was as good,' Skelly bites. He knows there is more than staying sweet with the priest but he can't intuit what. Why does she always cover for Edwin?

She pushes him hard in the chest and then, appearing to think better of it, lunges forward to steady him.

'Restrain yourselves,' Father Woods cautions. 'We must pray for those who administer justice. That they may show compassion. And that Edwin draws strength from his adversity.'

Mother begins to cry.

'Skelly and I will take some tea to the edge of the pond. I saw an interesting bird taking a bath there as I drew up,' the priest says.

He needn't have worried the rest of the family would fall into fisticuffs. How can Father Woods be so impartial? Rosanna looks as if her heart will break.

Eilish moves to the hob and reaches for the kettle while Father rambles on. 'It might be that in the future Skelly could come on a little trip with me and help me collect samples of fossils.'

'You would need to take great care of him. I cannot see another son at risk.' She bows her head.

Father arrives home subdued. Shattered by Edwin's departure, the family goes over the details of his arrest and sentencing, anguishing over how they will manage without him and their cut from his wages. Mother works hard in her garden that they might spend less money at the Gambierton store. Skelly reads to her from the play until she shouts at him to leave her be and he scurries away. The following day, Rosanna and Father, wearied in a way that signals more than bodily tiredness, ride silently to the station to resume their work, much as they always have done but heads bowed, as loury as a pair of lurchers without Edwin.

MRS ASHBY DEPARTS FROM THE STATION

For most of the week, time trails slower than mares' tails in summer skies. Mrs Ashby drives her friends into the township and returns without them, hand clutching her forehead as she stumbles from the trap. The blacksmith has been carried to his home suffering dropsy, and repairs on the Brigstocks' carriage will have to wait. Rosanna brings her employer tea in bed and carries the baby from room to room as she works. There is little good on the horizon. Mrs Ashby may not book her berth for months, depending on when her house guests leave.

George and Mr Ashby attend horse sales around the district and share the hospitality of vendors overnight. Rosanna knows the auctions to be an early prelude to the spring race meetings and, hard as it is to watch another rider astride Lucifer, she is placated by the fact that George remains in her vicinity. Once or twice they read early scenes from the play and enact swift love in the stables. Yet nothing is as it was. The household feels on the brink of something.

As she shoulders wicker baskets of soiled linen, pokes the clothes in the copper with a long pole and turns the mangle, her ears strain for the slightest sound inside the house or out. In the late afternoons, she squeezes the well-fed baby into the wooden cradle beside her employer's bed and makes her way to the stables.

Lately, it seems that Father has lost so much heart over Edwin that he relies on her to find her own way home. This blessing, coupled with the play manuscript left by George in the iron box, most recently stowed below the ladder to the loft, has enabled her to read, and transcribe when she has cajoled sufficient sketch paper from her mother. Not once has Mrs Ashby questioned why some days Rosanna's horse can still be seen tethered at the bottom of the garden for at least an hour after five. Preoccupied she has been with her own troubles.

The following Monday, Rosanna is surprised to discover that Mr Colyer and the Brigstocks have departed the station. The trap is gone, the house curiously quiet. To her great relief, she finds George's toiletries and shaving accoutrements in the bunk house, although there is no other evidence of him or Mr Ashby in the house or yard. Since Edwin's arrest, she has scarce seen him, but she feels confident that he will make arrangements to take her with him.

Rooms are stripped back, awaiting her attention. The baby, drenched in morning urine and clutching a bottle of warm milk, appears to be in the care of the dog on the floor. Freshly changed baby on her hip, Rosanna hurries to the bedroom where her mistress feigns sleep.

Mrs Ashby acts more than a little queer, spending the entire day in her dimly lit bedroom, with camomile-soaked linen squares draped across her face. Can it be that she misses Mrs Brigstock already, or should troubling Tasmanian news be presumed the root? There is sympathy and there is knowing your place. Since Bertram's dangerous escapade and controversial rescue, Jane Ashby has ceased confiding in her even the smallest household matters; indeed, she no longer seems to care about the project of improving her maid at all. Rosanna takes sole daily care of the baby, from whom she coaxes indifferent smiles contingent on the offering of food. It is now possible that the wee lad is in danger from his mother's neglect.

Her housekeeping informs her that Mr Ashby has been banished to the spare room vacated by the Brigstocks. Indeed, he makes quite a mess. During the day, she plays with the baby and ferries trays of delicacies to the bedroom, which Mrs Ashby turns over in her fingers and abandons. While the little man sleeps, Rosanna returns to the bunkhouse to examine George's belongings for some intimation of his immediate plans. She must speak further to him about Melbourne, about the opening of the play, which he rarely mentions; and about why a crumpled telegram from a Mr Magarey invites him to stable two horses in Adelaide this month.

In the afternoon, when the baby wakes, she jiggles him squirming in front of the sessions clock, feeling inexplicably cast down by the tedious *chink, chink,* of its rhythmic tick, and of the failure of all her plans to progress. In the shadow of Mrs Ashby's listlessness, she hardly dares dream.

Then one morning, Rosanna finds Mrs Ashby standing beside the stove stirring porridge. The baby is rolling on and off the braided mat, laughing at his own cleverness, the dog licking his face. Rosanna scoops him up and wipes his fingers with the hem of her apron. Kisses little Ashby's button nose. She looks to her employer for guidance.

'Finally, I am to sail for Tasmania,' Jane Ashby says, looking up as she whisks the porridge into an enamel bowl. 'Tomorrow ... My father ...' She sobs as she carries the wooden spoon to the wash bowl. 'I have booked Cobb and Co to Portland.'

Before she thinks of the implications of such immediate change, Rosanna sighs with something akin to relief at the end of the drudgery. On Saturday, her employer will be aboard the packet, crossing Bass Strait. But then what is to become of her maid?

They spend the day in a flurry of washing and packing. Both cry on the sly, inside cupboards and behind doors. Intuiting change, the baby gives up his mirth, resumes gluttony, vomits his lunch and dinner and bawls like a banshee. How will Mr Ashby manage alone?

By early evening, swift rushes of wind eddy from the south. The station atmosphere feels both cool and expectant. Rosanna reads Act Four with studied determination. Finishing her transcription of the play commingles with her larger ambitions and she has seen no sign of George all day.

It is a grim thing that Scene 1 of Act 5 relates Oscar's intercessions with God, whilst confined in a dungeon, and her own brother is locked up at the Adelaide prison. Of course, Oscar is in more danger than Edwin and *The Hibernian Father* is only a story. Rosanna reads in the dim evening light until the warden visits the prison and clasps his son, *a blissful tear of tenderness bedewing his parent cheek*, causing her to think of Edwin grieving for his family in his cell, so much that she begins to cry.

Warden   And as I traced
            In thee myself in miniature I thought
            How I might live, yet to behold my son
            Worthy inheritor of the stainless name
            So long and proudly borne in our house!

Had Father thought bleak thoughts about *his* son ruining the Lynch name—had he always feared the worst? Is it fear that makes men hard, caring only about stains and names? In the play an unruly crowd of citizens assemble at the gate, demanding the boy's release. Oscar's mother and sister must stand among them.

'*Licentious scum,*' says the warden. He will not succumb *to a ruffian band of Curs who snarl and bark*. Rosanna thinks he has no heart.

Mr Blake, the magistrate's friend, speaks up on Oscar's behalf:

Blake   Save your loved son from ignominious death!

At least Edwin will not hang for his sins. But nor will he be as comfortable as Little Dorrit's father in the London debtor's prison, whose daughter visits every day. Adelaide is too far away to visit, for Edwin or anyone. If only he were in Melbourne, she might visit him with the actor.

Next morning, relief swamps her when she opens the iron box to find the manuscript—only one act remains. She is glad to hear Lucifer whinnying not far from the house; not so glad to hear the baby crying and Mr Ashby's raised voice. Best to keep her distance, for he has not forgiven her for the lie about the fire, and today his wife departs.

She hurries inside in time to assist Jane Ashby with the last-minute arrangement of clothing in her trunk, following her from room to room like a poddy calf. Mr Ashby also lingers near his wife, a morose expression on his face, and sipping porter like water. Jane Ashby tells Rosanna to prepare several cold collations, for Mr Sutherland will stay two more days at the station to conclude some horse business. She hopes he will keep her husband company. William has expressed mild curiosity over Mr Sutherland's plans for Lucifer to be trialled in several races in Adelaide before he goes to the Melbourne Sweepstakes.

Rosanna sucks in her breath and tightens her cloth belt; there is truth in the telegram. Adelaide. Her belly hardens. Apart from knowing the play and the Lynch's story, she is no better off than when George arrived; and has no rights to his confidence. A boundary rider's girl, watching the world ride by.

Mrs Ashby farewells her husband in a brisk and determined

manner, as if she fears that he may break down. At the last moment *she* begins to cry, leaping down from the cart to stroke the side of his face with the back of her curled hand.

'William, oh, I do wish that we might all be going. You and I—and Baby.' She sweeps the landscape with a resentful eye. 'I will speak to your father when I arrive home in Hobart. He must understand that the situation is untenable.'

Mr Ashby flinches over the word *home* as if it is a blow to his solar plexus. She draws her hand across her mouth to acknowledge her mistake. Mrs Ashby's dog seems to smell unhappiness and howls, body bunched, head thrown back; jackasses drown out the last murmurs of the unhappy separation.

George arrives and assists Mrs Ashby into the cart. She will drive herself to Gambierton. Mr Ashby takes the baby's waving fist and smothers it with kisses. How would Father act if Mother booked her passage back to Ireland? Witnessing the touching scene, Rosanna's heart is strangely afflicted with sympathy for her mistress and a surge of affection for the wee boy. George melts away to his quarters before the cart reaches the gate. In timely fashion, she enters the house.

From the bay window, she sees Father leaving with three other riders to cut unbranded calves from the main mob and look for sick cows. Over his shoulder he throws dark looks at George, who has re-appeared at Mr Ashby's side. Quite soon, stock riders and horses—the size of ants on the horizon—and lowing cows are forgotten. Rosanna thoughts are now fixated on George.

She washes bed linen, then scrubs the kitchen dresser and the table where she and Mrs Ashby had prepared and packed food for the journey. At the same time, she tries to gather her wits. It is while emptying tea leaves in a pot of pelargoniums on the verandah that she overhears the object of her agitation electing to keep an eye on the house until the men return, for it is rumoured that a bushranger is at large in the district. In point of fact, George tells Mr Ashby, staying behind will not trouble him, now; the opening of the play at the Princes Theatre is delayed and he has made new plans to accompany the stallions to race in Adelaide. He has received instructions at the Gambierton telegraph station, from the Melbourne impresario, to continue rehearsing and come to Melbourne in a month or so. He must remind the maid about laundering and packing his linen before he goes.

Mr Ashby grunts and turns away and Rosanna scurries inside. Through the window, she sees him gallop west, following his men. Her mood has swung from torpor to terror; will she find herself, once more, entirely disconnected from the outside world? She pinches her cheeks and wets her lips with butter. 'May there be a fox on your fishing hook and a hare on your bait ...' she chants before the mirror atop the credenza.

THE ACTOR WELCHES ON AN OFFER

It is only a matter of minutes before George bounds into the kitchen enticing her with lines from Act Four, Scene Two, in which Oscar's friends have organised a vessel at anchor in Galway Bay, to snatch him away to safety. Two scenes remain in Act Four.

'You must speak *all* the lines until I finish here,' Rosanna insists, using the feather duster to keep him at a distance. How to broach the subject?

'Then will you love me, beautiful lady, my Anastasia?'

'Then we will read Act Five, together.'

'I can promise only to begin,' he parries. 'A man can endure just so much.'

It is an exciting scene, although Rosanna feels much distracted: Anastasia is rescued from the brigands by a fisherman, avoiding a forced suicide. She is surprised to find Alonzo alive after all and greets him with affection. In haste they descend the mountains, intent on saving Oscar, his execution nigh. George springs forward with a metal spoon to chime upon the lid of the butter dish. Can Anastasia find her way through the crowds in time to save her lover?

'Read her lines now,' says George. 'Such a dramatic scene will test your mettle.'

Rosanna feels overcome by emotion: the Lynch boy may be killed, Edwin languishes in a prison cell, and soon George will leave the station for Adelaide with Lucifer. She can barely find her voice.

George scoops her up. 'Dear love, let us go to the stables, where we can remember all the sweet times we have spent there together.'

'No, please, George. Wait. You must allow me to copy the last two scenes of the play for Skelly. He wants so much to know what happens. I do too. Then I will join you.' She must think what to do.

'The play. The play is all I hear about,' he snaps. 'Soon I shall be gone and you show me little affection.'

Rosanna makes a moue of her mouth and taps her foot.

He strokes and cajoles her. 'Do you not crave to see the play on stage? Private capital has been raised for a fine production with elegant backdrops of the mountain pass and Lynch's Castle in Galway's High Street. You will vouch that I know the lines of Oscar exceeding well, and you those of Anastasia?'

'George, can we not go to Melbourne, you and I, and I play Anastasia?'

'Nothing would please me more ... eventually ... but the impresario ...' He sighs. 'I fear I must delay my journey.'

'And why would that be? Tell me the truth, George.'

'The opening of the play has been deferred but it will be a long run, nothing is more certain. In Sydney the number of revivals was remarkable. In the meantime, I have to attend to my investment in fine bloodstock.' George glances uneasily over her shoulder to the window and checks his fob. 'I swear *you* care more about the play than me or your horse.'

'It is not true.' If he only understood her confusion. Rosanna twitches like a netted seahorse, as his fingers move compulsively to her blouse. 'Please, George. Let us race Lucifer together in Adelaide then. He loves me more than you. He will run faster if I train him. '

'I have no desire for your father to black my eye before I reach Guichen Bay.' He lowers his head to mouth her *ciochanna*.

She pushes him away. 'In Melbourne, do the ladies race at picnic meetings as they do here?' He will take everything away from her.

'They do, indeed, but respectable girls think twice before they abandon sidesaddle.'

'Oh mercy. Astride is so health giving and safer.'

'I will wager Lucifer on a wedding, if he will win for me in Adelaide, and resolve my bills at a Swan Street tailor's.' He fingers her chin. 'I own a small cottage and stables near the Brighton Racecourse. Perhaps not splendid enough for a haughty Lynch girl but I employ an Irish trainer and I have no doubt you will like him.'

Simultaneously crestfallen and excited, Rosanna's thoughts settle on a wedding. But contingent on racing luck. 'Please allow me to ride with you when you go tonight.' She leans forward and kisses him.

Suddenly she remembers Captain Ussher's lies to Feemy in her novel: *Don't make difficulties, love*, he said.

George frowns, cradles her back, and lifts her towards him. 'I fear not. But I will send someone for you soon. I know a man in Portland Bay. The same agent who buys poddy calves from your brother. Are they cadged?'

'It is nothing but a vicious rumour.' Edwin would knock George flat for saying such things.

George reaches into his fob pocket. 'Put these shillings in your pocket that you may travel in comfort on the stagecoach to Melbourne—when I write for you to follow me.'

'And Adelaide?'

'I have no time to make arrangements.'

Rosanna drops the coins one by one inside the neck of his shirt and, as they fall, holds them hard against his belly with her thumbs as she considers what they mean. It cannot be proper to take money from a man even if the reason sounds plausible. But how else can they be together? It seems she cannot ride away with him this day and Edwin's debts have subsumed all her wages. Surely George would not blacken her name when she loves him so fervently and with such confidence. But she cannot cry and faint like Feemy.

The old people used prophetic mirrors and the entrails of freshly slaughtered deer to read love in the shifting sky, their thoughts simmering with violence. 'If you do not send word within the month that I may come, I will kill you,' she says and sweeps away. But it is not true. If Rosanna cannot go to Melbourne she will dream a better death.

ROSANNA READS ON TO CERTAIN DOOM

Rosanna's hand aches from copying, and her head from crying. She slides her hand into her pantaloons to scoop out shimmering silky stuff that he has left inside her and rubs her thumb against her forefinger. He has, she must acknowledge, insulted her with his offer of money. And why has Mr Geoghegan written a play so cruel? Surely the Galway magistrate will save his son from the gallows. Her hand flies across the page. Pray that Mr Ashby will not notice that she has been forced to borrow another of his fine Indian pencils. She shaves it back, breathes in the clean smell of pine and graphite, and begins again, a callus swelling on the inside of her third finger.

While Rosanna struggles over the fading India ink copy of Act Five, Scene Two, Anastasia, Vice-regal pardon in her hand, runs through the crowds beside the river and into Shop Street, her thoughts dwelling solely on saving her beloved Oscar from the hangman's noose.

> *Anastasia*   Perhaps e'en now with agonising tears
> He feebly murmurs Anastasia's name
> And in the pining accents of despair
> Calls upon me for Comfort and for Hope.

Rosanna's hand quivers in sympathy, as the dear girl mourns.

Rising to stand at the open window she lifts her hand to George, cantering hatless on Lucifer, putting her horse through his paces. His hair is as yellow as mimosa, his mouth softly dropped open with exertion; a red cravat flies at his neck. She has kissed him there. Would he not make some signal, throw back his head in his surreptitious way—wave his hand—if Mr Ashby returned to catch her neglecting house duties?

The bells toll on in Galway.

> *Anastasia*   That fearful sound which, heavy on my heart
> Falls like the knell of happiness and wakes
> A thousand dire forebodings! Ah I know it now!
> It is the dreadful signal which proclaims
> The hour of execution is at hand!

Rosanna paces past the window, crying out Anastasia's lines to her own love: '*Oscar, I come—I come to bid thee live. To live for Anastasia and for Love.*'

George hears nothing of these details but smiles at her across the yard, touches his fingers to his lips, and puts Lucifer at a log. It is a great actress she has become, rushing past the curtains like the female lead in a play. It is not hard to imagine members of an audience, bodies closely pressed, shifting in their seats in the warm auditorium, hope and fear journeying across their flushed faces, necks stretched forward, nervous fingers fiddling with cloth and ornament, drawing in their breath in agitation as they lift out their fob watches to consider hailing a hansom cab on Bourke Street rather than look away to avoid the terror. Suspense eats at their faces.

The ink of the play-script darkens. Does Mr Geoghegan copy with more intensity? Does he wipe perspiration from his brow, reliving the agony of his own creation? Act Five, Scene Three, the last, set in the Grand Hall of the warden's mansion. The Galway City banner surmounts the arch. Rosanna copies the text as if her own life depends on it, only glancing to the window in occasional aggravation when she snaps her pencil lead. The yard is clear. Only the sound of the cottage clock and the rattle of brush bronze-wings can be heard above the beating of her heart. She scrapes the blade down her pencil stub, breaks the point and scrapes again, pinching the curls of shavings between thumb and forefinger and placing them in her pocket. On she presses, writing in thick swift strokes; there is no refinement now. She lays her head on the last page. Oh it is a terrible thing for wringing out a heart, a story.

Later George will find the manuscript slapped on the dining-room table, held down by a silver pickle-jar. Perhaps he will see her make her way on Glorvina, stumbling up to her hocks through freezing water. Perhaps he will watch her progress like a small green pennant flapping up to the ridge and over, disappearing into a silver mullet sky. He must love her. He has said so. Surely he will not forget her.

But for Rosanna everything is wrong: Edwin imprisoned, Lucifer sold; the actor leaving; and Moorecke not seen since Mr Ashby destroyed her camping places.

THE HIBERNIAN FATHER

Supper is quiet. Bowed over their beans, they industriously slurp to cover the dearth of conversation. Skelly cannot clean his plate, remembering that he has scuttered three times in the privy that afternoon. Mother stacks bowls and mugs and wipes the babies' mouths with a cloth. Water drips through the rafters into a bucket beside the hearth. Father slumps at the table, lungs whistling, his breathing shallow.

At the end of the meal he tells his wife that within a month he hopes to square off Edwin's debt and resume saving for a place of their own. 'Partly due to Rosanna's money,' he says, gruff with speech, 'helping at the Big House. I can do nothing about the bullocks. I think them a fabrication. And I am sorry to have kept you short of housekeeping supplies.'

Rosanna's eyes swell with tears.

Skelly's foot touches hers beneath the table but she pulls away.

Mother leans against her daughter to steady the plates as she clears the table. 'That's grand even if Edwin has to finish his sentence. We'll be fine. No one has starved yet. What news of Mrs Ashby, Rosanna? She has left for Hobart to see her ailing father?'

Nothing passes her. Rosanna nods. 'On Saturday's tide.'

'And the actor. Gone too?'

'He leaves with Lucifer tonight.' She casts her eyes down as if she has said too much.

'Damned pity Edwin sold the horse, thinking it would save his neck. He was a fool, dealing with a Kerry man.' Father drags on his pipe.

Skelly sees Mother's eyes light on her daughter's fallen face.

'We have the play,' she says. 'Let's do something to cheer us up. Celebrate the end of Edwin's debt, although the subject is bleak. Which act are we up to, Skelly?'

He shakes his head, feels disappointment swamp him. 'We don't have Act Five.' Now they will never know what happened to the Lynch boy.

Rosanna pipes, 'But Skelly, we have, for I spent my last hours at the Station copying it out. Without *herself* lecturing on and on about my Irish manners, I finished my work in a trice.'

Skelly's heart bounces with excitement. How lucky he is to have such a decent sister.

'Well then, shall we not have a reading, Eilish?' Father says. 'Skelly told me some details, about the early scenes. It is a familiar plot. In Galway Town, people tour the dreadful places where the events supposedly took place. Let us not be dull, without Edwin. We can make our own entertainment.'

Mother covers her surprise at her husband's loquaciousness, drawing Blinnie onto her knee. 'You did not tell me that you knew the play, Garrick.'

'I did not say I knew *this* play.'

Skelly thinks his mother calculates the number of tankards consumed by her husband that night as she rests her chin on Blinnie's downy head; no doubt fingers swiftly separate the beads of her rosary beneath the table.

'Get the new pages, Rosanna, and allow your brother to begin. Such a tedious day he's had, hiding from the rain.'

Skelly jumps to his feet with excitement. 'Act Five, three scenes, Rosanna. Have you brought the last?' He jigs around his chair.

'Well then, I shall fetch it,' she says and strides to her cloth bag hanging from a peg near the door.

'You have read to curtain close—Rosanna?' he asks.

'How could I not? You know that I have copied it all.'

Skelly takes the pages firmly from her hand.

His father nods and draws out a chair for his daughter.

Skelly thinks that he reads well, hesitating only when Rosanna's script is especially blurred or the lantern flickers. 'The warden's friend, Mr Blake, is present inside the mansion.'

'I know Blakes in Woodford.' Father lifts the rim of his tankard into his mouth and swallows like a draught horse.

Rosanna says, 'You're not expecting a Lynch father might take notice of a friend's advice!'

He raises one brow, in Edwin's way, but deflects her with less pronouncement. 'Mansion,' he croons. 'I like the sound of that.' Is he full of the grog or dreaming of building on new land?

'Well you would, *alannahh*.' Mother makes it her duty to smooth out dips in the conversation.

'You're like a chorus, the two of you. Let Skelly put us through it now,' Rosanna snaps. She nods at her brother, leaning sideways to inhale a plume of her father's plum tobacco.

'The boy's mother will raise her brothers from the inn,' Eilish says, 'just as I would. They'll not put up with such nonsense: fathers arresting sons. That would never happen.'

'Mother, shut it,' Rosanna cries.

'Rosannaaaa,' Father's voice inflects.

Skelly resumes his reading:

> *Blake*   But yet my lord bethink you there is still
> Much disaffection 'mongst the citizens
> And this the pretext on which they seize
> To arouse the angry passions of the mob.

'Did I not tell you?'

'Eilish, let the boy run with it now. Speak as one of the warden's true friends':

> *Edward*   To justice you have full adherence shown,
> Oh now let gentle mercy rule your breast
> Yield to the citizens' demands and spare,
> Oh spare the life of your unhappy son!

'They are wise words,' says Mother. 'And well read. Will the magistrate not concede them?'

Skelly stands up tall to play the magistrate. Cresting his father's shoulders, he clears his throat before commencing:

Warden   Tis pity and not fear restrains me now
             From issuing command by force of arms
             To sweep them hence and their insurgent mob.
             Behold the Civic flag long proudly borne
             Untarnished save by stern invaders' blood
             Thinks't thou within my grasp it shall be stained
             With taint of shameless partiality?
             Or cowardice of mine oppose the free
             And even current of the stream of justice?
             No, though the hour it brings before mine eyes
             The senseless corse of my still much loved son.
             Bring with it the horrors of the tomb
             I still as eagerly would welcome death
             As I would shun dishonour.

Skelly's performance as great tragedian falls away in the lantern-light. He has shocked himself. How can he act a part so unnatural? The Lynch father's words do not bode well for Oscar.

'It is an ancient story, Skelly, from bloody times,' Father rumbles, stroking his hand.

'Not a true story,' Mother reassures.

'A Lynch story oft told in Galway, most often by the city council to attract travellers. When I was a boy, another version, written by a Reverend, was performed in Galway. A Burke showed me the pamphlet.'

'It is unnatural,' Skelly says, 'a father not to save his son. He surely will by curtain fall.'

'Stories can be taken up or not,' Father soothes.

'*We* don't have to choose it, then,' says Skelly, passionate in the darkening room.

'And what if it chooses you?' says Rosanna. 'Fathers can be severe.'

Skelly would not blame his father, should he send *him* away with Father Woods, for he feels a burden, eating more as he grows, contributing little. But Geoghegan's play goes too far. No true Lynch father would act so stern. What of the playwright's?

Father bristles. 'Read on now, Rosanna.'

Crossing to Skelly's side of the table she finds her place. Then draws herself up full of angry pride; perhaps how Mr Geoghegan's friend,

Francis Nesbitt, plays the magistrate. She waves her hand.

Oscar enters attended by a monk and followed by two guards and Executioner. The Warden regards him for a moment with parental tenderness, then by a strong effort repressing his emotion takes the hand of Oscar.

'The warden, his own father,' she scores, 'delivers this verdict.'

Warden   You have asked
            For my reply. Behold I give it here!
            Here on the altar of my country's laws
            I offer up the sacrifice of all
            This widowed heart in this world held most dear.
            My son, thou now reached the utmost verge
            Of human life. A few short moments hence
            And thou wilt stand before thy maker's throne,
            Received I trust into eternal bliss.

'Oscar, kneel at my feet,' Rosanna whispers to Skelly. She holds the play in one hand and tugs at his buttoned-up coat with the other.

He supposes he can play the part of the Lynch boy well enough to make his mother cry. There is little doubt his sister will act the warden to the hilt. He shivers.

'*Nay to my arms!*' she orders, pulling Skelly roughly against her legs as she reads.

Warden   —to my last embrace
            And may thy fate to all example prove
            How unavailing every virtue else
            Within the heart where passion rules supreme
            Farewell farewell my boy—prepare for Death!

The Warden covers his face with his hands and appears for moment convulsed with agony.

Skelly trembles and pulls away. He looks to his father, his eyes wide with surprise.

'It is not over yet,' Father says, without conviction.

Rosanna nods, reads on: 'They embrace again.'

She pulls Skelly back against her and he feels her legs shake. She bends to hold him.

> *The curtain in front of the arch is drawn aside and discovers a large balcony on which are displayed the Block axe and other apparatus for the execution. Oscar is removed by guards to balcony and prepares for death.*

Skelly breaks away from his sister and clasps his hands in prayer.

Rosanna's face takes on a savage grimace, and she seizes a stool between her hands to rock in a semblance of private grief: '*Oscar at length kneels and places his head on the block.*'

Duly, her voice breaks, and Skelly obeying the strictures of the script lays his head upon the stool. He feels uncertain. Will his parents cope with the distress of the warden *and* that of their own children? He sees Mother wipes her eyes with the back of her hand.

7 3

A DECEPTIVELY CRAVEN IMPULSE

Rosanna narrates with increasing fervour:

> *A convulsive shudder runs through the Warden's frame, as casting one look to Heaven and another on Oscar he waves his hand as the signal for Execution.*

She takes her father's shotgun from above the mantle and raises it above her head. Then, seemingly overcome by horror, casts it at his feet.

'It is just as I thought, he cannot do it,' Skelly cries, exultant.

'God will stay his hand,' says Mother, counting her beads in frenzy.

Rosanna returns from the doorway where she has rushed to gulp fresh air. 'Friends beat at the door.'

'And the mother too?' cries Mother.

'The crowd roars,' shouts Rosanna, whumping the bellows over the fire. Fanning her face, she rushes back to the door.

Skelly holds his hand over his mouth.

Mother leans forward, furiously rocking Blinnie. 'He must abide by the wishes of the people.'

Father throws back his drink.

Rosanna again takes the part of the warden: '*Back Back ye Rebel Slaves!*'

'The warden must be mad, Rosanna,' her mother cries. Alarmed by the ferocity of the playing, Hugh frets to be picked up, rubs his face against the side of his mother's neck. 'Should we not wait, Garrick, until the little ones are sleeping?'

Grim-faced, he demurs. '*Arragh* ... finish it now, Rosanna.'

His daughter reads:

> *Warden*   Nor think that I
> Can thus be bowed to yield me to your will—
> But even as the patriarch of old
> when called by Heaven to devote his Son,
> So I when honour prompts obey the call
> And thus as ministering priest fulfil
> The Sentence of the law!

'It is Abraham, his son laid out on the pyre before him, pleasing God,' says Father. 'Just the same.'

'It is not just God afflicts us, husband. But Cuchulain in battle, he too, knife at his son's throat, the son of himself and Aoife.' Mother holds her beads to her throat and flinches.

'Mr Geoghegan writes of Brutus. As does Mr Dickens in *Hard Times*,' says Rosanna, her voice harsh and cracked. 'At least, despite every provocation, our father has not killed Edwin.'

'Nor me,' Skelly quibbles at Rosanna's feet.

Father stands and waves his unlit pipe in their direction. 'Well that's grand. You have the better of me now.'

'Holy Mary, Mother of God, what would Father Woods be thinking of our entertainment?' Eilish claps her hand against her mouth. 'We must not mention it to him.'

'Mother, ask about the Lady Anastasia,' cries Rosanna. 'She is close by, carrying the Viceroy's pardon.'

'She will surely save him, at the most dramatic moment. I had forgotten her,' replies Eilish, relief flooding her face.

'Nothing can surpass this sensational scene,' says Rosanna, making her way to the window, where she again takes up Father's shotgun. 'Once more, the Magistrate tries to quell the disaffected crowd below the balcony—before he turns back to his son. '

Then in one swift movement, she brings down the butt of the weapon on Skelly, who screams and slides to the floor. He twitches and jerks his legs like an animal in the throes of death and then holds his breath as long as he can. Rosanna's shawl swirls in the air above him, shielding the gruesome imaginary sight from their mother. Then she flings it over the joists above her.

From behind this imaginary curtain, she staggers, holding the gun across her arms, like a supplicant weighed down by sin. '*I now am childless!*' Her voice is high-pitched.

Hugh howls.

Really, Rosanna goes too far, Skelly decides, staring up at her. She is like a woman possessed. Perhaps, after all, she will become an actress.

'I will play Anastasia as she approaches Oscar's bier.' Rosanna shrieks more wildly. Is she in complete control? And bends to Skelly, kissing his hand. Then dies, in spectacular fashion, at their Father's feet. Oh, it is cruel to strike at Mother's last hope in this fashion.

She croons as if her belly pains her.

Rosanna rises to deliver the benediction:

From his entrance the warden appears Completely overcome and stupefied by the accumulation of misery and remains motionless and seemingly unconscious.

Tableau

Curtains

End.

Rosanna swirls her shawl one last time, drags Skelly to his feet and curtsies.

Skelly notes his mother's righteous anger. Pacing back and forth, she crushes Blinnie against her chest, and periodically peers through the window into the darkness. 'I am wishing we had not brought on this performance,' she fires at her husband. 'None of us will sleep, due to the terror of its conclusion.'

'Why it is just a story,' says Father, 'and Mr Geoghegan has shaped it in his own way. He is not a Lynch.'

'He is but a convict, and a rogue,' says Rosanna. 'Mr Sutherland says so.'

'*His* father would not believe him so,' declaims Father. 'You bring powerful feelings to acting our story, girl,' he says turning to Rosanna, and clamping his hands around her shoulders.

'Stories are often about death, Mother. The ones you tell, as well,' says Skelly, now recovering. His face feels flushed and he prods at it with his fingers; then places his stool beside the table to lean over and kiss her.

'Well, and I know that, Skelly, and it is not surprising that a dreadful tale should follow us all the way from Galway, but we have stood by Edwin, at least, in this God-forsaken place.'

Father puts an arm around her. 'I am glad we came here, away from village talk. When I have my land, we will be free.'

'The story will not imprint on our hearts,' Mother murmurs to Skelly.

'No one will know *our* story,' he rues.

'That is not surprising. It is so dull,' says Rosanna, her face darkening.

'We are living it,' his mother soothes. 'We have Skelly's sketching book to remind us.'

'That is only for the eyes of the family,' snaps her son.

'And Father Woods, I believe,' Rosanna says. 'Perhaps you should remember *that* when you choose your subjects.'

She looks as if she wants to run away forever. Why does she never think of him? He is a Lynch son, after all. The play is more emotional for him. The performing of it has made the story powerful. It has shipped pain all around his body, set it throbbing in his knee joints.

74

THREE CONVERSATIONS AND A CLOSE CALL

A severe head cold keeps Rosanna home from work, and during that time Mr Ashby sends a message that he will not need her for several weeks while he drives a mob of cattle to Portland. Time drags uneventfully by as Rosanna reads the play and sleeps. Skelly ferries her warm tea flavoured with eucalyptus leaves, whistling again, as if over the last month his old life has been restored. Rosanna wishes she might comprehend a life so responsive to simple affection. Then feels ashamed.

When she finally returns to the station, she thinks the rooms have taken on a masculine appearance, evidenced by mice waltzing over dirty dishes and through breadcrumbs on the tables. Dust has blown through the loose shutters. Fires not laid, beds not made. She flicks her duster around a letter trapped beneath a crystal whiskey decanter on the credenza, unable to resist scanning its contents.

Although I did not write on your birthday, I drank your health, Mr Ashby Senior writes, instructing his son to *dig in, work harder, employ some Blacks*—and to persist, until his investment pays dividends. *As you have four thousand head of cattle, you cannot be worse off than your neighbours.* In the evenings *why not play the piano*, he writes, *or backgammon? Make a practice of writing home each Sunday. I am afraid that you have not put your mind to all that might be done. With best wishes, I remain, my dear William, your very affectionate father.*

Fathers can be so warm and firm with sons. And cruel.

She finds Mr Ashby at his desk—dealing with accounts. He barely acknowledges her. 'Have you heard, sir, from your wife?'

He nods, barely lifting his slumped head from the page of figures he labours over.

'Her father has recovered?' She finds herself unable to veer from this presumptuous conversational path.

'Evidently so.' He peers at her through a flop of unbarbered hair, as if she is a troublesome stinging insect that he is inclined to sweep from his desk in a fit of temper.

'The child is also well?' Rosanna's lip trembles. 'And your guests Mr Colyer, Mr and Mrs Brigstock and Mr Sutherland too?'

'Bertram has recovered from his ordeal,' Mr Ashby replies, scratching out a calculation with his nib.

'It was most stimulating to meet an actor,' she persists, unfastening the string of her bag.

'I have heard nothing from him. I doubt that we will see him again.'

Rosanna stiffens, feels blood rush to her face. 'And what of Mr Sutherland's play? Perhaps the Brigstocks think of attending. It is not far between Melbourne and Portland.'

'I dare say, eventually, they will.' He pushes away from the desk and shepherds her towards the door. 'Your father has no doubt told you that the station is on the market. It doesn't live up to its promise. I doubt that I will require your services much longer.'

He does not listen to *his* father. 'Well then, I thank you for your trouble. If you hear of another situation you may let my father know about it. Please convey my respects to your wife and the little one.'

Rosanna curtsies. It is no more than a game, to survive such hardness. She plods through the decimated flock of turkeys roaming free between the stables and the house and vomits in perfunctory fashion in a corner of the tack room. Aggravated Irish pride rises with her bile. For her wedding portion Maeve asks for a man without stinginess, without jealousy, without fear. Anastasia dies on the altar of Lynch pride. Feemy's speechless death commits her brother to the gallows. Grim life. All Rosanna asks is love and a play. And not to identify with Feemy's entire circumstances.

Yet more trials present themselves on her wild ride home: O'Leary, the corpulent bag of pus, stands his massive bay across the bridlepath, obstructing her way.

'And how is your beautiful self today?' He touches the tip of his whip to her shoulder. She spits on the ground before him. He seizes her arm.

'When Edwin comes home he will flay you, you lying *pishrogue*,' she curses, pulling free and hauling Glorvina up the small incline behind him. What a blaggard he is, the black ruffian! Her mouth is sour with all her disappointments. In her mind, she touches the soft pulse in the hollow of George's throat, the scatter of freckles on his forearms, and the curve of his lower back where his dress shirt billows. Blotting out the fleshy neck of O'Leary proves even more difficult when he hauls his horse around to grab her by the waist. She struggles against him, nails flying at his pocky face.

The sudden arrival of Father Woods surprises them both; O'Leary releases her and, in a weak attempt at dignity, dips his hat before he scarpers.

'Dismount for a moment, Rosanna, and calm yourself,' the priest begs, leading Glorvina to a large rock beside the track. 'Such an unpleasant scene. You should tell your father.'

'There is little point.'

'How are you going? Are you happy in your life?'

Rosanna considers this and tilts her head.

'You haven't been to confession for a while. Would you like to make it now?' His face is sweet and understanding, his voice quiet. Surely, he is the instrument of God. He never gets in a huff with her.

Rosanna kneels beside the rock, hands clasped—eyes downcast. 'Bless me, Father, for I have sinned. It is at least three months since my last confession.'

'Tell me what has been troubling you.'

She hesitates. 'I have impure thoughts. I want a man to touch me.'

'You must stop them. They could do you harm.'

'It is too late for that.'

'Did you go further?'

She nods.

'Resist the urges of the body. Love God. Do penance now. He will absolve you of your sin.'

She nods again.

'Do you want to confess anything more?'

'No, Father.' She thinks of George's month-long absence and O'Leary's homage and feels ill.

The priest blesses her and she is shamed by his beautiful eyes—enough to say three Hail Marys in a rush. On his way to Penola he will say a prayer for her. And she will make rapid and pointless calculations that portend her doom.

75

ROSANNA AND FATHER AT THE STILL:
LUCK DIES IN MY HAND

Father arrives home late from the town where he has been sent by Mother to purchase paper for a letter she will write to Edwin. Rosanna follows him to the still and places herself beside him on the rock near the water, her head between her knees. Her reflection tilts and swims.

'When you feel tired and crabbity you must also think of her.'

'I may be home to help sooner than you think. Mr Ashby is to sell the station and I am to be dismissed.'

Father raises his eyebrows and leans close, better to hear her words. 'He has said so?'

'Now that Mrs Ashby has left *him* he has no need for temperance in anything. His wife warned *me* not to tipple in her cellar but I swear he will drink it all before I get there!'

'Of course, we will miss the money.'

She sniffs.

'You have grown up, *mavoureen*, since the summer. Try to see it from a man's perspective. He must be lonely.'

She wants to say that men bring suffering on themselves but not while she plays at challenging Edwin's place in her father's heart. If he does not love her now that Edwin is disgraced, then he never will. 'Reading the end of the Lynch play was a terrible thing. Did the story hurt you when you heard it in Galway?'

'It is not the end of the story—only where Mr Geoghegan chose to end it.'

'What more could be of consequence? Oscar lies dead.'

'The death of your firstborn is a terrible thing. Imagine if you were the instrument.'

'I do not feel for the Magistrate. He is a fool of a man. Why should name matter before love?'

'Name and pride help families survive. He did not waver, even as he grieved. Cuchulain, too, slayed his son. Then took his sword and strode into the sea—mad with pain, like a speared bullock.'

'You know about the bullock?' Rosanna blinks and ducks her head. Oh what a fool she is—not to concentrate in conversation.

'William Ashby needs every one of his thousands of bullocks to thrive to repay his father's loan. Each dead one grieves him. I fear that the Blacks left in haste because of a problem with some cattle.' He stares into the fire. Perhaps the whiskey has also affected *his* concentration.

Rosanna changes tack. 'I am anxious about Moorecke's safety.' She bites her lip. 'I have not seen her or Jack for a long time.'

He places the back of his hand against her cheek. 'She will take her stories wherever she goes, just like Eilish.'

'I hear stories about *Booandik* falling ill. Dying.' She doesn't know why she tells her father this.

'Don't dwell on everything so much. You're worse than the poets. Everyone knows things they can't explain.'

She considers this. 'Mr Geoghegan's play is a tragedy, much like one of Shakespeare's. Oscar is doomed from the outset. His father's name is more important than his life. I hope Moorecke's fate will be different.'

He shakes his pipe from his pocket and taps it on the rock before him. Sucks on it and taps again. 'It was not the end of the Lynch tribe, as we know. Nor will it be the end of the *Booandik*.'

She hesitates. 'Edwin is lucky, Father. Luck dies in my hand.'

'I'm sure Edwin does not think so while under lock and key—you sound like Skelly. You'll be all right, Rosanna. I hope you will learn resilience. We're fools to think our lives should be better than anyone else's.'

She breathes slowly, placing her hand on the rock to steady herself. Lately her stomach churns.

'Where does Mr Geoghegan live? I should like to know why he wrote this play.' Father packs his pipe in his gloomy way. 'At least he did not make the magistrate a potato-head peasant with sprouting hair and seed-fested pockets.'

'Mr Geoghegan is raising money for a revival of the play in Melbourne and perhaps in Geelong; and Sydney where it has been wildly successful and acclaimed by all the critics. George says the man has had deuced bad luck, since he came out from Ireland. It is because of money troubles that the play's Melbourne season has been delayed. '

'George Sutherland, the actor?'

Rosanna looks away and then returns his gaze. When George sends for her she will take care of him in the cottage near his stables. And when investors in the play have signed off on their contracts, she and George will travel on the train together to dress rehearsals. Oh, if only she might play Anastasia! She must be careful not to let anything else slip to Father, who looks hard at her as if his thoughts commingle with hers. Guilt runs through her, as sharp as Cuchulain's sword. And a softer feeling that perplexes her.

She tilts her chin. 'If the play does not go ahead *we* can tell the magistrate's story. It is a shameful one, but, all the same, it is ours. We are nothing but actors in our own plays.'

'It is true. The Lynch story is uncomfortable, but we will bend it to our purpose. I doubt that it is true. Go tell your mother I'd like to have a drink with her beside the pond.'

He is bound to tell Eilish they can no longer depend upon their daughter's money. Heaping more shame on Rosanna.

76

AUGUST 1859: A SURPRISE VISITOR

Morning rain thrums on the roof. Wind rips up the surface of the pond. Skelly and Rosanna take turn about to bring damp rough-cut logs inside from the stack beside the stables. All day they huddle around the smoking fire. Mother picks weevils from the flour, her deft hands slapping the dough into a glistening ball. Rosanna, hair awry, smudges of ash from the fender darkening her face, shawl about her shoulders, tends a pot of broth while she reads her novel. *Dishabille*, she mouths, and *dissolute*. Skelly recites lines from the Lynch play, and prods at her foot with the poker, no doubt hoping to gain her attention. Mother begs her to read to the little ones, who sing-song over their fingers and toes, and roll tins across the dirt floor.

For two long days the weather holds them all to ransom. The days being short, but feeling long, they take early to their beds, piling on clothes for extra warmth, clinging to each other like human water-bottles. On the third night, when they fear the storm will never shift to the east, rivulets of water rush beneath the door. Rosanna tries to ignore the scrapings and howlings, the shriekings and creakings. She sleeps fitfully, lurching from one half-familiar nightmare to another. She gallops to her wedding on Lucifer, through the Woodford High Street and on to Loughrea; the scalloped train of her gown speckled with mud; her veil streaming behind her like that of a warrior queen—Maude's or Aoife's. George must send for her soon. She lies on her belly in the hayloft where he inveigles his way into the picture, loosening the ties on her gown, nibbling the base of her spine. She bucks and groans. Her father stalks them with a coil of hemp rope. Is it simply that George refuses to say his marriage vows, or has Edwin caused Father's ire? Her father plays the Magistrate of Galway, his face savage with anxiety. But then she dreams Moorecke running along the banks of the windswept pond, away from Mr Ashby, who is chasing her on horseback.

Rosanna sits bolt upright in complete darkness. It is a long moment before she remembers that George has gone: Edwin too, Moorecke and Lucifer. A schism of loss opens in her body. Blinnie cries out in bed and she goes to comfort her. Mother stirs. Hugh has found his way into the space Father usually fills, and sleeps with a hand on his mother's breast, a leg flung over her hip. It is a fitting night for loss. Is Father safely swagged down at a station? Rats squeal and scrabble, gnaw wood and nibble paper—pray God, newspaper plugs and not the manuscript, or the book by Mr Trollope. Truly, she has gone to hell in a bucket. Luck has deserted her.

She does not wish her crying to disturb Mother and the others. What should she do? Struggling from her bedclothes, she jumps up to wedge newspaper between the lintel and the wall, stepping along the planks Father has laid across the muddy floor. Dragging the chamber pot a few yards closer to the warmth of the dying fire, she tosses on wood with one hand. Draughts as cold as knives attack her bare legs; rain washes soot from the chimney onto the sulking coals; and her heart feels weighed down. If Irish ancestors come they will not stay long, the house being so poor with clothes drying before the fire and mice scurrying across the hearth. The dead—would they speak?

She crunches her body over the steaming pot, warming her thighs with her hands. Even after the job is done, her belly bloats. Wind whistles through the gaps in the walls. Her breasts ache. The last act of the play flutters on the table where Skelly has left it, weighed down by a candle in a can.

The sky splits open and eerie light floods the yard. Horses whinny. Rosanna moves to the window. Has Glorvina been spooked by the wind? Lucifer has been gone for weeks, and she has heard from Father that the darling thing won two Adelaide races and placed well in a third. It is a travesty of justice that he should show his mettle with a rider who was not a Lynch. Would selling him to the poet have been more satisfying? Does Edwin hear of Lucifer's success whilst languishing in his debtor's cell?

Sorely troubled she must be, conjuring Lucifer when surely, by now, he is on his way with George to Melbourne for the Champion Sweepstakes. She peers into the darkened yard, jerking back when a fist of thunder pounds the house. For a moment the wind drops and

she hears horses again. In the dark, she finds her feet like a tardy shepherd. The moon slides behind heavy clouds. Lightning splits a tree
like kindling, behind the hitching place. Something is happening in
the house yard—thieves or dogs? Nothing could prepare her for the
next shock when the moon reappears and bathes the yard in light. It
sends her crashing outside in boots and shawl.

77

LUCIFER RETURNED

Tears run down Rosanna's face as she squelches through the mud; for it is a miracle and must portend some good. Lucifer rears behind a fallen tree, the small dark figure of Moorecke clinging like a whelk to his neck. His feet land, jarring his rider, wildly scrabbling at his mane before she is thrown across the trunk of the fallen tree.

Rosanna searches for her in the wet darkness. Lucifer prances around the yard, then, dolefully, legs splayed, drops his head to bunt her. Her friend finds her feet.

Rosanna holds her hard against her chest. 'Are you hurt?' Rain runs down their faces.

Moorecke takes her hands to her temple and shakes her head. The horses jostle against each other in the mud. Lucifer barges between them, blood caked on his flanks, nosing Glorvina's tail, biting her back, as he attempts to mount her. She shunts him sideways. The stallion throws down his shoulders and jumps away, pawing the ground, ears twitching with aggravation.

'How did you come to be riding Lucifer, and where have you been?'

'Lucifer came dancing in the storm, past our *ngoorla*. He let me catch him with string. We've been camping back by Carratum, waiting to shear them sheep.'

Rosanna pushes wet hair from her face, brings a halter-rope over the bridge of Lucifer's nose, and fastens it. She croons and soothes and strokes, walking him around in circles as she guides him towards a post and rail. 'You caught him with just string and rode him home twelve miles? You one brave, *ngat-mal*.'

'I see him running. I feed him. On I hopped. Home he run.'

'I have been so worried about you since Mr Ashby smashed your *ngoorla*.' Rosanna points. 'He was cranky about that boy you rescued in the swamp. When I came to warn you, nothing. Gone.'

'*Bung bung*. Bullets all in the trees. Kicked up plenty of dust. Jack and me, we hide. Then we run to Kongorong.'

'I looked everywhere for you. I was afraid you'd been *kilt*.' Rosanna bites her lips in puzzlement. 'Why is Lucifer not with George?'

Moorecke shrugs. 'Lucifer belongs to Lynches.'

'Well darling he did, but Edwin, the right fool, sold him to Mr Sutherland. Lucifer has been winning races in Adelaide.'

Moorecke cocks her head, her mild eyes look doubtful. She shrugs again. 'Jack saw *oorincarto*, big ship, stuck on the rocks. *Coomimor paron*, white people, crying out and falling into the sea.'

Rosanna slaps her hands to her mouth. Nausea guts her.

'Men coming from every place—from Gambierton, Carratum—to help people caught on that ship.'

'And Lucifer ran from the sand hills? Is that what are you are saying?' Rosanna cannot think what it all means.

78

A DANGEROUS RIDE

'You must take me there, now. I will tell Skelly that there has been an accident.'

Moorecke shakes her head. 'Long way to me and Jack's camp. Maybe eight more miles to the wreck, Jack says. Lucifer all knocked up.'

'Glorvina, then.'

'No. She is too old, that mare. The sand will suck her off her feet. Water is flooding everywhere.'

'The stallion can do it. He has wonderful strength.'

Lucifer accepts the bridle and the bit, with sugar. He will not stand up politely for the saddle and swings sideways, throwing his head about. It takes ten minutes to manoeuvre him against the rail so that they can both leap on. Faint pink light suffuses the sky. Moorecke guides them around the swamps, along the banks of debris built up on the eastern sides, all the time coughing, coughing and prattling in Rosanna's ear about the significance of certain stars, about how she and Jack's family curl like lizards around the remnants of their campfire, and how above the wind they hear voices—'*oooaaaii*'—spirit ancestors.

Moorecke directs Rosanna due west. Up to his girth in water, skirting sink holes, Lucifer crosses deep bogs. They pass through long grasses, scrub and stands of black-wood. He takes logs in his stride with Moorecke jolting like a post office package, hands on his haunches, and Rosanna standing on the balls of her toes in the stirrups. They curve their backs against the stiff salt wind like crooked trees—like *carratum*, Moorecke says. A swamp harrier drops before them and screams as it rises, a scrabbling creature dangling from its talons.

White mist settles like a ration-blanket around their shoulders. They approach the sea, making their way with caution past sinkholes and through limestone-littered clearings. Sea heath and spear grass cling to the dunes. Lucifer begins to flag. Fingers stiff with cold,

Rosanna lengthens his reins. The hollow roar of the sea reminds her that she has seen these limestone cliffs undercut by ferocious waves on a ride with Edwin. 'I know this place. There is a spring.'

'No stopping here.' Moorecke lifts Rosanna's hair to bellow in her ear. 'Blackfellas' caves.'

'All caves, blackfellas'.' Rosanna's eyes try to penetrate the blur of fog and sand and scrubby trees. Yellow pollen stains the horse's neck where he has nosed his way through stands of early wattle. A channel overflows its banks and fans into the sea. Lucifer slips about on the rocky footing; the sound of surf is loud.

'Bad stories happened here. *Manyoon*, long ago, many *druel* die.'

They follow the path past the cliff-tops, curving around the bays and across two sharp points. Rosanna stops to listen to the sea, then turns north, resting Lucifer at frequent intervals while she shouts into Moorecke's cupped ear. Crests of sand hills collapse beneath his feet. He flounders in deep drifts. Rosanna slips sideways and Moorecke uses her shawl to haul her upright. 'Lucifer—he bucked near here.' Moorecke guides her along the sedge-tangled path between high dunes.

The fog breaks up; daylight seeps into the sky, casting pink and yellow rays over the low eastern hills.

Moorecke strains her ears over the crashing of the surf and the roaring wind; she listens, and nods. 'Tie him up now. We'll walk a bit more closer.'

'Should I not take you to your camp?'

'First see about that boat.'

They slide off and tether Lucifer to a tea-tree. Rosanna fossicks in her pocket for more sugar, then follows her friend through the dunes past clumps of bower spinach and spiky grasses. On the last sandy rise before the sea, they haul each other up to peer onto the beach. *Rasach*, it is a wild place and difficult to see through the curtains of spray, with sand whipping the beach, and fresh rain on their faces. A pitiful sight confronts them.

79

THE WRECK OF THE *ADMELLA*

Appalling enough to see a vessel, mostly obscured by the rising swell, and so stricken upon the reef that the mast and sail have been ripped asunder; but, most distressing of all, a man runs along the deck, his hands thrown in the air in wild gesticulation. The agony of his cries can be faintly heard above the wind tunnelling along the beach. Suddenly, he claps his hands to his head and throws himself overboard.

Rosanna clutches her belly and retches, grasps Moorecke's hand. 'He is *Booandik* man. Did you see?'

She shakes her head. 'Might be American whaler or sealer man.'

Holding each other up, they peer again over the dune grass. Split asunder, the deck of the ship is set at an alarming angle, and continually beset by waves. The sea bucks like a live creature, slurping and sliding, washing and sucking at the boat thrown up on the rocks. If only, in some miraculous way, it would withdraw, leaving behind sand mountains and the wrecked boat on rocks, the survivors could climb down and scramble to safety.

A horse's body lies sprawled on the beach. Rosanna begins to shake. Her mind turns over and over the single dreadful thought that, in plunging onshore, Lucifer has left behind George Sutherland, who must be one of the distraught people balancing on the rigging or clinging to the rails of the deck. All the while she had worried that he had jilted her—not a letter, nor a note to tell her how Lucifer had performed like a champion on the Adelaide track, nor any details of his departure for Melbourne to run the sweepstake—and now he may be trapped on a disintegrating boat in the worst imaginable weather.

Instinctively, she turns to the hillock behind them, where Lucifer stands tethered, back turned to the scouring wind. Two more fine horses graze in the tussocks beside the beach. Lucifer must have swum ashore with them earlier, led them perhaps, and found his way to Moorecke's camp. She drags her mind back to the main event.

'We must ride for help. People will die, if we don't.'

'Jack told me the policemen are coming and more boats.'

For hours Rosanna is transfixed by the horror. Moorecke curls up her long legs and falls asleep beneath the woolly tea-tree. Rosanna strokes her hair, easing her possum-skin cloak around her shoulders. If help is on its way, what harm is there in staying, while her exhausted friend rests? Lucifer lies on his side in the knoll of a sandhill, legs outstretched as if he is dead. Eventually, she hears the sound of horses approaching from the northeast.

A party arrives on the beach in a flurry of sand. Rosanna squints through the blizzard of spray and sand. It is not William Ashby but the manager of a neighbouring station, accompanied by several men, including her father, sucking his unlit pipe, hat pulled down hard on his dark head, long legs slapping around the girth of a small mount. Is it comedy or love that makes her cry over her father, a tall man, arriving on a donkey?

The men walk their horses along the beach, their heads turning in unison to survey the wreck and the flotsam and jetsam strewn along the shore, including the comatose horse. They dismount and struggle in the shallows in their high riding boots. Father stands apart. In his silent way he seems, nevertheless, one of a fellowship, in a way Rosanna had never imagined possible, but she must stay out of sight.

Within minutes a second party arrives, a dozen men on horseback, one carrying a doctor's kitbag. They light a driftwood fire and the men wave and shout and signal the wreck. The sea calms long enough to reveal crewmen waving a flag in frenzy. Rosanna stands up, hand shielding her face from the wind and grit, eyes drawn to the disastrous scene; stupidly, she has shown herself. She pulls back, too late to protect herself from her father's angry words, when he arrives beside her on the sand hill.

'Why are you here? Go home.'

She cowers.

'Men's business. The inter-colonial steamer. Nothing pretty about it. Git.' He glares at Moorecke, who has roused herself.

'Father, please.' She begins to cry.

'You'd rather be one of those little girls on the deck of the *Admella*, naked apart from their petticoats, I suppose, waiting for the next wave to take you to God.' How distressed he sounds.

And, indeed, she can just make out the shape of a small poorly-clad woman swaying against the rails. 'We will go.'

'How did you get here?'

'I rode.' She gulps. She cannot say the word: *Lucifer*. Filaments of cloud wreathe the moon. She waits while Moorecke picks up her digging stick and skin bag. 'We have to go.' Father retreats to the beach. For all his tiredness, Lucifer pulls himself up from his knees.

The *Booandik* shearing camp is small: half a dozen huts clustered beneath paperbark trees. Jack emerges wearing a trailing overcoat and a knitted hat. He shouts at Moorecke and points in the direction they have come from. Three or four children run out to take her hand. Rosanna's belly hardens in sympathy. She hugs her hard, thinking of the bones in the cave, as she helps her slide from the horse.

'After shearing we come back to smoke eels at *Ngaranga*. When the sun is hot again,' Moorecke says.

'I will see you here before that. I cannot stay away.'

A CATASTROPHIC WEEK

Rosanna feeds and waters Lucifer, checks a superficial cut on his foreleg. When she removes the saddle he shakes himself and rolls in the mud. She limps to the house and crawls into her bed, whispering to Skelly, 'Lucifer has come home. He has swum off a great boat in the storm. Do not tell Mother, yet.'

In the late afternoon Father shakes her awake. 'Explain yourself.'

She seizes his hand. Tears trickle down her face. 'Moorecke found Lucifer and took me to the wreck.' She holds up her hands in helplessness.

'What has the horse to do with this disaster?'

'He ran to the *Booandik* camp near Carratum. You saw the horses at the wreck. Do you remember that Mr Sutherland was taking Lucifer to Melbourne? Pray to God *he* travelled ahead.'

'Don't concern yourself with him, girl. Not one of those people deserved their fate. More'n a hundred men are gathered on the beach, hoping to rescue survivors before they die of thirst and cold.'

It is best that Father never understands. She keens a moment, feels faint. 'Will they get them off Carpenters Rocks? The water is so rough.'

'I'm leaving again now, to help take the station dray and the life boat from the lighthouse to the wreck.' He shakes his head and turns towards the door. 'Tether the horse behind the pond and take care of him. I'm not sure when I'll be back.'

When he returns, hours later, he is falling-down tired. He and the station men have seen the dray safely to the beach, at three o'clock in the morning, on the authority of Mr Ashby's pocket watch. They have remained on the sand, anxiously watching until morning, when a small steamer comes close to the wreck but is unable to effect a rescue. During the day several passengers have died, either by toppling overboard or making desperate attempts to take themselves ashore.

Grey-faced and tired, Father whispers confidences to Eilish. Men's business, Rosanna thinks, straining to decipher details, yet something he cannot bear alone. She prays and prays to the Holy Mother that if George is among the passengers he will be rescued.

Next morning she rises early and prepares food for her father. 'Please let me come with you today.'

'It is only men on the beach, doing dangerous work.'

She drops her head. 'Is there any news?'

'Two crewmen from the *Admella* made it through the surf on Monday and raised the alarm at the lighthouse.' Father sucks harder on his tea.

'Did the storm drive the ship onto the rocks?'

'It has been said that a horse fell in his stall. By the time they righted him with ropes they lost sight of the coast in the dark and the boat foundered.'

'Lucifer was among the racehorses.'

'Yes, I think so.' He looks severely down his nose at her. She knows that he thinks of Edwin. 'It is the horse that *you* should be concerned with. Take care of him for your brother and leave saving souls to men.' Inexplicably, his face softens, and he reaches out to touch her hair.

She smiles thorugh her tears. 'It was such a blessing to see Moorecke riding him in on Monday night, but you know that Mr Sutherland bought him off our Edwin. And it was Mr Sutherland that kindly allowed Skelly and me to copy out the Lynch play.'

'Well and I can't be sure if that particular thing has had such a good effect, but I wouldn't be hoping a man would drown for the trouble he took stirring the hearts of my children. I heard Ashby talking about the owner of some of the racehorses, and an Irish groom accompanying them, but he didn't mention Sutherland. Nor Lucifer. No doubt, in time, a passenger list will be published.' He places his tin plate on the table and wipes his mouth. 'I can't take you, *alannah*. Stay and help your mother.'

An hour after her father leaves, halter in hand, she skirts the house and Mother cries out to her from the leek-bed, 'Where are you going, girl?'

When she canters out of the yard on Lucifer, she swings her head and sees her mother watching.

WHERE IS GEORGE?

Rosanna is not the only rider on the *boreen*. On the heath she thinks she approaches the poet but it is difficult to see in the dark. Edwin told her that Gordon had been seen with a married woman in Gambierton, but he has shown not the slightest interest in Rosanna since their encounter in the sand hills. George would never speak to the poet about her—surely.

Creamy tea-tree blossoms fall, washed by rain. Wattle drifts on the wind. The man, after all a stranger, lifts his hand, grim-faced, his face slick with rain; they are both preoccupied. People are drawn to the Carpenters like flies to a wound. Crouching in the dunes, she observes stockmen clustered around the large bonfire, fed by driftwood and despair. A young Livingstone Black in stockman's hat and torn velvet trews takes care of the horses. She has seen him with Moorecke at the camp.

Hope flares and dies with every failed rescue attempt. Rosanna watches, curls her nails into her palms and rocks her body to the eerie sound of the flightless bristle-bird—*reeor, reeor, reeor*—rising from sand gullies.

Each day her father has returned with new horror stories, whipping like wildfire through station communities, about survivors trapped on the truncated deck—starving, dehydrated, demented by exposure to the elements. Cries can be heard from shore. It is increasingly difficult for Rosanna to slip away in the bright moonlight, past her mother, who rolls and groans in her sleep at every creak. Each morning more passengers fail to survive the bitter night. Boats go out. Boats come in. The coast community weather-watches. Father intones bylines from torn out pages of the *Register*, reporting that crowds weep in the capital cities and both Houses of Parliament—in Adelaide and Melbourne—adjourn.

One night, Rosanna dreams that Lucifer swims with a rider between the waves, foam glistening on his powerful shoulders, sand matting his mane. 'Wait,' she cries, for it is George's head she sees, bobbing red and blotched by wind and weather, holding the Geoghegan manuscript above his head. Even as he is swamped by waves, and sinks below the surface, he manages to keep his sheaf of papers aloft—the fool. In her dream Rosanna reels from the sand hills, and is swept from her feet in the surf. But she rights herself and staggers on, her skirts tangling around her knees. Once she sights George beyond a line of breakers, then he dips from sight. He sinks and rises. Splutters. Petrels cry on the wind.

Mother hauls her upright, shushing her mouth with the palm of her hand.

'I was in the water, Mother, with George and Lucifer.'

'Rest. The wreck is playing havoc with everyone's imagination. I don't know how your father bears it, or the other men.'

'I was reading the play with George.'

'What a fool you were to be doing that,' Mother snaps. 'Even in a dream.'

'But I love him.'

'Is that right, Rosanna?' Her mother sweeps wet clothing from the floor beside the bed and sharply cracks it like a whip.

'I love him more than Ireland.'

'Enough of your wild talk.' She purses her lips with worry. 'Nothing can be done if the man has drowned. Prayer is all you have. Keep away from the whiskey now.'

Rosanna claps her hand against her head and throws herself onto the sham to wail. It dawns on her that she is never going to be an actress. Nor ever go to Melbourne. How can she ever explain the worst of it to Mother? Soon she won't be able to dissemble over her mortal sins.

82

DANGER ON THE HEATH

Father is coughing up phlegm and Mother withdraws to her corner by the stove. Rosanna hears them, spitting at each other like cats.

'I fear for her.'

'She'll be all right.'

'You must speak to her.'

'It will work out, Eilish. Leave her alone.'

Rosanna grinds her teeth. All week she has ridden out in the full-moon light rinsing the Carpenters, managing to stagger home before her father. Even so, shameful apparitions leap from the shadowy landscape. She is afraid to go, afraid to stay at home. She thinks of the bats in their torpor, safe in their winter caves. Only foolish humans push against the elements. Father brings news from the would-be rescuers on the beach and those in boats, and from more newspapers passed hand-to-hand around the bonfires fed to blazing heights, to lift the morale of the survivors. They can only bear witness.

On Thursday, a telegram bungle results in the *Havilah* steaming from the port of Adelaide to Melbourne instead of the Carpenters, abandoning the passengers to their fate.

'Those fools in Adelaide have failed us,' shouts Father. 'Secession is the only way. Only Victorians can save the day.' On Friday, all hope is dashed when he brings home the news that the Victorian Premier, an Irishman no less, has refused to underwrite a rescue. 'They are between an Irish devil and the deep blue sea,' he moans. 'And our own Parliament hovering over the wrong telegrams, looking after their friends in the city and ignoring the poor suffering beggars on the boat?' Meanwhile, a pilot boat from Guichen Bay battles the waves, approaching the wreck, again and again. They will never reach it unless the rough seas subside.

Returning home late at night on Lucifer, Rosanna surprises

O'Leary making water behind an acacia. 'Riding at night don't signify,' he sneers at her, clutching his pants with one hand.

She raises her crop to him and digs in her heels.

'I still recognise that stallion of your brother's,' he shouts. 'There'll be questions. Mark my words. Unless we talk.'

Lucifer obliges her with a show of silliness, rearing before he bounds past. It is a pretty pickle she is in. Will O'Leary peach? Cream light shafts the sky. Rosanna arrives home and falls fully clothed onto her bed. O'Leary, ham-fisted, fat hairy-*bod* dangling from his trews, chases her from one dream to the next until, flailing and sweating, she shudders awake, pulling her night wrapper around her.

On Saturday, despite high seas, the Portland Lifeboat rescues nineteen passengers from the wreck, one a woman: a little Irish girl, journeying to her sister in the goldfields. Tales abound of the rescue; enough men gathered around the bonfire on the beach to form a government, and Rosanna does not know why they don't form their own, instead of relying on Mr O'Shannassey and the colonial government of Victoria.

No survivor lists include George Sutherland. It seems that he did not accompany Lucifer on the boat that sank. Or, if he did, and an agent failed to record his name, only sharks will know of his friendly disposition. But she refuses to be convinced by the government reports, newspaper stories or shipping logs which are, after all, written down by men like O'Leary, and not to be relied upon.

After supper she makes her way to the pond and smokes a pipe with her father while he pours and measures at the still. 'O'Leary saw me on Lucifer last night. He threatened me.'

'He did not touch you?'

'No he did not.' She gulps. 'If only Edwin were here.'

'Edwin.' Father shakes his head disparagingly. 'I am no horse thief but I see no harm in lying low, at least until we know the facts. Hobble Lucifer in the scrub. Do not ride out on him and O'Leary'll not bother you.' He strokes the curve of her elbow and drops his great high forehead against hers. His eyes hold her. In his fearsome way he loves her.

It sorely grieves her that while Edwin is detained at her Majesty's pleasure Father has paid off his debts and leased his bullocks back to that pustule head O'Leary. Losing Edwin's salary has near driven them to the wall even without his debts. Oh yes, her brother is lucky. What a fool to trust the filthy *gombeen*. Father Woods has asked the policeman in Gambierton to keep an eye on O'Leary's activities at the bay. Meanwhile, Rosanna is left behind with the crows and dingoes, a shattering sense of loss, and her growing shame.

83

REVELATIONS AT THE PENOLA RACES

Three months later, Edwin completes his sentence and rides home, surprisingly subdued. He puts down his head and works to repay Father, who needs the money back for land of his own—a government block in the Hundred of Caroline, all he can afford. Rosanna follows them to the creek and eavesdrops on their conversation about Mr Ashby. They speculate on the bleakness of his mood, as he battles to rid his stock of coastal fever and cattle tic, and spends his lonely evenings pining for his wife. Men-folk of Gambierton know that William Ashby cannot find a buyer for his run, and that he drinks enough muscat to refloat the boat that brought Lucifer home to the Lynches.

Rosanna has more pressing concerns. During daylight hours she mopes in her mother's shawl, as she has every day since the week of the wreck. She patches splits in her dress and dreams of running away from black shadows biting at her heels. Every day she imagines a letter arriving from George inviting her to join him in Esperance, or Moreton Bay, or Melbourne. She takes long rides Carratum-way to see Moorecke; many of her people are ill.

Chores half-done, or not at all, incite her mother to reprimand her. Worry etches lines deep into her face. 'And what if someone sees you on that horse? What does your brother say?'

Rosanna shrugs. 'Lucifer does not belong to Edwin any more. Let him say one word to me.'

'Your reputation will be in shreds, and I blame you for bringing home that dreadful play and souring Skelly's mood. If only Father Woods could pay another visit. There must be a nicer play about Walshes.' Mother tugs at Rosanna's clothing, and when her daughter steps back, resisting her, she turns away frowning. 'Oh, the weather is so drear.'

'Skelly follows me everywhere with his damned sketchbook.'

Mother turns away.

Skelly's reproachful looks weigh Rosanna down—and his veiled threats. Was he worse when she worked at the Big House every day? Father Woods has invited her to confess again, although he doesn't know the worst thing.

To please Edwin, Rosanna enters the ladies' race at the picnic race meeting. She will not let him or Lucifer down again. Riding is the only thing that makes her feel like her old self. Fleeing around a racetrack, she leaves her troubles behind.

When she takes the lead this time, there is no rush from the course and no fighting before or after the race. Although she fears that someone will come forward to claim the horse, it is especially satisfying to win. On account of Mr Gordon away training a horse for Mr Livingstone, Edwin wins well on Lucifer, too.

The sun sparkles on the sea, warming her back and lifting her spirits. For a moment she forgets the events of the past months—it is only a moment. Draping her plaid carefully around her shoulders, she edges closer to a conversation between Edwin and Mr Ashby. It is the first time she has encountered her employer in months, although he pays her scant attention. She clutches her brother's arm, and over the thrumming of her heart she hears Mr Ashby's careless words.

'Charming man, George Sutherland,' she hears him say. 'No doubt his absence from the stage will be mourned.'

Something hard and indigestible lodges in her gullet.

Edwin nods, glancing across at Lucifer. There is always a point to the peregrinations of Mr Ashby's conversations.

'I see you have his horse, Edwin. I heard that, while in Adelaide, George stabled it with Magarey's stallions. Magarey, Fisher and Rochfort planned to attend the Champion Sweepstake in Melbourne. Alas, Fisher, Magarey, and his groom perished in the wreck.'

Rosanna forces herself to pay attention. Her chest tightens. Dust motes float in the air before her. She squints and blinks into the glittering sunlight.

Edwin nods. 'Someone brought the horse to us, found him running wild.'

'It is most peculiar. Sutherland was not initially listed on the passenger list, nor has he identified himself as a survivor. He may have travelled under Magarey's name. Boarded late, perhaps. In any case, arrangements have been made for his wife.'

It is possible that Rosanna will expire from shock as quickly as a bird smoked slamming into Moorecke's net.

'George was damned keen to run him in the sweepstake—thought him a dead-set walloper.'

Edwin shakes his head as a tide of details swamp Rosanna; she flounders in the backwash. Perhaps she will swoon. It is as if she doesn't exist. George is married. George *was* married. She feels her knees dissolving.

'Look after the horse for now,' says Mr Ashby. 'As you know, I am planning to finish up my business here, sell the station lease and join my wife in Tasmania. I have received a letter from an attorney representing Sutherland's wife. She and his parents have heard nothing from him since he landed in Adelaide. They read all the newspaper reports about the boat going down, never dreaming that he might be on board. But with the passage of time ... the presence of the horse is, of course, rather damning: *ipsa loquitur*. Not a trace of Sutherland can be found, and, despite advertisements, no correspondence. If Providence divines it so, he may turn up in another colony. I will write to them about the horse, but the wife may not be in fit condition to make an immediate decision. Quite understandable.' Mr Ashby strokes his beard in a ponderous way. 'He won well today.'

Mr Ashby gazes over Rosanna's head. Is he watching the shags drying their wings on the rocks beside the track? Does he bear her a grudge for attempting to protect Moorecke, or is it simply that she no longer works at the Big House and has become invisible? Well, that is how she likes it, and the curse of Cromwell upon him. No wonder his wife left him. She knows he looks down his long nose at Edwin. 'Your business seems to be picking up,' he adds.

Edwin assents. 'We would be glad to agist him for the moment, until the Sutherlands make arrangements.' He leans up against Rosanna.

Oh he is bold; there is no doubt about that. Rosanna wants to hug him. He tightens his hold on her arm to perambulate her away. Even while Mr Ashby patronises him, he appears, on the surface, solicitous. And he is not long returned from the Adelaide jail. It is the way of men.

George has a wife—it cannot be true. Did he not love *her*? She flattens her hand against her belly. Lucifer remains and George has disappeared. Lynches survive to tell the tale. It is the way of things. In the end, Lucifer will make his way to Melbourne to George's family, of that Rosanna is sure. But he has left behind a problem.

The heat beats down on her head. A buttery haze has settled on the hills behind the bay. Her mouth dries and she gulps the salt breeze. The green ribbon on her hat flutters in front of her eyes, as pressure builds in the back of her head. Light fractures into shards of dazzling colour.

Images of George disrupt the pattern of her thoughts. In pirate smock he swordfights to save the Lynches' honour; he opens his mouth on the flesh of her hip. Rosanna rides along the banks of the Shannon, crosses the bridge into Tipperary. She rocks on the balls of her toes—heel toe, heel toe. Mrs Ashby waltzes past in the lemon gown. The poet babbles. Moorecke runs through the scrub and Skelly limps behind. Arms outstretched, Mother leans over the rail of a ship slipping on the tide.

Rosanna's body sags, a hand grips her arm—Mr Ashby's? Would *he* step forward to catch her? Edwin slides an arm around her waist. His shrewd eyes bore into hers the moment before the black closes in, and she goes down like a packet of salts.

84

MARCH, 1860: THE SCORPIONS OF REMORSE INVADE MY BREATH

Edwin brings bird samples wrapped in squares of muslin and scented by rosewater, which does not do much to disguise their odour. The last, an emu wren, its feathers smudgy blue and rust coloured, is missing a leg. Swatted by a swamp dog perhaps.

Skelly unwraps the gifts tenderly, splays their fragile skeletons on pond stones and works with his pocket knife to free them from meaty rot. He stuffs their chests with patchwork scraps and sutures them back together with silk. He knows that, really, Kitty sends the birds. Edwin's general tardiness may explain the advanced stink of the carcasses.

Lately Edwin craves praise. He affects seriousness when carrying out the simplest tasks at home. Anyone can coddle an egg, Skelly thinks. Much has changed since the wreck. The townships have grown, offering his brother more chance to tender deals and then to tear up the paper on which they are written when they no longer suit him. In wondrous acts of theatre, bragged about at home, Edwin stands on his dig. Idiots populate the south-east, Edwin says, who want the shirt off his back. Money is as short as ever for Lynches. He continues to court Kitty at a new hotel, the first built from stone at Port MacDonnell.

But she is not the only girl to catch his eye. Skelly has always known about this. At midnight rooster-crow one night, he has sneezed whilst stowed away in Edwin's cart: an unwitting witness to his brother wrestling on the balcony with a stout, yellow-haired girl. In fierce temper she had pushed Edwin in the chest, without a wink at Skelly peeping from beneath a large paulin. The rotund publican arrived shouting. Down the verandah posts shimmied Edwin. All the way home, his brother had berated him.

'Please, Edwin, allow me to help with your accounts. I want so much to be useful.'

'Ask me when you understand more being a man.'

Skelly strikes the side of the cart.

For a little while, when the actor left, Rosanna had been affectionate with him again. Now she avoids them all. Yesterday he found her panting on her knees at the edge of the pond, head hanging over the water, and when he rushed towards her, she had waved him off. He is sick of her preening in front of her reflection.

Blinnie and Hugh inhabit their own world, playing by the pond and in the bush behind the house. For him, nothing changes. Months go by. His heart lurches as he crosses to the rear window after dusk.

Since the wreck, six months ago, he cannot help but listen for horses in the night, thus he is not particularly surprised now to see Moorecke leading Glorvina down the hill towards the house, and Rosanna slouched over in the saddle. They have been to the shore perhaps. Rosanna will smell of crayfish pulled by Moorecke from crevices between the rocks. Or fiery crabs. It is jealousy he feels, imagining them watching the tide, building up a steaming fire between the dunes, laughing their heads off as they smash the red shells and suck out delicious meat. It has been months since his sister thought of him, and yet he loves her more than ever.

In fact, Rosanna has been missing all day. Early in the morning he saw her trudging past the pond in the direction of the horse yard, head down, Mother's cloak with the claddagh brooch fastened around her shoulders. Lately, Rosanna reads and reads, as if the real world has lost all meaning. As if she is waiting for something to happen.

It is the disappearance of the actor, Skelly is sure, that is the source of her pain. Rosanna begins to resemble *Booandik* women he has seen on market day in Gambierton, stumping about in outsized overcoats, on the edge of the boggy rutted streets. Oblivious to the rising miasma of cattle dung and mud, Rosanna often forgets the one item she has been sent for. At home she creeps about the house, rarely washing or changing her clothes. Over the summer she's been missing from the house—from early morning until late at night. Perhaps she hunts with Moorecke. It seems that no one can stop her doing anything she likes.

He has become so accustomed to her absence that he no longer reaches out to place his hand on her shoulder in the night and share his confidences with her. Nothing has been the same since she stopped working at the station and went back to drifting into the bush, whey-faced, deaf to everyone's requests. Now she rides Lucifer late at night, jumping big timber—hoping she'll die, so she says when he confronts her. Perhaps another fight will erupt between Rosanna and Edwin about Lucifer losing condition. But Lucifer is the kind of horse that can win a steeplechase at Lake Hawden and gallop home again. And it is none of Skelly's business.

Nor is the Melbourne newspaper cutting that he carries in his pocket, passed to him that morning by his brother on a lightning visit. 'It was given to me by William Ashby,' Edwin said. 'Tell her gently.'

So Skelly waits to disclose to Rosanna the news that the planned Melbourne performance of *The Hibernian Father* is once again cancelled, this time because George Sutherland is missing, and that members of the Sutherland family had been asked by police to view a badly decomposed body dragged from the River Torrens, a knife lodged in its spine. He will withhold the most important information because he doesn't want to hurt his sister. Does Rosanna know that George Sutherland was married? Why can't she be happy? The Lynches have Lucifer back and Mr Geoghegan's play.

Pulling on his boots he goes out to greet her riding in, lifts his hand to Moorecke leading Glorvina. Blood trickles down the mare's back. Have they fallen? His sister lurches forward in the saddle. 'Rosanna,' he hisses, clutching her leg. 'Where have you been? Is Glorvina hurt? Are you?'

She makes a feeble attempt to stay upright, cradling a bundle of clothes in her arms. He tries harder to steady her but she fends him off, her brow tight-knitted with concentration.

Moorecke reaches past him to help his sister down. 'No, Skelly boy.' There is blood on the possum-skinned cloak slung around her shoulders. She turns back to him, the whites of her eyes shining in the dark, her expression tender and angry at the same time.

Rosanna slides to the ground in a heavy way, favouring the bundle in her arms. Moorecke half catches her and breaks her fall. Skelly scarce hears his sister's hoarse whisper over the susurration of the trees. 'Skelly, it's all right I am. I've been at the cave. The moon lit everything up outside and in the main chamber. I wish you could have been there.'

Skelly looks askance at her. Is she drunk? Then she almost faints, black cloak outstretched, landing like a large bat, prostrate on the path. Glorvina stands over her, legs akimbo, eyes gentle as she drops her head and blows into Rosanna's face.

Moorecke struggles to tidy the layers of clothing flapping around his sister. A gurgling cry fills the space between them. He thinks of the bats roiling in and out of the cave for food, of the tiny white bones in the aperture, of owls barking, and dogs howling in the bush outside. In trying to make sense of it all, he thinks that, after all, his sister must be fitting, and he runs to fetch his mother.

When he returns, Moorecke lifts the skin cloak higher, releases Rosanna into Mother's arms and leads Glorvina away. Inside, Mother settles Rosanna into a chair and stokes the fire to warm her. Skelly is sent to mind the little ones at the front of the house, where Hugh is wheezing like a possum. At least an hour goes by before the little boy has fallen asleep in his arms and Father joins the women inside. Skelly hears the rising and falling of their voices. He must not take the newspaper clipping to his sister now.

'We should have kept to ourselves,' Father cries.

'I should have done the same when I met you, you fool of a man,' Mother yells back.

Through the bedroom window, Skelly sees his father leave the house, clutching his pipe and tobacco as he stomps towards the pond. Father crying. Over the chittering of night birds and beyond the verandah he hears Moorecke exclaiming *Aiigh* in her sympathetic way. Animal sounds cause him to clutch the soft little bodies next to him. Hugh coughs and coughs, as if he will never right himself, and Blinnie snuggles up against him. They throw themselves from side to side, roll their eyes at him, and eventually turn back into peaceful sleep. Sweet Virgin of God, he is always the watcher but now he sees. Before dawn, he rises to make water behind the house.

Father comes weaving from the pond, knocking into Skelly. Has he been out all night? Turning in a fury he clips his ear. 'Agh, Skelly, you're always in the way,' he roars. Wounded, Skelly slides off into the trees.

In the morning, if she is well enough, he will tell Rosanna that a Mr Magarey loaded Lucifer onto the *Admella* at the dock because George was late. The body pulled from the Torrens did not belong to the actor.

She is bound to turn to Skelly and confide in him. He will not tell her about the wife yet. Later, when he thinks back over the events of the night, he supposes that the actor tore out Rosanna's heart—because he stayed so long in Adelaide and never sent for her. He is probably drowned. He mulls on this with sweet satisfaction.

Skelly broods. Watches. Slow to act. When should he speak to her? He waits for his sister to remember his existence. Each morning, an unnaturally persistent curlew cries from the scree on the eastern side of the pond and Rosanna rushes from the stables, where she has taken to sleeping in Edwin's old box bed; shunning the house. Even at a distance, she looks such a fright, her body heavy under layers of clothing and a cloak, dark circles under her eyes, a bundle hooked under her arm. Her bitten lips offer the slightest softening of expression when she turns to wave, flapping her hand as casually as a card shark.

She catches and leads Glorvina towards the first glimmers of sunlight on the water's surface. Next, he sees her bent over, atop the mare's broad back, reins loosely knotted at the pommel, Moorecke astride behind her, visible only from the waists up above the line of reeds. Her posture bunched and sloppy, riding side-saddle—a new habit. The old mare plods through a gap in the bush, her mammoth hips undulating, away from the house. Skelly does not know their destination—Moorecke is distinctly unwelcome at the Big House, perhaps Rosanna too. On principle he will not follow them.

All day, he listens for the sound of Glorvina whinnying or clomping through the reeds, signalling Rosanna's return. After supper when the light has gone, his sister reappears alone, munching singed meat that reeks of eucalyptus smoke, out of her kerchief. He recognises the top note smell of echidna. She really has become a savage.

Skelly suspects their parents no longer allow Rosanna inside. What can she have said to Mother? Edwin is equally scarce of late, choosing to frequent Miss Lallah's most nights unless he is collapsed with exhaustion. Skelly supposes that he has run out of money again but has persuaded Kitty to lie down with him in sympathy as often as he pleases. This thought evokes an immediate response in him and he fidgets with his fly buttons or simply rubs himself against the verandah post like Lucifer, yearning for the sweet sensation that promises some kind of freedom.

Since their final reading in the kitchen, he no longer studies Mr Geoghegan's play, now entirely transcribed in his sketchbook. Why should he care about it when Rosanna does not? The death of the boy in the play brings him very low. Does he not know, now, everything there is to know about Lynches in Ireland? But not about those who fled Galway for South Australia.

PART 4

SKELLY'S LIFE TAKES A TURN (1864)

8 5

APRIL

Skelly wakes to a brittle blue sky and shards of ice on the grass, re-membering that on his way to Melbourne Father Woods will visit Gambierton to meet with the new priest. It is of little consequence, for the Lynch family will not attend mass. They keep to themselves. They will wait as they always do for a priest to visit them. Skelly longs to talk with Father Woods. For four years he has floated through days and nights like a sleepwalker, knowing only that the world continues to spin, taking him with it.

He is not the only young man whose plans have come to nought. His envy of the Galway Irishman Robert Burke and his companion William Wills setting off from Melbourne's Royal Park, crossing the interior from south to north, swiftly faded to disappointment when the expedition was unsuccessful: two young men dead and buried. But he wished that he had done something equally interesting. Any-thing. Skelly knows things now; knowledge burns inside him. For he is past fifteen years, frustrated, stuck. Living an unnatural life.

The last few winters have been the wettest on record, with bullocks bogged and ducks and geese skittering across the main streets of the town. Hugh wheezes through each day; indeed, on profile his chest is marked by a pan-shaped depression below his ribs that makes him look deformed and thin. Yet, unlike Skelly and Rosanna, he is cheer-ful. Father worries, snapping at him to clear the decks, cough it up, the filthy stuff that obstructs his breathing.

Sometimes Edwin acts so jubilant that Skelly needs to leave the room. A causeway has been built across MacDonnell Swamp and there is no doubt that his brother's carting business has benefitted. Now perhaps Father can put more money towards buying land for Mother. Skelly wonders whether Edwin should propose to Kitty before he has no choice in it. She has waited an interminably long time already.

Mother and Rosanna fuss and quarrel over Arlen, for that is what they had named the baby, now a sturdy three-and-a-half-year-old with a face like an angel. Blinnie, at seven, resembles Rosanna, with her ring of toffeed curls, streaked with the blonde remnants of babyhood; with her keen brown eyes; with her strong legs clenching the girth of her pony; with her temper. Skelly watches her now, leaning forward over the stove, wielding a wooden spoon in a preserving pan of lilly pilly jam. Mother relies on her more and more because Rosanna is useless for weeks at a time. Vacillating moods govern her demeanour. She rides wildly around the district day and night, or casts dark looks from the high branches of elderly gums, or lies mute and senseless in her bed, refusing even Arlen's affections. Father has struck her with a willow switch to no avail. In her own time, she calms, but then it all starts over again.

Meanwhile, Skelly eavesdrops on his parents' conversations; he reads the newspaper. He knows that Mr Geoghegan's play ran at the Prince of Wales theatre in Sydney and at the Royal Haymarket in Melbourne. He knows that George Sutherland's wife has recently died of a diarrhoeal disease and he cannot decide whether to tell Rosanna. Lately she has confided more in him. He prays that the actor's parents drop their claim on Lucifer so that they can forget the year George came and went, and they can all get on with their lives. Perhaps they will come asking questions about Arlen.

Mr Gordon is married and lives not five minutes' ride away at Dingley Dell. Once, Rosanna broke her girth strap on the clifftops where the poet was exercising his dogs and he led her to his cottage to repair it. There she met his small, kind wife, who pressed tea and oatcakes upon her, telling her that her husband was writing a novel but that his spirits were low. Rosanna should have been excited about the book. Skelly doesn't know why his sister cares that Gordon acted terse, abandoning her in the kitchen like that, for she must understand his moods, they so closely resemble her own. Day after day she cannot rise from her bed to help their mother. Some things are unfathomable to Skelly. Sometimes he thinks he should have been born a girl in order to understand feelings.

He is filled with shame and loneliness so profound that he

understands why Rosanna harms herself. His skin feels crusty under his nails—he must not abrade it and risk infection or bleeding—his clothes stink of mildew and various other unmentionable excretions that he has neglected to remove. The droppings of various creatures driven inside to shelter from the cold so pervade the house that the smell no longer makes him nauseated and he merely sweeps them sideways with his hand. His tooth aches. Even should a travelling dentist arrive in Gambierton, the risk of bleeding after the tooth is pulled would be too high. He moans and drops his head.

Today nothing will divert him. Father Woods will likely berate him for neglecting his prayers. But has he not been trapped inside, living the life of a girl: kneading his mother's bread dough on a slice of contoured red gum, carrying water from the pond, reading stories to the little ones? Sketchbook in hand he creeps to his bed place.

Late in the afternoon, Mother rouses him up to shear matted curls sticking to his forehead and hanging limp on his dirty collar. A few clippings slip inside his shirt and add another layer to the prickling surface of his skin. Trailing his blanket, he hauls himself shivering to the pond, where he hangs it on a tree branch before sluicing icy water over his shoulders. Then he dips the rest of his thin body, lower first then upper, into the chilly water that rakes him with its talons. He pats his skin irruptions, rubs beneath his arms with hard tallow soap, and rinses; he gathers his shrivelled manhood, persuading his fingers between the crusty wrinkles. Perhaps if he can get his heart started, his eyes properly open, he will ask to tag along with Father to Gambierton, and take his sheaf of drawings of pobblebonks to show Mr Crouch at the store. He had followed the frogs' *'bonk, bonk, bonk'* until he found them in the rain and sketched their shining copper markings.

A cold wind hounds him up the slope to the house. Rosanna passes the verandah, humming something cheerless that ceases in an instant when Father appears from behind the house, crop dangling from one work-worn hand. He clamps his hand on the back of her head to steer her towards the stables. What has she done now?

Mother hitches up her skirts and flaps behind them. Half breathless, she turns back to shout at Skelly, 'Fill the bowl with water from the kettle for Hugh.' She pauses by the pit and puffs, finds her voice again. 'Hold his head over it as long as he will allow.'

Weak sons obey their mothers. Strong ones are killed by their fathers. But surely only in stories. For a long time, Hugh coughs as if he will never again draw breath; hacks and rasps and chokes. Falls to his knees clutching his throat. Skelly counts. Finally, he hauls him up against his chest and half carries him towards the stables, where in the gloom he can make out the shapes of Mother, Father and Rosanna gathered around the fire in fierce battle, snapping at each other like seals over a penguin carcass. Heads swinging, completely absorbed, they step forwards and backwards in the straw, pointing their fingers at each other, chopping at the air with the edge of their hands. What can they be arguing about now?

Father, all wattle and comb, leans forward to shout into Rosanna's face, raises his fist in the same motion; she steps up to receive the blow, holding her side and her belly as if in pain until he retracts his hand and curses, hawking onto the dusty floor. Mother slaps at his arm, glances to appeal to Edwin for assistance; but he, back half-turned, elbows resting on the crossbar of a stall, continues to drag on his cherry pipe, offering no counsel. Mother then throws her head in her arms against the wall of the stables to wail. Skelly clutches Hugh against his chest, cries out to all of them and to God but cannot attract any meaningful attention.

Hugh vomits down his arm and begins to take small ragged breaths, his hoarse metallic cough hacking into the air like a faulty band-saw. He cries out, 'No, no! Leave me alone, Skel.' Perspiration streams from his small head and body. Skelly shakes him. The light is poor. He rests his hand on the steaming forehead, one finger clinging to the boy's curls. Hugh's whole head emanates heat. Will it explode like a pumpkin in the sun?

Finally, Skelly drags him in the opposite direction, thinking it best to dip the delicate boy into the freezing shallows of the pond to break the fever. Stumbling down the steps to the brink, he sinks to his knees in mud and stinking pond slime, to toss handfuls of water over the boy's brow; then lowers the top of his head into the water, which swirls and runs in little rills around his ears. Hugh gurgles, throws back his head and rolls his eyes until only the white shows.

Above the wind Skelly hears the scraping, raucous cries of brolgas. Mother will come to her senses. Whatever Skelly does, Father will call him a useless *boccah*.

Hugh begins to babble an incomprehensible string of words that rise and rise and turn themselves into the snarling, growls of terrifying animals; his mouth gawping open and closing in a rhythmic way; his tongue sweeping around his teeth as if searching for an obstruction. His arms and legs begin to twist and flail, stiffen and jerk; he drums his feet on the ground.

In an effort to control him Skelly seizes his thin legs with their clamping toes. In doing so, he raises them above the boy's head and breaks the rhythm of the convulsion; limbs and body settle in the grass and pulse in a pitiful way. Hugh curls and uncurls his long fingers as if suckling once again at Mother's breasts. In the moonlight his pale freckled skin looks blue.

SKELLY WEIGHS HUGH'S LIFE IN HIS HANDS

Skelly lifts Hugh higher, arms braced beneath the now floppy, sodden legs and *thóin*, from which rises the reek of urine and something worse. The boy has pissed and soiled himself. It is a relief to imagine something freed in him, something released after all the heat and tension. Grubby hands clutch Skelly's damp clothing, sweet brown eyes flash white, brown, white; then close. Skelly sees his brother inhabits his body once more but has fallen into a deep sleep. He glances back towards the pond, from where the sounds of birds die down. A smoky moon rises in the darkness, as if a malevolent *Booandik* spirit glides away in the fog, relinquishing his brother.

Relief steals through Skelly's body and he staggers to his feet, attempts to lift Hugh in order to take him to the house. Hugh murmurs in the small moment before a cloud darkens the moon and Skelly hears the crack of splintering wood, a whoosh of air, the detonation of a cloud of angry bees, leaves thrashing down upon his back. Somehow he throws Hugh forward, up the bank, managing to cover him with his larger body, keeping the weight of the falling branch from crushing his brother's weak lungs and chest. He circles his arms to shield Hugh's hot face. A second limb attacks Skelly's legs, skewering his thick worsted trousers. Ricocheting foliage settles heavy on his back; there is a crack as pain pins his attenuated upper arm to the ground.

Lightheaded, alone in a dream, he begins, like Father Woods, to hallucinate blood. He hears Hugh whimper then howl, as if from the base of his belly. In the corner of his eye he sees his father, and Edwin leaving the stables, carrying a Tilley lantern, its dancing flames making shadows that leap and stretch and collapse. They have heard the wind attack and fell the river gum beside the pond; far enough from the house, Edwin tells Skelly later, they are not at first especially concerned. It is only when he notices his Goliath Father with Hugh flopped like a pillow over his shoulder, attempting to drag the branch away from Skelly, that he runs. Afterwards, abed in the house, Skelly sees Father pass Hugh back to Mother and swing from the room, fist jammed into his mouth.

Days later, Skelly lies swathed in blood-soaked bandages, which his mother changes at frequent intervals. His breathing is shallow and an enervating weakness threads through his veins to the mysterious junctions where blood readies itself for the climb to the heart.

Mother presses damp, folded strips of calico against his forehead, lifts his chin with her small fingers to spoon in goat milk and clean the slop that over runs his chin. Every so often, she applies more compression to the wound on his back and the place on his arm where the bone has pierced skin. Her face is damp with tears. She cannot, it seems, stop weeping: for everything that has gone before; or in relief that her sons live; or perhaps in terror that worse will come to pass. Her misery appears much the same, he is sure, as the kind that drives his father to the creek. No one talks about the smell of blood.

Skelly cannot know her womanly complexities but he is grateful for her care. He hovers on the edge of darkness, his skin white, too nauseated to eat because of the smell and taste of blood: like iron filings and putrefaction. Skelly has known since he was very young that blood loss swells his joints and makes walking any distance a chore, makes running impossible, never mind the kind of dangerous sacrifice he has just made for Hugh. He strains against the bandages as if constrained by a hand-stitched shroud.

Each day, Rosanna pauses at the door but does not enter, hooded, black clad, face a pasty moon of concern. Where does she go between these visits? Skelly hopes to hear something beyond the confines of bandage and bed. She should not take the blame for Skelly's suffering this time and yet he infers that she does. He would not be surprised to see her tongue rise to touch her upper teeth and susurrate 'sorry', like a creature expiring on a wharf or landing. Self-loathing informs her nature. When she enters at night, bows over his limp hand and lifts it to her lips, lays it against her cheek, places it gently back against his side—he knows this.

She says very little—'Thank God you were there when we were not'—bites her lips and bows her head, darts away.

He calls after her. 'Why was Father angry with you that night?'

The hours blur one into another.

Mother lowers Hugh's cheek against her own. Even at eight years of age he is lighter than a bundle of sticks. 'You saved your brother's life, Skelly. God bless you, darling, but get well.' Blinnie appears beside the bed with an old curtain swept around her shoulders. Another actress in the making. Skelly tries to laugh without setting off a warm surge of blood. Edwin brings Doctor Wehl, who sets his arm and issues instructions. Mother clutches Hugh against her chest, as if in fear that even professional strangers could murder one of her sons. Every visit, the doctor applies pressure to Skelly's leg, readjusts and tightens bandages, instructs Father how he should do the same. Father takes on each task with grim determination.

On the fourth day, Skelly no longer feels the throb and pulse of blood deserting his body. He can stand a little; hobble outside to release his water. But he feels low. As if his spirit drags in the mud. A large swelling remains on his upper leg. The praise for saving Hugh when everyone else was shouting and tearing, screaming and stomping, has died away to nothing. The throbbing has eased in his leg and the wounds feel more brittle than cuttlefish, under his worrying fingers. Strips of calico bind his ribs. People warn him to be careful from daylight to dark.

His thoughts return to old preoccupations. He broods over Father's comment, the night the war of words began with, when Rosanna came home with Arlen. Skelly *is* always in the way and not much more than useless.

SKELLY ANSWERS THE CALL

Father Woods appears, head bowed over his prayer book, his gentle face as serious as a cadaver's. Kneeling beside the bed, he espouses a plan that fills Skelly with more dread than his mortality. Leaving home. Mother cries. Father squeezes Skelly's hand. He swears that such a thing will be more than one family can bear.

In less than a fortnight, Skelly will accompany Father Woods to a seminary. If he returns while there to his former jocund disposition, attending to prayer and scripture, the priest may recommend him for a permanent position as a geological assistant to one of the Brothers. He is too young to take church vows. Who knows what will happen after that? In the meantime, he must work at something productive before he becomes a burden on his family.

'No, Father, for he has saved his brother's life. I want to keep him near me.'

'You must allow him this opportunity, to make something of himself, Eilish. He will be safer in a monastery and he will learn important lessons that will better fit him to serve the church.'

Until he goes, Skelly must practise his scientific drawings of shells and bones and sharks' teeth from the ancient seas. He must mind his health and try to be more useful. He must not worry so much about what people say but judge them by their deeds; for sensitivity, Father Woods says, can be a kind of selfishness. And he must put aside Mr Geoghegan's play about the Lynches, stop reading it to Blinnie, Hugh and Arlen, and take God into his heart as often as he can. Mother flings a white cloth over the stump that serves as altar and lights expensive white wax candles. She clasps Skelly's hand while they recite the Lord's Prayer together.

He tries. He does his best. But he has lost enthusiasm—for almost everything. Slumped over on his seat by the pond, he returns on the sly to reading the Galway play. He cannot completely give it up in convalescence.

He recites the opening lines of Act Five:

> *Blake*   Ask your own heart, explore its secret springs
> Search out the cause and you perchance may find
> That pride as much as principle there weighs
> With justice thus to counterbalance mercy.

He follows the verses with his fingers, from line to line, flicking the pages of his sketchbook, dipping his fingers in the water to smudge the hard lines of a sketch, dabbing away spots of charcoal excess with the sleeve of his jacket.

Was it pride that made Father hit out at Skelly, or whiskey, on the night when Rosanna rode in from the cave? How can he forget him swaying in the doorway, eyes ripe with suffering, fists clenched, barking at anyone who approached him, attacking his own family as if they were the real cause of his rage? Blaming himself for Rosanna's unhappiness. For Skelly's too.

A considerate son must resign himself to the plan that Father Woods has spoken of so many times. If God does not have a better plan for him, nor does anyone; his only duty being to stay alive until he leaves for Victoria and a new life at a seminary. Father and Mother now agree that he cannot live a useful life here. At least, his sore tooth has settled down, eliminating one source of pain.

The weeks pass quickly in an agony of dread for Skelly, until the day he farewells his family on the verandah. Father holds both his hands in one big fist, murmuring—*show dignity and return without shame if the risk be higher*—and strides away. Mother hands her son his swag packed with parcels of smoked mutton, a water canteen and several pairs of knitted gloves, instructing him never to chip or cut open quartz with his small hammer, without their protection. Father Woods has promised her he will instruct the Brothers on the particulars of Skelly's illness; that her son must abstain from heavy work. It is on this condition that she has agreed that he may leave her care.

Father Woods returns from nursing the needy in Gambierton, dressed in a workman's shirt rancid with possum fat. 'I wish that you had accompanied me,' he says in his sweet English voice, that makes Skelly's eyes shine with reflected fervour to help, 'when I removed the lice from their hair with steel combs.' The priest is thin and passionate with fierce dark eyes. Like a God walking among mortals. Everyone feels reassured by his presence and surely they must spare him one Lynch son. He cares about suffering children everywhere; that they might have a chance at life. After all, Skelly is one of them, and how can he complain when he can read and write and draw? He would drink kerosene for Father Woods.

He will go. In Victoria, he will be less of a burden to everyone. One less mouth to feed.

His father chokes on 'Skelly boy' and turns away.

His mother blows her nose on a rag and flattens the palm of his hand against her cheek. 'Go darlin'. You have cared for us all. Your own mother at her lowest.'

Rosanna presses her brow against his lapels and whispers, 'Don't concern yourself about father and me rowing in the stable that night. He was angry because I camped with the baby near Moorecke's *ngoorla*. Remember? If I had not, I would have gone mad.' She pushes a strand of hair behind her ears. 'He thinks that I am no use to Mother when I am tired and he is right.' She shrugs her shoulders. Then she pulls away. 'Now you have your chance. Good luck with it, darling.'

He glances up at his father, who is destroying a log with his axe. Weak sunlight seeps through the clotted sky. At the edge of the pond, swans make high-pitched scraping noises, worse than distressed violins. Blinnie proffers bread to the birds; they walk ungainly up the slope, long necks intertwining and retracting, rushing at her in a hissing flapping show, until she kicks at them—the darling *phookah*—dropping the crust at their feet and running into his arms. Hugh passes him a grubby letter and begins to cry.

Beneath his jacket, Skelly fingers the small leather bag tucked in the waist of his trews, with which he cannot bear to part. Each time he opens it and takes the precious items out, he will smell home.

88

FOLLOWING THE SEVEN SISTERS EAST

For the first part of the journey they ride in silence. Skelly knows that Father Woods keeps a gentle pace for his sake. Doctor Wehl has placed his arm in a sling and described to him the general malaise brought about by loss of blood; thus Father rests the horses more frequently than he would travelling alone, forgoing the all-night journey along the beach from Nelson to Portland. He says heavy clouds make him cautious and that he can no longer ride fifty miles a day or through the night. Skelly knows both these reasons to be nonsense. The priest is twenty-seven years old, young, and intrepid in any weather. He has ridden through flood and fire and storm. Skelly registers his kindness. If only they might ride on forever. Never arrive. Already the jingling iron links and rings on the tack have worried small abrasions into his legs and arms and *thóin*.

His serge hat pulled down over his dusty face, Skelly fingers the bag slung round his waist, containing the treasures of a childhood spent largely by the pond: the desiccated bat, a crumbling piece of limestone, a fossilised shell, a photo taken by a snake-oil salesman of the entire family after Edwin was released from gaol. The real source of his pain eludes him. He thinks about the preservation of bones—the science of it, not the sad passing of their owners—creatures mired in mud, victims of accident and aggression. Horse girth-deep halfway across the river, reins knotted at the pommel, he cradles his healing arm, trying to quell the memory of his father crying and the wrenching feeling in his gut when looking back at his mother. Surely, criminals feel like this. Useless *boccahs* causing everyone pain. Dying would be easier.

Portland is dark and forbidding, its basalt houses perched above the wild and windy sea. Skelly remembers little about his family arriving at Discovery Bay on the *Emma Eugenia*. He'd been about the same age as Arlen is now, but sicklier. Rosanna once spoke of a ghost appearing at the guesthouse on the cliff and of Mother screaming. He and Father Woods stay in the very same lodging house overlooking the bay.

After dinner they break bread with the priest's friends, singing and arguing about the temporal nature of scientific discoveries, the exact location of an extinct volcano as well as the love of God.

'The number of books I can carry in deep Bush is limited; not enough, Skelly, to satisfy my thirst for knowledge; thus I draw on nature. As you do. What say you, Skelly? You have learned so much this way.' Father Woods angles his face in the firelight, leaning forward to make his point, his voice affectionate but weary. In company he proves such a wonderful listener, his handsome face alight, delighting in humanity. While they prepare for bed the priest's spirits slump; the book he writes for scientific readers has many imperfections. Were he not so peripatetic, he says, he might seek assistance from museums and libraries, although the Geological Society has been most supportive. Skelly feels at a loss to comfort him.

The next day, morning sun dispenses the bright dew on the leaves as they warm their backs at the outside fire. Before setting off, they eat fried eggs in the guesthouse and share tender conversations about Mother and Rosanna and the children; and measured ones about the country through which they are about to travel. They leave the limestone of Whalers Bluff in Portland and enter a vast volcanic tract of land extending miles to the north-east. Beside them shines the sea. Through dark stringy-bark forests, over grass tree heaths and along coastal bridle paths that follow dune ridges, Father Woods points his whip at wondrous sights—in truth, many times this resembles a lecture—a tuff mountain once a volcano, spitting koalas and flocks of emus striding away like indignant feather-clad show girls; Skelly does not share this last comparison with the priest, having learned about such things from Edwin.

Unaccustomed to riding any distance, Skelly's body accumulates layers of tiredness, more and more apparent as they approach the serpentine driveway to the seminary and his new vocation. He improves his posture in the saddle and pats at small abrasions on his arms in order not to inflame them. For his family's sake, he must make a success of his stay. Part of him registers a frisson of excitement.

At the head of the driveway, they make their way like royalty along an avenue of Canary Island trees, passing a statue that appears to command them on rather than beckon them in. The angel figure looks a cut above them, its noble shaven head tilted skywards, its physiognomy high-browed, strong-featured and patrician, softened only by a chin cleft suggestive of humanity. The horses scent air heavy with eucalyptus and pines, seemingly hopeful of a feed.

When the steep angles and planes of an extensive red-shingled roof come into view, Skelly loses his bravado. As he surveys the building's painted finials and gables, louvered shutters and wrought iron weathercock, he hopes that his faith will firm into something more optimistic. Father shows him the Stations of the Cross on the limestone hillsides: north, south, east and west. Skelly imagines walking between them, on low days, and talking himself back to the house. Never has he travelled so far from home. Apprehension tightens its grip on his throat.

89

AN ELECTRIFYING INTRODUCTION

'You will come back to see me before Easter? And talk to me about my progress?'

Father Woods nods. 'You may send a message through the Monsignor if you have any problems.' But nonetheless, Skelly feels abandoned. Gang-gang cockatoos drift over their heads, serene until suddenly the picture breaks up, the golden sky split by a loud shot and piercing cries, flashes of red crests, dark grey wings with cream lacework, fiercely flapping. The head of the flock wheels and cries, turning swiftly away from the house. It must be an omen. But it is only a thickset Brother standing on the verandah of the seminary, stirring the sulphurous air with his rifle, picking off birds that fall like hailstones onto the fruit trees they have just marauded.

From behind a low line of scrub he hears a series of fearsome whoops and pounding footsteps. His horse startles, jumping sideways, and he grips its mane in terror of a fall. He wants to piss himself but remembers the embarrassment last time when the fingers of his fractured right arm cramped and Father had to release him from his trouser buttons. A skinny red-haired lad in overalls darts in front of their horses, then twists away down the hill, two others in pursuit, one of them black and the other large and lumpy, hurling clods of dung that thud against the boy's worsted shirt. Holy lamb.

'You'll be in lively company.' Father offers him a lopsided grin and begins to hum a Scottish air. Skelly finds he cannot join in. Yes, he feels excitement. About the work. But, nevertheless, his lungs are full of trepidation about the company. Twelve boys aged twelve to twenty reside in the house, training as farm workers until they find a placement in the community, but few of them read or write. Perhaps they will chase and hurt him too. How will he manage the companionship of these young men when he has been little more than a spectator during

Rosanna and Edwin's horseplay? Even little Hugh finds Skelly dull.

He must concentrate on the new life ahead, working at something he enjoys. Through the grace of God he may toughen up in this Holy establishment. Over the last miles of their ride, Father has spoken at length about the Brothers' geological discoveries in the local area and how well pleased one of them in particular will be to gain a geological assistant.

While I might groom them, this Brother has told Father Wood in page after perfumed page of a letter agreeing to take Skelly on, *not all boarders show a dedicated interest in fossils.* A *keen* apprentice will delight him, he writes.

Once more, boys' shouts rupture the peaceful pastoral scene. From the top of the slight incline, Skelly sees the large suety boy sling an arm around another's neck and wrestle him to the ground. For a while, the black one observes from a distance, hands on hips, then dashes away towards the back of the house. *That would be me.* The pair roll together in the dust, pulling at each other's clothing until the larger boy gains the advantage and throws his leg over the other, pinning him to the ground before pushing his face into the dust. The boy coughs, struggling as hard as a calf at the end of a rope, with no mother to defend him.

Father Woods stands up in his stirrups and raises his hand. The wind takes his indignant growl and smothers it. Together, they rapidly descend the slope. The plump boy shouts into his victim's ear as he snatches something from the boy's breast pocket and rises on his haunches to hurl it over his shoulder. It looks like the paw of an animal. This incenses the redhead, who struggles violently against him shouting, 'You filthy *gugusse*, Henry, you'll get hung beef,' until raw sobs pepper the air.

Father Woods shouts too, pushing his horse towards the pair but struggling to be heard. 'Enough, boy. Enough.'

The lad named Henry eases off the smaller one's chest, enough to roll him onto his side; then, seizing his leg from behind, bends it hard back until the angle of thigh and hip becomes incalculable; the redhead begins to scream. Skelly hears the familiar crack of bone and cartilage separating and gags. He finds himself unable to interpret the grim lines furrowing the priest's face or the fussing of his gloved hands around the throat of his whip before he hurriedly dismounts and strikes it against the ground.

The victim collapses in an apparent faint, and at the sound of a slamming outhouse door the perpetrator leaps to his feet and bolts. Father Woods stoops beside the boy whose face is contorted with pain and Skelly notices contoured stains of pink and yellow lapping the linen covering his muscular arms. As he regains consciousness the boy begins to moan, his hand striking the side of his head in despair, his upper body thrashing in unison. Wiry red hair flops over his freckled face. Then he faints again. Father kneels beside him, splashing water from his canteen on his forehead.

Skelly raises his head to the sky, preferring to watch the birds, little more than smudges of black to the west. A blister on his calf where the stirrup has rubbed over many miles tightens in sympathy for the victim. His arm aches; his skin stings in the wind. Shifting in the saddle, he eases his leg away from the horse's mud-caked flank and follows Father Woods, who is carrying the boy.

He tethers their horses to a hitching post beside the verandah from where he can hear a thrashing being administered with great energy and commitment at the back of the house. Father leaves the boy and strides up the steps beside him. The whump of leather and accompanying wails cease abruptly when, after a discreet amount of throat clearing and boot scraping, he rings a bell on a metallic chain. A Brother with sleeves rolled up to his elbows greets them. He says he has been working in the herb garden. Father Woods immediately directs him to the victim, who they find attempting to drag himself behind the stables.

FAREWELL GOOD FATHER

An hour has passed since the Brothers, with some difficulty, carried the unfortunate lad up the stairs to the dormitory—his leg broken during the shenanigans. Skelly casts his eyes around the cathedral-sized dining room, into which they are led to dinner by a limping housekeeper with a phlegmatic cough and a face like scone dough. When offering refreshments, she ducks her head, her fingers strangling the skirt of her starched white apron.

Through the window Skelly sees the boarders uninjured in the melee, much subdued, balancing themselves with scythes on the back of a rough cart jolting up the slope, towards a yellowing crop. The black boy has tied a red rag around his head. Father Woods remains upstairs administering laudanum to the injured boy, whose name is Samuel, while he awaits the arrival of a doctor.

Skelly is seated next to Brother Mitchell and Brother Aloysius at a long refectory table made of some carved native wood, receiving a lecture on his future duties, the first of which will be reading daily scripture to Samuel. He thinks longingly of Mr Geoghegan's play, hidden in the gum by the lagoon at home; perhaps he will retell the sensational family events in his own words to entertain the boy. Skelly keeps largely silent, only half listening, as the Brothers rehearse Henry's preliminary trial.

After several minutes, Brother Aloysius scrapes his dining chair sideways and places the flat of his fleshy hand on Skelly's arm. 'I am sure that Father Woods has schooled you in the importance of taking the utmost care when describing and classifying delicate specimens.'

'Yes, sir.' Skelly recoils from the brother's odorous breath, noting a black stub of tooth on the lower jaw. The man's linen collar is stained with golden spatters and his fingernails rimmed with grey—nowhere near as immaculate as Father Woods, who keeps up his toilet while travelling hundreds of miles on God's behalf.

Brother Mitchell leans forward, tongue poking into the side of his cheek. 'You will be working with me, not Brother Aloysius, and my standards are most exacting.' He winks.

Winks are complicated and sometimes dangerous. Skelly has observed this Brother arriving at the table, the author, he suspects, of Henry's beating. The man is tall and athletic, and throws himself forward from the hips, when walking, like a simian man. Skelly once saw a loping ape in Tenerife, a port of call on the voyage out. He had endured the thick and soupy air long enough to sketch it, along with cages of little yellow birds and hungry children diving for coins on the wharf. Brother Mitchell resembles an ape in other ways. His small head cocks to one side in conversation and his brown face rapidly mobilises when he smiles, splitting into two half moons. Beneath the table, his fingers press against Skelly's upper leg. Perhaps he is a friendly simian.

Father Woods arrives at table with tears in his eyes but seems in a terrible hurry to take his leave. Never before, he tells Skelly, has he experienced such a thing and he has seen a great deal of evil. He has spoken to another Brother about the excess of violence required to break a leg.

Brother Mitchell's eyes widen and he twists his left ear with his long thin fingers. 'Indeed, sir, Henry invites constant surveillance,' he says.

They make their farewells over a pot of tea in a courtyard rose garden with borders marked out by English box hedge. The scent of roses is unfamiliar to Skelly, although he has seen them growing in good seasons at Mount Gambier Station. He slides a fallen bloom into his drawstring bag and his spirits spiral to new depths. Soon he will be alone here with the leg breaker in this beautiful but dangerous place. Tilting his cup to slurp out the dregs, he looks to Father Woods for reassurance but the words remain unsaid.

Skelly *should* transfer his affection from his priest to Brother Mitchell in one smooth transaction, when all three shake hands, standing on the lip of the flagstone verandah. Would it not be easier than the waves of misery now racketing around his body?

Father Woods leans in to take Skelly's hands in his larger ones and clasps them hard, bows his head as if in apology—then lightly steps away, his stole swirling around his body in the breeze blowing across the valley. Skelly's face is damp, his emotions fragile; a lump calcifying in his gullet feels harder and more intractable than granite. He gazes hopelessly after Father Woods.

A MONSTER POUNCES

'Come now.' Brother Aloysius rocks back on his heels, one hand resting at Skelly's waist. His ample girth sticks out as he twirls the frayed cincture knotted at his waist, setting his cross swinging in unison. Brother Mitchell places his hand upon his shoulder as if together they have choreographed his entrapment on the verandah.

Attempting to step further away from both, Skelly drops from the edge onto the track, thinking should he break into a trot, wondering if he should—in all his newfound fitness, he *might* vault onto Father Woods's packhorse and return home with him. Had he not managed the ride through the night to Portland on Sunday with only the slightest stiffness, a few blisters on his arms and numb *thóin*?

When Brother Aloysius waves to Father Woods and returns to the seminary, Brother Mitchell points to a stone hut on the hillside where, he explains, he classifies and sketches his fossil collection. They stamp side by side through bleached grass the colour of kangaroo hide, stopping at the third station of the cross where the Brother fusses at the shrine with sacred ornaments and dried flowers, lights a candle, crosses himself and says a little prayer for Skelly's happy induction into seminary life.

Over the next rise, they reach the hut, door swinging on its hinges in the brittle sunlight. Skelly tries to put aside the loss of Father Woods, reminding himself that the Brother may grow in his affections and that he will find his specimens interesting; that this kind of work will not be onerous, nor endanger his life. Perhaps he might hide up here if the cruel boy becomes unpleasant to *him*.

Brother Mitchell props the door open for him. It is a very narrow doorway and Skelly feels awkward pressing past him, the man now breathing heavily through his linen handkerchief to avoid inhaling dust. Perspiration beads the Brother's hands; his dark hair falls lank on his shoulders. Inside, they each take a moment to become accustomed to the poor light. The brother bunts him forward like a wayward lamb and Skelly clenches his teeth in embarrassment.

'Here, son.' He tugs at Skelly's arm to indicate a box of matches on the shelf inside the door. 'Light the Tilley lamp on the table.'

Darkness presses around them until the match flares. Skelly smells a faint, sickly odour: floral store soap perhaps. The Brother grunts as he attempts to close the door but it sticks against the rutted earthen floor. Some light filters through a small window spattered with grime and fly *cac*. On three of the walls, heavy packing boxes and jars have weighed down wooden shelves until they have bowed. The jars must contain the specimens. A rough couch covered with a crocheted rug extends from the door to the sidewall. Beside it sits a metal bucket and a sluicing pan.

For no more than a moment, Skelly takes stock of this austere workplace, before something erupts in a flurry of dust from the far corner of the room and hurtles toward them. He flails his arms like Don Quixote, attempting to protect his face, dances about like a lunatic. An even more putrid smell assails him, skin as dry as cured hide scrapes across his lower arms, and something heavy and sharp clambers up his chest and mounts his shoulders.

There's a hard-edged shriek like that of an old woman, a string of violent blasphemies, and the Brother spluttering like an engine. Skelly cannot make sense of his predicament even now that large claws dig into his shoulders and something leaps to the top of the rough shelving. A box clatters down, breaking open to scatter yellow crystals. Even though his eyes grow accustomed to the light, he dares not turn his head an inch to look. Brother Mitchell curses with frustration that his specimens will be damaged and lunges forward to grab a staff and knock down the creature.

The large goanna bounds onto the table, knocking scientific tools to the floor; then in a leap of faith onto the Brother's head, beaming his yellow eyes on Skelly who, to his relief, now sees the scene is almost comical. The reptile resembles an eastern gargoyle, with three cascading chins, a grotesque expression and protruding devil tongue. He rides the Brother like a buck rider would a nervous yearling.

Oh wouldn't Moorecke love to commandeer such a gift. Dare

he offer to butcher it for its sweet, white meat? Skelly reaches for a claw hammer leaning against the wall and stealthily approaches the two-headed creature but, in the end, the reptile bites the brother's neck, rides him to the floor and clambers off. It rises up on its quilted feet, head twisting to protect its back from predators. The monster flees and so does the angry Brother, hand clutched to his neck.

BREAKING BREAD

Skelly sweeps and tidies the battle zone, feeling a grudging respect for the creature. When he returns to the house, the housekeeper directs him to his sleeping quarters—one cot in a row of narrow bunks covered with serviceable grey blankets, a small bible on an upturned fruit crate beside it—the window being the only saving grace. He unpacks his swag and washes in a jam preserving pan. Leaning on the windowsill, he views the hut on the hillside and imagines trudging up the slope to it each day. The wooden sash is warped by weather, leaving a one-inch gap at the bottom.

During the evening meal, shifting his gaze erratically from a portrait of old priests to the rows of diners crumbling their bread on gold-rimmed plates, Skelly feels overawed by his inclusion at a table more formally set with fine linen and silver and in the company of two companion priests so old they look barely alive. Wearing Edwin's pants, turned by Mother to freshen their colour, and the knee-high boots favoured by Father and Mr Gordon for riding, he feels a fake duffer that is for sure, his jacket buttoned over his vest. He is as gangly as Glorvina's foal, as awkward as a fledgling bat. And tired: a young man who has rarely left his house, riding hundreds of miles into the colony of Victoria to live in a palace with strangers, who seem more unpredictable than a nest of vipers.

A dozen boys hem him in on long pews either side of the table, offering him such profound terror that he dare not meet their eyes as he studiously works his way through two dreadful plates of food passed along the row. He imagines how Rosanna would behave, the darling mouthy thing. Eventually he forces himself to look up across the table at the two lads he recognises from the contretemps on his arrival. The black one named Nathanael has been rescued from his people, during an epidemic of scarlet fever, to be educated. The bloody bone-snapper, large Henry, delivers this information with arresting pleasure, begins to snigger, and punches the black boy's arm. The boy ducks his head and punches him back. Henry turns to snatch Skelly's damper and throw his fork clattering to the floor. When Skelly bends to pick it up the *gasún* kicks him in the head.

Henry is uplifted from the table by his freckled ears in a Brother's pincer-like grip. 'Half rations and two weeks' daily confinement in the punishment cupboard,' Henry recites under duress. He has attended his Last Supper.

Brother Mitchell, one hand nursing his neck with a wad of gauze, notices the disturbance, rises and crosses the wooden polished floor to the boys' table. Hands splayed like a fishmonger on the table's edge, he sways from side to side in way that renders Skelly paralysed but fixes all other attention on Henry. 'Leave the table. Stand at attention outside my door.' Brother Mitchell removes himself to the head table, twitching, bandaged and doubly affronted. He glares across the dining room at Skelly.

NIGHT GAMES

The first night Skelly doesn't know what disturbs him, the sounds outside being much the same as those at home—a possum growls on its scuttle along the balustrade before it drops to the ground, birds chitter, a vixen yelps. Those inside are as harmless as heavy boot treads and creaking boards, and the odours of carbolic soap and urine are no more distinct than at home. He drifts in and out of sleep.

Once, on waking, he sees a face mottled in the half-light, peering around the doorjamb. He sits up upright in his sweaty cambric nightshirt, and the figure flaps an imperious hand in the air, signalling him to lie down. Skelly cannot do more than feign sleep. The black boy cries out then sings in language as euphonious as Moorecke's, until his body thrashes against the wall and falls back again. At the passing of each hour, the cedar grandfather clock chimes in the hallway, reverberating through the dormitory floorboards.

After several hours, Skelly makes his way to his first-floor window and leans out over the sill. His eyes sweep across the soft horizon—dark sky, yellow hills, stone angel lit by an incomplete moon and shadowy groves of native pines and shea oaks. The air sliding below the window sash stinks of grass and cow manure. More than anything he misses the sea. Even though he rarely made the bumpy descent to MacDonnell Bay his body swells with pleasure at the memory of it. The salt tang, the crash of breakers, the fishy smell; the sea makes him feel most complete.

He alters his scansion, peers again and startles. Through the window, in the foreground of a composition he will surely replicate the next day in his sketchbook, he notices the tall, thickset figure still clasping the mournful rag to his neck and gazing up at him from the rose garden. Heat invades Skelly's face. Partly shamed, although not afraid, he thinks it polite to withdraw back into the shadowy room. Perhaps Brother Mitchell has not noticed him.

The morning breaks with rain clattering on the Blackwood roof tiles and Skelly makes his way to the kitchen, where the housekeeper sequesters him to wash dishes and fold linen. He has crept there in order to avoid Henry, carrying his boots across the upper floors, and he is glad when he hears the work cart creak away to the paddocks. Clouds scud swiftly east and blue sky can be seen behind them.

It seems the boys will take shelter outside until work can commence. They carry their food for the day in a large hamper and will not return until dark. Two boys, feverish with chicken pox, breakfast with Skelly. At midday the sky clears completely and a different boy comes to fetch him. He sluices his dinner plate in the washing-up suds and follows him to the hut, where he finds Brother Mitchell writing at a makeshift table by the window.

'I want to show you something,' he says.

It is nothing much. Just a feather star. A crinoid with no stalk. Father Woods has better specimens. The Brother draws a stool close to his, takes out a new notebook and instructs him on his official duties. First, Skelly is to write about commonplace objects as a test. On days when he finishes his house chores early, and if his notes have shown acuity and grace, the Brother will talk to him about Julian Woods's lectures on sea moss and corals. The man leans towards him, thin lips pressing against each other like a pair of annelids. Dumbstruck, Skelly perches, his thin arms dangling at his sides, fingers loose as if in surrender, as if he has lost all will. He strives to be polite.

'I am grateful to Julian and our Lord for delivering me a geological assistant. Our conversations will prove most stimulating, but reassure me that you don't suffer too cruelly from homesickness,' Brother Mitchell intones and smiles.

'I am managing well, sir.' Skelly leans back, stands abruptly, his hands gripping the specimen table behind him. The Brother's habit swishes across the floor, throwing up little flurries of dust as he opens the door and turns back to Skelly, holding out his arms as if to embrace him. Skelly moves towards the door.

Days follow each other, in much the same way. Weeks. Confined to the house most of the time, Skelly carries well water to the table and wood for the housekeeper's oven; he polishes silver cutlery and fancy goblets. Every afternoon he works in the little hut, sketching and describing the Brother's samples. Perhaps, after all, he can experience happiness. Despite occasional footfalls on the shale outside the window, no one troubles him while he is employed this way.

One day, he hears Henry's voice outside and moves to the window to assess the risk. Perhaps he has broken out of the punishment cupboard, because he wails as he attacks the trunk of a tree with his feet and then his fists. Skelly crouches below the ledge and observes him until Brother Aloysius recaptures the boy, prodding him down the hill at the end of a long stick. Another day, a German doctor arrives to remove the oiled linen bandages stabilising Skelly's arm. The cloth sticks to his skin and the young man snips at it with great patience, using warm water and a scalpel. The skin looks pink and new and clean; it appears to breathe, Skelly thinks, like him, in tender hope.

The doctor is kind. 'How are you getting on?' he asks.

'Fine, sir,' Skelly replies.

From dawn, most boys work long hours in the paddocks, stumbling up to the house at nightfall. Within two weeks, Henry accompanies them again. During long afternoons, when excused from his usual tasks, Skelly hikes away to the hills behind the seminary to search for fossils. Twice a day he climbs the stairs to read to Samuel. He has also taught the injured boy some letters—useful work for a pale weak thing who skulks in the shadows, he thinks.

Each night at dinner he surveys the Brothers bent over their platters of roast meat and root vegetables, and occasionally spies himself in the sideboard mirror, subdued, uncertain, still pale. At frequent intervals their voices explode into rich, ribald laughter as if they were Edwin's friends rather than men of God. At first Skelly feels a kind of contentment that as the hours slipped by in the little hut he is achieving something useful until Father Woods returns to visit him. Would Mother not be proud?

On the second Saturday night, the boys bathe in the open air, sluicing their brown, farm-hardened bodies with water heated over an open fire. The housekeeper makes tallow soap.

'Rub vigorously, boys,' Father Mitchell instructs, 'under your arms, behind your sprouty ears, and in all the dark places where boyish perspiration and grime gathers.' When he demonstrates all the places requiring attention, the boys laugh.

Skelly does not find ablutions to be fun like the others; fear of damaging his scrawny body and vulnerable skin almost overpowers him. Has Father Woods told them about his affliction? But he tries to join in, not wishing them to think him dour. The Brothers encourage wrestling and water throwing and general running about the garden. The old ones shoulder each other on the bench, tap their pipes on the bench arms when a boy goes down, and snicker as if bath night plays out for their entertainment.

Skelly recoils from Henry whirling a piece of dowling around his head, whooping like a banshee before bringing it down upon Nathanael's back.

The black boy snatches the cane and breaks it on Henry's shoulders.

Henry turns on him and shouts, 'Get off my neck, you black bugger.'

In an act of kindness, surely, Brother Aloysius intervenes, then beckons Skelly. 'Fetch another canteen of water, lad.' Relieved, Skelly scurries away.

Some time after his return, the Brother, pipe dangling from his mouth and sleeves of his habit rolled to his elbows, snatches the soap away from them with admonishing growls, and mock-sniffs its slippery surface odour. 'Hurry now, lads. Time for prayers and rest.' Nathanael cocks his head and apes hands clasped in worship, receiving a biff in the ear.

After the bathing, Brother Mitchell, who smells of aniseed and peppermint and something odd as well, brings upstairs tin mugs of Godfrey's Cordial, on a tray embellished by a decoupage image of Our Lady. Despite the grit of extra sugar that sets his teeth on edge, Skelly experiences a rush of warmth that brings back memories of passing the cup at home, but he drinks less than a quarter. Father Woods would not approve of the way the boys cavort naked and then glide into heavy sleep. Only temperance leads to Godliness. Within a short time, Skelly sees Henry and Nathanael and the others sleeping the sleep of the dead. At least their shenanigans have wearied them enough to bring Skelly peace. He lies back in the hope of a restful night.

But nerves keep him awake until finally he jerks upright in his bed, knowing that he will shortly vomit, and he rushes downstairs to find a garden bed. The cordial had been fearful strong and sweet. He dallies beneath the walnut trees below the dormitory, one hand on his belly, until he feels an urgent need to fertilise them. Queasy, glancing up, he sees a string of little bats sway like smalls hung on a washing line, and emotion surges through his heart. Surely they are bent-wings like his babies at home. Higher still, he observes the spray of stars that form the Southern Cross; it is always brightest in the autumn. On the way to the seminary, Father Woods had told him to think of Rosanna and his entire family viewing the constellation from not so far away, and to remember that they will be praying for him. Shadows flit. Is Henry on the wallaby?

Against all good sense and shielding his bad arm, Skelly climbs the tree to look through the window. Two Brothers move from bed to bed in the dim light of the dormitory. Pray God they do not notice his cot is empty. The tall black shapes hover over each boy, adjusting coverings and tidying nightclothes. When Father Aloysius moves to Henry's bed and covers the boy's body with his own and begins to move in a familiar rhythmic fashion, Skelly almost falls from his branch. Henry lies prone, upon his belly. Why does he not fight back? Skelly waits and waits, until it is safe to creep back to his bed, then clenches his teeth for hours in the dark, listening for footsteps on the carved staircase.

SINS AND PUNISHMENT

The following Saturday he offers his cordial to Henry, which the boy ungraciously accepts as Skelly's extra devotion to Trinity Sunday. After days and weeks, Skelly has heard nothing from home. At bedtime, listening, listening, he slides down, blanket pulled over his head, back against the wall.

'There, lad. Lamb of God,' he hears one of the Brothers murmur on his rounds. Skelly wonders why he has not been selected for special attention but is glad. One night, when he wakes in the middle of a thunderstorm, Skelly finds himself close to tears, to see Nathanael, arms pinioned to the bed and roughly rolled up against the wall. The black boy does not struggle upright in fright or cry out during the assault. Skelly wakes again and again during the long hours before morning, dreaming of blood. Once more, he has become the watcher, but who will watch over him?

When Monsignor visits next Wednesday, Skelly will send a message to Father Woods asking to be sent home.

When the day dawns he waits for an opportunity. Soon he will be with his family again. But the Monsignor spends most of the day closeted in the office with Brother Aloysius, poring over legal documents, and dines in the library where he may not be disturbed. A boarder, even one under the patronage of Father Woods, cannot possibly request an interview. It is not until all the lights have been snuffed that he struggles to the window for fresh air and sees the great man saunter past the stone angel and across the lawn, glass of wine in one hand and book in the other. He will run down the back stairs and attempt to speak to him.

On the first landing, he peers down at the French doors that open from the dining room onto the lawn, through which he can just make out the Monsignor, who has put down his book and is bent over a cigar being lit by Brother Mitchell. When he hears them laugh at something Brother Aloysius has said he despairs. For sure, they are all close friends.

Turning back up the staircase he trips and stumbles against the wainscoting. One of the Brothers starts and looks up, calling out his name. Skelly leaps from the doorway to his bed, reaching out to wake Nathanael, who punches him in the arm.

'Come, Skelly,' Brother Mitchell bids the next morning, leading him to the hut to work. 'How is your health? You must miss Father Woods,' he remarks. 'Did you not confide in him all your thoughts and desires?' He pulls out a chair and settles himself on it in front of his favourite display cabinet. 'You were as close as a man and a boy might be, yes?'

Skelly nods dumbly.

'Kneel down then, boy. Here, in front of me.' The Brother leans forward, hands sliding down his strong legs, composing his face in a way that is supposed to look avuncular but then, once more, he winks. Skelly wants to leave, but the man seizes him around the neck, pulling him hard towards him. A tug of war ensues until he opens Skelly's mouth with his long fingers, running them over his teeth as a Lynch might inspect a horse, at the same time hauling him closer still. He pushes his fingers deeper, almost down his assistant's throat, with his left hand, and violently twists with his right Skelly's mass of dark curls. 'Are you sure you have you no sins to confess?'

'No sir.' Skelly struggles to speak.

The Brother grips the back of his neck forcing his head forward beneath his holy garment, symbolising poverty and chastity, forcing his mouth hard down on his *boddagh*. Skelly gags and struggles; tries to resist the sickly smell of talcum powder and body odour; the slick of moisture. Edwin makes jokes about Lucifer nosing his way into Glorvina's urine stream and Skelly, choking, has seen dogs in the town licking each other in a firm and eager way. But never like this.

The punishment, for what crime he does not know, takes interminably long before the Brother pushes him violently away and Skelly overbalances, staggering against the display cupboard, breaking several marsupial skeletons assembled inside, and then finds himself sprawled on the floor.

He caresses Skelly's cheek as he hands him upright. 'Clumsy. Next time, remain in bed unless a visitor invites or requests your presence. And don't give Henry food or drink again. Even should you hear him whining outside. Clean up, and finish sketching my molluscs before you come down the hill to tea.'

Skelly dowses himself in the bucket of coffee-coloured water used for cleaning and polishing rock samples; he wipes out his mouth and attempts to staunch blood seeping from a small cut on his forehead. All Skelly lets himself think is that he must survive.

95

FLIGHT

The wound bleeds, this day and the next until Brother Mitchell berates his pale complexion. 'Eat more heartily, boy.'

Each morning, Brother Aloysius chides and pets him in front of the boys pressed on either side of him on the breakfast pew, something Skelly fears will turn their hearts against him. As a consequence of his unfortunate accident, he is to receive an extra serve of porridge dolloped with clotted cream, generally only available to Brothers. He is excused from household chores and given permission to sit in the pale sunshine sketching flowers—arum lilies, perfumed roses, and chrysanthemums, white and yellow daisies. Mrs Crompton likes to remind him of another young man whose father sacrificed him and who bled.

The Monsignor pauses before him to unwind bandages binding the wound on his forehead, to witness the drip, drip, drip. 'You must ask the housekeeper to change these cloths more regularly to prevent the overflow.' He stares deep into Skelly eyes, as if seeking the answer to a worrisome problem.

Skelly nods. He feels as feeble as a newborn marsupial might, before attempting the furry climb to the warmth and safety of a pouch; in the same way but different, he makes his way up the rocky slope to the hut, lead-footed but conscientious. Banished to the hut, he enters details of the broken treasures and the contents of the broken cases and describes the contents of two new boxes placed inside the doorway. He crouches miserably on his stool, sketching—thinking, thinking, thinking—numbering the ribs, repairing the diaphragm with resins and flour paste. The Brother must have misunderstood Skelly's relationship with Father Woods?

On the third day, the door creaks open and he swings around on his stool. Brother Mitchell fills the doorway, blocking the light with his black-clad bulk.

'I have farewelled the Monsignor. He spoke most affectionately of you. A small injury can evoke tremendous sympathy in a great man. Indeed, Skelly,' he murmurs, offering a smile resplendent with his own magnanimity and warmth, 'with any man.'

Beyond him, Henry passes the doorway and the Brother steps towards him in a swirl of black cloth and hard muscle to shoo him off. He closes the door before he spins on his heel. 'Come, lad. No hard feelings. It was an accident. Brought about by your clumsiness in the first place. By disobedience.'

Skelly shrugs. From dealing with his own father in his cups he knows to make himself small. Recovering the rag he presses it against his forehead, resumes his seat at the worktable. Trapped like the artefact before him awaiting description.

'You must learn humility. If I catch you out of bed again at night, I will report your insolence to Father Woods.' The Brother's kick upends him and his stool. Winded, Skelly clutches his side. He cannot mouth the word *sorry* or any other. Nor can he defend himself when the Brother beats him with a closed fist, perhaps in an effort not to draw further blood. A large hand pins him like a specimen to the earth floor, while its owner whips the leather belt from beneath his robe, applying it to Skelly's flat belly in increasingly heavy strokes, first clothed then bare. The Brother rough handles his clothing, before flipping him as Edwin might a silver mulloway before he gills and guts him; mashing his mouth against the floor. One hand clamps his buttocks; fingers work him into a state of terrible pain until he thinks he can endure no more. And then he does.

The next few moments remain indelibly printed on his mind until the day he dies, for the door flies open and a terrible oath swells the air, unrecognisable in tone and argot. The Brother withdraws his weight from Skelly, roaring like a mallee bull at the intruder in the melee who, it transpires, is Nathanael. Bare-chested, the red rag tied around his head, he exudes confidence until his head tilts on its axis under the smack of a vicious blow that lays him flat. The older man stands over the sprawled boy. With uncharacteristic but finite strength, Skelly lunges behind him, leaps like a salmon, like Cuchulain, to seize the shovel leaning against the wall and brings it down upon the Brother's head.

Nathanael regains his feet, face filled with battle fervour. 'Dress up quick. Keep away from that prick-batterer. I will get the horse.'

Skelly feels faint and falls to the ground. He wakes next, trussed across the neck of a large bay, which Nathanael urges towards the township, one hand bunching the reins, the other balancing his load. 'You always bleeding too much.' He sighs, his face comical with regret. Skelly slides in and out of consciousness, waves of pain circling his head in the purple dusk. So much trouble. Too much. Rocked in a long loping canter, he closes his eyes for several minutes until they approach the outskirts of the town.

Nathanael jumps down from the horse, looping the reins over a picket fence before he vaults it to tap on the front door of a neat timber cottage. Tree branches heavy with almonds dance on the thatched roof. By the time the satchell-arsed doctor appears in the doorway and carries Skelly to a cedar miner's couch covered in thin canvas, the black boy has gone. They hear the retreat of hooves behind the hill and Skelly lifts his hand in weak protest. 'He must not go back.'

The doctor shakes his head. 'He will not.' He bites his lip. 'But they will round him up and flog him home.'

Skelly ducks his head. He cannot meet the doctor's eyes. 'No need to bleed me,' he says before he faints.

96

SKELLY CONFIDES IN ROSANNA

As time goes by, Rosanna notices that Hugh breathes more freely. Blinnie reads *The Water Babies* by Charles Kingsley. Moorecke is nowhere to be seen. Rosanna imagines her walking into the wind on the limestone coast, beeswax in her hair, a necklace of King Parrot feathers and reeds swinging between her breasts, a swan bone piercing her nose. Mr Ashby has long sailed for Tasmania to join his wife. Baby Arlen has long grown out of the cradle carved by Father. Adam Lindsay Gordon is rarely seen in the district unless visiting friends or steeplechasing but, nevertheless, his exploits on horseback and paper command conversation at Miss Lallah's *síbín*. More than likely George Sutherland is dead.

It seems interminably long since Skelly left home in autumn. Now returned, he occupies some kind of suspended animation, a stasis that suits the season but suggests distress. One hundred brolgas have fled the screaming wind and driving rain on the coast and gracefully descended—bugling *garoo*—around the marshy sedges beside the pond. The bentwings have mated for life; deep inside each tiny female abdomen lies new life. Rosanna watches Skelly cut one open after its unfortunate collision with a fence, finding the tiny secret nestled within. The bat colony will soon swing from the roof of the cave, somnambulant, until its babies reach full gestation.

One afternoon, Rosanna and Skelly set off for the cave pretending that nothing has changed but the customary tricks of light and weather, stopping to fill a canvas waterbag at the pond, to stir a stick in their reflection: two tall things with untidy curls and dark circles beneath their large increasingly adult eyes. Fine lines mark their exposure to rain and wind and sun; and to suffering. They speak little.

It is Skelly's birthday and three weeks since Father Woods drove him home from the German doctor's surgery. A month earlier he had lain close to death's door in the goldfield doctor's parlour. Seven Hail Marys for that man. And for his young Scottish wife, who fed her brother and debarred all visitors, especially those that the wife secretly named the Brothers Grim.

After the telegraph the doctor sent to Father, Skelly's recovery took some time; and more waiting until Father Woods rode to fetch him in his new buggy. For more than a month, he had been sitting in a hospital chair between rosewood cabinets of Bavarian fruit plates and a tiny clavichord. When Herr Doctor's wife's fingers danced along the keys, so Father reported, Skelly had gazed over her neat little head and through the window, until the day that Father Woods brought him home.

Rosanna observes her brother's unnatural quietness. He becomes more and more like her. Surely he must never leave home again. How they had missed him: quiet, kind, self-effacing Skelly, who read, sketched, watched the younger children at play and helped their mother. No one could draw a bat or a possum as well as he. Much as she understands Father Woods's affection for her brother, she hopes he will forget his plans for the priesthood. It seems not as much her brother's haemophiliac tendencies as his sweet languor that draws danger from every quarter. And he had been homesick. He will be safer on Lynch land.

They dismount at the cave and ease themselves down side by side onto the granite boulder that guards the entrance.

'It is not your fault,' they say to each other, 'the things that happened,' passing the cup between them to suck back mouthfuls of warm sharp *uisce beatha*. They sigh and bump shoulders. They stare in an imbecilic way at each other, pulling faces. And at the sinking sun.

'You must stay with us always,' Rosanna remarks. 'We are your family.'

'I must go back,' he says.

'Skelly, no. Why would you do that? You were so unhappy there.'

'Nathanael saved my life and I his. I need to know if he is still at large, I mean safe.'

'Who is he, Nathanael?'

'He is a Black fellow much abused by life. He took me to the doctor when I near bled to death. After ...' He clears his throat and turns his face away from her.

A little breeze lifts the corkscrew curls that curve around his ears. She slings an arm around him, flopping her head down on his shoulder. He is taller now than her but his torso and hips are narrower.

'I asked Father Woods. His enquiries were not conclusive. Nathanael is accused of stealing the horse, robbing a store and bolting for the Grampians.'

Rosanna squeezes his arm. 'I am sure he will be safe if he has the horse. They will never find him in those mountains. He will go to ground.'

'And what if they send troopers? What then? I blame myself. What if the Brothers snatch him back.'

'Why worry so much? What can a good lad like you have done to endanger a Black?' her mind gnaws at this problem, sees that he is thinner and paler than she thought and full of immutable longings.

'We must exchange stories.' He drops his head to his chest. 'That way we cannot betray each other. Mine is the most shameful.'

Rosanna stands up and stretches out her hand to beckon him into the cave. She is full of love for him once more. 'All right then, now that the drink has loosened our tongues, let us have a good *craic* together.'

He tells her first of a conversation overheard between Father Woods and the doctor who demurs releasing Skelly into the custody of the church.

Their voices rise above the cockatoos they have disturbed in the wattle tree.

'You must trust me to deal with Brother Mitchell,' Father Woods had entreated him. 'I have already pursued Father Keating in Melbourne and in Adelaide, petitioned the highest authorities.' If only they took notice of him. But he is no longer popular himself. 'You see, Rosanna, that is the point. Everything is hopeless. If I return to seek justice for Nathanael, Brother Mitchell will attack me as he did before.'

After she knows, Rosanna blisters the air with her fury. In the morning she descends into the cave and weeps beside Moorecke's shrine of bones. Night after night she hurls filthy curses into the sky; she kicks the trunks of trees until her feet bleed.

97

THE TROUBLE WITH SONS (1868)

For four years, the memory of Skelly's flight from the monastery builds fierce grief in Rosanna; her heart still as gravid and tender with feelings as if pierced by a poker. She has tried to make things up to him. But swearing an oath never to tell Mother and Father the true story has been an impossible strain. Can it be that a person's silence perpetuates such evil; that keeping secrets compounds damage?

Without a single word or hint, she knows that her mother knows. Despite the regularity of their life and work, shafts of sadness penetrate everything they do together. If Edwin and Kitty ever marry and begin their new life in Nhill and if they all stop pining for a better Lynch story, can they begin anew?

Rosanna spends more time with Skelly, reading library books nearby while he fossicks near the creek and sketches samples, after which they stew a pot of tea. Some mornings, he lies abed nursing plaguing headaches or small bleeds. Some afternoons, while Arlen sleeps and Hugh and Blinnie bend over arithmetic and geography, Rosanna rides hard, trying to make sense of her brother's experience; each time she returns overwhelmed by sad stories—imaginary and real. For instance, what has happened to Moorecke?

Edwin sees the black girl, so he says, drifting past Mrs Smith's school gate in Mount Gambier, but when Rosanna rides into town to the circulating library and stops at the school to make enquiries about the *Booandik* girls, the housekeeper replies that Moorecke has been gone 'long time.'

They last met at Racecourse Bay, during the week that Skelly rode away with Father Woods.

'I am leaving too,' Moorecke had said, hands resting on the head of a small child. Rosanna had rejoiced to see the little girl tugging at her friend's pinafore. 'Going with the aunties along the *Coorongk*. Maybe to three-mile-camp.'

'Cranky Jack, also?' Rosanna had asked.

'He fell down dead on the boards at Carratum shearing shed. I touched the bone in his nose sometime and he shout.'

How had Rosanna not heard this? Father must have known. She drew out a photograph of Arlen and Moorecke had stroked its shining surface, joy filling her eyes, before she turned away to spit.

Together, they had moved away from the crowd and onto the dunes, to pick muntries and place them in Moorecke's flat basket. Was it the ripening tartness of the berries that brought tears to Rosanna's eyes, or her friend's sympathetic face? Or was it the glistening necklace of blood that Moorecke had coughed up at her feet. In any event it was a day when words failed, *Booandik* words, Irish ones, and English, all the same. She had unpinned her claddagh brooch and placed it in Moorecke's dillybag.

Since George's wife died, news announced by Edwin, there has been more uncertainty about Lucifer. A Melbourne lawyer called Levy had arrived by coach, appearing, Edwin told her, at the station, with a fancy leather satchel stuffed with papers.

Some uncanny thought that day had sent Rosanna scrambling behind the cook place to the stables, to slide a leg over Lucifer's bare back and rush him away to the *Booandik* winter camp where, placing all her body weight against his shoulders, she had backed him into the cave until only his head stuck out. What a fuss the horse'd made when she'd woven branches across the entrance to hide him. After she'd boiled tea and covered the fire, she'd watched him push his head through gaps. 'Don't be poking your silly eye out.' He'd cocked his head on one side, the portrait made more ridiculous by the green tendrils dangling from his forelock.

Later in the day, Edwin came crashing through the scrub, dander up, spitting through his moustache about warrants and stupidity and shouting at her to stay hidden. Staggering drunk, he'd been carrying soda bread and hunks of smoked kangaroo in a bag around his neck, his pockets weighed down, or so he said, with the lawyer's coin won at tables at Lallah's *síbín*. Oh, she was a bad young woman skiving off work at home but she didn't need persuading that he was awfully pleased with her for saving the horse. Not having always been on the right side of the law himself.

Rosanna had been happy enough to spend two days smoking the green tobacco he had left her, thinking about Moorecke and wishing that her friend might materialise between the trees as she always had, drawn by her acute sense of smell. Instead, encouraged by the smoking, Irish banshees arrived, cutting her sleep to shreds with their shrieking.

Sleet and rain drove her home. 'I thought you had forgotten me,' she spat at Edwin, wringing water out of her hair on the lip of the verandah.

'I put Levy on the Cobb and Co for Victoria this morning,' Edwin placated. 'First I cleaned him out at the card tables, but I doubt he'll give up on the horse.'

Lucifer was deemed safe from the Sutherlands for the moment. And Edwin offered her a stake in his takings for staving off the abduction. In the meantime, threats or promises flying back and forth between Melbourne and Mount Gambier aside, Lynches would keep the stallion and breed from him.

98

THE FLIGHT OF BATS AND FENIANS

Eilish removes her husband's dinner plate and he pulls her hard against his side. 'Where have you been these last two nights?' she asks.

'Working at Suttons. I met a Cork man and rode with him to a meeting at the Tarpeena Hotel.'

'Not Irish plotting, you fool?' Eilish bites her lip and tries to pull away.

He keeps the pressure on. 'I want you to read a pamphlet. It makes sense.' He releases her hand to take a creased and folded bill from his pocket.

'Holy Mother of God, not Fenians now is it? And written in Gaelic. Who says *you* have to take notice of what they're doing in America, or Ireland, for that matter? Did we not come here to escape all that? Now that Edwin is making his own way again, can you not leave politics alone?'

He pulls her closer; the plate tilts. Gravy drips on her arm. Bending to kiss her wrist, he licks at the juice from the meat. It is the drink, Rosanna thinks, as she stands in the doorway, pretending to survey the children acting like jackasses by the pond, and trying to shut out her parents' quarrel. Most of all she needs be sure of Skelly's well-being *and* only she really knows the reason. Mother might intuit the worst and still fall short of the truth.

'Leave well enough alone,' Mother tells Father. 'You have land now. How can you pay for it and food for our table behind lock and key at the gaol? Remind yourself of the house you're building. Tasmanian shingles. Extra rooms. The children going to Dismal Swamp school. I have taught them all I can. Rosanna too.'

The daughter turns her head to glare at her mother.

When Father Woods left for his new appointment, Rosanna had cried. He rarely writes to her now, forgetting it seems that he had offered her a letter of introduction to a school in Penola, looking for young teachers. Rumour has it that another school will open in Mount Gambier, for that is what everyone now calls Gambierton, but she has lost her confidence in paid employment.

Father lowers his voice. 'You know I've never talked about secret societies to the children.'

'Nor should you. Leave Edwin out of this too. I have no wish to lose my firstborn, who has already sashayed on the wrong side of the law.' Mother's voice catches.

'It is a great joy to see O'Leary installed in the new Mount Gambier gaol.'

'Too bad we couldn't afford a lawyer to restore Edwin's reputation. A pardon …'

'We have thrashed this out and you know it.'

'St Patrick and the Holy Virgin, if you have the means after all these years you should clear his name, or I've never been to Galway.'

'It is not that simple. O'Leary brought stray beasts across the border. Responding to that *gombeen*'s extortionate demands put Edwin in a difficult position. Sure he didn't mind a little remuneration for his trouble—nor would any man.'

'Next you'll be telling me my son was gully raking. Were the cattle branded?'

'Some were. Some weren't. It seems your daughter is implicated in the disposal of at least one Ashby carcass. O'Leary was after ruining our Lynch name. Edwin has served his time and doesn't wish to pursue it.'

Mother touches two fingers to her forehead and closes her eyes.

Rosanna glides guiltily onto the verandah and down the steps, wanting more than anything to make things up for everyone. If only she had protected Skelly. Where can he be now? Pray God he never takes off to find Nathanael.

'Law is not the only measure of justice,' she hears Father shout before she blots him out. She pauses by the pond and scans its reedy circumference.

Turning her back on her parents' quarrel, Rosanna joins Edwin at the chess set, which he has placed on a small tea chest at the edge of the pond. He smiles in welcome but then complains that she is too quiet; that she coughs too much; that she eats too little. That she presses harder than she ever did on a horse. Busy making money, does he never think to ask how life treats his younger brother?

'And yet ...' she argues to herself, 'some good things have happened.' What a miracle, Glorvina throwing a foal at her age, and the others sired by Lucifer. For the moment Rosanna is to ride the stallion, because Edwin should never have sold him in the first place. They will not give him up until they have to. She feels a surge of renewed energy.

The children lark about on the grassy knoll. When Arlen stumbles against her arm and knocks the chessboard flying she does not strike him but gathers him in—her seraphic pale-skinned child, with golden butter curls—revising the rules of the game as she replaces the board and pieces.

Edwin calls to Hugh, 'Come, take away your pesky brother, or you'll not be moving to Nhill with Kitty and me.'

Rosanna wishes she had put her stamp on Arlen earlier. Go hang the *chúlchaints* in Gambierton.

Edwin replaces the pieces from memory. 'Father can not afford to feed all of you with more on the way.'

Despite his sunken chest, Hugh grows taller, looking more and more like Skelly. Arlen, not entirely resembling any of them. Finally, Rosanna notices Skelly bunched over his sketchbook or, perhaps, the play manuscript, on a rock platform beside the lagoon, oblivious to children squealing, parents squabbling, Edwin bragging and berating. Blinnie and Arlen take up instruments, a whistle and a skin drum, and Rosanna leaps up to dance, in the same motion calling to Skelly, but he doesn't look up. If only he would.

Edwin fishes his mouth organ from his pocket, raises it to his mouth and leans into the song, a lock of hair falling across his forehead, his elbows sawing the air, his hips set forward to balance the tapping of his right foot. Arlen bows to the opening chord. Blinnie throws herself into the set. The music travels faintly up from the pond to the house. Their mother begins to jig on the verandah. When the younger ones cavort like fireflies around Edwin, Rosanna stops dancing to hold her side and cough. 'I am *all right*,' she calls up to her mother. 'In a moment

I'm taking Hugh and Arlen and Blinnie for a little ride to see the bats.'

When the dance finishes, Edwin stops to help his sister, slinging an arm around her shoulders as they make their way to the horses, the children prancing behind them. He lifts a protesting Arlen up to her, the boy clutching the pommel of a big stock saddle on Glorvina's foal. He is too old to ride like this but they are one pony short. She feels his breath on her arm and tousles his hair.

'Can we see the little huts and the camp, Rosanna?' Arlen coaxes, as they approach the cave on horseback. She nods. Blinnie and Arlen dismount and burst through the shining cobwebs laced between the huts and trees; they poke their heads into doorways.

'Watch out for snakes,' Rosanna cries, her voice swelling.

'Where are the little people who live in these tiny houses?' Arlen always asks, his face alight with curiosity.

'The Blacks have gone,' says Blinnie, kissing him. 'Father says,' her voice rising with importance, 'that the Big House people have scared them all away, and *kilt* a few as well.'

'Not entirely so, *alannahh*,' Rosanna soothes. 'For many years a *Booandik* girl lived here—and her husband—all the summer. Surely you remember. Has she not left behind her rugs and tools? If we were nicer, they would come back sooner.'

'I am very nice,' says Blinnie.

'I think they are dead,' Arlen decides, 'like the baby bats in the cave.'

'I once saw *Booandik* black people winning running races in the town,' Blinnie remembers.

'Of course, and why not? Arlen, put back the digging stick,' says Rosanna. 'You would not like it if someone touched your things. Perhaps people in Ireland think us dead. We have left no family to tell them different. Even Thomas, Mother's brother, has passed on to the next world.'

Arlen's face turns glum. 'Can we go to the bats now?'

Business-like, Blinnie hauls her horse's head from a feed of cutting grass and flings the reins over his head before she jumps into the saddle.

The sun sinks behind them as they dismount next at the cave, tie the horses to a tree branch, and settle on a smooth rock in front of the entrance.

'Will they come?' Arlen whispers, his face dipped into Blinnie's.

'They will, of course,' she says.

'What do the little bats eat?'

'I think mosquitoes, darling,' Rosanna says.

'Ain't that lucky because I don't like mosquitoes.'

'Pull down your shirt, for *they* love a fair-haired Celtic boy.'

She kisses their upturned faces. Rosanna doesn't know why she brings them to watch the bats fly out, perhaps because they keep returning and she feels lost. She leans back on her hands, allowing the breeze dancing along the ridge to lift her hair. She coughs, crosses her legs, and coughs again. She will never forget the taste of the actor's mouth, the warmth of his skin; the mellifluous tones of his voice; or, indeed, the poet's kiss. It had been a ripe time that year. She hunches her body and wonders if she is dying, any more than she has ever been.

'One is coming,' cries Arlen. 'Oh, it is a bird—a little owl—come first.'

'Hundreds will come,' says Blinnie, kissing Arlen's cheek.

Arlen jiggles happily. 'The sun is going to Ireland and the bats are coming here.'

Out they fly: one, or two, half a dozen, then enormous numbers swooping from the black hole of the cave's entrance into the trees, breaking the skin of the mottled air like dragonflies piercing water; not the least like birds. Rosanna hears the familiar whirr and flap and creak of their flight, imagines the shape of their leather wings against the darkening sky. But bats are barely visible in flight and she sees only the shimmer of disturbed air where they have been, hears only the faintest sound of their leaving. The children point and laugh and hold up their hands to swish them away from their faces.

'How will they come back home?' Arlen worries.

'They will carry the knowledge in their blood,' Rosanna says.

'But what if they are *kilt* by dogs or peoples or snakes? What if they die while they're away?'

'Their children will come. And their children's children.'

BAILED UP

At dawn, Skelly waits in the hide. It is not the first time he has seen the great cranes soaring, their necks outstretched, or spiralling out of sight on currents, in the air far above the water. But it is the first time that they have nested within walking distance of the house. He leaves Mother bent over the griddle and Rosanna working at the stove to set himself up on his limestone seat near the reeds: sketchbook across his lap, hat low on his brow to block the early spring rays of the sun, wedge of bread in the breast pocket of his jacket.

He will make a new beginning, by working on his folio of local fauna sketches. Father Woods has promised to take these illustrations to the Melbourne publisher of his natural history book. When he comes tomorrow, Skelly will ask him again to enquire about Nathanael.

He waits for the cranes. He remembers waking to their bugling, and how they had shattered the quiet dawn, distracting him from *his* wounded pride.

At the same time, he examines the striations of a resolving yellow bruise on the inside of his wrist. The injury is tender still and angry looking but he is almost well now. Blood makes its troubled way around his body, pressing against his skin like a caged animal, swelling around his joints, protesting against the least activity. When he was young, Father Woods told him that sons of European queens suffer the same complaint, and that he must not mind for it is the will of God. The mere thought of anyone else suffering as he did at the seminary brings on nausea. He hopes never to leave home again. Skelly has always been afraid of death. Blood flows in his dreams.

But it seems that, after all, he is not to die. He is now full grown, a man, half a head short of Edwin. He remembers his foolish dream of running away to the gold with Rosanna. He understands more now. About everything. Rosanna looks at his drawings, and he is grateful for her renewed love. He is not jealous that her slow wide smile is for Arlen. As years pass by, she works with fewer complaints but her happiness fluctuates—it being such a fleeting thing. And he knows that his experience has harmed her. It is languishing in bed Rosanna likes, as if she is dying of a terrible affliction, and when she has more freedom than most, especially Mother, sick with another pregnancy. He hopes she will read the play with him again one day. But perhaps now she finds *The Hibernian Father* such a terrible story that it could not possibly be true.

Nevertheless, the play belongs to Lynches, and through reading it they have learned more about themselves, if only that hearts have as many cavities and passageways as karst. Skelly is more than ever horrified by the fate of Oscar Lynch; he cannot desist from dwelling on it, as he reads and re-reads the carefully copied scenes in his sketchbook. And he wakes at night disturbed by dreams of the injustice inflicted upon him and the other boys by the Brothers. Why should the magistrate's story not be true?

Mother has threatened to remove the pages and throw them in the fire. 'I find it so unnatural. Morbid,' he hears her berating Father Woods on the verandah one day, both hands cradling her heavy belly. 'Whoever heard of such a thing, a father hanging his son? Someone made it up for a purpose, of that you can be sure.'

Father Woods places his hand on Mother's shoulder. 'He will get over it.'

Skelly had moved away from the window. The priest had kept his confidence, Skelly was sure, insofar as he had not told Mother the details about what happened in Victoria. He knows she has some inkling. Perhaps she believes her son was whipped by willow rods or starved. The next part of the conversation makes his heart constrict.

'I have another plan for Skelly,' Father Woods had reassured her.

Kurr. Kurr. Kurr. Skelly starts. It is the music of romantic cranes. He has seen them touching bills and leaping three feet into the air. Such graceful creatures, prancing and dancing on their stilt-like legs; bending their delicate necks to pluck tubers and insects from the grass. The reeds shift in the slight breeze, tickling his chin, and he parts them to see more clearly.

The brolgas alight less than twenty yards from him, and form in lines like choirs of angels: feathered arms outstretched, robes falling in crenulations the colour of Loughrea linen or the underside of mushrooms, dewlaps as vivid as the blood of Christ. Then their dance begins and they lift their heads, stepping forward on their elegant stilts. Skelly sketches furiously. The birds advance and retreat, dip their heads, and throw them back again.

Scratched-up grass flies around their ears; the largest bird leaps into the air, collapses its wings, shudders; again draws up its shoulders, proud and tender, advancing and retreating on its mate. Skelly's eyes glaze over in the brightness. He angles his body to hold back the reeds so that he can better see the birds as he sketches them, pushes up his sleeves to accommodate the sweeping arcs required of his pencil to shade the massive fringed wings on his page. Skelly is always the watcher. Squinting through the sunlight bouncing on the surface of the water, he is so intent on drawing brolgas that he is only faintly aware of their trumpeting cries and of a shiver of skin passing over tuberous fronds, and the gulp and plash of frogs on half-submerged rocks.

Small black ducks scatter in the shallows. Skelly's eyes penetrate the foreground of the larger picture and widen when he sees gold-rimmed eyes watching him. At first, he worships the yellow variegations, lightly sketched, the mosaic of scales perfectly attenuated on a thick body, the dove shades of the snake's fish-like mouth, the black dart of the tongue, and the elegant cord of the tail completing a lap of the body. Sunlight throws apricot tones into Skelly's composition.

Then he stops breathing. His heart lurches. Ever the intruder, he has stumbled over yet another doorstep—into territory where he doesn't belong. He waits and watches. Considers hurling himself sideways. The reptile's head emerges from the glistening coil; it sways and weaves the air; it takes him in. Does it think him predatory? Its body, thicker than wurst made by Prussians in Gambierton but far more beautiful, unknits itself and follows its shining head.

It moves towards him as naturally as wind or rain. Skelly feels the light punch of its head against his trouser leg and finally—as his pencil spears the water—the stab of its fangs into his bare arm. He throws up his hands. An image invades his stricken consciousness, of his sister wrapping his sketchbook in oilskin, and placing it back inside the knotted hole of an elderly gum, where he keeps it safe from the younger ones.

Scrambling hopelessly to his feet, Skelly clutches his throbbing arm as the snake hoops across the open ground towards the house. He turns his eyes towards the bridlepath. His feet squelch. He smells the blue smoke coiling from the house chimney and sees Rosanna, Arlen leaning against her hip, hand to her brow, pointing up at the soaring cranes. She looks preoccupied, serious, as if it is her only duty to reveal such wondrous things to Lynch children. In any case, history has shown her and Skelly that for all their wheezing and blowing, neither of them can protect the other.

He cries out to her as he bounds from the reeds onto the path, where the slight incline destabilises him, and he crashes full-length like a felled stringybark, air leaving his lungs with a *whump*. It is too late now to agonise over whether he will bleed to death like the sons of European queens. His sketchbook flies from his hands. He rights himself and staggers forward. A child waves both hands above its hyacinth head; clouds block the sun; shadows fall in the blackwood trees beside the path. He hears the clicking and whirring sounds of the bush. Is it Moorecke rolling her tongue? Has she come? The great cranes abandon him, crying out as they flap away to the south.

His lips try to form his sister's name as she runs towards him, dragging Arlen by the hand behind her. Where is the snake? He has dropped his sketchbook. He raises his hand. No. And his hatless, grey-headed father, gun jouncing against his hip, pounding in heavy boots across the hollow ground, falling to his knees on the rise below the house to take his shot. Will he be angry? If only Skelly has time to show him the liquid brilliance of the snake now veering towards the outhouse. Gunshots pierce his eardrums. The snake will be dead, an explosion of spangle and scales. He closes his eyes and thinks of the great Irish champion Cuchulain who cared not if his life would last one day, provided his name, and the story of his life remained.

100

LIFE HANGS IN THE BALANCE

Skelly has not been dead a month when Rosanna sees her mother yawing along the black-pitched edge of the pond, during the darkest part of the night—jaws clenched, arms pinned to her sides, tears truckling down her cheeks. Even from the privy, she knows her mother's intention, and she screams loud enough to be heard in Ireland as she runs towards her. Swooping like an angry gander, she knocks Mother off balance and onto her back on the bank, throwing her arms around her. They hold onto each other and weep.

Father bursts from the house and stands helplessly, as if tethered to the verandah. 'Come inside,' he cries. 'I will warm you.'

'Can I not be alone, even by the pond?' Mother calls back. 'Leave me now. Life is not the same for men.'

'It is harder, for all you know.' Father cries, butting his head against the wall.

Rosanna steers her mother beneath the trees beside the pond, to sit on a log out of sight. '*Tha, tha,*' she murmurs, hand curled into her mother's neck. 'Skelly would never want you to leave the rest of us. And what of the little one inside you?'

Mother keens, her voice piercing the night sky until Rosanna's voice joins in and then, eventually exhausted, trails away. 'Bloody woe, we'll have him rising from his grave,' Eilish laments.

Grief has bleached her mother's hair white and lined her face almost overnight. Incumbent beside her at the water's edge near Skelly's limestone seat, Rosanna waits until the first flush of dawn before easing her mother onto her feet. Father broods in the doorway, clouds of smoke swirling round his heavy shoulders, reaching out for his Eilish as they reach the step.

Father Woods rides in weeks too late to comfort them, his tears suggesting he bears sorrows and regrets of his own.

'Love God, Rosanna, and our blessed Mother Mary,' he says, shaking her hand as he leaves. 'Ride hard, read well, and take care of your family. God will light your way.'

'Yes, Father.' She weeps in any case.

'Honour Skelly's memory. I think of you both, often.'

'Father, what of the Brothers? Skelly is dead, but they can harm others.'

He shakes his head in apparent distress. 'There is nothing more I can do.'

To steady herself as he leaves, she looks away from Father Woods's black flapping garments and his tall shape, focusing on the gang-gang cockatoos rising on the wing behind the pond, until she knows that he has begun his descent to the bay.

Inexplicably, she feels angry with Skelly, for leaving them all in such a dramatic way, before she had half a chance to seek revenge on his behalf.

She may never again read Mr Geoghegan's play—tangled up as it is with her brother's death—now safely stored on a high shelf for Arlen when he grows. He is far too young to understand dying for greed or love, let alone on the altar of a father's pride. Once she had thought she might apply to housekeep for a priest in Melbourne but now doesn't know how she would keep herself from strangling him.

PART 5

MELBOURNE (1870)

101

ON THE ROAD TO RETRIBUTION

Rosanna waits. Some years go by after Skelly's death when very little happens. It is often the way with families after terrible suffering. Now Father owns the land on which their house stands, and they make a paltry living from cattle, but not enough to feed them well and he has loaned more money to Edwin. The lawyer Levy's letters on behalf of George Sutherland's estate have become more humourless in relation to Lucifer, more strident, accompanied now by writs and court orders, until Father, Mother, Edwin and Rosanna hold a council of war.

They will submit. Edwin and Father have had their day in court. They will give up Lucifer to avoid another. Edwin will sell some of his steers and yearling stock at Portland market to pay for materials to build a house on government allotted land in Nhill, and they will relinquish the horse to George's estate. If Levy will meet them halfway to Gambierton.

Rosanna wishes more than anything to accompany her brother for the handover, riding Lucifer and leading two of his colts demanded as compensation for the delay; and there is something to which she wants to attend, once she finds herself within cooee of Portland and a monastery. Night after night images of the cruelty suffered by her brother disturb her sleep. Skelly rarely leaves her thoughts.

Edwin refuses her this one small favour, until Kitty intervenes. 'For goodness sake, darling, why ever not, when she rides him better than any of you?'

She is a soft little thing, Rosanna thinks, but stubborn when it suits her. She curls her arm around Kitty's waist.

'He'll never agree to help me, nor you. If I were you I'd find some-one else, without a knee problem.'

'What do you mean, then?'

'Choose someone younger, a man not so stiff with pride, who'll bend his knee to propose marriage. My brother is not worth it.'

Kitty raises her apron to cover both their faces and they choke back laughter. Then tears fall.

Shame suffuses Rosanna's face.

Edwin returns, grasps the tail of the conversation, his face mottled like a turkey cock. 'Shut it, Rosanna. I asked her already and she agreed. We're to wed in the spring.'

Rosanna doubts any girl could manage her brother's ambitions. 'Oh, that's your business, but I'll come with you to Portland to make sure you return and honour your promise. For I cannot bear to lose this lovely girl.' She dips her brow against Kitty's shoulder. 'At least she will not need to live in a tent now.'

When Edwin finally agrees Rosanna may ride with him, nerves attack her. She has vowed for so long to travel to the monastery and now she has no excuse. How will she contain her feelings? But she must. Then she must return to Arlen and protect him better than she did her brother.

First she will leave a message for Moorecke with Patchuerimen, a Mount Schanck man. If Rosanna has a winter cough, Moorecke's must be more persistent. It is dangerous for a *Booandik*. She fears she may never see the girl or her child again. For now, it is enough to go to Portland with Edwin and the horses.

Rosanna holds herself upright, feeling as righteous and murderous as a snake. For weeks before setting out with Edwin she has hardened herself, preparing to gallop two hundred miles through swamps and low-lying coastal scrub, along shores and riverbanks, and past townships; preparing to control her anxious mind bucking against the restraints he will impose on her. To press Lucifer more than she should to jump chaotically eroded creeks and fallen red gums from Gambierton to Portland. Soon she will relinquish him and his colts to that tetchy legal sometime cripple—and Edwin has described him—representing the actor's Melbourne family. In their ignorance and pride, they have refused all correspondence with her, an Irish settler girl— have inflicted on her their grief and loss.

Unbeknownst to them she holds one more card. She knows how

to hide her feelings and will meet them on her own terms. Like any brother, Edwin would not have wanted her company on this expedition had he known her plan.

The bullet-pocked signpost to the priest's hole barely registers in her mind as she wheels Lucifer up the steep gradient to the head of the valley. At the summit, he shuffles his unshod feet, setting off a cascade of stones and she drops back into her creaking saddle, an ungloved hand pressing against his broad black back, her thin wrists gathered and laid one atop the other over the reins and pommel. She holds herself stiff enough to be *feiseanna* dancing but her tanned, callused fingers belie such soft diversions.

Behind her lies the settlement of Portland, where Edwin will spend the day argy-bargying with squatters over land and cattle. She has left the colts with him. Oh he is lucky, but had she not thrown in her lot with him and used some of her savings to piggyback his bets on steeplechases, she would not have heard the sweet jingling of florins in her velvet purse, that had enabled her to contribute to their expenses, ongoing, as they journeyed towards the final heartbreaking handover of Lucifer.

Edwin brings her good luck *and* bad but at least not boredom. Fingering a jabot of lace at her throat, she angles herself forward in the saddle, bruising herself in an easeful way against the pommel—everything aches or tingles uncomfortably—and thinks of Gordon who once brought her such discontent and confusion, and of the other, whose name she will not discuss with Edwin until her affairs with him and the boy have been finally brought to order.

Before her, a bluestone bell tower floats above a sea of eucalypts. On its bellcote, fierce winged gargoyles augur badly for a happy day. Perhaps the main monastery building hides its face, in the knowledge of her brother's death. Skelly must have waited just like this, courage knotted in his gut, on the same rise, before he descended, point of shoulder to point of shoulder, beside Father Woods, between vegetated swales lining the valley.

She nudges the horse forward and he steps off, nose down, picking his way between pieces of scree, lifting his feet as if she had weighted them with bags of rattling beans in preparation for trot work.

Throwing his head he prances, flesh glistening with health and all the confidence of his lineage. Hands low, torso steady, she directs him towards the head of the driveway where a stone angel, Uriel perhaps, beckons her with outstretched hand.

Amos said, 'Hate evil, love good, maintain justice at the city gate.' Rosanna taps the sign with her crop, and glares up at the silent seraph, suddenly conscious of the isolation of this place.

Hobbling the horse by a magnolia tree, its funereal-white wax flowers wreathed by summer-spoiled brown foliage, she kisses his muzzle for luck, and crosses a rough path circling the garden to hammer at the front door. Stepping back from the verandah in a moment of panic or defiance, she raises her head to see the liquid shapes of faces, pooled like ghouls in the dirty attic windows of the eastern wing.

Her mouth feels dry, her head thick. The door handle grates in its track, splintering wood sticking against the jamb until an ancient woman, with a shrunken apple head and stringy hair plastered against her neck, levers it free and heaves herself over the step, rubbing her fat fingers fretfully against her stained calico apron. She stares up at Rosanna. 'Good morning.'

'I've come about my brother,' Rosanna proffers employing hard flat vowels. 'Father Woods brought him here some years ago.' Had the woman worked here then? Even so, she could never be blamed.

The woman nods. 'What was his name?'

Rosanna swings her head—she should not have come—and bites down on her lip. He would not thank her for this shameful naming. 'Lynch.'

'Oh, then. Dear boy. We shall see. I will ask.' The woman waves her into a majestic foyer, in which a ruby leadlight dome disperses the early morning light, scattering it over gold-embossed representations of our lady, silver candlesticks, and prayer books atop cedar devotional side tables. A burnt sugar smell travels along the hallway towards them and Rosanna's stomach snarls, having shrunk to the size of an almond since she'd finished the last of her mother's griddlecakes below Mount Richmond. If they turn her away without speaking, she will never forgive herself.

BOYS AND BROTHERS

A holy Brother materialises as silently and economically as anyone might expect of a corpulent man in split satin slippers—all squelching bunions—why does she care? She is a woman now, who knows what he sees but doesn't see. Does he note a resemblance to Skelly in her high cheekbones, in her flushed oval face, her thick dark hair? *Calm yourself.* Rosanna talks herself up in her terror. He cannot intuit that on the journey, her eyebrow-quirk now as habitual as Edwin's and her ironic smile, have turned heads in every commercial establishment from Nelson to Portland. The Brother looks fleshy and self-indulged, worse than O'Leary at the bay.

'You might remember a boarder ... Lynch.' Rosanna stands tall in the hall of the Brothers who failed to care for *her* brother; as tall as many men, as she looks down upon the fleshy red-faced plum duff on the doorstep, chin slightly raised, head tipped on one side like a docile dog.

Over a silver brooch engraved with his name, Brother Mitchell surveys her with no apparent enmity. She steadies her breathing, leans back on her heels, clenches her fists behind folds of black velvet that she has fashioned with her mother's help into a riding skirt, and thinks of beautiful Skelly, his heart filled with wonder and reverence in the presence of any living creature, snake or swamp dweller, perhaps even this one.

'He left us some time ago,' he remarks, pulling up his lip in a show of carelessness. Then suddenly smiles, exposing a gap between his front teeth. Charm brings people together. To begin with.

'Oh yes and I know that,' she begins.

On his fat knuckle gleams a black diamond solitaire ring. On his freckled brow, grey hair recedes, sparse remnants splay like autumn bracken. The Brother smiles again. 'Why did he not return to us? It was Father Woods's wish that he remain here learning scientific skills.'

'I think you know why.' A lump rises in her throat.

'It was unfortunate. We were not told on his arrival that he suffered a weakness ... that he might over-exert himself. Then there was an accident using geological tools.' The Brother shrugs in a helpless way.

Rosanna's voice catches on the first two words but rises at the end of her speech. 'The church ... should be a safe haven ... for fragile souls. You did him harm. Brought him shame. Shame that he would not confide to his mother.'

'We arranged for a doctor and transport home. He was a boy too delicate for the work of the Lord.' The Brother crosses himself and eyes her with the surety of a man of faith.

Liar, she thinks. 'I am his sister.'

The silence that follows hollows out the hallway and surges at the vaulted ceiling, becoming something palpably more than humbug.

Rosanna pauses. 'One of you wounded him.'

'You are mistaken about ... us. Ask God for forgiveness.' Something ripples across his face, some semblance of a long-forgotten emotion.

Nothing more than fear, Rosanna concludes, gathering her wits. 'Had Father Woods known of my visit he might have entrusted me with Cretaceous samples. I hear that you have a fine collection.'

'Indeed, donations are always appreciated.' His fingers worry away at the knotted cord beneath his chasuble. 'Your brother showed interest worth encouraging in natural history.'

Rosanna lowers her gaze. 'He did of course. He and Father Woods spent many hours conversing about geology. You might remember that's why he sent him here.'

'How is Father Woods?'

'He is well, so I hear. Busy setting up a school with Mary Mackillop and the Josephites.'

A gangly young man rushes from the corridor forking to the left, running towards the middle door of the dining hall, but the priest hooks him as he passes, bringing him to a skidding halt with all the strength of his suety arm. 'Samuel. Speak to Lynch's sister.'

Rosanna starts. At least one of Skelly's friends remains. She fears for the other. The boy slaps his head with the heel of his hand, drawing attention to vivid scars darting under his hairline.

'Samuel, please. Some decorum.' The priest rests his hand on the lad's shoulder and he shies away; bows his head to Rosanna, claiming he must attend to pressing administrative matters. They anticipate the arrival of the bishop that very afternoon to discuss their preparations for liturgy during the Sacred Heart of Jesus. When the other boarders leave to work in the vineyards, this poor boy will take her on a tour of the house, an historic Primitive Gothic building. He will reveal where Skelly slept and carried out his ablutions: the lavatorium, the night stair. He will show her the place of his daily work. He will ensure her safe departure from the monastery.

The Brother sets off; Samuel uncurls after his rude arrest and tugs at his ear, then shakes Rosanna's hand firmly. He limps as he guides her, to the kitchen to drink tea with the housekeeper before they begin. Past the long elegant room in which four old priests fraternise, heads bowed over the grape poured from a crystal carafe, sawing their way through generous slabs of meat. She will have little to say to them for her brother has named them. All. He had been apprenticed to Father Mitchell and tormented most by Henry.

The dormitories are austere. Samuel explains in a husky voice that Skelly had slept in a narrow cot by the door and that he had worked each day organising and transcribing on neat cards Father Mitchell's notes on his collection of fossils, in a hut out of sight and hearing of the main building. It had been his job to lecture visitors on the geological significance and locality of the samples. Rosanna knows he would have been good at that. Father Woods had long held out the carrot of employment as geological assistant. If only *he* had taken Skelly on.

Through the garden and up the hill track the boy leads her, to the slab hut housing the Brother's collection, past the rise where she had first waited, girding herself up to descend the hill. The steep climb intimidates her because she knows at the end of it she may know nothing new. When she trips on the roughhewn steps up to the hut, he reaches out to steady her.

'I was worried about your brother.' He slides past her into the hut and lights a bush lantern inside the doorway.

Rosanna hesitates before advancing into the room and placing her hand on his arm. 'Skelly said two of you stuck together before that day he left.'

The boy shakes his head. 'Nathanael perhaps ... not me.' He hangs his head. 'It would have been pointless. When you finish, come past the stables. I'll water and feed your horse.'

She lifts her hand. 'I won't stay here long.'

Poking around the stale room, Rosanna fingers dusty rock picks and hammers mounted on wooden display boards, a spade and axe leaning against the far wall. She recognises Skelly's elegant handwriting in notebooks, on tags and labels. Dear God, had he arranged the displays in such artistic fashion to please Brother Mitchell or himself? Although she acknowledges the bleached and fragile beauty of the samples, she thinks surely it would have been so dull for her brother—breathing dust, living in a charnel house, piecing together the bones of long dead animals, shaving back limestone to expose its secrets, confirming Father Woods's theories about the pre-history of the south-east. The place stinks of mould and the alcohol in which small animals have been pickled. But the collection overflows the space; through the window she sees samples in buckets and boxes awaiting classification. A second, less elegant new hand writes the scientific labels now. God forbid, this enrages her further.

She picks up a leather sample bag, secreting it in the pocket of her cloak. A longing to flee back to Portland almost overpowers her. But first she must do something for Skelly. If only she can concentrate long enough. Can put aside memories of George and her dream of living in Melbourne. Can forget the bitter things that have happened to her family. Can dismiss the fading memory of the actor's mouth nuzzling her breast, and the feelings he elicited all those years ago, when she was little more than a desperate girl who quivered like frog spawn when a man, any man, placed his hand, in kindly fashion or otherwise, on her person. Gordon had touched her too. Was he settled now? After the worst things happened, she had focused on the sweet toughness of his dear little wife, who rode a horse near as well as Rosanna, who, like Moorecke, understood better than her the loss of a child, and who once had been kind enough to invite her into their cottage, pressing a cologne-seeped handkerchief to her nose, after she'd almost been thrown from her horse on the cliff.

She closes the door of the hut with a bang and strides down the slope. She needs more time to attack the task at hand. The walls of the monastery rise before her, dark and forbidding; even so, they had not managed to hold Skelly.

103

ROSANNA YEARNS TO MAKE AMENDS

Leading Lucifer from the stables, she hears sudden footfalls behind her and she turns, savagely brandishing her crop. Dressed in workmen's trousers held in place by a thick leather belt, due to his extreme thinness, a black lad leaps out of sight.

'Wait,' she cries. 'Come back. What is your name?'

He turns. 'Nathanael.'

Surely not. Why has he returned to the seminary, when Skelly saw him galloping hell for leather for the Grampians.

His head and torso re-appear around the heavy sliding door of the stables where he had been tending a horse in another stall. He steps out to face her. Around his neck hang boxing gloves tied together with string. Had there been horseplay during Skelly's stay? She pictures them scrapping in a dirty space behind the buildings and a gaggle of boys cheering them on. Skelly, fists held up, bare-chested, dancing his feet in futile circles, trying to survive the punitive discipline of the institution while ill.

Nathanael's face puckers with shyness and something else, his dark skin greyed. A facial tic jerks in his cheek. His upper body looks more strongly built than the lower and clad, despite the cooling autumn air, in a thin chambray shirt, sleeves torn off at the shoulder. He has the body of a mature man with all its musculature. And scars. But then he must be twenty. Her brother could never have worked or played as this lad did. Pugilism and hard physical work had always been out of the question.

'Do you remember my brother, Skelly?'

He ducks his head, the leather gloves hanging uselessly on his chest.

'He told me that you once saved his life,' she adds, drawing herself up to meet his eyes.

'Might be,' he answers, gesturing to her to walk behind the out-buildings and out of earshot of renegades from prayers. He looks at her queerly; then continues on, head angled on one side, chancing glances at her, his concentration repeatedly drawn back to the main building. 'I have something for you.'

She follows him up the slope to a bloodwood tree below which he begins to dig with his pocketknife.

When Nathanael hands over the leather drawstring bag and she draws out each item contained therein she weeps anew: the desiccated bat, a crumbling piece of limestone, a fossilised shell from the ancient seas, a photo of the family taken by a snake-oil salesman. 'Skelly told me what happened to you and Samuel. And Henry and the others. And about Brother Mitchell. Why did you come back here?'

'Troopers caught me sleeping. Dragged me on the end of a rope and I come behind their horses as long as I could until I fell. They told me if I run again they would flog me.'

'I said a novena for you. Wished that you had ridden so far north, that you lived happily ever after like a character in a book.'

His face contracts. She thinks he might like to punch the wall, or her perhaps, without any further provocation. But then the fight leaves him. His hands shake.

'They beat you, don't they? That's why you suffer so much pain.' Of their own accord, her fingers trickle down the side of his twitching jaw and across his neck bone.

He pulls back, muttering.

'I'm glad that Skelly didn't know what they did to you,' she says.

Nathanael turns away. 'I ran three times after your brother left. I was afraid if I left again it would be in a box.'

'I wish that I might make it up to you,' she murmurs. Her voice turns hoarse, something the size of a plum catches in her throat. And to Skelly, she thinks. How she had neglected him when he most need-ed love and support.

After their meeting Rosanna shakes the black boy's hand and rides the horse away from the monastery, at least a mile, to squat beneath a peppermint gum and relieve herself of all the irritation in her kid-neys, hoping not to poison the tree. She no longer feels frightened. But she will wait with Lucifer, one hand cupping his nose, head resting against his sweet side. For vespers. These men do not keep dogs and leave their doors unlatched, but they have sharp ears. From beneath the tree she hears choral waves of thanksgiving rise in the air, and she reconstructs from memory the placement of items of interest in the fossil room. Then with this map laid out in her head, she sets off under cover of shadowy twilight. In full confidence, she locates the claw hammer, still faintly visible through the glass of the grimy hut window.

On seizing it, she begins to smash to smithereens the Brother's precious collection. Dust chokes her throat. Debris clings to her hair, spider webs and plaster. And what if he reports her to the Portland police? He will not have the hide, she decides, the yellow-bellied coward, saving her strongest emotion to slam an axe through drawer after drawer of the rosewood specimen cupboard: shattering bird bone, marsupial teeth, lungfish, vertebra, mollusc burrows.

Has not Father Woods spoken to the Bishop of Melbourne about his concerns for the welfare of monastery boys? Nothing more could be done, he told Rosanna. Brothers give him more trouble than the Sisters of Mercy. One of them, Father Woods's own flesh and blood, his brother, has fathered three children. Rosanna had chewed on these morsels of information for months. Years. The priest had been cooler with her since she had committed her worst sin; he had no longer cared enough to divert or placate her. Now he spends his time with the MacKillop girl and warding off his own problems with the Diocese of Adelaide.

104

NEVER RELY ON A MAN

By the time she returns to her lodgings in Portland the sky turns pitch black and salt wind blows straight off the Southern Ocean to whip at her cloak. Even so, she cleans herself with icy water from the pitcher and bowl set upon a carved wood table, and combs her fingers through her tangled hair before she seeks out Edwin. He will otherwise berate her for her filthy boots, her riding habit smeared with limestone powder, her tear-streaked face. She sniffs beneath her arms. She stinks no worse than most people.

Mrs Critchett, who had welcomed them not twelve hours before, sets bread and gruel before her without comment. Rosanna wolfs the meal, casting her eyes around the room as she mops the last dregs of grey potato with her crusts. Her brother, she thinks, will be enjoying hospitality in the bar. But Edwin can not be found and the publican has no clue to his whereabouts, since her brother saddled up a fresh horse in the middle of the afternoon and rode out of town. In the stables Rosanna finds Lucifer and the colts in stalls and the woman's husband sprawled drunk and snoring across a sheaf of hay, half rising to defend himself only when his wife appears and begins to kick his *thóin*, all the while shouting questions at him.

He leaps up, blinking at Rosanna with some recognition. On their arrival, he had regaled her with a ghost story—a ship captain and his murdered child may yet appear by her bed. 'Your brother's gorn. Read the telegram from the Post Office and rode off.'

'No message?'

'He wrote to you.' A weather eye on his wife, the man manages with some comical contortions to release a wad of paper wedged in his hip pocket, and falls back again into the hay. Rosanna shivers as she unfolds the paper:

Kitty has a dangerous fever.
Where have you been?
Levy arrived today expecting delivery of the horse.
Wants to leave for Melbourne at daybreak.
Arrange for Lucifer and the colt to be saddled and fed and tap
on his door tomorrow.
Room 4.
Then follow me by coach to Nelson.
You made me look a fool, Rosanna.

'No that will not do,' she shouts at the inebriated husband. 'I refuse
to believe my brother so inconsiderate.'

'I've never relied on a man,' encourages Mrs Critchett, tonguing her
gum.

Then Rosanna feels overwhelmed by guilt. 'His fiancée is ill.' Sweet
Kitty.

'What could he do then? With you on the wallaby. Stay until morning. Room's paid.' She holds the door ajar for Rosanna.

Half the night Rosanna paces the perimeter of her simple room. Why
had she expected that visiting the seminary would stopper her unsettled feelings? At dawn, she makes her way to the cookhouse, where
she finds a man who must be Levy, in shirtsleeves, mopping up fried
duck eggs with a heel of damper. He swivels his head as she enters.
'Miss Lynch, I presume. Where have you been?' His eyes are red, his
nose inflamed; his voice barks hoarser than a hawk owl.

She surveys him warily. 'Restoring justice.'

'I too. And there will be more to come. Please have the horses ready
in one hour.'

It had been wrong to call the man a cripple, but it has always
grieved her that she must one day give up Lucifer and now, worse, his
colts as interest. Cruelty drives people into the arms of the devil and
she wagers he has suffered too. She stares at his haggard, handsome
face and soft boyish neck, at the line where the sun has kissed it. On
his feet to carry water to the table he leans to the left, adjusting his
posture to accommodate his dragging leg.

The man looks ill and more unpredictable than a one-eyed,

one-legged *balor*, staring her down with his evil eye. Rosanna's heart leaps from Skelly to Lucifer. Jesus in Heaven, seated at the right hand of God the Father, what can be the matter with the man? It will be hard enough to part with the horse without placing him in the hands of an aggrieved man. An ill man.

After that she will have to load herself onto a coach and go home at Edwin's instruction. And for three days be shaken about like a bag of bones or strain her arm hanging from the strap as miles of grey bush swim past her window? It will be near as bad as taking a switch to the soles of her feet for her selfishness. The passengers will reek of eggs and dirty clothes and talk about the dullest topics. By the time she arrives home, Kitty will be well again and she, Rosanna, will have wasted her florins for an imperfect revenge.

She fears for Lucifer's safety on the long ride. 'Indeed, if justice exists I will do better than acting as your groom. I will deliver the horses myself to the Sutherlands in Melbourne.' Even as she says this, she knows it to be what she had wanted—planned—all along. Possibilities rush like a fright of ghosts through her head. Melbourne. Besides, it will be one less mouth to feed at home and perhaps she can strike some kind of advantage in Melbourne Town.

'That was not the arrangement I made with your brother, nor one they would welcome.' His large brow crinkles with irritation.

'Edwin was urgently called away. He instructed me by note.'

'May I see it?'

'I'm afraid not. It includes private family business.'

He pushes his enamel plate aside and uses his hands to raise his sturdy upper body from the table. Limping alters his stature but she should never call him cripple.

'I do not want the responsibility.'

'You will look a chump reporting to the Sutherlands without horses. Leading a pair with so much spirit across unfamiliar country will sorely try you. They could bolt.'

'I fear that should I allow it, *you* will sorely try me.' He pushes his chair beneath the table with such conviction that he rattles the enamel plates.

'I will make the journey an easy one. I have ridden each of the horses to victory on various racetracks. I have trained them. You know this.'

She softens her tone. 'And I have enough money for my lodgings.'

He looks twice, up and down the length of her, slyly fiddling with the chain of his fob, looped between two waistcoat pockets. When he does not immediately answer, Rosanna thinks of appealing to him further but decides to remain silent. Lawyers are vipers. Edwin is right about that. And what could she be thinking of suggesting such a thing—a girl who until now had never travelled beyond Mount Gambier, riding all the way to Melbourne with a slight cough of her own?

She makes to turn from the kitchen outhouse but the man hobbles away first, wiping his mouth with his handkerchief. When she catches up with him outside her room he is shielding a cigarette from the breeze with his cupped hand, even as he wheezes over it worse than a consumptive, as if in danger of falling through death's doorway.

She shoulders past him, knocking his hand; then hesitates, before turning back to take match and flint from his fingers. Smoking is a wonderful antidote for bronchitis. It gets people going in the morning. She lifts the cigarette to his lips and parrots her father speaking to Hugh. 'Cough, now. Clear the decks, so.'

105

THE PORTLAND HANDOVER

Propped against the guesthouse stable wall, prominent authoritative nose running like a faucet, perspiration beading his distinguished forehead, he glares at Rosanna, holds her gaze, as if she has measured him for a rosewood coffin instead of offering to help. The night before, his hacking cough had savaged her sleep until she had tapped and left a jug of water at his door. But she had not felt sorry for him. Not at all. Well, not for long. For ten years he has threatened her family with lawsuits on behalf of the actor's family. Edwin most of all should have taken them more seriously.

It is a shame that Levy had not been killed en-route by wild Blacks, for then she and Edwin *might* have honourably pressed on to Melbourne through Thursday and Friday, stopping in Geelong on Saturday to watch a race—or better still, to ride in one—resting before they rode the last fifty miles to Melbourne, delivering Lucifer and his colts themselves. Rosanna dreams of riding a horse to victory in steeplechases at Flemington or Caulfield. Now Edwin has abandoned her, his sister, leaving her without farewell. Poor Kitty. If she lives through her illness, he should marry her in the spring. What is a promise worth?

Levy lifts his crop as he pushes past her.

'Do not strike Lucifer,' Rosanna shouts, moving between him and the horse. 'Let me help. He loves me well.' Straddling the crossbars of the stall she holds the stallion's head against her bodice. 'There, *cushla*.' She cups his muzzle, fingering two new grey hairs; then tugs him away from the feed and leads him outside to the water trough to take his fill. Levy barks stentorian behind her, one hand on his chest as he hawks into a boobialla bush below the verandah pole and attempts to draw himself upright. Rosanna has seen worse behaviour in her brothers but she glares at him as she hauls down on his horse's stirrup irons, shortening and lengthening them to accommodate Levy's uneven legs. Mother of God, the man is a challenge. How can she trust him with Lucifer?

She stands back to observe him mount. On horseback, with two leads fastened around his wrist and tied to the girth strap, he looks a different man. Hard. Handsome enough. Someone who avers pity, but who does not?

'Go now,' he rasps. 'Speak to the woman about your coach and I'll be on my way.'

'I have done that of course. The stage will not be coming here today or tomorrow.' She needs Mrs Pritchard to refund her fare. 'The driver is laid off three days in Nelson until the blacksmith returns from his mother's funeral to repair its broken axle. If you refuse to take me with you, I will be waiting here; and for even longer if it rains and the river floods.'

She knows he can not blame her for this new source of irritation. Face red, mouth dry and chafed, knees high on the saddle like a jockey, the lawyer sways sideways for several seconds, as if hypnotised by her, before he falls.

Rosanna leaps forward, drags him by the sleeve of his navy peacoat from beneath Lucifer's surprised feet, props his head between his knees and, in the process, snags her best petticoat on a large bent nail. 'Jesus wept.' The man is a caution. Charles Levy shudders and closes his eyes. His forehead feels molten under her hand. Might he convulse? She digs her heel into the turf and works harder to put him upright. 'You cannot ride. How far had you hoped to travel today?'

'Church Street.'

'Church Street where?'

'Brighton.'

'Well you're raving,' she says. 'I'll be calling Mrs Pritchard for a doctor to have you committed.' In the same moment she decides that, if he allows it, she *will* accompany him all the way. Keep the foolish *gossoon* alive. She takes a deep breath, having frightened *herself*.

He tugs at her arm in an attempt to struggle into sitting position and falls back again. 'I'm fine.'

'I'll ride along beside you. Help you manage our horses. I'm stuck here for a short while in any case.' Her smile offers all the equanimity and confidence that she can muster.

He glares at her. 'Out of the question. If your family was more law-abiding, the horse would have been siring champions in Middle Brighton and I wouldn't be finalising an 1860 deceased estate.'

'You're forgetting I knew the man.' She flushes with annoyance. 'Do you have a corpse yet?'

The body found at the approximate date of the wreck, Edwin said, had been claimed by Government House, it being their footman, who had become shickered, cleaning crystal in the dining room in the wee small hours, and crossed the road to the River Torrens to avoid detection. In any case, a groom on the *Admella* swore that while George hadn't appeared on the passenger list of the tight, streamlined craft, he had spoken to him on boarding. On hearing both pieces of information, Rosanna had simultaneously felt grief and resignation, finding little benefit in choosing between two dead bodies. George must be dead but, in any case, back then, a married man, he would never have mentioned her to Levy the family lawyer.

He sways again. His face pales. 'All right, then,' he says, no doubt feeling sorry for himself. Leaning up against her to recover his balance, he lights another cigarette and draws deeply. Then steps away to prop himself against the wall. He watches her face with studied nonchalance. Then coughs again. 'But you can't travel with me *all* the way to Brighton.'

Rosanna recognises weakness in a man but feels as sick as an eel on a bone hook at the thought of him ordering her about. It is a concession and she will take it.

'How far do you think then?' She lifts her chin.

'A brave little bird to risk catching influenza,' he manages before turning away to cough up his stomach. 'I'll doubt that I can allow you to travel much further than Port Fairy.'

'Pfft, and we shall see about that.'

Yet, the lawyer walks his long fingers across her belly, and in bold steps towards her waist, where he pauses a crooked little finger at her cloth belt. Tremors of pleasure run in the opposite direction until another storm of coughing overwhelms him.

'Would you stop that? You're ill.'

'I'm not dead yet. Can you not find a little sympathy for a man?'

Oh, men are full of bravado even when they are vulnerable—she knows that much. Averting her face she pulls away, hoping that her body has not betrayed its hunger to be touched. Criminals facing Levy in court have her sympathy. He attacks on all fronts at once. But Mother of God, she has every confidence that she may manage him; at least as far as Melbourne.

106

CHURCH STREET, BRIGHTON

On Judgment Day, she hopes that Our Lady will remember how she saved Levy's life, because he has sorely tried her. Three days and three nights of riding with horses knee-deep in mud, along boggy tracks, with a grey-faced cadaver swaying in the saddle who will not give in and who eats nothing. Drinking intermittently from the silver flask in his coat pocket, he thrashes his body like a stuck lizard, coughing and complaining next to the small fires she lights each night. In the mornings he berates her—'leave, go home, I do not need your assistance'—lapsing, when she ignores him, into sullen silences.

When they finally splash along Church Street, bedraggled horses and riders sliding sideways in the slanting rain, he drops once more to the ground, as if he has reached the limit of his endurance; no more than a bundle of filthy clothes and muddy boots, so ill that he is finally and utterly speechless. His sister Etta, short for Henrietta, helps Rosanna brush down the horses and settle them in the stables that comprise the ground floor of their home. His mother whispers her thanks over her shoulder as she steers him, lurching from side to side into the balustrades, by the elbow up the stairs to his sleeping quarters.

Mrs Levy and her daughter nurse Charles Levy through the night, holding hot whiskey to his lips, changing his nightclothes and bedding as his fever rages, cradling his head over steaming bowls, pressing mustard poultices against his throat and chest. Etta relates this at midnight when she returns to lie beside Rosanna beneath her patchwork eiderdown. At three, Rosanna hears St Andrew's clock chime and the women arguing about sending the neighbours' boy for a doctor. Hours later, she hears one of them crying on the landing outside the bedroom door. 'I fear he might die like his father,' the mother wails, 'to finance other people's troubles.'

Rosanna wakes next morning to a silence so profound that she fears he must be extinct. Ill or dead, either way, the woman will pack her off home and the horse to its legal fate at the first opportunity. They must know about George's estate and the Sutherlands' claim on the horse.

First, she plans to ride Lucifer along the beach, because she knows that any day now someone will come to take him from her. She presses her head through thin muslin curtains at the window and throws open the shutters, inhaling the usual miasma of cattle dung and human waste, made worse by memories of the night, of sounds made by Levy—coughing, groaning, raving and vomiting—travelling through the wall between his room and the one Rosanna shares with Etta. It reminds her of Hugh, now aged thirteen, struggling to breathe for weeks, through winter and in spring.

Sea air drifts into the room, salty and sharp. Fish and boat smells swell on the wind whistling from the end of the street and through the dormer windows. The chill bites into her skin, pinkly rumpled from the bed linen. She buttons her only jacket, now mud-spattered, and ties her shawl tightly around her shoulders. Nothing can be done about her petticoat until she borrows needle and thread. Removing the newspaper from her sodden boots she pulls them on with difficulty. Craning her neck through the window she muses on the whereabouts of the Sutherland mansion; imagines things differently, imagines herself petted in George's arms in a four-poster bed—a beloved daughter-in-law. Imagines being waited upon by servants.

Downstairs, Lucifer dances out of his stall, placing his muzzle in her hand before spinning in a circle at the end of the row. 'Oh, you old show horse with your cloudy eyes and grey hairs. I hope you can still give their dams satisfaction. It will be a bitter life without you.' Two inquisitive colts poke their heads over the loose boxes and whinny. 'Shoosh now.'

She heaves her shoulders against the heavy stable doors, prises them open, saddles and mounts, canters along the muddy street, past the railway station, across New Street and along Normanby, making her way through a stand of shea oaks onto the sand at Brighton Beach. Gaslights flare on the pier. Through the early morning mist she sees ships anchored and rain falling in a shimmer above the pale grey sea. It is a beautiful sight—not so different to MacDonnell Bay.

She has hardly a moment to enjoy it before a horse and rider thunder across her path from the northern stretch of New Street. She slips sideways, jerking against the pommel and bruising her shoulder. The man's large black hat is pulled down against the cold over the collar of a heavy coat. He carries himself in a strangely familiar posture, head rearing a seeming pace behind his body, knees high in the saddle. The figure starts when it sees her and adjusts the horse's trajectory. Mr Adam Lindsay Gordon. Now famous colonial poet.

Throwing his head as if tossing off a bucket, Lucifer startles into a rocking gait, careering through the sand to the water's edge, where he prances in aggravation. By the time Rosanna regains her balance, Gordon, long-limbed, grim-faced, has set his horse's chestnut nose for the far end of the beach. Nursing her shoulder, Rosanna follows him at some distance. When he rounds the curve where the wooden beach houses stand on the edge of the water, she pulls Lucifer skidding to a stop. No sane person would swim in such bitter cold weather.

What is he doing, coat tails flapping, riding at such a dangerous pace on Brighton Beach? Rosanna dismounts and sits down on the beach to wait until he returns, although she has no particular reason to think that he will. But the cloud of sand kicked up by his horse as he galloped at furious pace along the shore proves to be her last view of him that day. The truth is that he has always rendered people invisible as he passes them on the street, on the cliff top, and especially in a race, and he is wilder in the saddle than Lynches.

Back home, Gordon has doffed his hat to her on rough turf roads. Once, he had touched her. Skin to skin. Mouth to mouth. Once he had slighted her because she had chosen another. This morning his long face and heavy eyes, his slumped shoulders, had reminded her of Skelly, and of Edwin too, when things go wrong. Gordon is not kin, but cliff paths and fast horses connect them, sink holes and limestone streams, Father Woods's books and tragic family histories—although they have never spoken of the latter.

She crosses herself. God, save him from all harm. Men have given her nothing but trouble but she shall spin the pot—widdershins, wid-dershins—until they serve her better. Home she will go, reaffirmed a spinster, done with men forever and their greedy, needy ways. And yet ... how strange to see Gordon in Brighton and contemplate what might have been. Years ago, she had found George Sutherland so much sweeter, simpler than the poet.

107

HOME SWEET HOME

Levy remains abed and Mrs Levy has also lain in exhausted. While Etta corresponds with suppliers, Rosanna tends them, carrying bowls of boxty, tepid tea and lemon curd on thick toasted slices of bread purchased from the baker across the street. For more than a day and night, Levy drifts in and out of sleep, one hand clutching a book of verse on the coverlet. Mrs Levy also succumbs to the influenza and, over the following days, during which Rosanna toils in house and stable, repeatedly thanks her guest through a fog of overheated dreams and congestion.

One day, Charles Levy appears suddenly at Rosanna's shoulder as she dusts the office desk with one hand and straightens papers with the other. From behind, he circles her waist with both hands. 'Etta tells me that Gordon is an acquaintance. I know some of his poetry.'

Rosanna feels his warm breath on her neck before she spins around, unhanding him. 'You must recite one to me. But Charles, first tell me how you injured your leg.' Boldness never deserts her, often bringing ruinous consequences and because of this she flinches, expecting him to seize her or turn away in anger, but his expression softens. Has illness humbled him?

'I fell at Flemington. From one of Harry Powers's horses. A quack set my broken leg at the track. My doctor broke and re-set it weeks later, under opiates, with no better result.'

'Oh, poor you. You were lucky to survive then.'

'Richardson suggested I try spiritualism but I am a cranky rationalist.' He sighs in a world-weary way.

The revelation of this vulnerability surprises her. Is he undecided about furthering his suit, or simply changing tack? 'That is all you have to show for your escapade?'

'My ribs healed but one had punctured my right lung; although

Richardson drained it, I am weak on one side. There. Now you have it. A full report.' His face pales before her and she reaches out to grip his arm. Then he turns and moves swiftly, sliding his bad leg across the floor, through the door, and dragging it upstairs.

No doubt she has offended him, confirming her mother's belief that if you think that life is greener for other people it simply means you do not know them well enough. Mother of God, thoughts bounce inside her like loquats on the boil for jam. She thinks only of the immediate, of dealing with what lies before her. Putting from her mind her rage at the monastery. Bother Levy. She will continue to assist his family as best she can and ignore his pot shots. Taking a book from a glass cabinet she reads for a short while by the kitchen fire, waiting for the kettle to boil for a tea tray.

Back turned to the cooker, Rosanna is soon engrossed, her fingers moving lazily under her skirts to disperse uncomfortable heat into delicious warmth. Only the stink of singed cloth and smoke rising from her petticoat alerts her to sudden danger and she leaps away, shaking her tail like a duck. She flounces upstairs carrying the book and a tray of scones and tea, remembering a story she'd heard back home about the Station's little Irish girl catching alight while warming her *thóin* before the fire. Mr Ashby had rolled her in a braided mat on the earthen floor to save her life. Yet another humiliation for her.

Rosanna's regular irritable cough has quietened in Melbourne. Part of her knows it would be wise to leave for home, perhaps this very afternoon, before she becomes overburdened. Yet Mrs Levy looks so pitiful lifting her hand to receive the refreshments—what will one more day matter?

108

DELIVERIES AND BILLS

Two days later, Rosanna feels just as indecisive about abandoning Etta to run the stables while her brother and mother are ill and, more truthfully, does not wish to explain her extended absence to Father or Edwin when she returns home. As they approach the city by train, she observes Gordon stomping along the platform at St Kilda Station wearing his navy wide-awake hat, the same long coat and too-short breeches that reveal the tops of his boots.

Walking does not appear to improve his mood.

It is not so long since he and Edwin had mashed each other's faces in the dirt after an argument at the card table. Since then, Mount Gambier drinkers frequenting Miss Lallah's *síbín* to drink *poteen* had followed Gordon's undulating fortunes with increasing ardour and sympathy. As one who rode among them and against them, who drank and gambled and yet always held himself separate, Gordon commanded local criticism and attention: a maverick rider who suffered serious injuries after heavy falls from horseback, who entered Parliament and left it, who bought land in Western Australia and lost it, and who took over stables in Ballarat with an old mate, who threw away the profits through sheer incompetence—each achievement and its reversal a saga in itself. Before he moved to Brighton he won the Ballarat Steeple, rode Babbler, Viking *and* Cadger to victory in a *single* afternoon at the Toorak Hunt Club Steeple. He wrote for *Bell's Life* and the *Australasian*. The south-eastern *síbín* goers passed these news bulletins on to their women with suitable embellishment, blandishment and envy, before putting in their boots. In their minds Gordon was as sensational as theatre.

She knows all this. Although Gordon has always been morose, Rosanna sees that something troubles him now, and she remembers his nervy tobacco-stained fingers, his nails bitten down to the quick;

she imagines his head aching as a consequence of all his head injuries.

Twenty minutes earlier she had stepped from the platform onto the train at Middle Brighton Station as if she'd been doing it for a hundred years, pressing down folds of the plaid dress lent to her by Etta and altered by her mother, who was a dressmaker as well as licensee of stables. Since Mrs Levy's husband died, she had related to Rosanna, fewer Brighton men were building mansions and agisting their horses at the stables. She had been forced to take in lodgers as well as sew costumes for the Theatre Royal and the Haymarket. Thus, borrowing a needle and thread to mend her petticoat had not been necessary; a convalescent Mrs Levy had laundered and mended every item of Rosanna's clothing in gratitude for accompanying her son home from Portland.

A gooseneck station lamp frames Rosanna's reflection in a soot-stained window as she lowers herself onto the carriage seat. Oh my. If only Mother could see her prancing about in velvet when she should be home helping with the children. Certainly not gallivanting across Melbourne on a train. But Mother will manage without her, even with the twins born at Christmas who sit fat and smiling like a pair of wombats braced in a packing box.

And Rosanna must do her duty, but never, well at least never in the last ten years, has she felt so stimulated. She now sees why many south-east people wish to secede from South Australia and throw in their lot with Victorians. To canter across the border, to make regular the sale of stock in nearby Portland, and to visit Melbourne by coach or train or on horseback; it is their plainsong.

She and Etta run errands in the city, for Mrs Levy has begged Rosanna at dinner time, plucked at her hand in desperation, to remain in Brighton a few days longer, to help Etta keep the house and hostelry business afloat until she and Charles recover. This afternoon, they must deliver mended costumes to two theatres as well as leave a note for Charles's friends at his club located in the little archway room above *The Argus* newspaper office in Collins Street east.

The note is unsealed, vulgar and late. It informs members of the Yorick Cub that Charles Levy will be unable to partake of social intercourse on Saturday evening 25 June, as he is recovering from influenza, but that he welcomes company at home, particularly if dissolute. Rosanna refuses to feel shocked either by the content of the message or by Etta reading it. Charles's friends are writers and he writes too, according to his sister, in a very colourful, amateurish kind of way. His friends will write anything for money and out of wickedness. Etta is as open as her brother is closed.

109

SILLY BOYS

'There goes Mr Gordon,' Etta remarks. 'On the platform. If you gain his attention, he can take Charles's message.'

Rosanna tugs at Etta's arm. 'Won't we embarrass him?'

'Oh pfft.'

Rosanna taps her clenched fist against the carriage window, torn by indecision and uttering little cries. Head stuck out like a longneck tortoise, the poet turns but seems not to notice them.

'He is short-sighted, you know.'

Etta sighs. 'We shall have to go to the Yorick, after all.'

'I have never been to a club,' muses Rosanna with some relief.

Etta rolls her eyes. 'It is a sacred place dedicated to male symposiums.'

'How well do *you* know Mr Gordon?'

'Why do you care?' Etta has been rolling her gloves off and on in an effort, she says, to ease chafing brought about by nursing her brother. She flaps them at Rosanna, who reaches out and lifts the soft kid to her nose. They exude bergamot and neroli, mixed by Etta and kept it in a silver phial on the shelf above the bed they share.

'Perhaps he makes me homesick. Not so long ago, he lived in a cottage on the cliff tops near my home.' Rosanna sinks back into the plump upholstery. 'He won races on our horses. My brother Edwin knew him better than I.' Men think they know everything. She turns to view the platform along which Gordon has disappeared. 'Why do you suppose that he was walking so briskly? Perhaps he has business in St Kilda.'

Etta looks deeply into Rosanna's face, as if intuiting more; then drops her gaze. 'Gordon is in dire straits. Everyone says so. He probably had no coin for the fare. He and his wife lodge in Mr Kelly's cottage on Lewis Street because he owes money to every trader in Brighton. My brother will cover him if he asks. If Gordon chooses not to libel him Jew.'

Rosanna looks askance at Etta. Debt can be cruel. *Jew*.

'What I meant was that he frequently walks home from the city and in the other directions as well, due to lack of funds. All the *real* writers in his coterie—Henry Kendall, and Marcus Clarke, for instance—are poor. Apart from Mr Haddon, who entices professional men, shop and business men, quacks and little lawyers like Charles to write for free, working on their memoirs or scribbling an essay on the dung beetle. They shore up the club with their membership fees to guarantee good whiskey for the men Charles believes to be true geniuses.'

'Oh that is unkind,' Rosanna says.

'Not so much.' Etta smiles. 'Clarke, the Yorick's present spokesman, insists they emulate the affectations of Bohemians and they savour controversy and disputes over class and hierarchy. They have carried out some disrespectful japes—switching the brass plates of doctors' rooms nearby, stealing door knobs—and I am certain they are known to all the policemen on the Collins Street beat. They act like silly boys.'

'You sound angry.'

'Charles works harder than any of them at his rooms and finds time to write as well. The others lay about, sucking on their churchwardens while they made their erudite way to drunkenness in the early hours of the morning on Little Bourke Street.'

'Church wardens?'

'A kind of cigar. Are you a good girl, Rosanna?'

'Indeed.' Rosanna's mind has leapt to Trollope's warden at Barchester Cathedral. She rolls her eyes. 'And you, Etta?'

'I am not a baby. Since Father died we have all worked hard to keep the stables, the only roof over our head. Charles suffered such bad luck, injuring his leg at Flemington and then compounding the problem with bad treatment. Then he had to study dreary, dusty books late into the night, to sit for the bar. The Yorick Club has saved him from certain *ennui* and provides me with stories you could not make up in a fit. Girls dancing without their underwear, freaks and showmen placing their heads in the mouths of Bengal tigers, and a medical museum of enormous human organs of *every* kind!'

Rosanna is not prim, and Etta's worldliness is frank enough to make her wish for a plain-speaking friend at home. Of course, she would like to see a tiger before she left Melbourne. Years ago at home, she saw one streaking between the shadows of trees. Edwin had ridiculed her almost to death but, since then, there have been rumours of a renegade from a circus.

The locomotive whoops across the Yarra Yarra River, sending out clouds of steam as it reaches the station.

110

DOING THE BLOCK

They alight at Flinders Street and are soon swept along by people rushing towards the turnstiles. Gathering up their skirts against the mud they stride past the Princes Bridge Hotel. The air is thick with soot and coal dust, making Rosanna cough. Bodies press against her, causing her to stumble into filthy pools of water. Smoothing collar and cuffs, she clings to Etta's hand along Swanston Street, stepping carefully over wagon ruts. Drizzly rain has eased to almost nothing over the past few days, but intermittently Etta secures the parcel of costumes beneath her arm to open a large umbrella above their heads and rush them past narrow lanes. Chill winds shunt heavy grey clouds across the steely sky.

'You'll like doing the block on Collins,' Etta murmurs, squeezing her arm as they cross, 'It is Melbourne's premier street.'

Rosanna ploughs along behind her friend, turning her head when she can, to take in fashionable ladies and their companions. Etta offers only a flap of her hand and cursory explanations when they pass gargantuan buildings, including the Town Hall where crowds of people stream in and out. They stride past elegant women lifting their plaid skirts over metal ramps carefully positioned to prevent people falling into water-logged gutters. Men secure their felt hats with one hand, slanting their bodies against the wind, and dash across the street in front of trams and covered conveyances. Rosanna likes being part of a purposeful, surging crowd. 'Etta, must we hurry so, past all these wonderful sights?'

Etta pauses to wait for a fancy buggy. 'We have at least three calls to make and I'm worried about leaving Mother and Charles alone.'

Rosanna nods. As they climb east up the steady incline of Collins Street, she glances at her profile in luxurious shop windows, and sure there she is, reflected against draped fabric, hats with elaborate pins, soft leather shoes; her hair dark and curly, her cheeks flushed, her mouth eager and her waist waspish. Despite the Levys' troubles her time has passed pleasantly. Only one more thing can satisfy her: meeting George's parents to determine their trustworthiness, should anything terrible happen to her. She must think of a way. At the Russell Street intersection, she stops beneath a statue depicting two men. 'And who might they be?'

'Burke and Wills and I haven't time to relate the tragedy,' Etta snaps.

'Oh, I know about Burke, the poor thing,' Rosanna cries, 'for he was a Galway man.' She tilts her head to take in his tragic Irish face, her gaze lingering over the plinth depicting him atop a camel—she has never seen such a creature. Poor, brave fool.

In the moment of their pausing, a small dapper man carrying a rolled up newspaper bumps against them and they all teeter before regaining their balance on the kerb. He straightens, tugging at his three-piece suit, and appears to recognise Etta. His sable fine moustache looks painted on but in a show of animal energy kicks up at the end points like dancing feet. He lifts his hat and bows slightly before hurrying away.

Rosanna watches his retreating back. 'Did he injure you?'

'No, he did not. But Mr Marcus Clarke cut me dead on account of my fair sex and my name.'

'I will go after him and demand an apology,' Rosanna says, retrieving their fallen umbrella and brandishing it like a crop. 'What could be wrong with you being a woman or your name?'

'He dismisses me as Charles's sister.' Etta purses her lips. 'Had he been more polite, I might have dispensed with carrying Charles's note any further. Pride is my vanity.'

Rosanna's mind hovers over the word *Jew* again before she squeezes her friend's arm. 'Don't give him another thought on a gorgeous day like this; look at the wind pushing the clouds away.'

'Oh, I shan't.' Etta sniffs. 'We'll find a friendlier chap at the club.'

YORICK CLUB AND HAYMARKET THEATRE

Cheeks pink, Etta rushes up the hill past tobacconists, undertakers, fruiterers, cafés and hotels where waiters dressed in white serve customers from silver trays, towards the Yorick Club rooms. Finally they reach an archway, above which they see a window lit by a lamp. A horse and buggy are parked in the laneway. Etta continues past them to the adjoining two-story building, on which the name *Argus* had been mounted in brass letters on a plaque. 'Wait here.'

Rosanna tickles the ears of the gaunt old horse. Nothing but bone and gristle, poor mare, her right eye winks with blight. Few things make Rosanna angrier than the ill treatment of horses. She unties the knotted lead and leads the horse to drink at the water trough between the verandah-posts, attracting the smile of a tow-headed scoop boy gathering manure from the street. What an odious and odorous job, that must be poorly paid; the boy looks more emaciated than the horse. Would he not fare better begging?

Etta returns puffing with indignation. 'I expected to find one of them upstairs scribbling verse, nobbler in hand or, at any rate, playing billiards. How difficult their day must be, reading newspapers and cheating at bezique. Then perambulating off to a swank hotel for a meal that will extend until the money runs out in the early hours of the morning. I left Charles's note with a reporter from *Punch* in the office. Now we must hurry to make our own deliveries.'

Rosanna reties the horse and on they march, across two intersections, past several elegantly appointed shops and a closed wet market that takes up several blocks, before turning into Bourke Street and sighting the Haymarket Theatre. Here, people mill about; newspaper boys ply their trade beside little girls hawking posies.

'Peep in the foyer,' Etta urges. 'You'll find a fountain. And a candelabra in the auditorium.'

Rosanna hesitates. Here she is, at the theatre where George prated and pranced for Mr George Coppin. Here lie the ashes of her foolish dream; that George might transform her, a boundary rider's girl, into an actress on a stage. Nothing had been more unlikely. And yet … She *had* acted. She *had* loved. And she *had* survived, whereas George's ambitions had likely come to nothing at the bottom of the Southern Ocean. Soon enough, Rosanna's memories of Melbourne will appear only in brilliant dreams—the real alternatives for a spinster being drudgery, loneliness or death.

'Or stay here, if you wish,' Etta teases, observing Rosanna's fixation with a billboard and several sandwich frames advertising the entertainment. 'I must deliver this costume.' She turns to rush away along the laneway to the tradesmen's entrance at the side of the building.

'No, I'll come with you,' Rosanna replies, glancing over her shoulder and up at the steep walls of the theatre's magnificent façade. She wants to see where George trod the boards.

Backstage, she ducks her head to avoid the low raked ceiling and moves into the room, fingering costumes and noting creased manuscripts, face down on covered tables, with all their ink blots and scratchings-out. These are lit by sputtering lamps, lying beside rusty pens and bowls of desiccated flowers that stink of rot. There are congratulatory perfumed notes, pots of face paint, thick Kohl pencils and fine brushes. A black cat curles like a mollusc on a silk cushion. Signs on the wall caution quiet: Wings; Stage Door.

Members of the cast, Eva the wardrobe mistress explains to Etta, have retired to a nearby café to eat before the evening performance. Eva, hair partially covered by a green turban, ears pierced like a savage's with heavy gold hoops and a mouth full of rotten teeth, is as tall and blonde as a Nordic maiden. When she wants to smoke, she removes dressmaking pins from her mouth and pushes them into the blue Indian shawl furled over her shoulder, adeptly rolling tobacco papers with spit. Etta unfolds tissue paper wrapped around the costume and smooths out wrinkles in the skirt. Eva's voice crackles with intelligence and humour. 'Etta, your mother is an angel from God.' She places a cigarette between her thin lips.

'Eva, meet my friend. She brought my brother home when he was on the brink of death from pneumonia.'

'Women never get credit for their selfless deeds,' Eva replies, as she lights her cigarette.

Rosanna laughs and holds out her hand. 'Her brother is recuperating. Did you ever meet a Mr Geoghegan?'

The woman rests her cigarette on an upturned shoe. 'Geoghegan. The playwright who wrote *A Trip to Geelong*?'

'I know *The Hibernian Father* well but not the Geelong play. It must be him, I think.'

'No one has seen him in half a dozen years. Disappeared like smoke. I remember him because when *A Trip to Geelong* ran here I was afflicted with a woman's problem.' She bites her lip and frowns. 'He'd been a doctor once and helped me.'

Rosanna feels her heart beat in an irregular fashion. 'Do you also remember a Mr Francis Nesbitt? But perhaps you are too young. '

'The great tragedian? I never met him,' Eva demurs, crossing one leg over the other, and swishing her skirt. 'But I know that he expired on stage in Geelong. Poor old McCron.'

Destabilised by the woman's frankness, Rosanna loses all sense of caution and propriety. 'And Mr George Sutherland?'

'Now he was a little sweetheart. We all fell in love with *his* pretty face.'

Rosanna drops her gaze to Eva's stockingless legs. Such plain speaking. Waves of pain crash in her head. *A Mhuire*! A fool she must be to mention George.

The woman's eyes widen as she leans towards Rosanna and prods the air with her cigarette. 'You've been here before then? At the Haymarket?'

'Oh no. I knew someone who knew these people.' Rosanna turns sharply away.

'We must hurry to the Royal,' Etta reminds her, tugging her towards the stairs.

The woman drags hard on her cigarette and stares hard after Rosanna. She calls out. 'Come back and talk to me again.'

Etta urges Rosanna onto the street, an arm encircling her waist. 'Are you all right, darling? You look so pale.'

THEATRE ROYAL

Etta continues to strongarm Rosanna along the laneway and back onto the street. They turn at the corner and descend the hill down Bourke Street. 'You'd better wait outside next time.' She touches her knuckle against her friend's cheek.

Rosanna feels admonished and she buttons her lip until they reach the Theatre Royal.

'Don't wander too far until I return,' Etta commands. 'The passers-by are more colourful, in Bourke and Little Bourke Street, than in the respectable parts of Collins, and it's getting dark. Lively. You must take care.'

Crestfallen, Rosanna trudges up and down the ill-made street, viewing the theatre from both sides; smelling green tobacco and something else: something like sugar syrup burnt in the bottom of a pan. She craves something for the headache brought about by thinking of George. A patina of filth and smoke stains the buildings. Jostling patrons purchase tickets from the booths, girls with cocky hats arranged over their rouged cheeks laugh as they promenade across the foyer; and oyster sellers shout from barrows on the street. Gangs of colonial larrikins, who look no worse than those at home, gather in larger numbers.

Rosanna does not immediately notice a plump, dark man observing her from a doorway, hands glittering with jewellery clasped before him. He looks a proper dandy with his seal-sateen lapels and waist coat, a gold watch chain hanging from his fob pocket and a moustache extending almost to his ears. He holds her gaze as he turns to pluck a satin-clad young girl from inside the house, hauling her onto the street and primping her pale shoulders above her lacy corset in a way that makes Rosanna think she must be partially compliant. His fingers dance across the girl's décolletage, lift her skirt to expose her suspenders and cup her *thóin*. He massages her like a pet; all the while watching Rosanna.

The little girl first kicks him with her yellow shoes and slaps him hard on the side of his glossy pomaded head, ruining the severe central part of his coiffure. The pair resembles roughhousing marionettes—a Punch and Judy show. The man sweeps his hand through his hair in irritation and slaps her. It seems romantic but a performance to attract attention, and sure enough a man shaking out a birds-eye handkerchief approaches the pair. The men confer, the girl half turning sideways until addressed, her pouting lips as red and succulent as floribunda. She follows the men through the doorway next to the hairdressing shop. The dandyish man reappears and beckons Rosanna; raises a glass of sparkling liquor. She scowls and turns away.

Moving past a coffee cart towards a row of shops beyond the theatre, she recognises Henry Tolman Dwight's: Father Woods's favourite place to publish and purchase books. Oh, she can not resist, and through the door she goes, banishing the insolent pair from her mind.

Within minutes she is deeply absorbed, picking up books and placing them down, delighting in the smooth boards of their covers, the gold emboss beneath her fingers, as the proprietor reads behind the counter. Apart from her own copy, she has never seen Mr Trollope's *The Macdermotts of Ballycloran*; not in the Mount Gambier Library, in peddlers' packs or in catalogue selections. Neither does the shop have a copy. How lucky she has been to read a book so colourful, so instructive. The bell ringing over the door breaks her reverie and causes the proprietor to glance up, fanning his copy of *Lorna Doone* against his chest.

'Rosanna.' Etta steps through the doorway, damping her finger and patting wisps of hair behind her ear. 'I should have known you'd be here. After all that nosing amongst Charles's intellectual tomes?'

'I had no idea you were such a little spy.'

'Miss Levy,' calls a man in his thirties reaching the door behind her. 'How pleasant to see you.'

Etta turns and nods in an uninterested way. The pair lower their voices, his still animated, hers reserved but thawing.

After several minutes, she beckons Rosanna and introduces her companion. 'Mr Alfred Telo will escort us to the theatre vestibule, where he will respond to Charles's note as I have related it.'

'I am meeting Kendall soon at the Café De Paris,' he adds.

'Kendall is the best Yorick writer next to Mr Clarke, who made us victims of a hit and run accident today,' Etta says po-faced.

Telo lifts a hand to his chest and swallows as if suffering indigestion. 'I am sorry to hear that. I must confess that I have also quarrelled with him this afternoon, about payment for some work.' He smiles at Rosanna, and under Etta's instruction they shake hands.

'It is a pity that your brother has been so ill,' he remarks to Etta. 'We have capital plans for Saturday evening ... Perhaps he will recover by then.'

They leave the bookshop and progress towards the theatre vestibule. Accosted in the doorway by a hawker with a tray of mutton pies, Rosanna is struck by the size of her hunger and the misfortune of possessing only a few coins. Etta has pocketed the costume money. Inside, people stand shoulder to shoulder. Telo moves past them to approach the bar. On his return with three glasses of Chablis she notices that he also limps. Poor fellow. Can none of these writers keep their seat on a horse? He is otherwise solid and imposing, with his patrician nose and wild facial hair that froths like vegetation from beneath his nose and chin. He acts kindly, inclining his head and stroking his beard with concentration as Etta asks him about borrowing a volume of *War and Peace.*

Sipping her wine from a pewter pot, Rosanna's spirits lift, until she is surprised to notice the unhappy couple from across the road slide into a nearby booth. Up close, the girl looks dirty, with skin eruptions and a burn on the side of her neck. Drunk perhaps, she twists the man's ear, and he clouts her with the back of his hand; his diamond rings draw blood. Rosanna half rises, as the girl staunches the cut with her handkerchief.

Mr Kendall arrives beside Telo's chair and plonks down a bottle of absinthe. 'Perhaps we will meet Gordon at the Café de Paris,' he says by way of greeting. 'Neither the promise of a good steak or reading my *very* favourable review of his *Bush Ballads* tomorrow will shake his melancholia. I swear his mood is contagious.'

'We saw him earlier today, walking towards the town,' Etta says. 'So, at last, the book has been published then? We would have congratulated him had he looked up from his reverie.'

Choosing between George and Gordon had not been a difficult calculation for Rosanna. Gab and wit and *badinage* she loves. Darkness in a man is often dreary and of dubious value to a girl who recognises the same shadows in herself. But she feels pleased that his collection has been published.

'Look, there he goes,' shouts Telo.

Rosanna looks up to see Gordon, hat pulled down over his brow as he rushes along in front of the window. He gesticulates with his pipe at Telo, who, in response, pushes up the sash and calls, 'Come and talk to me about the Mallarmé.' A waiter hurries forward to close the window and Gordon continues on his way, head shaking as if in disbelief. He has seen Rosanna and Etta too—was that why he elected not to join them? What makes him such a contrarian? Telo winks. These men are no better than Edwin and his friends; completely self-absorbed and incomprehensible.

'He will be looking for Clarke, God love him, who also owes *him* money.'

'Why do you think so?' asks Etta.

'He is always on the cadge for money or a feed. Let me buy you another drink before you go.'

'No, thank you, Sir. And for the note for Charles.' Etta stands and waves her glove at Rosanna. 'We must leave to check on our invalids at home.'

113

A DISASTROUS ACCIDENT

Outside, the Town Hall clock chimes five; winter dark descends and fog comes drifting on a light wind, along with the sharp egg smell of gas-lamps. Along the street, young men carrying fire-lighter poles appear and balance on small step ladders to ignite them. On turning her head, Rosanna sees the Theatre Royal lit up—sixteen gas chandeliers blaze inside, Etta says—and thinks it God's mercy the place has not burnt down.

On Swanson Street the quarrelsome couple trail behind them; he hauling on the sleeves of a matted blue fur coat slung around her partially clad body, she shouting obscenities, advancing and retreating, and trying to pull away. Both are staggering drunk, of that Rosanna is sure. The girl cannot be more than fifteen.

'Hurry, we must catch the last train or we'll be stranded.' Etta dabs at her lips with a small handkerchief on which Rosanna has seen her embroidering sprays of lily-of-the-valley, seated at her brother's sick bed.

At Flinders Station, Etta moves below a row of clocks displaying imminent departures, and towards the ticket office. Rosanna waits, taking in the sights: mainly men in office suits slouching on the footpath, tapping their canes, enjoying a cigarillo, leaning against a wagonette dispensing hot cider in front of Mrs McDonald's, a pork butcher. Newspaper boys unpack new papers and wave copies in the air.

Etta returns with their tickets and jiggling, damp-shoed, the warring pair arrives alongside them on the platform, as noisy as a fighting cock and hen. His small, waxed moustache quivers as he tries to unhand the girl seizing his chin. She bleats into his face, her wide red mouth working; her earrings resemble golden scarab beetles swinging against her cheeks. In the next moment she sways sideways, releasing him. He staggers back, then, recovering his balance, jumps up at her, repeatedly smacking her ruddy cheeks and ears.

Rosanna winces, draws in a panicky breath. The hard sound of it, the way the beaded clasp in her hair falls forward and dangles over her left eye makes the girl a pitiful sight. Within a matter of seconds she bends to vomit a lurid-coloured liquid, spraying across his flashy waistcoat.

On the last punch, a right hook to the side of her head, the girl collapses like a bag of silks tossed on a dressmaker's floor and slides sideways across the platform. Rosanna and Etta rush towards her as she ricochets onto the track, into the path of a Sandringham engine.

Brakes screech a hag's scream, and soot swirls as Rosanna reaches the edge of the platform, cloak skirling like one of her beloved bent-wing bats, in time to see the iron wheels slice into the girl's bare leg, unleashing a flush of blood onto the grimy tracks. Etta drops to her knees, clawing Rosanna back by her dress. They hold each other, their eyes fixed on the scene playing out before them.

From every direction railway workers and members of the public run towards the track, leaning over the siding and pulling back, their faces contorted with horror. The screaming girl manages to crawl forwards, dragging one leg, her soiled costume clotting behind her.

After a burly ambulance driver carries the poor girl away by stretcher and the police have questioned onlookers about the actions of the dapper man, it seems bad form to bother the platform guard about their onward journey, or the officer roping off the section of track where the accident occurred. What can be the matter with the little pimp that he would treat a girl like that? God damn him to hell. And he has run like a fox from the scene. The skulking coward. The bilking bastard.

114

A CHANCE ENCOUNTER BY THE YARRA YARRA

Etta has torn her dress and scraped her leg in her efforts to secure Rosanna on the edge of the platform. They bind the wound with a silk scarf and she hobbles forward; then begins to cry as she makes her way to the ticket office to enquire about the likelihood of another train. Five minutes later, she returns clutching her ticket and no reassurance for their return journey to Brighton. 'What shall we do?'

'Let us,' Rosanna suggests, 'come back and ask again when we have collected ourselves.'

Arm in arm, they turn towards the river, walking east away from the Princes Bridge where rats skitter through yellow pools. Debris litters the riverside paths, reminding Rosanna of the deluge on the night she arrived in Melbourne when, according to the *Argus,* the Yarra Yarra had broken its banks and surged through nearby streets. Seagulls seeking inland shelter perch on broken fences and tree stumps. A light breeze chops at the oily water, sweeping paper and broken tree limbs back towards the railway station from whence the girls have fled. The air stinks of rot.

Espaliered across the fork of a fallen branch, they see a small, billed grey creature with leathery feet. Perhaps it perished upstream and rolled in its rigor mortis, like a Catherine wheel, for miles and miles along the river. If only Skelly were alive to sketch its remains, its duck bill, its vicious spur; if only he had lived long enough to see more of the strange things he had only shared in books with Father Woods. Rosanna reaches out for Etta's hand. Tears well.

Under the black dripping trees they notice a camping place: a sheet of canvas; a tin billy; rags; smoky wet coals. Almost at once a black man in a shoddy suit jacket and bare legs materialises, cigarette drooping from his lips. Etta starts back, hand to her breast. Rosanna begs a shilling from her purse and offers it to him.

'*Birrarung,*' the man says, pointing to the river. Fog swirls around him as he swings back to face them. Then he bounds up the bank, directing them to a horse and growler cab, offering the coin to the driver snoring in the seat, head tucked inside his coat like a grey-headed possum.

'No, no,' Rosanna cries and offers the coin again. 'Etta?'

'*Wurundjeri.*' The black man steps onto the riverbank path and then turns. 'Charles Dickens is dead,' he calls back. 'Apoplexy.'

Rosanna seizes Etta's arm in surprise. 'It must be in the newspaper. Do you believe him? Will we go back to the station?'

'I don't believe I have the strength to walk back for a paper or a train. We could wait hours.' Etta's face reflects her tired bemusement as she hands the driver a second coin. 'We will use Eva's payment for now. Mother will understand.' She hesitates and turns to the driver. 'Drive us to Brighton, please?'

Rosanna puts the great author from her mind. Perhaps the black man made it up. She knows that neither she nor Etta will forget the unfortunate girl lying ruined on the railway track, who now faces an even more uncertain future. She stares back across the dark water.

Clopping through fog comforts her. The horse snorts companionably and lights along the roadside sway in the breeze. Drops of rain freshen Rosanna's face when she leans from the window; Etta dozes propped against her as the driver sings 'Paddy and the Railway' and 'Homeward Bound'. In that moment, Rosanna feels homesick. But despite Charles Levy's irascibility, she has grown fond of his family and of Melbourne too.

Life would have been different living here with George. As the wife of a wealthy only son, she could have patronised the Yorick men, paid them for their writing, enabling them to establish another small journal that would bankrupt. Gordon, Kendall, Clarke and Telo are drawn to each other by failure; she reads this in their haunted eyes. They have no right to her concern but, all the same, she feels sorry for them. Failure is something familiar to Lynches.

In any event, she will soon be gone. Etta has promised to write. Mrs Levy has offered her a portmanteau to carry on train and stage in a day or two. Perhaps she will be well enough tomorrow for Rosanna to book her seat. Nothing will make her consider boarding a boat after the wreck of the *Admella*. Leaving Lucifer remains the hardest trial of all; she'd rather cut herself with knives.

115

MORE DISCONCERTING NOTES

Rosanna retreats to the kitchen stove, where she throws up her skirts and warms her *thóin*—Jesus wept, she never learns from her mistakes—then smooths a page of her book, open on the wooden table. All morning she has thought about Dickens. According to Charles the news is true and can be found in all the morning newspapers. Etta has found another peremptory note dropped onto the mat below the brass letter slot in the front door. She carries it to her mother abed upstairs.

A lady demanding the delivery of her costume for *La Traviata* has penned it and, as a consequence, Mrs Levy will stay up half the night hemming and sewing on pearl buttons. By dawn she collapses with exhaustion, crying out to her daughter, who must, she begs, deliver the paper package to the Sutherland household immediately. Rosanna, who has followed her friend upstairs, starts at that lady's name. Holding her tongue, she straightens the bed cover and lifts sewing supplies, cloth scraps and empty teacups onto a tray. Inexplicably, she slides Mrs Levy's ivory-handled embroidery scissors into her pocket. Her nerves jangle at the mere mention of George's name.

Etta folds the voluminous froth of satin and all its petticoats, kisses her mother's pale cheek, finger to her lips—'lie back'—and leads Rosanna across the landing.

'To the Sutherlands?' Rosanna whispers to Etta.

'You know them?' Her eyebrows arch in surprise and then deflate. 'Ah, the business of the horse.'

'Yes. No, not exactly ... but I knew their son.'

'Their son is dead.'

'Yes.' Rosanna forces the blades of the sewing scissors hard into her hip through the fabric of her pocket. It is too much. She burns to meet George's parents; at the same time nothing terrifies her more. Her heart seems to have capsized but she must stay afloat for Arlen and the other children. 'May I come with you?'

She straightens up and stills her hand at her hip so that she can hold Etta's attention with her eyes. Pain blossoms in her side. The ghostly voice of Skelly murmurs in her head. 'Rosanna. Why?' Well, he would shake his head. Of *course* he would. She can hardly explain it herself. *Shut it, darlin'. It's none of your business.*

'Why do you want to come?' Etta echoes Skelly's question in an eerie way.

'I promise that I will tell you everything, tonight when we retire.' Etta is a darling girl and Rosanna must learn to trust people. She cannot go on forever thinking the entire world against her. Oh she has resolved to change before. To become a kinder person. To create a better future for her family who depend on her—more than ever. But how to make it come about?

Etta sets off down the stairs, tugging Rosanna's skirt behind her as they descend. 'We shall see, then. Come.' They pull on hats and gloves and set off for the stables. If only she had made a plan instead of stuffing her head like a sausage with prevarications. Part of her dreads approaching George's childhood home, another part yearns to see the place where he was raised, where he played and rode and sang and recited.

After all that, craning her neck as Etta hurries along the narrow hedged path to the Sutherlands' kitchen door and taps with the handle of her umbrella, Rosanna sees little more than the service lane behind the house, and the frowsy face of a little maid who takes the parcel, dropping coins into Etta's upturned palm and closing the door with her foot.

'Wait,' Etta says, wedging in her own. 'I need to speak to your mistress about a hat.'

'She ain't at home,' the maid replies. 'She ordered the carriage early and I'm to follow her with the dress.'

Etta hugs Rosanna. 'We will come back, I promise.'

116

GORDON AND ROSANNA ON THE BEACH

Rosanna takes the last rise before the beach in a flurry of sand, reining Lucifer in to prevent it from endangering early-rising promenaders, before she hurtles over the small enjambment. What must Etta think of her? Rushing away like that. Reckless. But she will need to leave Brighton very soon and Etta need never again vex herself over her friend's bad behaviour. An intractable sky of icy grey shards joins in reproaching her. She removes her gloves to wipe her eyes and rub thumb and forefinger together, each red and irritable from the cold. Before her, breakers roll towards the shore.

A tall grey horse whinnies from where it is tethered beneath a spindly tree. Rosanna lifts her eyes by degrees, to follow sandy footsteps to the water, then halfway to the thin insubstantial line between sky and sea, where silver lights ghost the surface like airborne iridescent particles or tiny flying fish.

A small dark head bobs and surges forward, such a long way out. She glances back to a jacket tied by its sleeves around a branch behind the horse, and again at the deep impressions in the sand where someone has walked down to the beach. The swimmer will drown; his balls will likely turn to ice and snap right off. Her horse skitters and neighs, moves towards the other one in a show of bravado. Oh lord, is the swimmer *trying* to kill himself?

Dismounting and placing her hand to her brow she observes the figure sinking in troughs of wild water. Wind bites at her skin, at her neck and wrists and ankles; sand swirls into her eyes until they sting. If only she had brought Father's oilskin coat. For a long time, the swimmer bobs between breakers surging towards the shore. Then, just when she thinks he might disappear from view and never be seen again, he turns and strokes slowly back to shore, veering slightly in the direction the waves are running, correcting himself, lifting his head to aim for some point on the land he has memorised, a study in concentration.

He finally stumbles out of the surf, regains his balance in the shallows and shakes out dark ringlets clinging to his neck like seaweed. Rosanna realises that she has moved almost halfway to the water's edge, drawn by his apparent calamity. She sways in the wind, one hand over her mouth, the other pushing down her habit. He is a full six feet at least, and stamps towards her through the sand, trousers flapping against his calves, cream shirt clinging to his back and waist. She had never doubted that the swimmer would be a man. No woman would act such a fool in these conditions.

Looking up and noticing her, he turns sideways, she surmises to hide his expression, for she sees that despite his chattering teeth and shaking limbs he is full of exhilaration. It is Gordon, his face now breaking up like the weather. He catches her eye severely as if daring her to say a word. She lowers her head to gather her wits. She thinks of the day he caught her bathing at Ashbys' station and then tried to take advantage of her.

Rosanna remembers wonderful wanton hours spent diving and splashing in the pond with Moorecke; how they had laughed like hussies even on days they both felt sad. Water heals. But neither of them would dive into a winter sea. Only Gordon has a reputation for it. The Levys had told her so. Fair weather and foul he swims every morning, tearing up the surf as if it were his enemy, stroking across Port Phillip Bay towards the city as if he has an appointment with madness.

'What are you doing in Brighton, girl?' he asks, pushing his hair from his face.

She feels discombobulated. Looking up at him, she tries to pin down the reflective sadness in his eyes.

Weak sunrays dart at them from behind a cloud, offering pale encouragement. Gordon looks entirely different to the gentleman she observed two nights ago, striding past the Café de Paris along Bourke Street.

'I was sorry to hear about your daughter,' she says. Gordon will not back away from this, she knows, for despite his faults he has a reputation for honesty.

'There cannot be a worse tragedy than the loss of a child. It brings abjection to everyone,' he admits.

She inclines her head. 'Perhaps there will soon be another child.' But even as she speaks she recognises her lie. The unfairness of mentioning such a thing. Her hand grazes his wrist crazed with scars.

He whips his hand to his head and grimaces. 'My constant companion, pain.' The inside of his head is likely scrambled, the result of falling from horseback. Gordon shakes himself like a shaggy dog. Water sprays from his hair and reddish beard, onto his milky skin. 'I did not recognise you earlier this week, Miss Lynch, although I thought I remembered the horse. And on Bourke Street, the circumstances were awkward. I was hurrying to meet someone.' He stares hard into her face again. 'You've been weeping.'

'It was nothing.' She brushes her cheekbone with her fingers. 'You look unwell yourself, sir. And why would you take your headache out for a swim?' In an effort to recover, she cocks her head and parts her lips to form an impersonation of a smile.

He also makes a futile attempt at cheerfulness. She has never seen him smile. It is but the ghost of a smile and swiftly retracted.

'You have not led an entirely fortunate life?' he says.

Oh, he is canny, she thinks. Perhaps he has not heard of her wins at picnic races and on the track. Perhaps he has heard only that for the past ten years she has been as old and barren as Sarah in the Bible, marking her time by grinding work, sustaining herself by telling stories to Lynch children but not knowing how they will end, by reading new ones obtained from the Institute library and falling asleep on the pages with a quaff of grog in her hand, wondering when she too will disappear like her brother. Stuck. Like a little bentwing, flapping in the deep recesses of an isolated cave. Edwin has built himself a tidy little business, and lost it several times over. Soon he will have land proferred to him by the government of Victoria and leave them all behind. Cuchulain shone with his own light; Cuchulain owned his name; and Cuchulain's story will remain. Edwin's too. Rosanna's—not a chance. Nor Skelly's either.

117

A LATE REPRIEVE

'Tell me something wonderful, Gordon,' she challenges him, staggering a little in the soft sand beyond the tea trees.

'I am on my way to the city to borrow money.'

'*Alilu*,' she says. 'More wonderful than *that*, please.'

'The money will pay a printer that I may hold my first collection of poetry in my hands.' He spreads them out before her, indeed, looking full of wonder.

'Huzzah,' she says.

'Tell *me* something wonderful,' he says, spraying her with sand.

'I will bring to Melbourne three more horses sired by Lucifer and you will race them to victory. They will win every race that afternoon. I will back them and become richer than Croesus.'

'*More* wonderful.'

'I will bring a champion filly to town that will win the Melbourne Cup. You and I will escort Mrs Gordon, Etta and Charles Levy, and your Melbourne friends to Parliament House where the new Irish premier will toast us,' she crows.

He begins slapping at his clothing in an effort to reduce his saturation but with sardonic amusement. His teeth chatter. 'Ride with me while the wind dries my clothing.' After all, he looks at her kindly, his eyes glittering with something resembling exhilaration.

'Do you know the most wonderful thing of all?' she asks.

He unties his horse from the tree and mounts in a clean smooth motion, looking down at her.

'One day you will be so famous for your poetry that the mayor will give you the keys to the city and the people of Melbourne will cheer you in a street parade.'

She thinks he would like very much to laugh, for she has become so absurd—oh if only Edwin or Skelly were here—but, nevertheless,

Gordon has entered into some sort of contract with her; just for a few moments, to become part of her game. And he urges his horse forward, rising up in his stirrups to point at the sea.

A pod of dolphins cavort across the bay. She has never before seen such creatures, let alone heard them laugh. In any case, the wind blusters in, throwing up sand and drowning out their chatter, until the dolphins are scarcely visible and she and he canter up the beach away from them. Back and forth Rosanna and Gordon weave, jumping their horses over wooden fences along the roadside, turning each time on a threepence and leaping away again. A mangy yellow dog follows them, yapping with excitement as they gallop along the beach. Rosanna begins to feel warm in the face and happy, as if the pair of them are young again, pounding along the road to Penola or across the cliff tops to Carratum Station.

As the horses flag, he manoeuvres his mount beside hers and shouts over the shushing sound of the waves, 'I liked you then, girl, your sweetness, the way you sat a horse, the way you sassed your brother, and chucked a race on his horse. Such courage. You reminded me of my mother. My father would have told you that when I was young, I acted the same. I fell into so many scraps but, even so, he loved me.'

Her heart swells with indecipherable pride. But her father will never be *proud* of her, although in recent years he had spoken to her with more civility. He will say an Irish girl's place is with her family. They can only be strong together. When she departs for Mount Gambier on the next coach as planned, she will remember Melbourne as a place of failed dreams. Not her place at all. Skelly had been the watcher and she will take his place, guarding her family with much more grace from now on: drawing on memories of Etta and the city, of the wild seas along the coast road, of her beautiful act of destruction at the seminary. She will give up her dreams for them. But though she accepts all this she feels confused. Perhaps she will stay.

As she and the poet ride towards New Street, where they will go their separate ways, Gordon raises his whip and points in a northerly direction—'you can find me some days at Lewis Street'—and she lifts hers and turns into Church Street on her way to Levys' stables.

'I want to hear from you, girl, when the horses are ready!' she thinks she hears him shout.

118

BAD NEWS

That she and Gordon might race Lucifer's colt, an untried two-year-old, at Caulfield in the spring is surely no more than an empty notion, although it interrupts her sleep. She feels a cautious happiness. But then one day at breakfast, Etta returns from an early walk and hands her a telegram; Rosanna stirs her porridge with more ragged gaiety.

> Come home immediately. Kitty recovered.
> Wedding in ten days. Mother ill with worry about you.
> Garrick Lynch

All at sea, she considers her options. Every day, Mrs Levy shows her gratitude for the selfless and confident way Rosanna, a stranger, winds red flannel around feverish necks and heads, exercises horses, takes millinery orders, delivers sewing and carries messages to the courts on behalf of Charles. When bills arrived from testy creditors and the stables fail to attract new customers, lines of worry deepen on the lady's forehead.

But Arlen and the other children at home play on Rosanna's mind as naturally as wind. Mother cannot go on forever, bearing and burying babies, even with twelve-year-old Blinnie's help. If Rosanna remains well enough, she can send money home. She could fetch Arlen and perhaps Hugh to work in the stables, but she doubts the enterprise would generate enough in wages without further burdening the Levys. And Mother would miss the boys; both so precious in different ways. No matter how useful she has been in bringing Charles home, in becoming a chum to Etta, and in nursing members of the Levy family after they succumb to the influenza, she can impose on them no longer.

In any case, Father would not hear of such a plan. What would be the point, he would argue, of family emigrating to strange new places and then deserting each other; when they can pull together and lift themselves out of the bog? Before she left, everything he said had a desperate edge. After dinner he took his medicinal whiskey, his anxieties about daily setbacks—imagined slights and innuendos—until his granite-carved mask blurred, his head slumped on his chest and, Rosanna suspected, he cried with frustration. She longs. Oh she longs.

'Good morning.' Rosanna swings her head. Charles Levy stares at her as if he has forgotten her name and, certainly, the reason for her presence at the family table. It is the right time to go. In convalescence his limp is more pronounced, his cravat clumsily tied, his toilette incomplete. Compassion wells in her and she reaches across to steady the chair he has seized in agitation. 'It is not a good morning then?' She concentrates on his weary eyes.

'Gordon is dead,' he announces.

Rosanna's body arrests; air sucked from every pore. 'That cannot be so. I rode with him on Monday around the bay. He seemed quite hale. No more despondent than usual and he is not so old. We made plans to meet on Friday and talk about a horse.'

Charles grips the top rung of the chair.

Etta floats behind him, placing a hand on his shoulder and then drifting towards Rosanna, her eyes widen with concern. 'Today is Friday.'

'I saw Kendall on my morning walk. He was very cut up,' Charles says in sombre tone, 'I know Gordon meant something to you.'

'I ... my brother and father ... knew him in Mount Gambier. When we meet, not often, we speak of those times, of horseflesh, of steeplechases. He is lately down on his luck but ...' Rosanna smooths and smooths the folds of her gown, perspires, smooths again.

'Quite.'

She stares at him; scans Etta's face. 'Was there an accident?'

'In a manner.'

Etta pushes bowls of food towards her brother; he pushes them back. 'Poor Mr Gordon,' she cries. 'Did he fall from his horse? I hear he is quite short-sighted.'

'I'm afraid not. Look, I have to go. A few of his friends are meeting at the Marine Hotel, where he left his mount. We're driving on to the Yorick for drinks and then to lunch.'

'You must tell us what befell Gordon,' Rosanna interjects, rising to her feet. 'Poor Mrs Gordon has already lost her child.'

'It would not be proper to talk about that lady or the particulars of her husband's tragic death,' he says, looking askance at her. 'Indeed, this is a terrible loss for her, for all of us.'

Etta passes his coat, hat and an ironed handkerchief, which he places in his breast pocket. She kisses his cheek. 'It is too sad that the life of such a clever man should end so soon. You were fond of him as we all were.'

Rosanna pushes her chair hard against the table and runs.

119

EARLY MORNING GRIEVING

Levys are not like Lynches, Rosanna decides as she turns Lucifer down Church Street, across New Street and canters into the shea oak scrub fringing the sand hills. Charles is a stitched-up prig. The horse, the sky, the sea amplify her melancholy; wind slapping at her cheeks, drying her tears that begin to fall the moment she disappears between gnarly trunks and untidy foliage tipped with the remains of the frost lying in melting piles on the ground. It would be indiscreet for a comparative stranger to make enquiries about Gordon in the street; perhaps Charles's account isn't true and Gordon is alive. She will ride until the stallion begs to stop and that will be a very long time; she'll probably find herself halfway to Black Rock.

When she returns, no doubt, she will find Etta and Mrs Levy sitting by the fire, stitching golden spangles on red satin or black frills on circular taffeta skirts, pasting decorations on flim-flam hats. They will look up from their work and try to read her face. Etta will rise and take her arm to offer consolation. 'Sit down. Here, eat a little pastry. Let me bring tea in your favourite cup.'

Rosanna will say, 'Darling, it was not true about Gordon. He and I just rode to Sandringham and back.'

Paying little attention to the great boats on the horizon or those moored at the wharf, Rosanna follows the curve of the shore. A strangely docile Lucifer moves smoothly beneath her on the hard corrugations near the water and picks up pace when she urges him on with her legs. Not wanting him to lunge into the surf for a swim, she loosens his left rein in her glove and veers up the beach through softer sand, in which he momentarily sinks.

A breeze swings around from the south throwing grit in her face and she raises her hand to her forehead to protect her eyes. At the top of the rise, close to Park Street, she sees two policemen hammering pegs and tying them with rope. One of them tips his hat to her in a solemn way, the other waves her off, which piques her. She has never blinkered Lucifer and he turns too, to assess their risk or interest, although it will not do to be too inquisitive about police business. Around the next bend she rides, making her way between the trees, out of sight where she can still observe them working.

To her surprise she finds herself with company. A boy, of about Skelly's age the year he died, steps out from beneath the canopy of a sprawling tree. He has evidently been sleeping there, for she sees dirty, crumpled bedding and a water container hanging on twine from a branch.

When she dismounts beside him he grins and points. 'See the coppers? Some bleddy old poet shot himself before breakfast.'

'What do you mean? Do not be disrespectful.' She begins to gag.

He eyes her resentfully, preparing to withdraw beneath his curtain of needles. 'All the same to me. Why should I care? Just some clumsy toff.'

Rosanna steps towards him and offers him a halfpenny. 'Please, tell me what happened. You were here? It must have been terrifying.'

'Safe as houses, I was. Who knows, if I went down there they might have tried to hang it on me.'

'I understand.' Tying Lucifer's reins to a branch near a patch of green feed, she subsides in the sand like a sea anemone, skirts billowing around her. She takes in the boy's fixed address, the pitiful details of his housekeeping: unripe fruit, no doubt scavenged from neighbouring yards, coloured glass bottles and rags.

'I was at the back of the Hotel where I sell stuff I find. *He* told me it was a poet.'

'Oh, so you didn't see it happen?'

He shakes his head.

She tries to imagine Gordon's spirits low enough to be sucked out by the tide on the dawn of a grey day: 24 June 1870. Now, dreams of their shared enterprise evaporate; of racing the colts and running a book at the Brighton Races; let alone attending the Melbourne Cup with Charles and Etta, to cheer their investments around the bends. She will never raise a glass of porter with Gordon and his wife, on the lawns at the finish line, or share any kind of victory with him. It has all been daydreaming. It means nothing in God's grand scheme.

She gives the boy another halfpenny and leads Lucifer away through the scrub to the hotel. She, at least, is still alive, and what happens next will determine her future—different to the one she had imagined, in which Gordon was to be lucky and she was not.

At the Marine Hotel, a dried-out husk of a woman named Ailsa offers her warm toddy and she stands some distance from a group of sober men, more than likely jawing over the tragedy. Ailsa tells her that Gordon carried his service rifle past the hotel at six a.m., perhaps on his way to target practice, and finding the publican Mr Prendergast abed, continued on.

What had happened after that? Images of Gordon's lonely, loveless death flooded Rosanna's thoughts. She pictures him trudging across the sand to sit in gloom, rifle tucked under his arm, collar turned up to protect him from the biting wind, fingering a few paltry coins in his pocket, barely enough to buy a drink or a newspaper. What had crossed his mind as he sat hunched over in the inadequate shelter of a belt of shea oaks? Had hungry gulls shrieked overhead? Had he recited a few last lines of verse, his own or Lord Tennyson's perhaps. Had he knelt to face his beloved sea and placed the rifle between his knees, resting the tip of the barrel on his forehead? Had a gull alighted beside him and cocked a pink eye in curiosity, before it'd been flung skywards in an explosion of skin, feather, shell grit, brain muck and fabricated cloth? What if the publican had been awake? Would Gordon still be dead?

Back along New Street Rosanna rides, crying but fortified by rum, trotting Lucifer towards Lewis Street, where she sees half a dozen people, including men she recognises from the Yorick Club, Charles Kendall and co., clustered at the small wire gate that opens onto the cottage pathway leading to Gordon's lodgings. Charles stands with his back to her.

Pretending no interest she rides past and pulls up to observe them from an avenue of trees at the house nearest to the beach. For what, she knows not. Sympathy for Mrs Gordon is soon overtaken by self-pity. Although neither of them will receive a penny, Gordon's Annie will not be left as compromised as Rosanna was when George drowned. But then, she thinks of the magnitude of the breaker poet's financial problems, the debilitating debts that probably drove him to his death and trumped his granite pride. The Galway magistrate, Father and her own pride come to mind. For sure one of Gordon's rich friends would have loaned him enough to keep him from ruin. Had he exhausted all avenues of help? She bends to pluck white chrysanthemums through the iron wicker fence, a raggedy bunch, and through her tears watches Mrs Gordon's visitors disappear inside the house. The yard is empty of well-wishers when she lays the bunch across the woven doormat and retreats.

120

ROSANNA HATCHES A PLAN

Rosanna gallops along New Street, retracing her route to the beach until she finds herself on her knees in sand at the makeshift shelter above Gordon's place of death. The boy is nowhere to be seen. The police cordon remains, the beach empty of live souls. For an hour at least she sobs into the gritty wind that knots her hair and scratches at her skin, even as Lucifer munches contentedly nearby.

Who would commit such an act of violence when furnished with resources and in full possession of their wits? Of course, any death is sad, and the death of someone you know quite momentous, but it is more than this that troubles her. In some way she feels Gordon's spirit is commingled with hers, for they have both ridden hard against the odds; both made mistake after mistake; both found solace in books. They are both tragic characters; no different to Anthony Trollope's Feemy Macdermot of Ballycloran and all the others. Although he is a genius and she is not. Life is surely no less than froth and bubble and, without money or luck, barely tenable at all.

She sits for a long time, arms hugging her knees, attempting to dispel prophetic visions of another young man suffering similar penury in the future, and finding it more than she can bear. She does not want this suffering for her brothers and sisters—but especially not for Arlen. The sun breaks through a tempera of yellow clouds and inexplicably her spirits lift. Why should anyone die in poverty? Why has her family struggled to scratch out a living all these years, when they are clever enough and hardworking? George has gone and now Dickens and Gordon too. Life is truly precarious.

Deep in her heart something shifts. Within the darkest caves she had always been able to locate an arrow of light and move cautiously towards it. This very day she must visit a second Brighton mansion and make a sacrifice she has long considered. It may lighten her parents' load. Another daughter might have married well and assisted them in their older age—perhaps Blinnie will create a different fate—but Rosanna must make the most of the fortune she has been allotted. She swallows an irritating cough as she mounts Lucifer.

The stallion puts on a good show, makes his way to the house with unusual decorum, as if he senses the momentousness of her decision for them both. Staring over the privet hedge at the substantial grounds, she almost turns and runs. She checks the name on the painted sign: *Cedars*. French doors have been flung open onto the garden; topiaried trees fringe ornamental ponds and a croquet lawn; opera music issues from a piano in the morning room. Horses neigh, and chickens cackle in the walled kitchen herbarium; putrid smells pervade the pit outside the washroom. The normality of such sights and sounds reassures her as she leads Lucifer to a loose box in the stables. But how can she relinquish him on such a terrible day?

No one stirs about the house, which owns so many rooms, attics and cellars that humans might disappear inside and never be seen again. The place seems bigger than a village. George's family must be grander than the Ashbys. Quite by chance, Rosanna encounters the singer when the piano ceases its noisy outpouring and she steps out onto the verandah.

'Good afternoon. I am sorry to trouble you,' says Rosanna, stepping from the shadows thrown by European trees into the light. 'Have you heard that a man died on the beach this morning?'

The woman clasps a sapphire necklace at her throat in a compulsive gesture made more dramatic by her royal blue opera cloak, pinioned at her wrists with velvet ribbon. In her right hand she holds an ornate silver lorgnette. Has she been rehearsing for a musical production? Had George learned theatrical effect from his mother?

'Where is Jane?' the woman asks, turning her head from side to side in a way that sets blonde cascading ringlets in motion. Her large green eyes and retroussé nose lend her an easy beauty that must enchant her dinner guests. But she has a faint sour line around her mouth when in repose that suggests disappointment.

'Surely, you must be Mrs Sutherland.' All at once, Rosanna drops her arms to her side and sways, feeling unexpectedly faint.

'Oh, my dear.' The woman gasps and rushes back through the

French doors, lifting out a small velvet parlour chair. 'Do sit down. I'll call for a glass of water.' In and out of the house she wobbles, several times, the last time bringing a second chair and a hobnail glass of water, but all the time keeping surveillance over Rosanna. 'My husband is out. How fortunate not to have to explain yourself to him.'

Peacocks cry mournfully from the trees.

'I delivered napery here last week. Sewn for you by Mrs Levy. So I knew where to come.' Rosanna loosens her belt and straightens her spine against the hard chair.

'Indeed.' Mrs Sutherland looks perplexed. 'And your name?'

'My name is Rosanna.' She elects not to offer her surname until she feels more composed.

Mrs Sutherland shifts a little on the padded chair, lifting her small plump chin, no doubt speculating on how she will get rid of her unwelcome guest and resume her music practice. 'Well then, I am sorry that you feel ill on such a difficult day. Who died, did you mention?'

'Mr Gordon, the poet and steeplechaser.'

'Oh my goodness, I do believe he came to one of our musical recitals. My husband met him at the rifle targets and invited him. He didn't stay long. Seemed a morose sort of fellow ...' She catches her tongue and stops.

'He was discovered by a passer-by on the beach below Park Street, with a bullet in his head.'

Mrs Sutherland begins to fan herself, as if Rosanna has dragged the body up onto the verandah and demanded that she inspect it. Her bosom quivers, her lips tremble. 'You must go. We are no strangers here to tragedy. Not so long ago, *my* son drowned in the wreck of the *Admella*.'

'I lost someone in the same wreck and, soon after that, two brothers.' Rosanna places her empty water glass on the top of the balustrade.

'George was my only child,' Mrs Sutherland continues, her voice catching. 'A beautiful boy.'

'Yes,' Rosanna replies, fixing her eye on her face. 'Indeed.'

Mrs Sutherland cocks her head. She thinks perhaps that she has misheard.

'You should return to the Levy stables now. They will take care of you. I can't imagine why you came here.'

'I took flowers to Mr Gordon's wife. In the next street.'

'I would offer any woman sympathy in such circumstances. Do you have a means of conveyance at the gate?' She tips her head askance at Rosanna's dishevelled lemon riding habit, one of Etta's, now greased and rained upon.

'I boxed my horse in your stables, there being no groom in attendance.'

Mrs Sutherland looks alarmed and utters 'pffts' and 'pshaws' in rapid succession.

'Mr Gordon's terrible death reminds me of the dangers of unpaid debts. I am determined to act against injustice.'

'Of course, we all wish to do that.'

'My brother sold his stallion to your son, and during the drama of the *Admella* wreck the horse galloped ashore. He is rightfully yours.'

Mrs Sutherland begins tapping her foot and turning her body towards the refuge of the house. 'You are one of the family—the Mount Gambier people. Why have you not settled this before?'

Rosanna smooths down her dress and wets her lips with the tip of her tongue. Oh, she is a gambler. No doubt about that. And a mother. She will risk everything for *love*. Unlike the Magistrate in the play and God himself, she will sacrifice *her* happiness for her son's. 'I daresay you'll forgive me, ma'am, when you know that I loved your son.'

'You could not have.' The woman drops with a little bounce onto her chair. 'George married young. The shock of the *Admella* hastened Petronella's death.' She draws her cloak closer around her shoulders. 'I really am at a loss as to how to end our interview. You must go.'

'Your son was not a gentleman but he promised to marry me,' Rosanna says. 'I have brought the horses as a demonstration of good faith, although it will kill me to part with one of them.'

'You have brought the horse because we sent a lawyer after you. I really am all at sea. What is the purpose of your visit?'

Leaning forward, Rosanna places her hands firmly on her knees. 'Mrs Sutherland, George and I had a child together.'

'Oh no, it cannot be that you would turn the knife on my grief after all this time.' Mrs Sutherland begins to gasp like a pretty goldfish: all sparkle and splutter, her sad eyes agog.

'Surely it is reason to rejoice?' Rosanna draws from her reticule a small photograph that she carries always. 'Cast down as I am in shock over Gordon's death it has crystallised my thinking. I cannot imagine how hard it is to lose a son in such circumstances or any other.' She bows her head. 'I have always wished that you would take a hand in Arlen's education.' She places the photograph in the woman's hand and rises to leave.

Mrs Sutherland turns the portrait in her hands and stares deeply into the little boy's face; she must note its likeness to her son. Neither of them speak. Rosanna feels faint again. Is it not enough, for Mr Gordon, to throw his life away while he possesses so many talents, but that those remaining must also choose between love and luck, and tragedy?

121

BREAKING EVEN

The following evening Mr Sutherland summons Rosanna by note to Cedars, and she approaches the visit as Edwin might a high-stakes game of craps. When she arrives at the mansion at six p.m., she sees more evidence of habitation: a groom stables her horse; a tiny French maid answers the front door and strands her in an opulent atrium, where a floor-to-ceiling portrait of George, aged about eighteen and dressed as Hamlet in doublet and hose, reproaches her. Wilting beneath the cut glass chandelier, recoiling from the sombre sound of organ music, smelling the preparation of boiled crayfish, which makes her feel homesick, she almost turns and runs. But they have Arlen's photograph and she must reclaim it or his future.

A butler ushers her into a library of overwhelming dimensions; a kind of heaven in which she finds Mr Sutherland presiding over a large desk covered in parchments and his wife perched opposite, hands clasped and seated on a chaise. Very soon it becomes clear that the pair may accept her proposal. Rosanna feels unaccountably torn by this miracle, surely a result of Arlen's uncanny resemblance to their dead son. Both became emotional when Rosanna answers questions about his abilities and nature.

Mrs Sutherland floats before Rosanna an armada of questions about her plans for the future and, with little conviction, asks whether a small birthmark might be hidden on her grandson's person. Rosanna suppresses a rebellious wish to describe the small red crescent located below George's right breast, in the face of the overall ghastliness of the meeting and its serious purpose.

If she had dreamed of weeklong sojourns staying with the Levy family to visit her son, of taking Arlen for hot chocolate at the coffee palace in Church Street, or setting off on the train from Middle Brighton Station to Spencer Street and laughing with him during pantomimes in city theatres, these ideas are soon dashed. Mr Sutherland drives a hard bargain. It seems that in withholding Lucifer and forcing him to pursue the horse through the courts, the Lynches have exceedingly displeased him and, he claims, despite deeds of inheritance, he has lost years of bloodstock breeding. This doubly insults him after all the loss they have suffered. Moreover, he is not as convinced by Arlen's portrait as his wife, although he sees some likeness to his son. However, if his wife is willing to undertake the raising of another child, that may necessitate her drawing back from some unsuitable theatre circles—Rosanna winces at this. Had George lived, would he have treated her with similar disrespect? In her imagination Mrs Sutherland sneaks out under the cover of her opera cloak, and imbibes opium whilst reclining on a couch in Little Bourke Street, a young oriental man feeding the hookah.

Mr Sutherland proposes that Arlen will attend St Andrews School in Brighton before preparing for university. The Sutherlands will maintain his ridiculous name but with the addition of another. He will learn German and violin from a private tutor. Mr Sutherland leans back in his leather chair and taps the end of his cigar into a fine brass jardinière on a pedestal. 'You may take it or leave it,' he says. '*Your child* has a chance to prosper. If we raise him.'

Rosanna takes particular note of the veiled aspersions he casts on Arlen's paternity in the interests of blackmail. Bluff, surely? She fingers crab tartlets placed on an occasional table beside her, knowing that she will never be offered the crayfish. Mrs Sutherland sips from a heavy crystal tumbler and perspires in the way of women in their prime. A sessions clock chimes seven as Rosanna sits in calculation.

'I may visit Brighton. Perhaps once a year, to see my son.' Her voice quavers. 'To meet friends and to place flowers on Mr Gordon's grave,' she says. The morning newspapers had been full of the poet's tragic story and Rosanna is in no doubt that it is familiar to him. George was just as arrogant as his father, she thinks, as she holds his gaze.

'You must give us a chance to realise our experiment without interruption and regression. After all, this is what we all wish, and he is ten years old; it may be too late to make an impression. Think how much we can offer him.' He smiles as if a girl like her might be better disarmed than insulted.

'I must insist,' she says with great conviction. Even so, she cannot be sure that he will not cool off on the deal. Mrs Sutherland, no doubt accustomed to her husband's business dealings, chews her fingernails.

It is not too late for Rosanna to run home and seize her son in her arms; to take him on a wild ride on his pony to the caves; to read with him Mr Geoghegan's play and argue about the influence of ancestors; to retell the tales of Cuchulain and Maeve. She will never allow Father Woods to intercede and take him to the unholy Brothers for education. Although Mother presently lives in a state of profound ignorance of Rosanna's plans for Arlen, this new development runs the risk of breaking her heart. Oh, poor Mother. Such thoughts are both comforting and nerve-wracking.

Then she remembers her father, scratching away at the land he bought and cleared such a long time ago; and how he struggles on, his family still expanding, prices rising and profits dropping. How will they manage? She makes an inventory of riches available to Arlen in Melbourne—tennis lessons, university study and rowing on the Yarra Yarra—and sets them against the unknowable. Who will listen to him, take care of him and watch out for him? Arlen may not be safe at St Andrews school or in Brighton. He may be as vulnerable as Skelly. The new world holds so much danger for boys. Even Father Woods has lost faith in the church and she has not been to confession for longer than she can remember. On God's breath, she hopes that her son teaches Mr Sutherland senior a lesson for his presumption and his manipulation.

In her furious processing of these conundrums, her musing over Arlen's future, she loses concentration and catches only the last sentence of Mr Sutherland's lecture. 'I will make sure that he writes to you on his eighteenth birthday. You must allow him this chance, a boy who knows no better, to make a different life.'

Rosanna wants to shout, 'He can ride and sing; he can read and write. He is a gifted mimic, a compassionate brother.' If she does not bring him here she can kiss him in the flesh: the dirt and soap commingling, the generous mouth smiling just for her. Every. Day. She straightens up abruptly, jolting sweet wine across her wrist. Her mind circles and circles the same ground. What if they are bad people? What if they fail to protect Arlen as she failed to protect Skelly, even with the best of intentions?

She takes the rest of the drink in a rush, throwing back her head in distress. They are George's parents. She loved George. They are *good* people who have suffered a devastating loss. Surely. 'I will need to think some more,' she mumbles, lurching to her feet and the door. She leaves her son's photograph with the grandmother, who leans forward on her chair and clutches Rosanna's hand.

On the day she rode south-east with Edwin, the three older children and their ponies had followed them along the road to the bay: Hugh, Blinnie, Arlen, heads held high, backs straight as whips, hair thick and black as a moonless night, eyes dark and sad as lagoons. Back then, the pain in her heart had been only for Skelly, whose life had been dishonoured; the knots in her brain for Arlen, who needed protecting from whatever lay ahead. He brought her so much joy. The gift she had carried from all of them lay wrapped in oilskin and tied with a leather thong. Its contents not dissimilar to Skelly's memory bag of fossils, eviscerated bats and sketches, pressed flowers and bird feathers, but Arlen had included a poem.

It is as if she smells clean, sweet, sea air issuing through a vent in the bat cave and draws it in with perverse gladness as she marches away towards the Levys' stables to make her farewell to Lucifer. Desperate she feels to hold Arlen in her arms. Etta and Mrs Levy will understand her sacrifice; Charles will not.

Before she passes on foot, unescorted between the Sutherlands' majestic gates, she strikes the carob trees on the avenue with her now useless crop and, on impulse, doubles back to bury the children's memory package beneath a large stone that sits among the pods and strewn leaf matter. From home, she will direct her son to its location; perhaps in the early days of his adoption he will take comfort from a few mouldy treasures that smell of home. Next, she places the crop, hand woven by her father with strips of station leather hide, in a forked bough, the highest she can reach. Taking action changes everything. It is her way. Only indecision brings her down.

Gordon's funeral tugs at her heart but she has almost made her mind up to take the train to Ballarat the very next day and then the coach to Portland, into which she will collapse. She must not begin to think of Mother, who will seize Arlen and lock him in her arms, who will collapse with grief as her daughter tears him away. Rosanna feels cruel, adrift from her old self. But Mother will take comfort from the twins and, despite what Gambierton people think, Arlen is not her child.

PART 6

NHILL (1880)

122

CODA

Rosanna cups her hand to extinguish the fringed lamp beside the ledger books in which she totes and tallies figures three days a week. She likes her little hidey-hole beneath the carved oak stairs that leads to the guest floors. Most weeks the door stays closed but today a steady stream of punters poke their heads in, trusting her shrewdness about horses. They bring their bets rolled up in darning eggs, silk bags, fob pockets. She counts the coins on the baize cloth and leather-edged blotter. How does she pick the winners of country sweepstakes? Locals never ask. Only hotel guests wonder. For her luck has turned since Gordon died in every respect but one. And Edwin's has waned.

She glances at the rough curtain drawn across an alcove at the apex of the stair space, wherein hides a sturdy safe. In a rush, she pulls the door to and steps out, looking neither left nor right, as she moves along the burgundy hallway runner, through the double-bolted front door and onto the shady return verandah. She scans the dusty, heat-fatigued street before setting off for the railway station.

As if she hadn't enough to occupy her the day before the races, without Edwin imposing himself on her goodwill. She is to meet the Melbourne train at four p.m. and pick up a registered parcel from the stationmaster. Apparently, no one else can be trusted with this mission. Oh yes, Edwin is still precious about his self-important business. Hardly hoping any more that his marginal land will support four small children and poor little Kitty pregnant with their fifth; now he is threatening to sell up and take them all West.

The train must be late. In irritation, she marches up and down the platform, tapping verandah posts and planter boxes with her crop. Savouring the officious crunch of her capped soft leather boots on the gravel. While relieving herself in the outhouse, she spies her reflection in a cracked, fly-spotted mirror, dangling over a rusty bucket.

She glances long enough to note the deepening lines on her weather-brown skin. Skelly once compared her to a yellow peach and she had snapped at him but been secretly pleased. Now, she no longer owns a bonnet. Her round belly will never carry another child; her full breasts never suckle one. While she has not inherited her mother's distinctive and distinguished streak of hair, grey flecks her crown. Her hands are still whip strong on reins, her legs know when to tighten, to squeeze and relax. Horses accept this, and the guests she entertains from out of town, punters willing to share their winnings after she takes her cut and visits them upstairs in their chintzy rooms, or for whom she backs up against the office door to talk horse sense.

It seems that she cares less and less about what people think since Father died. Had he not set her a fine and prideful example until the end? Tending his brew late at night, he had stepped back into a sinkhole, fractured his skull and drowned. He might have disappeared forever, had not his horse broken its tether and come home alone, dragging his reins behind him. After an exhaustive search around the house, they had found two neatly arranged boots behind shrubbery not far from the cave.

For years, her father had preferred to stay close to home, disdaining all company and taking sustanance only from Eilish. Edwin managed the buying and selling of their cattle, even as the price of a side of beef dropped to an historic low, and they all cast desperate thoughts to the colony of Victoria. Their property had become Father's bolthole; he wished, it seemed, never to leave it—in fact that they could carry him out in a lead-lined coffin—and privacy had become his swansong. After his death, Mother had packed up and moved the entire family to Nhill, to be close to Edwin and Kitty and their little ones.

Rosanna squints up into a clear, blue sky empty of birds. Will it be cooler tomorrow? Nhill summers arrive earlier each year, drying up the swamps and creeks before November. The decision to hold the race meeting late in the year came about for municipal reasons that have nothing to do with good sense but heat will not trouble Lynch horses; three are racing. Rosanna has been out at dawn on a beautiful streak of grace and light: a keen descendent of Lucifer, she needs no urging along the road to the township and back. If she wins again tomorrow, Edwin says, they will take her to Melbourne for the 1881 season; to the cup. Rosanna chews the inside of her mouth. Oh yes, the filly shall have her chance; surely they all shall, after their disappointment, grief and sacrifice.

The stationmaster blows his whistle before the train pulls up at the platform. The tardy locomotive wheezes steam and soot as it approaches, screaming like a wounded animal. Half a dozen passengers disembark and step wilting into the sunshine. The guard, the Maxwell boy, throws a gallant smile at Rosanna as he springs from the last van. Patting his pockets, he gestures to her as he lifts luggage from the carriages. If the box weighs too much, she'll ask him for help in getting it across the main street to the hotel; enabling him to inveigle from her a tip for tomorrow's race. He has a good eye and a steady wage from the Victorian Railways. Arms folded, feet tapping, she waits beneath a hanging basket of geraniums to take delivery of Edwin's order.

'What do you mean, no parcel?' she berates the stationmaster, mentally transferring her aggravation to her brother once more for interrupting her afternoon. She follows the Maxwell boy, snapping at his heels like a lizard, while he searches again through small freight unloaded on a trolley by the ticket booth. He ducks his head around the door of the railway office and grins. 'There *is* one more item.' He moves again to the guard van and slides back the wooden door.

A young man of eighteen or nineteen steps out, dressed smartly, almost foppishly, in a grey suit with a black velvet ribbon looped around the collar, and he squints into the lowering sun. Loosening cuffs fastened with silver links, he clutches his small leather valise.

In her mind Rosanna begins to rehearse the dressing-down she will give Edwin for this further trial even as the young man holds her gaze. When he releases her by looking away, his eyes circling the dusty street and returning, her eyes scoot across his face, searching, searching. When one of his eyebrows kinks and rises of its own volition, she commences an inventory of features that resolve and dissolve into something dear and familiar.

His expression veers between uncertainty and cockiness, common enough in young men, and he steps forward to shake her hand. She lifts her head the smallest amount to take him in, for he is taller than her by at least two inches; slim and wiry, well-muscled. His eyes are a deeper blue than his father's. Rosanna's fury with Edwin dissolves in a rush, replaced by a new fear that the boy will climb back on the train with his bag and return to Melbourne, their meeting cancelled like an overdue cheque.

123

THE MYSTERY PARCEL

Leading him towards the hotel dining room, she makes brittle, awkward conversation about the weather—a drought on the cards, dire water shortage, hand feeding—until they are seated and the waitress arrives with a menu. Rosanna, accustomed to dining alone, makes no comment.

'I suppose you thought yourself an orphan, having a mother who abandoned you to strangers at such a young age and having never made your father's acquaintance.' She toys with the ruby glass decanter placed between them, her face suffused with blood and something else. Mother Mary he is beautiful.

'I might have liked more say in it,' he replies, with nonchalance that she feels sure is feigned.

'Leaving you behind in Brighton tore at my heart, especially after what happened to Skelly. But I wanted to give you a chance at living a decent life, to know more happiness than he did, and I couldn't guarantee you that in Gambierton. With the priest gone ... Edwin itching to leave ... We would have been an added burden to your grandparents ...' Her voice peters out and she reaches for her glass, moving it swiftly to her lips. 'Do you remember any of those people?'

'Of course I do.' His voice carries a new inflection that resembles the Sutherlands' speech.

'And are you happy?' She held his eyes. 'In Melbourne? At all? I prayed that you would be so.'

'Yes, I suppose I became so, once I got over the surprise. And became accustomed to a different life. I wanted for nothing. I came to know my father through photographs, play bills, newspaper clippings, school compositions that Grandmother kept in a camphor laurel chest at the foot of my bed. She told me stories. She sang. She thinks that I resemble him in looks and in character.'

'Well, I don't mind that you do.' She laughs. 'God love him, Arlen. He was a gorgeous-looking man. Clever, and amusing in the most challenging way. I was just a girl when I met him.' She feels suddenly wistful. But it hadn't been like that entirely. Her feelings had been full-throated and complicated. George had a greedy side, for horses, for her skin, for entertainment. Secretly, she thinks Arlen carries traces of Skelly's good humour, in his gentleness with her.

'I'm finished my schooling at St Andrews,' he says. 'I'm reading for the bar.' He throws back his drink.

'Oh, like Levy. He and his sister have kept me informed of your progresss. Every December, I receive a letter from Charles and Etta. They see you some days in Church Street, on the train to the city, in carriages on the road to St Kilda and sometimes at the bathing huts. They reported to me that you were alive, growing up, acting more and more confident. That you got about with friends.'

His mouth drops open in surprise. 'Until a month ago, they never mentioned you. Not even when I visited the stables on business for my grandparents.'

'And do you get a ride sometimes, darlin'?' Her voice totters and then regains its balance.

'I do.' He raises his renegade eyebrow. 'Grandmother is filled with terror at the possibility of losing another blue-eyed boy. I think she'd prefer that I stayed inside and assisted her with flower arrangements and turning the pages of musical scores as she plays. But Papa and I ride together. He takes me to Flemington and to the Brighton track. Did not my father love racing?'

Oh the joy of accompanying a boy to the races; this boy, who means so much to her. Jesus wept she had missed him.

'He did, darling. And what of those horses I brought to New Street to pay off his estate, now your inheritance most likely? You remember that I rode them over myself: Lucifer and two colts? Are they champions?'

His voice comes alive with pleasure. 'The Magistrate came second in the Melbourne Cup. You must have heard.'

'I did, and that you named the horse The Magistrate. You have read *The Hibernian Father*? I kept your father's copy for you.'

'Charles Levy discovered another copy in some gloomy archives in the Colonial office. My father drowned on the way to performing it. The story was a tragedy that spoke to him and many others, even though he thought it ridiculous, extravagant, theatrical, that a father might kill his son.'

'You should know that my own father, your grandfather, would agree with him. Perhaps on that subject only. He was an irascible man who rarely agreed with anyone.'

A long silence arrests the conversation and they stare at one another. Rosanna feels overwhelmed with gratitude that she has reached this moment. Lived long enough to enjoy it. 'Next year, Edwin and I will bring another horse sired by Lucifer and she will chance it in the Melbourne Cup. A strong filly, two years old. My old horse Glorvina was her mother's dam.'

'A filly?'

'Why not? You will see her spirit, and courage tomorrow. She has a long strong back and tidy forefeet.'

'It is most uncommon for a mare or a filly to win, but I believe you. You and I will cheer her over the finish line.' He touches her hand with his long fingers.

'So the Sutherlands cannot prevent you now from accompanying your mother?'

When he tries to answer she shushes him, touching her finger to his cheek. It is such a magical night and she doesn't want to spoil it. She beckons the waitress to hurry with the plates of roast beef, mashed potato and green beans. When the girl withdraws, Rosanna looks up, over her food, eyes questioning.

He meets her gaze. His hand shakes. 'I know why you couldn't write to me or visit. Since preparing for my legal studies with Mr Levy, he has explained the conditions of your agreement with Grandfather.' He twists his linen napkin into a hundred creases. 'I wish that I had written to you. Had I known ... You must have been so lonely and fearful for my future.'

'It was a cruel kind of pain,' she says, 'but you are not to blame. Tell me it was worth it. Can you? Turn your studies of law to fight for justice. Use them to get around all the humbug that oppressed your family in the old days.'

'I want to live a good life but I am horribly addicted to the track and the theatre. Just like my father and his friends, it seems.' He grins.

'Nothing wrong with either,' she jibs.

'Grandmother tells me that you knew Adam Lindsay Gordon and that you were very cut up over his death.'

'Mount Gambier is a small district. It is not surprising that I knew him. Edwin and Father frequently worked and raced with him. A few days before he died, I met him riding on Brighton Beach. He was frank with me.' Her eyes begin to water at the memory and she swipes at them with the back of her hand.

'Now he is a legend. If only he had lived, he would take comfort from this.'

She laughs at his boyish naivety. 'You are too young to have any notion of how darkness can pull at you, of unrelenting pain. Are you not?' Her face forms a quizzical expression. She is curious about Arlen's beautiful life.

He quirks his eyebrow in his automatic way, then shivers as if, she thinks, a goose has crossed his grave. Should she be displeased that he too has suffered?

'I do not know you well enough to tell my feelings,' he parries. His bottom lip quivers.

'Darling, keep your counsel. Pride works for happiness as well as sorrow.' She pushes her plate away.

'I have been reading Gordon's poems, brought to me as a birthday gift by Grandfather. "The Ride from the Wreck" meant a lot to him because of Father.' He breaks into a recitation.

> Look sharp. A large vessel lies jamm'd on the reef,
> And many on board still, and some wash'd on shore.
> Ride straight with the news—they may send some relief.

Rosanna admires the way emotions fly across his face, the way he modulates his voice to capture the excitement of the ride and the courage of the riders, as well as the cries of the poor souls trapped on board the *Admella,* wedged on the Carpenters reef in rising seas.

She toys with her napkin. 'It takes me back to the terrible long week of that event. I'm thinking of the people lost. Some of whom I knew. Apart from your father. And how my heart beat like a *bodhran* when my friend Moorecke brought Lucifer home.' She wipes tears from her eyes.

'Some say it is a true account. What think you?'

'It's a grand poem. But it isn't true that Gordon made that ride. I know because I was there. Riding on that heath and worried about your father.'

'I want to know all the stories. About your time with him, and about the Lynches.'

'After your study we will ride home, to the old volcanos Gambier and Schanck, and to the shore. Our stories will come easier there because the landscape will help you remember.'

Edwin has thoughtfully tied a Lynch horse to a walnut tree in the hotel yard. Perhaps he spied on Rosanna's tears and laughter from the saloon bar and kept clear. Arlen places his small case in the saddlebags and fastens the buckles. Rosanna takes his arm and points up to the highest branches, where a pair of small bats sway upside down in the breeze. Her son flashes his clean beautiful teeth at her and she rejoices in his good breeding, praying that some part of him is wild, although not as wild as Gordon: that poor, poor man and poor Mrs Gordon.

As she moves to untie her horse, her breathing quietens. She will know a lot more about her son when they race the filly tomorrow; he and the horse will show their colours then. And later, when they return to the house to greet Edwin and Kitty's brood, they will celebrate the day's victories and pass the cup between them. She tilts her head to the night sky. A million stars warm her and bring her hope. After Arlen returns to Melbourne on the Sunday afternoon train, the events of the weekend will collapse in his mind like a hand of poker, but they *will* change him.

ACKNOWLEDGEMENTS

Unsettled suffered a long gestation for complex reasons, its first incarnation a PhD that then lengthened and strengthened in a small writing group, and on the basis of feedback from family and publishers. I thank members of the Lynch family—Brian Lynch, junior and senior, and Martin Lynch senior, Helen Lynch and Justin Lynch—for reading early drafts.

First and foremost, I wanted to materialise Lynch girls, absent from every family anecdote and official document, church, state and school, apart from their birth documents. I found one reference to a Lynch girl, racing her brother's stallion Lucifer. Maria, the Lynch matriarch made it into *The Border Watch*, Mt Gambier's newspaper, for smoothing the waters during an altercation between the law and her menfolk and, on her death, she was eulogised as a pioneer settler. The girls' lack of documentation and therefore their invisibility reflects their early settlement status on the frontier, which I explore in different language in academic papers and in *Apocryphal and Literary Influences on Galway Diasporic History*.

The names of the Lynch settler family who settled in the Gambierton district in 1852 have been redacted and fictional names chosen from a roughly equivalent 1850 Woodford village list. In the same way, their real employers at Mingbool and Mount Schank Station, have been conflated to create my pastoralist family. Rosanna and Skelly Lynch exist only in my imagination but my lived experience as Lynch wife and mother, verifiable historical events present in family oral histories, and historical Lynch antecedents –haemophilia, horse breeding, Irish luck on the track, single mothering and rebelliousness—offered me the connective tissue I needed to link their fictional lives.

In the spirit of historical fiction, I have kept as closely as possible to official records so that playwright Edward Geoghegan, poet and steeplechaser Adam Lindsay Gordon and Roman Catholic Father Tenison Wood, appear as true as I can make them but, in the spirit of story, some events may not be verifiable.

Entering South-Eastern South Australian historical territory was not difficult for me because my Scottish forebears settled not far from the Lynches and I lived in the district as a child. As a teenager, my maternal grandmother Sarah Ann Teresa Fennell rode her horse several miles across country to work as a parlour maid at Yallum Park, a grand station property regularly visited by one of my protagonists, Adam Lindsay Gordon. The poet reportedly wrote his famous and disputed poem 'From the Wreck' whilst poised on a branch of a Yallum tree. Perhaps here my grandmother learned the aesthetics and management skills necessary for a young widow to later raise six children, run her farm and serve office in numerous community organisations.

Boandik people tell their own South-East story—they live still on that once dangerous frontier, on land they never ceded—of their attempted eviction and genocide. During the PhD process I benefitted from knowledge shared by Boandik custodian Ken Jones, who walked me through his country, revealing its wonders and terrors, including copperhead snake tracks under our feet. I was grateful for conversations with Boandik linguist David Moon who read the PhD manuscript. Any errors made are entirely mine. Thank you to Yunggorendi and the Flinders University Ethics Committee for helping me address important questions about voice and Indigenous historicity.

Huge thanks to Matt Rubinstein at Ligature for his enthusiasm for the novel and its intertextuality, in particular convict-medico Edward Geoghegan's play *The Hibernian Father* (1840), and his interest in publishing both.

Heartfelt thanks to Irish speaking Dymphna Lonergan, Richard Hosking and Jeri Kroll who supervised the PhD novel, and to Irish writer Niall Williams who mentored the manuscript to third draft. I received an Australian Postgraduate Award and a Flinders University Visiting Research Fellow Grant to work in Galway. I am ever grateful to the university for early brokering of this project, particularly close members of my writing cohort, Drs Sharon Kernot, Annette Marner, Michelle McCrea, Margaret Merrilees, Emily Sutherland and historian Dr Robin Haines. Thank you to NSW archivist and historian Janette Pelosi for her generous collaboration with me on the Edward Geoghegan restoration project. Thank you to Mt Gambier historian and friend Pam O'Connor; to my dear friend Gillian Rubinstein; and to my mother Elvin Crouch, who valiantly reads my novels in draft.

Further I would like to thank my Adelaide writing group whose members—Doctors Danielle Clode and Sharon Kernot, and Douglas Stevens—workshopped the new sections of the novel, set in Portland, Melbourne and Nhill, Victoria. Thank you also to Hannah Kent, and to Kate O'Donnell for trimming some early fat from the manuscript. This version has been read by very few people but at just the right moment, was spruiked by one of Australia's best critics, and by my sister Felicity Morley, a reader and passionate horsewoman. To writer and friend Laura Bloom, thank you for a sympathetic reading at the perfect time.

Gay Lynch works as an adjunct academic in creative writing and English at Flinders University, publishing essays, hybrid memoir pieces, novels, papers and short stories. Her first novel, *Cleanskin*, was published in 2005. She now lives in Melbourne but spent most of her life in rural South Australia. You can find her recent work in *Best Australian Stories, Bluestem Journal, Edições Humus Limitada, Island, Meanjin, Meniscus, Griffith Review, Westerly, TEXT* and *Sleepers Almanac*. From 2011–2015, she was Fiction and Life Writing editor at *Transnational Literature ejournal*.